MURDER ON COLD STREET

SHERRY THOMAS

BERKLEY
New York

BERKLEY
An imprint of Penguin Random House LLC
penguinrandomhouse.com

Copyright © 2020 by Sherry Thomas
Penguin Random House supports copyright. Copyright fuels creativity, encourages
diverse voices, promotes free speech, and creates a vibrant culture. Thank you for buying
an authorized edition of this book and for complying with copyright laws by not
reproducing, scanning, or distributing any part of it in any form without permission.
You are supporting writers and allowing Penguin Random House to continue
to publish books for every reader.

BERKLEY and the BERKLEY & B colophon are registered trademarks of
Penguin Random House LLC.

Library of Congress Cataloging-in-Publication Data
Names: Thomas, Sherry (Sherry M.), author.
Title: Murder on Cold Street / Sherry Thomas.
Description: First edition. | New York: Berkley, 2020. | Series: The Lady
Sherlock series
Identifiers: LCCN 2020015834 (print) | LCCN 2020015835 (ebook) |
ISBN 9780451492494 (trade paperback) | ISBN 9780451492500 (ebook)
Subjects: GSAFD: Mystery fiction.
Classification: LCC PS3620.H6426 M87 2020 (print) |
LCC PS3620.H6426 (ebook) | DDC 813/.6—dc23
LC record available at https://lccn.loc.gov/2020015834
LC ebook record available at https://lccn.loc.gov/2020015835

First Edition: October 2020

Printed in the United States of America
1   3   5   7   9   10   8   6   4   2

Cover image of woman © Joanna Czogala/Trevillion Images
Cover image of foggy street © Lee Avison/Trevillion Images

To all the women who have been
F.O.D.—First. Only. Different.—thank you!

One

A Norwegian fir occupied a corner of Mrs. John Watson's afternoon parlor, its scent green and resinous, its branches festooned with ornamental hot-air balloons and handmade horns of plenty. At the very pinnacle of the tree loomed a slightly tilted, plaid-clad angel. The angel, his expression rapturous—eyes closed, lips apart, face raised heavenward—embraced a large and surprised-looking goose.

This farcical display would have drawn any visitor's eye, were it not for Miss Charlotte Holmes, who stood next to the fir, clad with even less subtlety.

Her redingote was red on the top and brown on the bottom, open to reveal a seven-tiered white lace skirt underneath, each tier bearing appliqués of green spruce and golden candles. Moreover, the brown part of the redingote had been made to resemble a pinecone, rendering the entire outfit a literal representation of a Christmas tree.

The first time Lord Ingram Ashburton had seen Holmes in this dress, someone next to him had dropped a teacup. He himself had been incredulous that he not only knew this woman but corresponded with her—and had been thoroughly relieved that she had not walked up to him, obliging him to acknowledge her.

The next time he saw the dress had come four years and a lifetime later. By then he had become more or less inured to her taste in clothes. Another woman might have been swallowed whole by such an outlandish concoction. She, with her needlessly sweet face and her near-indestructible composure, somehow subdued the insurrection of velvet and lace, reducing it to merely another item in her gaudy wardrobe.

In the months since her public fall from grace, which had obliged her to run away from home and start life afresh on her own, he'd thought more than once of this particular dress, buried in her parents' house in the country, lonely and pining to be worn.

To be abroad in all its absurd splendor.

And he'd also thought, more than once, of the surprise and gladness he'd feel, if he should ever see it again. Of the smile that the sight would bring to his face.

He was not smiling now.

Nor was the other woman in the room. Under different circumstances, Mrs. Treadles, wife of Inspector Robert Treadles, Lord Ingram's friend and Holmes's sometime collaborator, would probably have grinned in good-natured appreciation at such sartorial hullabaloo.

But pale and stricken, her hands still clutched around Holmes's, she only said, "Please, Miss Holmes, I don't know who else to turn to."

Lord Ingram, travelling from his brother's country estate to his own, had stopped in London to see Holmes, with whom he shared a long, complex, and increasingly line-blurring friendship. He had intended to tell her that he was ready to erase the lines altogether. And as he'd waited in the afternoon parlor of Mrs. Watson's house to be received by Holmes, trying to rein in his anxiety and agitation at the enormity of what he was about to do, Mrs. Treadles had arrived, with the news that her husband had been arrested on suspicion of murder.

Lord Ingram was still trying to digest her words, trying to move beyond his initial and nearly overwhelming belief that it had to have been a mistake, pure and simple.

His friendship with Inspector Treadles had grown out of their mutual love of archaeology. This past summer, however, he had disappointed Inspector Treadles with his continued friendship with Holmes, given that Holmes was no longer a respectable young lady. He himself had been no less disquieted by this new coolness from Inspector Treadles.

But late in autumn, he'd had the feeling that the inspector was trying to see things from a different, less absolute point of view—and that their friendship was on the mend.

In the weeks since, he'd spent most of his time abroad. But all throughout that escapade, he had looked forward to returning home, seeing his children again, and hosting Inspector and Mrs. Treadles at some point after Christmas.

When Mrs. Treadles had first appeared in Mrs. Watson's afternoon parlor, he'd been both surprised and somewhat embarrassed to see her—a man about to make a confession of an extremely private nature could scarcely wish for the presence of a third party. But his self-consciousness had quickly turned into pleasure: They hadn't met in a while and her company had always been warm and thoughtful. He hadn't in the least anticipated the reason for her unannounced visit. Now dread invaded him, sinking down to make him heavy, while swarming up at the same time, crippling his voice cord.

Holmes gave her caller's hands a squeeze. "You must be Mrs. Treadles. How do you do? Inspector Treadles has been a great friend to and champion of my brother Sherlock. In his hour of difficulty, we will of course make his welfare our overriding concern."

"Oh, thank you, Miss Holmes!" cried Mrs. Treadles. "Thank you!"

She looked down. Her eyes widened, as if she'd just realized that she'd been clutching at someone to whom she hadn't been properly introduced. With a clearing of her throat, she let go of Holmes and took a step back.

Holmes, who couldn't possibly be unaware of the faux pas, managed to give a highly creditable impression of not having noticed. "I was just about to attend to my brother. Lord Ingram, would you conduct Mrs. Treadles to 18 Upper Baker Street in five minutes' time?"

Inspector Treadles knew very well that Sherlock Holmes was but a *nom de guerre* for Charlotte Holmes. But apparently, he had not yet informed his wife of this fact and Mrs. Treadles still believed that a bedridden savant dwelled at 18 Upper Baker Street and imparted his wisdom via Miss Holmes, his sister and oracle.

And apparently, Holmes had decided that this was not the moment to dispense with all fiction.

When she was gone, Mrs. Treadles turned to Lord Ingram. "Robert was absolutely amazed at what Sherlock Holmes and his friends were able to do for you at Stern Hollow, clearing your name so decisively. I can only hope that—that he will be able to do the same for Robert."

A desperate hope glittered in her eyes, but it seemed more desperation than hope.

He went to her, took her hands, and made himself speak past the lump of fear blocking his airway. "Dear lady, you have come to the right place. Holmes will not let h—his friends down. You may depend on that."

She smiled wanly. "Thank you, my lord. Thank you."

"Now, is there anything I can do for Inspector Treadles? He saw to it, when I was in police custody, that I was treated as respectfully as possible. May I do the same for him now?"

She shook her head. "He has friends in the force—I'm certain they have seen to his comfort and dignity."

She did not sound more than halfway sure. Of her husband's current state of comfort and dignity, or of the stalwartness of his friends?

Lord Ingram chose not to question either. "Then is there anything I can do for *you*, Mrs. Treadles, as the inspector's friend—and yours?"

"I—I can barely remain still now. Would you mind, my lord, if we took a walk outside while we wait?"

The day was cold and gray, the air so saturated with moisture it might as well be raining. Mrs. Treadles marched along the railing of Regent's Park, her head down, her gloved hands holding on to her forearms. Her garments were black—mourning attire, but not widow's weeds—he recalled belatedly that her brother had passed away in the summer, toward the end of the Season.

The pavement was crowded with hawkers, sandwich-board men, and children trailing in their governesses' wake; he steered her by the elbow to keep her from colliding with a woman selling roasted chestnuts. At the nearest park gate, they turned around and made for 18 Upper Baker Street, where he rang the doorbell and said, "I will leave you here, Mrs. Treadles. I'm sure you would wish for some privacy for your discussion with Miss Holmes—and her brother."

"Oh, no, please don't go! If I hadn't found Miss Holmes at home today, I would have called on you next, my lord. And cabled Stern Hollow if you weren't in town."

She exhaled, a trembly breath. "I'd like to be prouder and not need anyone's help. But it's Robert's life and our future at stake and I shall feel a lot better if I can have your counsel as well as Sherlock Holmes's."

In recent years he had begun to grapple with his own, sometimes overwhelming, desire to serve. Unchecked, that urge to be someone's knight in shining armor had led to an unhappy marriage—not to mention exploitation by a brother who understood his weakness. In fact, only days ago, Holmes had declared, her eyes boring into his, *You are not a tool to be deployed at the whim of some reckless master, and you don't have to prove your worth by leaping at every task other people are too afraid to do.*

For that reason, he had offered his help here, but not jumped in to take charge. But he was glad that Mrs. Treadles wanted him to accompany her—and humbled that she would have called on him specifically for assistance.

"In that case, of course I'll come up with you."

"Thank you. Thank you, my lord."

Perhaps because he had spent too much of his life helping those who either resented his aid or took it for granted, gratitude, the kind that misted Mrs. Treadles's eyes, always took him aback.

As if flowers had blossomed before he had even planted seeds.

Holmes answered the door and led them up to the parlor of 18 Upper Baker Street.

He had been in the parlor a number of times and had come to think of it as Holmes's office. But the room had been furnished with a homey ambiance, and to give the impression of a convalescent man on the premises.

The air held a whiff of tobacco smoke, mixed with the herbal, faintly alcoholic scent of tinctures. The magazines in the canterbury next to the fireplace were recent; the ironed newspapers on the occasional table had been delivered just that morning—seized from Mrs. Watson's house, no doubt, on Holmes's way out.

The only thing missing was the bouquet of flowers that usually sat on the seat of the bow window overlooking Upper Baker Street. In its place, a bundle of dried lavender stalks in a creamy white jar, which would have been the focal center of the room, were it not for Holmes and her Christmas-tree dress.

She poured tea and passed around gingerbread biscuits and slices of holiday cake, generously studded with morsels of glazed fruit and candied peel. And then, after another moment, she asked, "May I also offer you something stronger, Mrs. Treadles?"

"Yes, thank you."

Holmes rose, went to the sideboard, and returned with a glass of whisky. Mrs. Treadles did not hesitate in downing a sizable draft, grimacing as she swallowed.

Holmes gave her a moment to recover. "Has Inspector Treadles mentioned to you, Mrs. Treadles, how my brother and I work together?"

"Yes, he has," said Mrs. Treadles, sounding slightly hoarse. "I understand that Mr. Sherlock Holmes is beyond that door and that he can hear us in this room."

"And see us, too, via a camera obscura. Which is why his door is shut to keep out light, so that our images, upside down and backward, will render more vividly for him."

Mrs. Treadles gazed intently at the door, as if she could will the unseen sage to his greatest feat of mental acuity yet.

"We are ready to begin when you are, Mrs. Treadles," said Holmes softly.

Mrs. Treadles took a deep breath. She had seemed eager to answer the question about how Sherlock Holmes worked, but now she hesitated. "I—I can't be sure where to begin. As I look back at the events of recent weeks, I find myself wondering whether Robert—whether Inspector Treadles was where he said he was, doing what he told me he was doing."

The tremor in her voice indicated more than trepidation *for* her husband. There was a fear that *she* might further incriminate him.

Lord Ingram had to remind himself that at Stern Hollow, not long ago, things had looked dire, too, with all circumstantial evidence pointing at him and him alone. Still, he was troubled.

"Let's begin with known facts," said Holmes calmly. "And then, Mrs. Treadles, everything else you care to share."

It occurred to him that although he'd been in this space before, this was the first time he had ever sat in on a client meeting, if one didn't count his first visit with Inspector Treadles, which took place before "Sherlock Holmes" had officially taken up the mantle of the world's only consulting detective.

"Known facts," echoed Mrs. Treadles. "In that case I suppose I should begin with the arrival of Sergeant MacDonald at my house this morning, asking to speak to me."

There probably wasn't anyone with whom Inspector Treadles worked more closely than Sergeant MacDonald, his colleague and apprentice who had accompanied him on many a case.

"When did Sergeant MacDonald show up at your residence?"

"A quarter before ten or thereabouts."

Lord Ingram glanced at the grandfather clock softly ticking away in a corner of the parlor. Twenty past one.

"Are you usually home at that time, Mrs. Treadles?" asked Holmes softly. "I understand you took over the running of Cousins Manufacturing at the end of summer."

A look of embarrassment crossed Mrs. Treadles's face. "Typically I would have been at the office by then. But it was a late evening the night before, and I was not feeling entirely well this morning. So I had risen only shortly before."

Holmes signaled for her to continue.

Mrs. Treadles took a more measured sip of her whisky. "I was surprised and more than a little alarmed when I heard the sergeant announced. I knew *of* him, very well, since my husband enjoyed speaking of his work and Sergeant MacDonald figured prominently in that work. But we'd met only one time before, when the inspector and I ran into him when we were out and invited him to join us for a meal at a nearby establishment."

She did not elucidate why there was so little socializing between Inspector Treadles and his trusted lieutenant outside of Scotland Yard, but Lord Ingram knew. Mrs. Treadles had not been born into the same social stratum as himself and Holmes, but her late father's wealth, however new and sooty, meant that her station in life was far above that of the man she married—and therefore also far above that of the vast, vast majority of his colleagues.

He'd been to the Treadles residence, a wedding gift from her father. It was not large or showy, but sat at an excellent address and was beautifully furnished within—an acquisition that would have been beyond the means of any mere policeman, unless he were the commissioner himself.

And even then, to afford the house, he would probably have needed to economize in other areas of his life.

Little wonder then that Sergeant MacDonald had not been invited for Sunday dinners or other occasions.

"Sergeant MacDonald looked grave—and shaken—when he was shown in. My heart began to pound. I asked him if the inspector was all right. He assured me that he was well, and then said, 'But unfortunately he has been arrested for murder.'"

She shivered. Lord Ingram rose, went to the grate, and added coal to the fire.

"I stared at Sergeant MacDonald. I was sure he was spouting gibberish. And yet, after some time, I heard myself ask, 'For whose murder?'

"'That of one Mr. John Longstead,' he said.

"I became truly disoriented. 'Mr. Longstead—my father's old friend Mr. Longstead?' I cried.

"'I wouldn't know about that,' answered Sergeant MacDonald uncertainly. 'But I understand he did work for Cousins Manufacturing.'"

Mrs. Treadles pinched the space between her brows, her eyes half closed. Lord Ingram felt his own temples throb at the implication of her words.

"That man did far more than work for Cousins," Mrs. Treadles murmured, as if to herself. "My father supplied the funds and was deft at managing the business, but it was always Mr. Longstead's engineering acumen that gave us a competitive advantage.

"For twenty-five years they were friends, colleagues, and partners. Mr. Longstead's health led to his departure—his physician warned that he could no longer work at the sort of feverish pace he sustained. And he only returned to Cousins as a personal favor to me, after I took up the running of the enterprise."

A sharper focus came into Mrs. Treadles's eyes as she looked from Holmes to Lord Ingram and back again. "But I saw him last night, alive and well in his own house, only hours before Sergeant MacDonald knocked on my door. And as far as I knew, Inspector Treadles wasn't even in London—he was away for work.

"So there I was, staring at Sergeant MacDonald, my mind a jumble. Who would murder dear old Mr. Longstead? And why would my husband, who had sworn to uphold law and order, be remotely connected to Mr. Longstead's death, let alone generate so much suspicion—and evidence—that he was already arrested?

"'But the inspector barely knows Mr. Longstead!' I heard myself exclaim."

Silence.

Mrs. Treadles lowered her face, as if she preferred to address the next part of her account to the tea table. "You probably guessed, Miss Holmes, by the fact that Sergeant MacDonald showed up at my house, rather than my office, at that particular hour, that he didn't know about my recently acquired responsibilities at Cousins.

"You see, Inspector Treadles was at first not particularly . . . enthusiastic that I'd ventured outside of the domestic sphere. After he returned from the investigation at Stern Hollow, he began to express an interest at last. So I invited Mr. Longstead and his niece to dinner at my house. They then reciprocated the invitation at their house. On both occasions, Inspector Treadles was cordial and respectful to Mr. Longstead, exactly as one ought to conduct oneself before a much-revered family friend.

"The second dinner was more than two weeks ago. Afterward, he expressed an admiration for Mr. Longstead and thought it fortunate I had him as an ally. As far as I know, they never met again. And now to hear him named as a responsible party for Mr. Longstead's death?

"I poured out my shock and incredulity to Sergeant MacDonald. He was sympathetic, as he himself was no less shocked and firmly believed that Scotland Yard must have made a mistake."

"Did he see the inspector in person today?" asked Holmes, her tone reflecting none of Mrs. Treadles's confusion and turmoil.

"No. He said he asked to but wasn't allowed. And he was warned to keep what he'd been told strictly to himself, except for informing me. He did have a note from the inspector. I've brought it, but I'm afraid it isn't much more informative."

She took out a piece of paper from her reticule and handed it to Holmes. Holmes scanned it. Then, after a look at Mrs. Treadles for permission, passed it to Lord Ingram.

My dearest Alice,

I'm sorry that Sergeant MacDonald will be the bearer of bad news. I'm sorry that I will cause you much worry and uncertainty. And I'm sorry that it will most likely get worse before it gets better.

I will need to rely, as always, on your strength and resilience.

Difficult days lie ahead, but I remain,

> *Your most*
> *devoted husband,*
> *Robert*

P.S. I love you with all my soul, even if I do not always, or indeed often, deserve you.

Two

Mrs. Treadles gazed at her husband's note for a while, after Lord Ingram returned it to her. "It's true that he doesn't proclaim his innocence in this note, but since he does seem to believe that it will get better . . ."

"Then we should take his professional opinion into account," said Holmes.

Her client caressed the edge of the note. "After Sergeant Mac-Donald left, I went around to Scotland Yard. Since I knew that the arrest wasn't yet common knowledge, I pretended to be, of all things, an admirer of Sherlock Holmes's and asked if I could meet with Inspector Treadles to learn more about the great consulting detective. There I was told that he wasn't expected at the Yard today."

"So Scotland Yard doesn't want it known that one of its own has been arrested?" murmured Lord Ingram.

"Scotland Yard had a major embarrassment recently, my lord, when they arrested you in triumph and had to later release you with full apologies," said Holmes. "It's understandable that they wish to keep the matter hushed for now—or for as long as they can keep it hushed. That does not, of course, help us. The first person I—the first person my brother would wish for me to speak to would be Inspector Treadles himself."

"What will you do then?" asked Mrs. Treadles, her fingers now clutched tightly together in her lap, around a white handkerchief.

"We will try a different course of inquiry," said Holmes calmly. "My lord, I can hear the newspaper boy's progress on Upper Baker Street. Will you be so kind as to fetch a copy for us?"

He did and was back in the parlor in two minutes flat, still scanning the paper, an early-afternoon edition printed around noon, shortly after the daily meteorological forecasts had been received and typeset. "No accounts of sensational murders or arrested Scotland Yard inspectors. I also don't see any mention of Mr. Longstead, Cousins Manufacturing, or indeed anything to do with Inspector Treadles's current difficulties."

He looked up. "But one minute, Mrs. Treadles. What is Mr. Longstead's address in town?"

"31 Cold Street."

At the answer, something flickered across Holmes's face. An almost unnoticeable change, and yet for her, this counted as genuine surprise.

His fingertips tingled. "The house next door got a mention. 'A disturbance erupted at 33 Cold Street in the early hours of the morning. The police were called for. The house was apparently unoccupied and the nature of the disturbance has not yet been disclosed. It is not known whether the events of the night had anything to do with the nuisance of fireworks in the district previously reported in these pages.'"

"What was the nature of the gathering at Mr. Longstead's house?" inquired Holmes.

Mrs. Treadles twisted her handkerchief between her fingers. "It was a dinner, followed by a dance. A coming-out soiree for Miss Longstead, his niece."

The London Season ran from late spring to high summer; it had no definitive beginning but ended absolutely before the first day of grouse shooting. Granted, the season was for the Upper Ten Thousand, but Lord Ingram was under the impression that the merely wealthy emulated their "betters" and set their social calendar to similar dates. Besides, the weather in May, June, and July was simply more conducive to merrymaking.

A coming-out soiree, in town, in December—he wouldn't go so far as to say it wasn't done, but it wasn't done often.

Mrs. Treadles echoed his thoughts. "A bit of a strange time to be having a debutante party. I would have organized a New Year's ball, instead of a dance a few days before Christmas. Mr. Longstead was introducing his niece not to scions of the landed gentry, for whom leisure is a mark of gentlemanliness, but to families similar to his own, the fathers and sons of which were both needed at their businesses the next day to see to the closing of the year."

"How long did the gathering last?" asked Holmes.

"That I don't know. I felt a headache coming on after midnight and by one o'clock I was in my carriage, driving away. At the time I wouldn't have been surprised if the dancing went on until dawn— Miss Longstead looked splendid and the guests were enthusiastic. But as I reached home, a fog was rolling in. So it's possible—perhaps even likely—that the party dispersed not too long after my departure."

"Were you aware of anything unusual going on either at Mr. Longstead's gathering or in the house next door?"

Mrs. Treadles dropped her eyes to her handkerchief and shook her head. "No."

"And of course you never saw Inspector Treadles at any point that night?"

"No."

Lord Ingram glanced at Holmes. He did not have her observational powers. But he didn't need observational powers of such magnitude to doubt Mrs. Treadles's last two answers.

It was far more difficult to tell when Holmes lied, because nothing else about her changed as she shifted from truth to fiction, not tone, not posture, not eye movements or facial flickers. Part of it, he was sure, was because of her copious mental capacity, which easily accommodated the calculations and calibrations required for lying that strained the ordinary mind.

Another part, and he wondered how large this part might be, was attributable to the fact that she was impervious to the dictates of moral absolutes. Like most everyone else, she must have been told again and again that lying was bad. Unlike with most everyone else, it had left little impression on her and she viewed telling the truth as a situational, rather than an ethical, choice.

Mrs. Treadles, on the other hand, lacked both Holmes's talent for fibbing and her moral fluidity, and was clearly uncomfortable with her most recent declarative answers.

"I'd mentioned that I thought my husband was out of town, not expected for some more time," she went on. "In hindsight, he must have returned to London at some point during the night, if not sooner. Perhaps he entered the house neighboring Mr. Longstead's—I have no way of knowing. I can't tell you anything about his movements— or the rationales for them."

People who lie often say too much. With Mrs. Treadles's additional explanation, Lord Ingram grew more convinced that she *could* tell them something important on both accounts, if she chose to.

Or was forced to.

Holmes took a sip of her tea and did not say anything.

Silence fell.

Over the years, Lord Ingram had experienced a great deal of silence in Holmes's presence. In fact, he was certain that if a tally were made, their acquaintance would turn out to consist of more silence than speech.

This was, however, the first time he'd ever known her to wield silence as an interrogation technique, an intentionally unsubtle signal that she found the witness less than creditable.

Mrs. Treadles shifted in her chair. She picked up her hitherto untouched tea and drank. And drank. And drank.

"That the murder hasn't been reported by the papers is a blessing,

I'm sure," said Lord Ingram, breaking the silence. "But at the moment we need more information."

Mrs. Treadles's teacup shook visibly. "Please let me know what else I can tell you."

Holmes was still silent, but her silence was not pointed or reproachful. He'd left most of the questioning to her—it was her investigation, after all—but she'd have known that he would not let Mrs. Treadles squirm in discomfort for too long. She'd issued a warning, that was all.

"Did Mr. Longstead go in to work every day?" she asked. "Would his absence have been already remarked upon?"

"No, he didn't come into work every day," said Mrs. Treadles, setting down her teacup. "It was understood from the beginning that he would serve only in an advisory capacity. I would see him on a Thursday, then perhaps not until the Tuesday of the following week. He made sure to be present when I met with the managers as a group, for which I was immensely grateful, as they became less dismissive of me out of respect for him."

She laughed a little, mirthlessly.

Lord Ingram felt a surge of self-reproach. Great upheavals had taken place in his life around the time Mrs. Treadles inherited Cousins Manufacturing. Still, he could have spared her more thoughts, perhaps even a letter or two, asking after how she fared in her new capacity as the owner of a complex going concern.

He'd been pleased for her, as he'd thought that the running of a large enterprise, while demanding, would suit her well, given her energy and intelligence. And that after an initial period of adjustment, she would wrap her hands firmly around the reins of the company.

But the undertone of bleakness in that not-quite-laugh—of outright despair, even—made it clear that the initial period of adjustment had been far rockier than he'd supposed, that she still did not have control of Cousins, and that she had just lost her greatest ally.

Possibly her only ally.

"I'm sorry for your loss," he said.

Mrs. Treadles sighed shakily. "Just when you think things couldn't possibly get worse, you immediately find that yes, indeed, they can. Far, far worse."

Silence fell again, until Holmes spoke. "You are here, Mrs. Treadles, in the hope that Sherlock Holmes can help make things better. Or at least, prevent the situation from further deteriorating. But in order to help, we must know much more than we do now."

It became Mrs. Treadles's turn to be silent.

Holmes regarded her for some time. "Very well, Mrs. Treadles," she said, clearly deciding on a different approach. "Can you give me a summary of the inspector's movements in the seventy-two hours before the party?"

"Seventy-two hours . . ." echoed Mrs. Treadles slowly. "The party was yesterday, Monday. Seventy-two hours earlier would have been the Friday before. He left for an investigation in the Kentish countryside that afternoon. And he was gone until . . . until his arrest, I suppose."

Not very helpful, as far as summaries of movements went.

"Did anyone go with him?"

Mrs. Treadles hesitated. "I can't be sure. I'd assumed Sergeant MacDonald would accompany him. But when I spoke to the sergeant this morning, he assured me he'd been in town all the while."

Holmes pitched a brow, a deliberately exaggerated expression for her. "You didn't ask, Mrs. Treadles?"

Mrs. Treadles smiled apologetically. Uncomfortably. "I was rather distracted at work, I'm afraid."

Lord Ingram had to refrain from raising his own brow.

Not long ago he had envied the Treadleses for their affectionate and harmonious union, while he himself endured an embittered domestic situation. When he last saw them together, in summer, in the middle of Holmes's first major case, they were still devoted to each other, a couple who glanced at each other out of care and consideration, and leaned together without even being aware of the gesture.

The cooling of friendship between Lord Ingram and Inspector Treadles coincided more or less with the beginning of a chaotic period in Lord Ingram's life. He didn't see Inspector Treadles again until Scotland Yard dispatched the police officer to Stern Hollow in the wake of a murder.

Such circumstances did not lend themselves to intimate conversations between the investigator and the investigated. Near the end of the case, when they *were* able to speak as friends again, he'd inquired after Mrs. Treadles's doings, and received the distinct impression that Inspector Treadles spoke with pride at his wife's accomplishments.

But Mrs. Treadles told them just now that her husband had *not* approved of her foray into the world of business and manufacturing. Not for months on end.

Words Holmes had once spoken came back to him, words concerning Inspector and Mrs. Treadles. *I only hope his wife fares better, if she ever breaks any rules he deems important.*

He had the sinking feeling that Mrs. Treadles had not fared any better against her husband's judgment. But they had reconciled, had they not? And if they had, would she not have asked, even if only in passing, whether he was taking Sergeant MacDonald with him?

Mrs. Treadles fidgeted. Lord Ingram began to wonder if there were any avenues of inquiry that *wouldn't* make her squirm.

Perhaps Holmes had the same thought, for she indeed opened another avenue of inquiry. "Do you know, Mrs. Treadles, who would benefit the most by Mr. Longstead's death?"

Mrs. Treadles exhaled, as if relieved to be asked this particular question. "He never married and had no children of his own. His niece lived with him and they doted on each other. I understand that he is also survived by a sister and several nephews.

"As for who would be the greatest beneficiary of his will, I guess it would be his sister and his niece. I once heard him say that men should make their own way in the world, but that women, not being able to work for success in the same manner, should be given as many resources as possible, so that they do not depend on the mercy of men who do not have their best interest at heart."

"Did his nephews know they were not to expect much from his will?"

"I would imagine so. Nothing more significant than small annuities."

Nothing worth murdering for.

Although, if a discontented nephew knew that the bulk of his uncle's fortune would go to two women, who was to say that he wouldn't kill Mr. Longstead in the hope that he could persuade the women to let him have a lot more of the money?

"Is there anyone else, besides blood relations, who might want him dead?"

Mrs. Treadles bit her lower lip. "If he weren't dead, but had simply left, I would have thought that those at Cousins who oppose me had finally succeeded in persuading him that it was in everyone's best interest to let me fail. But as overwhelming as my own problems seem to me, I don't believe that is why he died."

Lord Ingram's interlaced fingers tightened around one another. The weary reluctance in her words—it cost her to speak the truth. She would have preferred by far to be the picture of confident vivacity, and present her tenure at Cousins Manufacturing as one of brilliant success. But for the sake of the investigation, she must swallow her pride and admit that she was foundering.

"It is early in the investigation," said Holmes, "too early to dismiss any possibilities, even ones that seem unlikely. Any other reason you know of, Mrs. Treadles, why someone might want Mr. Longstead dead—or gone?"

Mrs. Treadles shook her head. "He could be blunt, Mr. Longstead— it was the very reason that he and my father got along so well. My father used to say that one could depend on Mr. Longstead for the unvarnished truth, because he had no vanity and therefore no desire to embroider results or shift blame onto others. For the same reason, one could *tell* him the unvarnished truth, because he would never take offense at being informed that his work needed improving.

"So yes, Mr. Longstead spoke the truth as he saw it. But he did not use truth as a cudgel, as some do, or an instrument for the wounding of others. He was deeply decent and deeply kind, and his honesty was equally decent and equally kind."

Lord Ingram was beginning to regret not having met Mr. Longstead while the man still lived. Some men's deaths left little besides unfulfilled obligations and the inconvenience of a corpse. The departure of others tore holes in the hearts of those who were fortunate enough to know them.

Mrs. Treadles's eyes glimmered with unshed tears. "My father loved Mr. Longstead as a brother. More than a brother, I'd say. I don't remember him ever being as happy to see my late uncle, or having as many good things to say of him. He always did lament that it wasn't the same at Cousins after Mr. Longstead left. That he felt lonely without his brother-in-arms."

Holmes nodded, as if in sympathy, but not so much that she didn't immediately pose another question sure to discomfit her client. "Since you brought up the existence of those who oppose you at work, Mrs. Treadles, may I ask what exactly is the nature of your disagreement with your managers?"

Mrs. Treadles dabbed at the corners of her eyes with her handkerchief. It crossed Lord Ingram's mind that she might be trying to hide her reaction from Holmes's all-seeing gaze. He felt disloyal at the thought but nothing Mrs. Treadles had said or done since had dispelled his earlier impression that she was not being entirely forthcoming.

"I can answer that question, but Miss Holmes, you must understand, I never mentioned any of my difficulties at Cousins to my husband."

"It is precisely because we are trying to extricate Inspector Treadles from his present predicament that I am asking about matters unrelated to him," Holmes explained. "You affirmed Mr. Longstead as an ally. I take it to mean that he sided with you against your managers. Could that have been the reason he was killed? Such a line of reasoning would exclude Inspector Treadles, who was ignorant about the insubordination you faced at Cousins."

"Very well. If you must know, Miss Holmes—" Mrs. Treadles took a deep breath. "This is mortifying to confess, but the truth is, my greatest point of contention with the managers is how little I am allowed to participate in the running of my own company.

"I'd always found Cousins Manufacturing fascinating, and my father had enjoyed my fascination and indulged in my desire to understand both the technical and the commercial aspects of the enterprise. I learned double-entry bookkeeping when I was still a child. I've been tutored in enough physics, mathematics, and even chemistry to understand the concerns of engineers. I always read both the financial pages in the papers that my father followed and the scientific and mechanical journals that Mr. Longstead kept abreast of.

"But no matter how I enumerate my qualifications, no matter how I try to make clear that at the very least, I am far more prepared to run Cousins than my brother was when he took over, my words fall on deaf ears.

"The only thing that I am good for, it seems, is providing signatures. And they don't even want that: Every day I am urged to designate someone to act on my behalf, either one of them or someone they recommend—so I can return to the domestic sphere, where I'd be happiest, you see.

"I don't want to sign just anything put down in front of me. But when I ask for clarifications, for the context of the outlays and obligations, explanations are inevitably deemed too complex for my understanding. When I refuse to comply without explanations, I'm told that by my inaction I have delayed important sales, or prevented the arrival of crucial shipments. And when I demand to know why I was not properly informed in the first place, they take my ire as a sign of incipient hysteria."

Lord Ingram's stomach tightened. His had not been an easy life and on occasion he'd even wondered whether he wasn't being punished for sins from some prior lifetime. But times like this he realized anew that however many difficulties he encountered, there were still many hardships and stumbling blocks he would never experience, simply by virtue of having been born a man.

Mrs. Treadles gave a bitter smile. "I have wondered, frequently, whether I am indeed utterly irrational. Whether I indeed possess only the mind of a child. But so far, I have not returned to the domestic sphere. I suppose I must give myself some credit for sheer pigheadedness, if nothing else.

"Mr. Longstead shared my frustration. He didn't understand the opposition I faced, but as he was no longer a stockholder in the company and couldn't give orders to the management, he counseled patience and perseverance. He believed that I would eventually prevail, and I very much hung on to his reassurances."

"So he wasn't personally involved in the conflict between you and the managers?"

"No. He was on my side, but due to his health, he was unable to join me on the battlefield, so to speak."

Holmes nodded, a contemplative look on her face.

What was she thinking of? As far as Lord Ingram knew, at her work she had been spared such belittlements because to her clients she was only a messenger, and their faith rested on the near-mythical capabilities of a man.

But she, too, had chafed against the limitations placed on women, on what they could or couldn't do, and on what they ought or oughtn't even think. He was sure she felt for Mrs. Treadles, but then again, she had never been one to let sympathy, or the lack thereof, affect her investigations.

"Is there anything else you can tell us for certain, Mrs. Treadles?"

Mrs. Treadles shook her head.

"I'm ready to hear your conjectures," said Holmes, her voice crisp. "You mentioned earlier that you wondered whether Inspector Treadles, in recent days, was where he said he was and doing what he told you he was doing. Why did you think he might not be?"

Lord Ingram leaned forward. Their client had indeed brought up the subject herself, which meant that she was ready to make some confessions, at least on that front.

Mrs. Treadles drank again from her cup, several jerky swallows of tea that must have already cooled. "Two reasons. First, as I mentioned, he left this past Friday. Since then, I've received two letters from him. Today I found those letters and looked at the postmarks. They weren't from any post office in Kent, where he was supposed to be. One was sent from Manchester, the other from a little place in Cornwall."

Her voice quaked a little.

Lord Ingram's brows rose.

Holmes's expression remained unchanged, a placidness that must have felt oppressive to Mrs. Treadles. "Is Mr. Longstead's country residence in either of those places?"

"No, it's in Berkshire."

Then what was Inspector Treadles doing traipsing all over Britain?

"Is Inspector Treadles in the habit of misleading you about where he travels for work?"

"After I found those two discrepancies, I went back and checked the envelopes of all the letters he'd ever written me when he was away for work, including during our courtship. Thankfully, in all those other instances, the postmarks on the envelope accorded with the locations he'd given in the letters themselves."

She expelled a long breath. "A relief, of course. Which only made it more troubling that he did lie in this instance."

"You mentioned two things that made you wonder about the inspector, Mrs. Treadles. What is the other one?"

In a gesture that was beginning to seem reflexive, Mrs. Treadles raised her teacup to her lips again—only to set it aside with a small grimace: The cup was already empty. "Before I went to Scotland Yard, I thought I should at least gather a change of clothing for him. But when I went inside his dressing room, I—I saw that his service revolver was missing."

Lord Ingram sucked in a breath.

Holmes continued to be unruffled. "Does he normally carry his service revolver?"

"He does not. He said that sometimes night patrols encounter dangers but as a member of the Criminal Investigation Department, he did not really have cause to fear for his safety."

Mrs. Treadles's expression, that of someone about to dive off the headland into the pounding surf below, made Lord Ingram brace himself for what he might hear next.

"I'm afraid earlier I didn't give a complete account of what I learned when I went to Scotland Yard. When the constable I spoke to told me that Inspector Treadles would not be in that day, I pretended to be distressed and said I knew I should have come to town sooner, and now I'd missed my opportunity. The constable consoled me by saying that I wouldn't have seen Inspector Treadles earlier either, as he'd been out on leave for the previous fortnight.

"The constable didn't appear to be telling anything except the truth as he knew it. But if my husband had been on leave, then it was truly news to me. He was away a good deal recently. But when he wasn't traveling for 'work', I said goodbye to him in the morning when I normally did and saw him again in the evening when I normally would.

"Which makes me wonder—what if I'm not the only one he lied to? What if he was also lying to Scotland Yard? Could that be why they were so swift to arrest him, because he'd been caught so plainly in a lie?"

The hurt and bewilderment on her face at having been so excluded from her husband's life . . . Lord Ingram's chest constricted.

Holmes, not so easily distracted by sentiments, merely asked, "Is there anything else you can tell us?"

"Sergeant MacDonald said he would come by to pay his respects to Mr. Sherlock Holmes later today and ask that you would please receive him. Other than that . . ." Mrs. Treadles shook her head.

"In that case, would you mind, Mrs. Treadles, if I asked you a question?"

"No, of course not."

Yet she tensed. As did Lord Ingram.

Holmes picked up a piece of holiday cake and took a leisurely bite. "Mrs. Treadles, what is it you would like Sherlock Holmes to do for you? Are you more interested in the truth or in Inspector Treadles's freedom?"

Three

Lord Ingram stared at Holmes. The dichotomy in her question, as if the truth and Inspector Treadles's freedom were mutually exclusive . . .

Mrs. Treadles's jaw worked, then she squared her shoulders. "Both, Miss Holmes. The truth of the matter will lead to the arrest of the true culprit and my husband's release from police custody."

She said it with a fervency that seemed to be more than conviction. She *needed* for her husband to be thoroughly exculpated by the thoroughly above-reproach Sherlock Holmes.

"Everything that you have just enumerated—Inspector Treadles's lies to you on his whereabouts, his missing service revolver, and his omission of the fact that he had been on leave from Scotland Yard—do they not cast doubts as to what Sherlock Holmes might find out, if he looks closely enough?"

The thoroughly above-reproach Sherlock Holmes sounded skeptical.

"They are not what makes my husband guilty. They are only what makes his innocence difficult to prove," said Mrs. Treadles with a stubbornness that Lord Ingram found inexplicably touching. "Which is why we need Mr. Holmes's genius, to bring the matter to a satisfactory conclusion."

He cast a look at Holmes. She had managed to get to the truth of the matter in every case that had been entrusted to her. But truth had a vicious way of upsetting everything else on its way to the surface. And he was hard-pressed to say, as someone whose existence had been repeatedly convulsed by recent overdoses of truth, whether there had been anything satisfactory to the aftermaths.

"In that case, if you will excuse me, I will consult my brother."

She left in a flounce of velvet and lace. Lord Ingram stared for a moment at the bedroom door, closing behind her, then took a sip of his tea, which had become thoroughly lukewarm. He undertook the making of a fresh pot, glad for an excuse not to sit still.

But something as undemanding as putting a kettle over a spirit lamp didn't excuse him from conversation. He was racking his brains for a suitable topic when Mrs. Treadles said, in an exhausted voice, "This is a very nice parlor."

It *was* a nice parlor. Mrs. Watson, Holmes's benefactress, possessed excellent taste and any room she had a hand in decorating was bound to be both lovely and comfortable. There were still rooms at Eastleigh Park, the Duke of Wycliffe's country seat, that the current duchess had not bothered to alter, because when Mrs. Watson had been the late widower duke's official mistress, she'd remade them so admirably.

But at this moment, Mrs. Treadles could scarcely have any real interest in the color scheme or furnishings of 18 Upper Baker Street.

Even with the catastrophic turn of her own fortunes, she didn't want him to feel awkward.

"Yes," he said. "A very cozy place."

Although—the last time he was in this parlor, Holmes had managed to overturn his life.

"Have you eaten anything since Sergeant MacDonald's visit?" he asked.

When she had first appeared in Mrs. Watson's home, wild-eyed and short of breath, he'd thought she must have just learned of her husband's arrest and rushed over. But hours had passed since that heart-stopping moment.

She shook her head. "No, but I'm not hungry."

"I understand not feeling hungry. And I understand that at the moment, everything else feels more important than nourishment. But please believe me when I tell you, Mrs. Treadles, that these will be some of the most demanding days of your life. And it is the *least* you must do, to treat yourself with as much care and courtesy as you would a horse carrying you on an arduous journey."

He set a plate of holiday cake before her. She liked a good fruit cake, she'd once said in his hearing, because the taste made her remember happy childhood Christmases. "Allow me to be useful as a nursemaid, my dear lady, since I cannot do anything else at the moment."

She blinked rapidly—he realized with astonishment that she was holding back tears at his utterly insignificant gesture. She picked up the piece of cake and took a bite, smiling bravely. "I'd like to say that I'm following your sage advice because I've come to my senses. But right now I'll probably blindly obey any kindly voice of authority, if only to no longer be responsible for everything myself."

His heart ached for her: She had been exhausted long before catastrophe struck this morning. "Decisions are taxing—far more than I ever imagined they'd be, in those days when I longed to make all the decisions."

She took another bite of her cake. "I hope Sherlock Holmes is excellent at decisions."

He nodded with wholehearted endorsement. "Extraordinarily so. As is Miss Holmes, in fact."

"Do you have any guesses as to what Mr. Holmes will have us do?"

"No, but I've come to expect the unexpected."

She turned her plate in her hands, as if she wasn't sure whether she ought to ask her next question. "Robert said you were impeccable in your conduct at Stern Hollow. But were you—were you at all afraid?"

He also didn't answer immediately—the memories brought back a sensation of cold that had nothing to do with the December day outside. He suppressed a shiver. "I was deathly afraid."

"Even though Mr. Holmes had sent a brother to help you?"

Even though Holmes, in the guise of that brother, had been there in person, fighting for his life.

"Had I been an outsider looking in, I would have had full confidence in Holmes's capability. But I was the prime suspect, I was the one all the evidence pointed toward, and I felt as if I were drowning. Even having Mr. Sherrinford Holmes at Stern Hollow didn't change the fact that I was barely holding my head above water in rough seas. But he was the lifeline I held on to and eventually he pulled me ashore."

Mrs. Treadles looked toward the door through which Holmes had disappeared. "Do you think," she asked tentatively, "that Sherlock Holmes can do the same for Inspector Treadles?"

Yes, but you must place your complete trust in her. Tell her everything. Do not withhold any more crucial information.

Before he could answer, Holmes returned. "Ah, I see you have put more water to boil, my lord. Thank you."

"May I ask what Mr. Holmes counsels?" asked Mrs. Treadles, her voice sounding both eager and nerve-stricken.

Holmes sat down and arranged her skirts so that they cascaded with greater flair about her. "In situations like this, it is always advisable to know all the facts as soon as possible to avoid wasting time on unnecessary avenues of inquiry. My brother recommends a multipronged approach. We will need to know everything about Mr. Longstead, look into the doings of Cousins Manufacturing, and seek to speak and otherwise communicate with Inspector Treadles."

A commonsense—and commonplace—set of recommendations that Mrs. Treadles could have come up with on her own.

She tried valiantly to conceal her disappointment. "I see."

"In the meanwhile, can I count on you to be home tonight?"

"Of course," said Mrs. Treadles, rising wearily. "Thank you, Miss Holmes. And you must please convey my gratitude to Mr. Holmes."

Lord Ingram rose, too. "I will see you out, Mrs. Treadles."

At the bottom of the stairs, he asked, in a low voice, "Would you like me to accompany you home, Mrs. Treadles?"

"No, I shall be quite all right," she said rather quickly.

"I'm sure Inspector Treadles would wish you to have the support of friends, in times such as these."

"And I'm sure *I* shall feel more assured to know that you are at Sherlock Holmes's disposal, my lord, rather than wasting your time squiring me about town."

Her first refusal he'd attributed to a desire not to inconvenience him. But this second one, accompanied by a flash of apprehension in her eyes, was more adamant. She really didn't want him to escort her.

She did not want any further questions, from anyone.

"In that case, let me see you to your carriage, at least."

As he handed her up into her vehicle, she turned around in dismay. "Goodness, I forgot to inquire about Mr. Holmes's fees! Should I have paid a portion up front to retain his services?"

He put on a reassuring smile for her. "Don't worry about that now, Mrs. Treadles. You will hear from his bursar in good time."

—❖—

When Lord Ingram returned to the parlor at 18 Upper Baker Street, he was not surprised to see that said bursar had joined Holmes at the tea table: Mrs. Watson, his old friend, must have been in the bedroom, listening. But he *was* surprised—and delighted—to see Miss Penelope Redmayne, too, by her side.

To the world Penelope had always been presented as Mrs. Watson's niece. But she was Mrs. Watson's daughter, her natural father the late Duke of Wycliffe, Lord Ingram's official father. But since he was, in truth, the product of the late duchess's affair with a wealthy banker, he and Penelope were not related by blood. Still, he had always regarded her as a baby sister, one he didn't see enough of.

He exchanged warm greetings with mother and daughter. Holmes looked on, appearing bemused. With someone else he might worry she felt excluded, but that had never been a problem with Holmes, who did not weigh the affection she received against that bestowed on anyone else.

"When did you arrive in London, Miss Redmayne?" he asked. When they were alone, they called each other Penelope and Ash. But even in front of Mrs. Watson, he preferred to maintain the pretenses.

"I reached yesterday," she said cheerfully, "after a crossing that felled everyone aboard. I do believe I kissed soggy English ground in fervent gratitude upon disembarking. Presently I shall petition all and sundry to bring the tunnel under the Channel to fruition at the earliest possible date. And I refuse to hear a word about how such a shaft might undermine Britain's natural defenses."

He smiled. "And how are your studies?"

"Demanding and fascinating. I've become an ever more indelicate individual, by the way, having by now eaten pastries and cheese sandwiches next to still-open cadavers," she answered, sighing. "My friends say that my coarsification will be complete when I will have consumed a serving of *rognons à la crème* under the same conditions—which, of course, will never happen as I don't care for kidneys, even without human remains nearby."

He laughed. She was a second-year student of medicine at the Sorbonne in Paris and enjoyed making light of her anatomy classes.

"But enough about me. How did Mrs. Treadles look to you, my lord?"

"Indeed," echoed Mrs. Watson. "Is she all right, that poor woman?"

He glanced at Holmes, who nibbled on a slice of cake and said, "I told them she wouldn't buckle under yet."

"No, not yet," he agreed.

"But . . ." prompted Penelope.

"But it's also true that Inspector Treadles is in significant trouble."

"Surely it can't be anything except a huge misunderstanding," murmured Mrs. Watson, not sounding entirely convinced.

This time everyone looked at Holmes, who drank her tea and said nothing.

It had so often fallen to her, to be the harbinger of ill tidings. He decided to fill that function this time. "We are all hoping it will prove no more than a misunderstanding. However, given that Inspector Treadles was, until last night, as far as we knew, a member of the law-enforcement community in good standing, I cannot help but think that Scotland Yard wouldn't have arrested him unless he was standing over Mr. Longstead's dead body, the murder weapon in hand."

Mrs. Watson recoiled. "That bad?"

"That would be my guess. Holmes?"

"A likely scenario, yes."

"Is there any chance that he did do it?" asked Penelope, who'd met the inspector only once.

Lord Ingram shook his head. "I can't see him taking a life in cold blood. Or even in a rage. That said, he himself once told me that he had seen, in the course of his career, the most unlikely individuals turn to murder, when the stakes became high enough."

"And what would have been *his* reason to turn to murder, if it had indeed come to that?" mused Penelope, as if to herself.

His wife, thought Lord Ingram.

He did not peer in Holmes's direction this time, for fear that Mrs. Watson would take one look at their exchange and read his mind. Mrs. Watson was an integral part of any Sherlock Holmes investigation, but he did not want to lay bare his friend's entire private life before her.

Not yet.

Mrs. Watson broke the silence. "My dear Miss Charlotte, have you a concerted strategy for us?"

She must be recalling the case at Stern Hollow, where Holmes, upon learning of a dead body found in the icehouse, had immediately formulated a detailed master plan, a large part of which she'd entrusted to Mrs. Watson to execute.

Holmes shook her head. "Not at the moment. I must at least speak to Inspector Treadles in person before I'll know where to concentrate our efforts."

"When will that happen?" wondered Penelope.

"When the papers get wind of the murder. At which point, Scotland Yard will need to respond. And if they already have Inspector Treadles in custody, that, too, will become public knowledge. Then they will have to allow him counsel and visitors."

Mrs. Watson drained her teacup. "And how soon will the story be in the papers?"

"By tomorrow morning, at the very latest. If Scotland Yard suppresses this for too long, it will seem as if they are deliberately shielding the guilty, especially if the only suspect they have is one of their own." Holmes turned to Mrs. Watson and Penelope. "You may enjoy another evening of reunion before Miss Redmayne's holiday is interrupted by the work of the investigation."

A few months ago, when Penelope had come home for her summer holiday, she had been eager to take part in any and all Sherlock Holmesian adventures. But the complicated nature of real cases and the toll they took on real lives had sobered her. Now the young woman who nodded did so with a hint of trepidation, as if already bracing herself for unhappy outcomes.

Mrs. Watson rose, pulling Penelope up with her. "My dear, let's go back to the house. Mr. Mears has obtained bags of cuttings from the Christmas tree seller and we have much garland-making to do."

Penelope gave her a quizzical glance before agreeing heartily. "You are absolutely right, Aunt Jo. And I believe it's late enough in the day that we can have a bit of Madame Gascoigne's cherry brandy while we work."

They managed their departure with such grace and lightness that if Lord Ingram hadn't already known Mrs. Watson wanted him alone with Holmes, he might not have guessed.

But now they were alone. At last.

The fire in the grate crackled softly. A horse whinnied on the street below. Rain came down, a soft percussion on the roof. Holmes adjusted the lace at her cuffs—the Christmas-themed dress, in addition to everything else, also boasted two extravagant spreads of snow-white broderie anglaise that cascaded from the middle of her forearms and matched the white lace cap on her head. The cuff lace swished pleasantly with her motion.

Satisfied with the image of exaggerated domestic tranquility she currently presented, she said, "Shall I assume that you plan to be in town for the immediate future, my lord?"

He had meant to stay in London a few days, in any case. For her. So that they might spend some time together, after he had . . . spoken to her. But this was not yet the moment for it—she was still preoccupied with her newest case.

"I will better serve Inspector Treadles here, rather than from a distance," he said.

She gave him an even look. "Let's speak of what you chose not to share with Mrs. Watson. I admire your desire to guard your friends' privacy. But you of all people, Ash, should know that privacy becomes a mirage as a murder investigation gathers steam."

"Nevertheless I hope that Inspector and Mrs. Treadles will manage to keep a large part of their lives private, that not all of it will have become fuel for public consumption."

So many of the most pivotal events of his own life had been fodder for gossip. He wished, as much as possible, to spare his friends that particular torment. Life was difficult enough without one's most harrowing experiences splashed over every major newspaper in the country, for the bemused speculation of strangers at breakfast.

"You and Mrs. Watson are well-matched in your gallantry," answered Holmes. "However, you know as well as I do that Mrs. Treadles is holding something back—holding it back with all her might."

He did know, alas.

Mrs. Treadles had made a great number of confessions: that she'd been having a terrible time at Cousins Manufacturing, that her husband hadn't been where he'd said he would be, and even that his service revolver was missing from his dressing room.

However, everything she disclosed was something that a skilled investigator would have discovered within a day or two.

That she was having a difficult time helming Cousins would have become known upon interviewing, if not the men standing in her way, then the secondary actors, the clerks and secretaries, etc.

That Inspector Treadles hadn't been where he was supposed to be was, at this point, probably already known to the police.

And her candor with regard to the service revolver? His guess was that someone else—a maid in her household, perhaps—had already noticed its absence, which made it futile for Mrs. Treadles to lie.

"I know you don't wish to think unkind thoughts about your friends," said Holmes, "but we must ask why Mrs. Treadles has been so suspicious of her own husband."

The worst part was that he didn't disagree with her, which made it even more disturbing to hear her speak those misgivings aloud.

"But she said she believes the truth will help him."

"Allow me to rephrase: It behooves us to ask why she was so worried that *others* would think he did it. After all, if it is as she said, that Inspector Treadles and Mr. Longstead only met twice, and that the inspector considered Mr. Longstead a good man and a good ally, then even news of his arrest shouldn't have made her as frantically fearful as she was."

His shoulders slumped. Holmes was right. In Mrs. Treadles's place, another woman's first reaction would not have been to think of where her husband might have been when he had written her those letters. Nor would she have been rooting about in his dressing room.

That woman would have been stupefied by the turn of events, but she would have then marched directly into the office of his superior to ask for the misunderstanding to be cleared, rather than pretending to be a tourist at Scotland Yard, craning her head for a better view of the proceedings.

"But it's not entirely irrational to overreact when your husband has been arrested for murder," he still argued. "There is always the chance that there will be a miscarriage of justice, that an innocent person will be convicted of crimes he didn't commit."

She rose and brought back a glass of whisky for him. "True. But Inspector Treadles is a respected and respectable man. He is considered one of the more promising young officers at Scotland Yard. Not to mention, he is married to a woman in control of a considerable personal fortune: He is assured of the most formidable barristers for his defense, should it come to that. He even has Sherlock Holmes in his corner."

"All these advantages, and she was still petrified with fear. At this point it would be irresponsible not to assume that she is hiding something. Something that in her eyes, at least, is hugely incriminating."

His hands around the glass of whisky, he suddenly remembered. "Wait. I meant to ask this earlier. When she said Mr. Longstead's house was on Cold Street, you recognized that location, didn't you?"

"I did," she said slowly. "You know I have been keeping track of the small notices in the papers since summer."

He nodded. Lieutenants of Moriarty, a dangerous enemy, had used the papers to communicate with their minions, though those notices had ceased at the end of summer. But she still kept an eye out, not only for any movement on Moriarty's part, but also for any news from Mr. Myron Finch, her half brother, now on the run from Moriarty.

"I don't have my notebook with me now—it's in the other house. But yesterday morning there was a coded notice in the papers that said, 'Roses are red, violets are blue, on Cold Street one finds a wife no longer true.'"

He sucked in a breath. "Do you think Mrs. Treadles knows about it?"

"She doesn't strike me as the kind with time to decipher small notices in the papers—certainly not these days. And something tells me the notice was aimed not at her, but at her husband."

"So . . . a young woman in distress, a chivalrous older man, and a husband made suspicious by a notice in the papers . . ." His words came reluctantly, even though it was not the first time he'd had the thought.

"She admitted that her husband was not enthused about her new responsibilities at Cousins. And now we know that the situation at Cousins was difficult. We can be sure that she would have felt isolated both at work and at home. But as for what exactly transpired under those circumstances . . ." Holmes shrugged. "It may be something as simple as her drawing closer to a man who should have remained only a father figure. Or it may be something else altogether."

His pulse quickened. "And what might that be?"

She took a sip of tea and finished her slice of cake. "The nature of what exactly transpired almost doesn't matter, only that it's something that she believes would lead a man to kill."

—❈—

A silence fell.

After a while, his attention shifted from the problem at hand to the silence itself.

Their interactions had always been full of silences. The leisurely, almost opulent silence of entire afternoons spent together as adolescents: he busy with his interests, she with hers. The inexplicably awkward silences after she'd first propositioned him—inexplicable only to him, too young to understand that he'd refused her not out of virtue, but out of fear of what she and her autonomy represented— rejection of the very hierarchy he was still trying to embrace.

Then there had come years of silences extraordinary in their complicatedness. He'd been unhappy in his marriage yet clinging on to his vows, and any moment alone with Holmes had been a pleasure so dark and bittersweet it was at times indistinguishable from pain.

Lately, however, things had changed again. His marriage had effectively ended in summer—and soon it would end entirely, with a divorce to be granted by the High Court in the first half of next year. And the silences between him and Holmes, well, sometimes, like now, they could almost be called comfortable.

Almost.

If he were not so keenly aware of her presence, her soft, even breaths, the wisp of golden hair that had escaped the confines of her lace cap, the slowness with which her fingertip traveled the circumference of her now-empty plate.

"Have you been well, Ash?" she asked.

At her quiet question, he tensed: She would not have forgotten that he'd arrived at her doorstep out of the blue. "Well enough," he said. It hadn't been long since they last saw each other. Only days. And those had been peaceful days, spent in the company of his children. "You?"

"Very well. Girding myself for the onslaught of Christmas baking Madame Gascoigne is about to unleash."

He smiled a little. She had recently fended off an aggressive approach of Maximum Tolerable Chins, a natural consequence of her typically robust appetite, and must find it vexing to have to practice self-control again so soon.

As if in rebellion against that, she placed another slice of holiday cake onto her plate. "By the way, Ash, did you come to see me about something?"

His heart stuttered.

He; Mrs. Watson; Holmes; her sister, Miss Olivia Holmes; and Miss Olivia's beau, Mr. Stephen Marbleton, had lately returned from a fortnight in France, during which they'd burgled a tightly guarded château of some of its most closely held secrets. Much had happened that night. He'd always had the presentiment that repercussions would be felt far into the future, but for Mr. Marbleton the consequences had already been unkind.

Lord Ingram had learned of the younger man's forced departure this morning, as he'd been about to travel with his children to the Derbyshire countryside. Their original plan would have seen them change trains in London and continue on their journey, but the news had careened into him like a runaway carriage.

Mr. Marbleton had been so full of hopes and hopeful plans. Come spring he'd wanted all of them to go on another trip together, this time to warm, sunny Andalusia, a holiday that would have been delightful for everyone involved, but especially so for Miss Olivia, who loved warm, sunny places almost as much as she loved her rare bouts of freedom, away from her neglectful yet limiting parents.

And now, in the blink of an eye, Mr. Marbleton had become a prisoner, not behind bars, but fettered and held captive all the same.

Lord Ingram understood the chaos and unpredictability of life. But this time, faced with a fresh reminder that disruption was the very nature of the universe, his thoughts had instantly turned to Holmes.

She already knew that he loved her—he'd never said so *to* her, but she'd been seated beside him when he'd made that confession to a pair of policemen. And she already knew, too, that in some distant, hypothetical future, with all obstacles and complexities magically removed from their lives, he would be happy for them to . . . spend more time together?

They'd been too oblique. They'd spoken of going together to Andalusia and other southerly, beautiful places, perhaps all the way to the fabled hill stations of the subcontinent, but they'd never specified exactly what they'd *meant*.

Perhaps the oblique and unspecified had been all that they'd needed.

Perhaps that had been all that they'd been capable of.

But this morning as he'd read her letter about Mr. Marbleton again and again, growing more chilled with every paragraph, he had been filled with an urgent need to see her—and to turn all the lovely, insubstantial metaphors into something concrete.

"Yes, I did come to see you," he said in answer to her question.

She looked at him expectantly, her eyes at once limpid and fathomless. She must know what he had come to say, and yet, he found that *he* did not.

Not exactly.

It was not the first time he'd placed himself before a woman, his heart on his sleeve. The previous time, when he'd offered his hand in marriage to the then Miss Alexandra Greville, though his fervor had been sincere and his idealism real, he had nevertheless seen his love as a gift, a great and precious blessing upon his penniless future wife.

Who had instead experienced it as a great and unwanted yoke.

He would not do the same to Holmes, to blanket her, even if it was with love, when she preferred to be without encumbrances. Was there not something she desired that he could give her?

Ah, but from the very beginning, she'd always been clear about what she wanted from him.

Which he had been too proud—and too afraid—to give. Because . . . what if it was the only thing she would ever want from him?

But today, under her steady blue gaze—today he wasn't so proud. Or so afraid.

So today he set down his whisky, rose from his chair, and went to her. Today he braced a hand on the back of her chair and set his other hand against her soft, full cheek. And today, he dipped his head and took her lips in his.

Four

The first time Charlotte Holmes had kissed Lord Ingram, she'd been thirteen and he fifteen—and she'd blackmailed him into it by threatening to lure a horde of unruly children to the ruins of a Roman villa that he had been in the middle of excavating.

She remembered very little of the kiss itself. For a girl who possessed near-perfect recall, that had been a grand anomaly, as if for the duration of the kiss, her brain had suffered some sort of catastrophic mechanical failure.

She did remember the faint whiff of Turkish tobacco that clung to him. She did remember the stare he gave her afterward, his expression opaque and unfriendly. And she did remember watching him march away, his strides long and swift, while her fingertips prickled with remnant heat and electricity.

A dozen years passed before they kissed for the second time this past summer. Their circumstances had changed greatly, as had they as people, yet exactly the same thing had happened. She had emerged from that kiss, too, as if from a daze, aware only that she was holding on to him, her cheek against the lapel of his coat, his heartbeat drumming in synchrony with her own.

Much again had happened in the months since, most notably that they had slept together. Not as an ignition of long-suppressed desires—though she suspected they'd had enough of those to set a dozen beds on fire—but as a measure calculated to create a certain impression, while dealing with a dangerous adversary.

Thankfully, as driven by ulterior motives as those two bouts of physical intimacy had been, she remembered them very well. The very correct, very straitlaced Lord Ingram had been as depraved in bed as she could have hoped for—and she had hoped for a great deal, having had long years to contemplate, in theory, all manner of debauchery and indecency.

Present-day Lord Ingram leaned down toward her.

The faint scar by his temple that he had acquired after a trip abroad two years ago. The gleam of the tiny antique coin that adorned his favorite stickpin. The beginning of stubble on a jaw that had been closely shaven that morning.

Heat.

Pressure.

Incitement.

He straightened.

She panted, as if she'd just finished a session of *canne de combat* training. Her face felt hot. The soles of her feet tingled. And *still* she could only recall bits and pieces of the kiss—the texture of his hair between her fingers, the slight roughness of wool under her other hand, the slide of the tip of his tongue across the inside of her upper lip—as if she'd dreamt of it and most of the dream had evaporated upon waking up.

Silence.

Not a fraught silence, full of undertow and that asphyxiated feeling in the chest. Nor an easy, relaxed silence. More as if . . . as if they were two travelers who found themselves in a place not marked on any map, and were looking about for their bearings.

"So this is what you came to see me for," she murmured. "Does it have something to do with Mr. Stephen Marbleton's involuntary return to Château Vaudrieu?"

"Yes."

She gazed at him. "You gave in to an impulse. This is unlike you, Ash."

He made no response.

She, for all that she was often thought of as cold-blooded and unemotional, was rather free with her impulses—as much as possible, she preferred to indulge herself. Lord Ingram, on the other hand, felt intensely, yet kept a stranglehold on his emotions and his desires.

"You taste good," she said.

Another indulged impulse on her part, to give voice to this particular thought.

Was he carefully weighing his words, making sure that he did not answer rashly, impetuously?

He kissed her again.

The heat of his palm against her cheek.

The pressure on her chin, held firmly between his thumb and forefinger.

The incitement of being pulled up from her chair and set against the wall.

And then he was no longer kissing her, but gazing into her eyes. An entire minute passed before he said softly, "I didn't give in to an impulse, Holmes. I made a choice."

Her eyes were large and wide set, ringed with long dark lashes tipped with a hint of gold. Her irises were the vivid cool blue of northern skies in autumn—and sometimes they reminded Lord Ingram exactly of a transparent, impersonal sky, unclouded by emotions.

They were not quite as impersonal today. But they remained deceptively guileless, as if she had never experienced kisses—or even proximity to a man—before this moment.

She exhaled.

Into the silence came the enthusiastic cries of a prepubescent boy, somewhat muffled by wind and rain. "Scotland Yard inspector accused of murder! Read all about it! Read all about the murdering copper!"

They broke apart and rushed to the window. She knelt on the deep, cushioned sill, opened a casement, and asked the paperboy if he could toss one up at her. He did and caught a coin she dropped down in return.

"Keep the change!"

She closed the window and spread open the rain-speckled paper on the desk. They stood over it, reading, hands braced against the side of the desk, arms almost but not quite touching.

> *The Metropolitan Police has acknowledged that Inspector Robert Treadles, of the Criminal Investigation Department, has been arrested on suspicion of murder.*
>
> *He was found on the scene of the crime, 33 Cold Street. The two victims, Mr. John Longstead and Mr. Ambrose Sullivan, are uncle and nephew, and both said to have been longtime associates of Cousins Manufacturing, owned by Mrs. Robert Treadles, the suspect's wife.*

They exchanged a look. Not one, but two men killed!

The paper went into some biographical details about the dead men. Those describing Mr. Longstead accorded largely with what Mrs. Treadles had related, except the article neglected to mention that he'd only recently returned to Cousins Manufacturing after a long absence.

Mr. Sullivan, the nephew, had been at the company ten years. Accounted capable and brilliant, the handsome managing director was popular with both peers and subordinates. His death had left behind a grieving widow and two fatherless young children, one still an infant.

Inspector Treadles, too, received a fair number of column inches. Nothing of what was written could be classified as inaccurate, per se, but Lord Ingram's lips flattened as he read on.

The distinctive impression he received from those paragraphs was that of a man who had married above his station and then proceeded to be jealous of his wife, especially after she took over her father's enterprise and began associating with men of her own class, men better educated and more successful than he.

The article concluded with *Inspector Treadles has not confessed to the twin murders and Scotland Yard has released no additional details on the crimes.*

He was just about to state that the paper went too far in its conjectures when his gaze fell on a stub of an article directly underneath.

> *In what might be considered a highly curious coincidence, it has been pointed out that a small notice, carried by a number of London morning editions yesterday, reads, when deciphered, "Roses are red, violets are blue, on Cold Street one finds a wife no longer true."*

So much for hoping that the message would have gone unnoticed in the wake of the murders.

"It smacks of manipulation, doesn't it?" said Holmes calmly.

"Manipulation or not, the public will leap to the conclusion Mrs. Treadles feared: that those were crimes motivated by an insecure husband's intense jealousy. Men have killed for far less."

Holmes ran her fingers through her hair, shorn short several weeks ago so that it would be easier to don wigs. Her lace cap from earlier now lay on the floor next to the wall where they had kissed, the sight of which sent a rather adolescent thrill through him.

"And men have withstood far more without killing." Her voice remained dispassionate. "It's telling that Mrs. Treadles didn't mention Mr. Sullivan, whom she would have seen a lot more of, since presumably he was there at the office every day except Sunday."

He forcibly pulled his mind back to the case at hand. "Perhaps she didn't know he also died."

But even he didn't believe it.

A young man, handsome and well-versed in the running of the enterprise—whatever they had speculated earlier about Mrs. Treadles and Mr. Longstead was much more likely to have instead taken place between Mrs. Treadles and Mr. Sullivan.

Her conspicuous silence certainly didn't dispel the thought.

Holmes tapped a knuckle against the paper. "The article didn't say who would be the detective leading the investigation. I wonder if it will be Chief Inspector Fowler. I hope not."

They'd had more than a little taste of working with Chief Inspector Fowler, who had handled the case at Stern Hollow and had been rather overtly invested in Lord Ingram's guilt.

"Fowler has seen me as Charlotte Holmes the fallen woman, and he has seen Mrs. Watson, too, as my companion. If he's in charge, we'll need disguises." She patted her cheek wistfully. "And I'd rather not put on a beard unless absolutely necessary. My skin does not care for the glue."

"You have suffered for your friends," he said softly.

"In your case, I'd say I was also pleasantly rewarded," she said with a slight smile. "Very pleasantly."

He ignored the heat that surged through him, although the effort took a moment. "Shall I go find out who is in charge of Inspector Treadles's case?"

The bell rang. "Probably not necessary for you to make a special trip for it, if that's Sergeant MacDonald at the door."

"Let me go out the back door and come back in—so he doesn't get the wrong impression."

Her eyes twinkled with amusement. "So he doesn't get the correct impression, you mean?"

"That, too, I suppose."

She sighed softly. "It would be nice—"

"If he didn't jump to conclusions?"

"If whatever conclusions he jumps to with regard to my gentlemen friends did not affect his ability to work with me."

He wasn't sure *he* could do that. He, for one, emphatically did not want to judge Mrs. Treadles. But even so, he knew he was already beginning to wonder whether she was as competent and trustworthy as he'd first thought.

All in the absence of solid evidence.

"I'd better hurry," he said. "We don't want Sergeant MacDonald to wait too long."

"You don't need to go anywhere," she said.

"I don't—"

"You're afraid he'll wonder what we two might be doing here alone. But you forget: to Sergeant MacDonald we wouldn't be alone."

Of course. "Sherlock Holmes" was in the next room.

She touched him briefly on the arm, went down, and returned with their caller. As they climbed up he heard her say, "By the way, Lord Ingram is also here, Sergeant, to discuss Inspector Treadles's current predicament—Mrs. Treadles wished for his involvement in the matter."

"I would have wished for the same—this is a time for friends," said Sergeant MacDonald, as he walked into the room.

He was a young man of about Holmes's age. When Lord Ingram had met him before, he'd remarked on the sergeant's relaxed, smiling mien. Today he was not relaxed or smiling, though he was visibly relieved to be among his superior's supporters.

"I'll make tea. Would you also care for something stronger in the meanwhile, Sergeant MacDonald?"

"I probably shouldn't but I will, this time. Thank you, Miss Holmes."

"It has been a long day for you, I take it," said Lord Ingram, while Holmes put a kettle to boil on the spirit lamp.

"Unfortunately so, my lord. I don't know what to make of anything anymore. Rumors are rife within the Yard. I'm petrified to think that the inspector might have done the deeds—and I'm even more petrified that he didn't but will be condemned as guilty anyway."

"Do you think the inspector might have done it?" asked Holmes, taking her seat.

Sergeant MacDonald made a rueful face, as he sat down after

her. "The only reason I force myself to contemplate it is because the inspector taught me that I should eliminate suspects on evidence, and not because they seem unlikely.

"But no, I really don't think it could have been him. We are working men, us coppers, but we labor for different reasons. Some of us just want wages on the regular and work that isn't as grinding as what men do in factories. Some of us fancy it a bit more—I think my work in the Criminal Investigation Department is interesting, when it isn't too gruesome. But for the inspector—he's never said it in so many words, but I think for him it's a calling.

"He really does revere the rule of law, to an extent I find a bit . . ." The sergeant scratched his chin, searching for the right word. "Well, a bit old-fashioned. Laws are made by men, aren't they? Men aren't perfect. And even decent laws aren't enforced uniformly—I see that all the time. But the inspector, even though he's a tough investigator, has this idealistic, almost romantic view of a just society and all that."

It was precisely this quality that had drawn Lord Ingram to Inspector Treadles. He was a few years younger than Inspector Treadles, but by the time they'd met, his own romantic vision of life had already become badly eroded. It had been encouraging, almost restorative, to be in the company of a man who dealt with some of the worst elements of society, yet still held on to his ideals.

Not realizing at the time that Inspector Treadles's ideals also included a number of inflexible views on women.

Holmes passed Sergeant MacDonald a plate of cake and he fell upon it eagerly, consuming a slice before saying, "I imagine the inspector would kill in self-defense, or in the defense of others, if he must. But I can't see him killing with premeditation. If he was dealing with malfeasance of any kind, he'd let the law handle it. After all, he is an enforcer of the law; his words would carry weight."

But what about where the law did not legislate? What about matters of affection, of husbandly possessiveness?

"We just read about a small notice," said Holmes, "that would seem to indicate that Inspector Treadles would have arrived at Cold Street already in an inflamed state of mind."

"I heard about that, but Inspector Treadles doesn't read the small notices, as far as I know. And in any case—" Sergeant Mac-Donald again scratched his chin. "Forgive me if I'm speaking out of turn. I've known the inspector for a while. I won't say he doesn't get angry, but he isn't a man who lashes out in anger. He pulls in, if you take my meaning."

Lord Ingram did. He also "pulled in," so to speak.

Holmes nodded and changed the subject. "I believe Inspector Treadles enjoyed a stellar reputation at Scotland Yard. Yet despite his good name and his good work over the years, he was arrested for these murders. Should we take it as indication that his guilt, at the moment at least, appears overwhelming?"

Sergeant MacDonald sighed. "After I saw Mrs. Treadles, I went to the nearest two stations to Cold Street and got the gist of the story. A bit after three in the morning, I was told, a pair of bobbies were coming back from their patrol. A fog had rolled in. Because of that they changed their route to Cold Street, a shortcut back to their station house.

"The fog was dense. But with the light from their lanterns they could still see, when they passed before 33 Cold Street, that the front door was open. They went for a closer look, and saw that the house was unoccupied—cold interior, furniture covered, etc. Their first thought was burglary, possibly one in progress. They heard some noises coming from an upstairs room and climbed up, thinking to catch the thief red-handed.

"What they found was a room locked from the inside. They rattled the door and heard no response. They identified themselves as the police and still received no answers. So they forced open the door— and saw Inspector Treadles inside. He'd barricaded himself behind the bedstead, his service revolver pointed at them. Nearer to the door were the two dead men and a fair bit of blood."

The sergeant's recital was matter-of-fact, but Lord Ingram heard the catch in his voice at the end. His own stomach tightened. He could almost smell the pungency of fresh blood and feel the inspector's terror at the pounding on the door.

Holmes took the kettle off the spirit lamp and poured hot water into the teapot. "Had the victims been shot?"

Sergeant MacDonald took a swallow of the whisky he'd been given earlier—and took a deep breath. "Yes, they were."

"Had anyone heard the shots?"

"I asked the same question. Apparently there was a problem with miscreants setting off fireworks in the area. Some coppers blame Italian immigrants—word is, in some Italian cities, Christmas fireworks are a tradition. Others say there was once a tavern nearby that set off fireworks at Christmas and people are just nostalgic." Sergeant MacDonald shrugged. "In any case, the residents are annoyed by pyrotechnics going off at night. The news has even made the papers, but no one has been apprehended."

Holmes passed him more cake. "I see. Please continue."

Sergeant MacDonald accepted her offer with a grateful smile. "Right. Now where was I? Oh, the constables didn't have firearms, as they were patrolling a generally safe district. But one fought in Afghanistan and wasn't daunted by either the carnage or the sight of a man holding a gun. He simply told Inspector Treadles to hand over the revolver and submit himself to the authority of the police.

"There are different versions of what happened next, but most of those I spoke to agreed that Inspector Treadles questioned the men in some detail about their station house, their superiors, and their duties, which they answered earnestly enough, given that they still had a revolver pointed at them. And then Inspector Treadles gave his name and rank, and surrendered the firearm and himself."

Lord Ingram exchanged a look with Holmes. Whomever Inspector

Treadles had dreaded would crash through the door, it hadn't been the police.

"Once the inspector was handcuffed, one constable stayed to keep an eye on him and the crime scene; the other ran back to the station for help," Sergeant MacDonald went on. "Scotland Yard, I understand, was on the scene before dawn. I was pulled aside not long after I arrived for work and told to go see Mrs. Treadles."

"At which point you didn't know the details of the case, except that Inspector Treadles had been arrested for the murders of Mr. Longstead and Mr. Sullivan," said Holmes, pouring tea for everyone.

"That is correct," answered Sergeant MacDonald. He drank his tea rather thirstily. "And this is an excellent brew, Miss Holmes."

"Thank you, Sergeant. Now, when you called on Mrs. Treadles, I assume you informed her of the names of both victims."

"I did," said Sergeant MacDonald without any hesitation.

So Mrs. Treadles knew very well that two men had been killed. Yet when she had called on Sherlock Holmes, she'd omitted any and all mentions of Mr. Sullivan.

Holmes stirred her own tea. "How did she react?"

"She seemed completely cut up about the older fellow, said she'd known him all her life and that he'd always been a perfect gentleman."

Completely cut up about the older fellow. What about the younger fellow?

Lord Ingram rose. He hadn't touched the whisky Holmes had given him earlier, but now he was in need of a draught.

Holmes cast him a look, though her expression never deviated from that of mild interest. She returned her attention to Sergeant MacDonald. "Inspector Treadles had been on leave for a fortnight or so before the events of last night. Did he give you a reason for his prolonged absence from work?"

From the sideboard, Lord Ingram glanced sharply at the duo in the center of the room. Toward the end of Holmes's interview with Mrs. Treadles, the latter had given notice that Sergeant MacDonald would call on 18 Upper Baker Street later in the day. It stood to reason that Sergeant MacDonald also knew that Mrs. Treadles had been to see Sherlock Holmes.

Would he not wonder why Holmes asked him about something she should have already learned from Mrs. Treadles?

His brow indeed furrowed with puzzlement, but the next moment, he must have made the decision that Holmes was following sound procedure in obtaining her information from multiple sources. "He said it was something to do with his family and would require that he travel away from London."

"Did that surprise you?"

"Somewhat. I knew that his parents had both passed away and I hadn't heard him mention siblings. But the inspector wasn't one to speak of his private life, so I didn't think it was *that* unusual—family has a way of finding a man, especially if he's doing well in life." Sergeant MacDonald hesitated. "But I did wonder when he didn't come back after a week—surely a family emergency would have been resolved after that much time."

"Do you wish to hazard a guess as to where he might have been these past two weeks?"

Sergeant MacDonald began to shake his head, then said, "Wait. I did see him poring over some maps a while ago at his desk. I think they were of Yorkshire. I asked him then if we might be investigating a case there. He said no, but didn't give any explanations. And I didn't ask any more questions."

He smiled apologetically.

Holmes raised her teacup. "Did he seem different in the days before he went on leave?"

Sergeant MacDonald frowned again. "I've been asking myself the same question, wondering if there was something I should have noticed. But the truth was I didn't see very much of him even before he went on his leave—he'd given me some assignments to undertake on my own when he went to Stern Hollow with Chief Inspector

Fowler. When he returned, he was pleased with my work and gave me more assignments. I'd report to him either in the morning or in the evening, when we happened to both be at the Yard."

Mrs. Treadles had mentioned the same, that the young man was happy and proud to have been entrusted with this independence. But now, in the light of subsequent events, Lord Ingram wondered whether Inspector Treadles had been *that* happy with his subordinate's work, or had he simply wanted to be unobserved for much of that time?

"Very well, thank you, Sergeant. One last question. Do you know who will oversee Inspector Treadles's case? The papers didn't say."

"That would be Inspector Brighton. He's new to Scotland Yard, but he's said to have had a distinguished record in Manchester."

It made sense, Lord Ingram supposed, to have an investigator who wasn't a longtime colleague of Inspector Treadles, someone whose impartiality wouldn't be so easily called into doubt. And yet. At the thought of having a complete stranger in charge of his friend's fate, his hand tightened around the glass of whisky he'd just poured for himself.

Holmes cast him another glance. "Chief Inspector Fowler—he wasn't considered?"

"He might have been—Lord knows he has no allegiance except to pinning down culprits. But he just left for a case in Lincolnshire. In fact, he's gone to take over Inspector Brighton's new case, so Inspector Brighton could come back to London for Inspector Treadles."

"If Inspector Brighton got the summons early in the day and started, he should already be back in town, directing inquiries," mused Holmes. "I wonder what manner of man he is."

"I've only ever said 'morning, sir; good day, sir' to him. But he's said to be sharp as a tack."

Sergeant MacDonald hesitated. When he spoke again, it was in a lowered voice. "And he's also said to be thoroughly ruthless."

Lord Ingram's heart thudded unpleasantly.

The grandfather clock in the corner chimed the quarter hour.

Sergeant MacDonald glanced at it and rose slowly. "I'd better re-port back to the Yard. Once Inspector Brighton has seen Inspector Treadles—and the bodies—he might want to speak to me."

He spoke as if Inspector Brighton might put him to the rack.

"Have you thought about how you might handle Inspector Brighton, Sergeant?" asked Holmes.

Her tone hadn't changed, but Lord Ingram heard concern. For the sake of his livelihood—and as a policeman sworn to uphold the law—Sergeant MacDonald was obliged to tell Inspector Brighton everything he knew. But out of loyalty to Inspector Treadles, he needed to say as little as possible, lest anything he gave away further incriminate his superior.

Tilt too much one way, and he might never advance his career. Tilt in the other direction, and he would further endanger the mentor he admired, the man who had done more for his career than anyone else.

The young man gazed at the remainder of his whisky, as if in it lay the secret of how to achieve this impossible balance. Then he squared his shoulders and looked back at Holmes. "I'll look after myself. But I'll also look after Inspector Treadles."

An immense gratitude swelled up inside Lord Ingram. "Thank you," he said.

Sergeant MacDonald gave a rather wan smile. "Don't mention it."

He shook hands with Holmes and Lord Ingram, thanked them, took a deep breath, and showed himself out.

Leaving behind two very quiet people.

"Mr. Sullivan," Lord Ingram said at last.

The specter of the dead nephew, whose name Mrs. Treadles refused to speak, loomed large.

"Yes, Mr. Sullivan," echoed Holmes. "One begins to wonder whether anyone involved in this situation wanted the real truth known, now or ever."

Five

There was no time to lose.

Lord Ingram needed to be at Scotland Yard, where he would facilitate arrangements for Sherlock Holmes's involvement in the case. What good was being a lordship, an independently wealthy man, and a well-connected figure in Society, if he couldn't secure a few favors for himself and his friends?

"Not to mention that," he said as he helped Charlotte into a secondhand mackintosh—she was going out dressed as a laundry maid, "Scotland Yard, having wrongly arrested me not too long ago, owes me some reparations."

She regarded him rather cautiously, wondering if he meant to perform even more loverly feats—in days of antiquity, at the first house party he and his wife had attended as newlyweds, she'd witnessed him button up Lady Ingram's overcoat with an overabundance of husbandly zeal, sinking down to one knee for the lowest buttons.

But he waited for her to do her own fastening and, when she was done, kissed her lightly on the lips. "I'll see you at dinner."

Her hansom cab headed to Mrs. Treadles's house, where she had some pointed questions to ask her client. But as her vehicle bounced and swayed, her mind kept going back to his soft yet implacable declaration.

I didn't give in to an impulse, Holmes. I made a choice.

What kind of choice?

With the cries of the newspaper boy and the arrival of Sergeant MacDonald, they had not spoken again on his choice. But she had a fair idea: He had come to give her what she wanted.

She had always been the one to make demands of him, of his body specifically. She wanted him to be her friend and her lover. He had always refused, first because he couldn't possibly compromise her, and then because he'd been married, albeit unhappily so and no longer intimate with his wife.

That had been the stated reason: His honor forbade it.

She believed in his sense of honor—the man was practically a wellspring of honor. But she also knew it hadn't been the only reason.

He'd been . . . Well, not afraid, exactly, but wary of her, despite their long-standing friendship.

Unlike Inspector Treadles, who needed to think of society as just and justifiable, Lord Ingram had always been deeply ambivalent about the world in which they lived. But he'd yearned to belong, to find a place for himself. For this acceptance, he became not only acceptable, but the very embodiment of gentlemanly virtues.

She had been, in a way, the mirror image of him. As he'd left his rebellious days behind, she, too, had learned to speak and act in ways that were socially acceptable. But unlike his transformation, hers was only superficial. And she'd regarded his profound changes not with awe or gladness, but with skepticism.

Is this really what you want? Is this really who you are?

She'd never posed those questions in the open, but over the years he must have heard them resoundingly. Had he approached a different woman, greater physical proximity might signify just that. But getting closer to her would force him to face his doubts, otherwise ruthlessly locked away, on whether there wasn't another way to live, one that didn't clap his soul in irons.

And now this man who had not wanted to examine his misgivings and who had therefore carefully kept his distance, had kissed her three times in a row.

What choice *had* he made? The choice to overturn all the other choices he had made in his entire life?

---❉---

Miss Olivia Holmes groaned as she flexed her right hand. Her fingers were stiff and cold, which they often were in winter, but today every muscle in that hand hurt from having been made to labor since early morning.

On the desk before her lay ten more pages of her manuscript. She made sure the newest page was properly blotted. Then she rolled her wrist, rotated her shoulders, rose to her feet with another groan, and carried the pages across the room she'd once shared with Charlotte to hide them in a trunk.

Transferring her Sherlock Holmes story from the bundle of notebooks in which it had been drafted onto proper manuscript pages had seemed a monumental task. Yet in little more than eighteen hours of work, split between two days, she'd managed to reach the two fifths point in the . . . novel.

My novel, she tried to make herself say. *I've written a novel.*

A story seemed a small thing, but a novel had heft. If nothing else it testified to its creator's persistence, that she was stubborn enough to string tens of thousands of words together in the fervent hope that they would form a cohesive whole that not only made sense, but entertained.

Enthralled.

She caressed the edges of the pages already concealed beneath Charlotte's winter dresses. The stack was reassuringly thick, crisp and dense against its nest of silk and wool. She didn't know why she'd thrown herself headlong into duplicating her work by hand; after all, she wasn't in any great hurry to submit it—and have it come back rejected.

No, she was lying to herself here. She did know why she copied for hours on end, hunched over her desk, the sandwich that should have been her lunch still largely untouched. After a glorious, if also terrifying adventure in France in the company of Charlotte and a number of their friends, Livia was back home, where she least wished to be.

And yesterday morning, just before she departed London, Mr. Stephen Marbleton, the young man she loved, and whom she believed to love her equally in return, had told her that they were too hopeless a case. That he would no longer keep in touch with her.

Livia had been instantly heartbroken, and yet . . . strangely calm. She'd told Mrs. Watson, who accompanied her home disguised as a lady's companion, that she believed it very wise of Mr. Marbleton to act as he had. Instead of living on false hope and eventually being hurt and disappointed anyway, now their courtship had ended and she need no longer dread its eventual demise.

Mrs. Watson had comforted Livia as best as she could. And then, Livia had arrived home and no one had cared particularly that she was back or that she wanted to cry but couldn't. She'd gone up to her room, unpacked a few things, taken out her notebooks, and begun to copy her story.

To escape her own life in the only way she could, by immersing herself in the fictional lives of others.

She massaged the muscles of her right forearm. A cup of tea would be nice, but her kettle was empty. In other households, the daughter of the house would simply ring for a fresh pot. But Livia tried not to give more work to the servants, who already had to contend with her inconsiderate parents. And after an entire day in a chair, she could use the exercise of going down for a pitcher of water.

She hadn't yet reached the stairs when her mother's question exploded like an artillery shell. "And where do you think you are going?"

Livia stopped in her tracks, mortified. Would she be berated now even for fetching water?

"Ah, Lady Holmes," said her father, "I was just coming to say goodbye to you."

Livia blinked, realizing belatedly that her mother had been speaking to her husband, and not her daughter.

"You were not!" huffed Lady Holmes. "You would have left without saying a word."

"And could you blame me, my lady, given the harshness of your goodbyes?"

Women newly acquainted with Sir Henry sometimes considered him suave and charming. Livia, after nearly twenty-eight years under his roof, only found him both unctuous and mean-spirited.

"How could you leave now? It's almost Christmas, and Christmas should be spent at home."

"Since you think so, you should by all means remain home for Christmas, my lady. I wish you a most joyful holiday filled with warmth and festiveness."

The sound of footsteps headed for the front door.

Livia stole forward until she was at the top of the stairs and had a clear line of sight to the front hall. Her father, in his traveling cloak, stood before the door to the vestibule, a large satchel in his hand. Her mother had just caught up with him, her heavy bosom heaving, her fussy winter cap askew.

"But even if you don't care about spending Christmas at home," she shouted, "shouldn't you spare a thought for your pocketbook? You'll be spending money we don't have to please your selfish self!"

"Ah, but that is not true," answered Sir Henry, his voice dripping with smugness. "I recently came into possession of one hundred pounds."

"One hundred pounds? How? From where?"

The same questions echoed in Livia's head until she remembered the deal Charlotte had made with their father to give him one hundred pounds every year.

"You need not concern yourself with that, my lady, save to know that it is indeed so."

"Then how could you be so cruel as to not take me with you on holiday, if there is money to spend?"

Sir Henry grinned, a superior, callous expression that made Livia wince. "But you yourself insisted just now that you should remain home for Christmas. Who am I to gainsay you, my lady?"

And with that, he sauntered out, leaving his wife to sputter with impotent rage.

Had Charlotte imagined that Sir Henry would spend the entirety of his windfall on himself? Or that Livia would be left alone with a seething Lady Holmes?

She tiptoed backward, but not quickly enough. Her mother turned around and saw her. "You! Peeping from the shadows again! Did you see it all? Did you see what a dastardly scoundrel your father was? And why are you still here, you old maid? Why can't you find a good man—or any living, breathing man—to marry you and take you off my hands?"

Livia fled, back to her room, back to her desk, back inside a story where the villains weren't her own parents.

Six

Despite the rain, reporters and curiosity-seekers thronged the pavement in front of Mrs. Treadles's house, their small forest of black umbrellas spilling into the street. As Charlotte drew near, a large laundry basket under her arm to complete her laundry-maid disguise, a murmur of excitement rippled through the crowd.

She stopped beside a woman, most likely a maid from a nearby house, at the edge of the herd. "Pardon me, miss, but why are there so many people? And everybody a-quakin'?"

The woman placed a hand over her heart. "You don't know? Goodness, but the inspector what lives in this house got himself arrested for murder. *Two* murders. And they said another inspector from Scotland Yard just went in to see his missus."

Charlotte had come as quickly as she could, in the hope of speaking to Mrs. Treadles before Inspector Brighton did. It would seem she was still too late.

"Oh my," she moaned. "What's the world coming to? And me with washin' to deliver to the house."

This earned her an enthusiastic reply. "Well, then ask them on the inside what's going on. I'm dying to know!"

Charlotte broke through the crowd. As was typical of such town houses, next to the front door there was a wrought iron fence that enclosed a set of steps going down to the service entrance. Onlookers hung over the fence, watching her descend.

At the service entrance she knocked loudly. "I've yer washin' 'ere!"

The door was opened by a tense-looking woman of about fifty years of age. "We've already got—"

Charlotte handed over a slip of paper on which was written, *I am Miss Holmes. Here to see Mrs. Treadles at her behest.*

The woman's expression relaxed somewhat, but her tone remained severe. "You'd best come in out of the rain then and close the door quick. Never seen so many idlers in my whole life."

Once the door had been secured, the woman, who must have been the housekeeper, inclined her head respectfully. "Mrs. Treadles has the police inspector in the drawing room, miss. But she said to bring you by should you call. Do please come with me—I'm just about to take the tea tray up."

They walked down a spotless service corridor. The housekeeper picked up a laden tea tray; Charlotte divested herself of her mackintosh and her basket. Together they mounted the service stairs and exited two floors up.

The housekeeper indicated a nearby room to Charlotte, while she herself trundled toward a different one. Charlotte opened the door the housekeeper had pointed to with her chin and found herself in a dimly lit private parlor. In fact, the only light came in through a connecting door that had been left ajar.

On the other side of the connecting door must have been the drawing room, from which came the faintly ceramic thuds of teapots and teacups being placed upon a tablecloth.

"Thank you, Mrs. Graycott," said a woman. Mrs. Treadles.

The housekeeper left, closing the drawing room door softly behind herself.

Tea trickled gently into cups.

In the private parlor, the wall opposite the opening of the connecting door was dominated by a large mirror. Charlotte tiptoed until she had the best possible reflected view of the drawing room, standing almost immediately next to and behind the door.

The slice of the drawing room visible in the mirror showed the back of a man's head and Mrs. Treadles's pale face. She was trying to smile and not succeeding very well. "Milk, sugar, Inspector? Sergeant?"

"Both, thank you," said Inspector Brighton in a crisp, clear voice.

"Neither, please," said another man, who sat some distance behind Inspector Brighton, out of sight. He would be the one taking notes.

"Do please help yourself to the biscuits and the finger sandwiches," said Mrs. Treadles after she'd distributed the teacups. "It must have been an exhausting day for you."

"No more than it has been exhausting for you, Mrs. Treadles."

Inspector Brighton sounded cordial, yet Charlotte was put in mind of a serpent in the grass, flicking its forked tongue.

"I visited Mr. Sherlock Holmes today, and engaged him to help my husband," said Mrs. Treadles.

"Indeed."

"On my way back I heard a paperboy shouting about the murders, so I had my coachman take me to Scotland Yard, hoping to see Inspector Treadles."

Had she bought a paper? And had that newspaper also gleefully pointed out the small notice that aimed to goad Inspector Treadles into descending upon Cold Street?

"I do apologize that you weren't able to see him," said Inspector Brighton. "I spoke to him about an hour and a half ago. He is in reasonable fettle, if you are worried."

"I took him some food and two changes of clothes. I was told they would be given to him."

"I will make sure that they are."

"Thank you."

Mrs. Treadles's expression was one of weary relief, as if the assurance that some comfort would reach her husband was the most she could hope for from this encounter. And now that reassurance was out of the way . . .

No one spoke for some time, until Inspector Brighton said, "This is an excellent sandwich, Mrs. Treadles. My compliments to your cook."

Mrs. Treadles straightened abruptly, as if she were a small creature in that same grass, sensing the approach of a predator. "Thank you, Inspector."

"If you don't mind my asking, you and Inspector Treadles come from very different walks of life. How did you meet?" inquired Inspector Brighton, his tone conversational.

Mrs. Treadles's answer was muted. "At one of Lord Ingram Ashburton's archaeological lectures."

"And that led to your marriage."

"In time, yes."

"What manner of man would you say Inspector Treadles is?"

"Honorable, dutiful, sensible," said Mrs. Treadles with anxious pride. "He is also a voracious reader, very keen on broadening his horizons and understanding the flow of history—of British history in particular."

Inspector Brighton let a moment pass. "And what manner of *husband* would you say he is?"

That he had begun with the class difference between the Treadleses was a clear indication, to Charlotte at least, of the thrust of his inquiries. But Mrs. Treadles still seemed caught by surprise.

Or perhaps it was because she could never adequately prepare for this particular question. Because no matter how she braced herself, the unhappiness of having to answer it truthfully would always shake her to the very foundation.

"He . . . is a very good husband. As I said, he is honorable, dutiful, and sensible, so I never need to worry about dalliances on his part. Since we have no children, we spend a great deal of time together, reading side by side, sometimes aloud to each other, and generally treasure the quietness of domestic contentment."

"Most marriages begin well. The passage of time, however, puts all heartfelt wedding vows to the test. How would you say your marriage has changed over the years?"

If Livia were here, staring at the back of Inspector Brighton's head in the mirror, would she have imagined a sinister smile on the man's lips? Charlotte was less prone to such flights of fancy, but she very much felt that Inspector Brighton was enjoying himself at Mrs. Treadles's expense.

Mrs. Treadles swallowed. "I . . . Well, he has been made an inspector in the time we've been married. And I inherited my father's enterprise after my brother unfortunately passed away."

"Let me be more specific, Mrs. Treadles, since you mentioned your family. Your dowry, dear lady, could have served as a tremendous asset to your husband's career. You yourself, a cultured, handsome, and personable woman, could have been a similar boon. Why do you suppose he never put either to use?"

Mrs. Treadles raised her teacup to her lips—Charlotte was reminded of her nervous tea drinking at 18 Upper Baker Street. "I— I must assume it stemmed from his sense of fair play. It would be unfair to his colleagues if he were to advance faster due to his wealthy wife."

"Is that so? I understand that Inspector Treadles has risen as fast as he has because he has had the good fortune of being associated with Mr. Sherlock Holmes, whose insights have led him to solve several puzzling cases."

"That is . . . true."

"And he did not consider that an unfair advantage?"

"But he hasn't consulted Mr. Holmes of late. Not since summer."

Not since he'd found out that Sherlock Holmes was a fallen woman, thought Charlotte wryly.

"Nevertheless," Inspector Brighton hammered on, "he didn't mind help from a man, but he didn't want help from a woman, not even if that woman was his wife."

Mrs. Treadles stared down at her teacup.

Charlotte sighed soundlessly. As soon as she had learned of Mr. Sullivan's death, she had wanted to see Mrs. Treadles, to put those exact same questions to her. Both to wring out the truth, if possible, and also to prepare her for a similar extraction from Inspector Brighton.

Inspector Brighton was quick to press his advantage. "When did you realize that he was not happy about Cousins Manufacturing having come to you, Mrs. Treadles?"

Mrs. Treadles's head snapped up. "Did he say that to you?"

"You need not concern yourself with what answers your husband may or may not have given. Answer my question, please."

Her gaze dropped away. "It's true he was not greatly pleased. But he did nothing to hinder me from assuming my rightful place at the head of the company."

"Did he inquire into how you were doing at the company?"

Her voice grew smaller. "Not initially."

"And how long was that interval you referred to as 'initially'?"

"Three months or so."

This time, her answer was barely audible.

"A long time to go without asking questions of one's beloved as to how she fared at her monumental task. Would you have said that his resolute lack of curiosity was a strong rebuke of your choice to run the company yourself?"

Mrs. Treadles was silent.

Inspector Brighton tutted, as if he were speaking to a recalcitrant, yet none-too-bright child. "And how did you fare at Cousins Manufacturing, by the way, my dear lady?"

Mrs. Treadles remained silent for some more time; then she set her jaw. "Not as well as I'd have liked to have done."

"Why not?"

"My brother's lieutenants did not welcome me."

"Oh, how did they not welcome you?"

It was obvious to Charlotte that he already knew the answer and was only toying with Mrs. Treadles. *Mrs. Treadles must know it, too, and yet she must still give an account of her unhappy powerlessness.*

Her throat moved. "They resented that I was there, asking questions about how they did things. How they'd always done things. When I gave my opinions, they acted as if they hadn't heard. At every opportunity, they insinuated—nay, stated outright that I should return home, that my presence at Cousins was a waste of time for both myself and the men who had been entrusted with looking after that great enterprise."

"You were made to feel an intruder in your own domain."

"That is correct."

Inspector Brighton combed his fingers through his hair—he'd been laying siege, but now he was getting ready to storm the castle gate. "How did your husband react when he learned of your difficulties?"

Mrs. Treadles set down her teacup—was she too tense now to even drink tea? "I—I never told him anything of my difficulties."

"Not for three months or thereabouts that I can understand. But when he did eventually ask how you were doing, why did you not tell him?"

"There was nothing he could have done to help me. And I didn't want to worry him."

"Perhaps he couldn't have taken any direct measures to influence your subordinates, but surely his moral support would have been appreciated." Inspector Brighton paused. "You did not wish for even that?"

The question was uttered softly, as if in concern, but his voice was devoid of warmth.

"I was too proud. I didn't want him to know that I had trouble handling my own company."

"A man who disapproved strongly of your undertaking should

have guessed that he wouldn't be the only disapproving man you'd encounter along the way."

"He did guess, but I glossed over my difficulties."

Inspector Brighton shifted in his chair. Not a nervous or involuntary motion, but a deliberate exertion: He braced an elbow on an armrest, and stretched out his legs, the very image of a man at ease.

Mrs. Treadles, in contrast, brought her arms, and very possibly her feet—judging by the small, sharp jerk of her skirts—closer to her body.

Her instinctive reaction seemed to please Inspector Brighton. Charlotte heard a smirk in his next question.

"Did you have any allies at work, Mrs. Treadles?"

"Yes, Mr. Longstead," said Mrs. Treadles quietly, "whose departure I greatly lament."

"Mr. Longstead was not a constant presence at Cousins. He left many years ago. Even though he recently returned at your request, it was in the capacity of an adviser rather than an executor. Would you agree, Mrs. Treadles, that you worked much more closely with his nephew, Mr. Sullivan?"

At the sound of that name, Mrs. Treadles's jaw moved, as if she felt nauseated and were trying to hold down the revolt in her stomach. "I did work more with Mr. Sullivan. Unfortunately he and I did not get along very well. He was one of those men who made my life at work more difficult at every turn."

She even sounded faintly queasy.

Inspector Brighton chortled softly. "Did you always think so, Mrs. Treadles?"

"What do you mean?"

"Scotland Yard will speak to everyone at Cousins who had the remotest dealings with either of the victims. Or with you. Will we receive answers at variance with yours, Mrs. Treadles?"

"Of course you will. I have never known any group of people to give uniform answers to any single question."

Even a rabbit would snarl, when backed into a corner. Inspector Brighton evidently did not mind his prey's futile bristling.

"Mrs. Treadles, I do not speak in hypotheticals," he said cheerfully. Indeed, with relish. "Will those we interview at Cousins tell us that you were unfriendly toward Mr. Sullivan?"

Mrs. Treadles tugged at her collar, as if it had become too tight. "Very well, then. Initially I was favorably inclined toward Mr. Sullivan. When the other men, often older and more set in their ways, were openly dismissive of me, he appeared kinder, more liberal-minded. But I was deceived. He was a wolf in sheep's clothing, a man who seemed attentive and helpful, but in fact did more than anyone else to undermine my position."

Charlotte, unsurprised, shook her head. She understood why Mrs. Treadles had not been able to bring herself to make this confession before her husband's friends. All the same, it had been an unwise decision.

"Mr. Sullivan was, in other words, the ringleader of the disloyal opposition?"

"In retrospect, yes."

Inspector Brighton's tone turned more languid, as if his interrogation were but a chat between friends, over glasses of wine. "Why did you not let go of him?"

"I would have let go of the entire lot if I could," said Mrs. Treadles bitterly. "But they would have had a field day shredding my reputation. And how could I be sure that the men I hired to replace them would be any better?"

Inspector Brighton flicked a nonexistent speck of dust from the cuff of his sleeve. "I didn't ask why you didn't get rid of the whole lot, Mrs. Treadles. I asked why you didn't get rid of Mr. Sullivan, the ringleader."

His voice remained dulcet, but the menace in his words had become unmistakable.

Mrs. Treadles tugged at her collar again. Charlotte had the sensation that had she been alone, she'd have been clawing at the closure to breathe better. "I—I didn't wish to injure Mr. Longstead."

"I thought you said Mr. Longstead was your ally."

"Yes, but he was also Mr. Sullivan's uncle."

"Did you ever broach the problem of Mr. Sullivan with Mr. Longstead?"

"No."

"Why not?" said Inspector Brighton silkily. "Would it also have injured him merely to have brought up the fact that Mr. Sullivan was stabbing you in the back?"

The aversion on Mrs. Treadles's face was turning into pure fear: Inspector Brighton was drawing near what she most desperately wished to keep hidden.

"One wonders, Mrs. Treadles," continued Inspector Brighton, savoring each syllable, "what Mr. Sullivan had on you."

Mrs. Treadles's hands dug into her skirts. "Nothing. He had nothing on me."

"Not anymore, now that he is dead. But what could he have told Inspector Treadles that worried you so much that you dared neither to sack him, nor to confide your problems to your husband?"

"I did nothing remotely inappropriate with him!"

Her high-pitched words ricocheted around the room, at once a furious denial and an anguished plea.

In contrast to her risen volume, Inspector Brighton spoke ever more softly, more sinuously. "I am not saying you did, Mrs. Treadles. In fact, I very much do not believe you did. But what about Mr. Sullivan? Did *he* think to maintain propriety at all times?"

"I much prefer not to speak of Mr. Sullivan," said Mrs. Treadles. She pressed her lips together in a mulish line.

It pained Charlotte to listen to Mrs. Treadles's futile refusal. She should have either lied convincingly all the way, or divulged everything from the beginning. To have the truth dragged out of her piecemeal helped neither her cause nor her husband's.

"But you have no choice in the matter, Mrs. Treadles. Mr. Sullivan is dead and your husband was in the same room with a firearm in his hand. Notice that I haven't even brought into consideration a certain small notice in the papers."

Did Mrs. Treadles cringe? "Be that as it may, I still have nothing else to say about Mr. Sullivan."

Charlotte winced. *Dear woman, brace yourself. You have given your adversary his opening.*

Inspector Brighton straightened in his chair and leaned forward, the king cobra at last ready to strike. "Then let me tell you what I think happened, Mrs. Treadles. You love your husband and value your marriage, but his willful spurning of your work at Cousins cut deep. And given that at Cousins you had to fight tooth and nail even to be heard, you felt embattled and alone.

"Into this desolate landscape strode Mr. Sullivan, by all appearances an excellent fellow. His virtues might have been only skin-deep, but you did not know this. What you saw, in your hour of desperation, was a sympathetic figure, someone who, even if he didn't slay dragons for you, was at least willing to listen to your problems, and make such reassurances as 'Let me talk to Mr. So-and-so. I'm sure he didn't intend for it to come across quite like that.'"

He paused, as if taking a moment to bask in the incipient panic on Mrs. Treadles's face. "Friendship has not been easy for you. The young women you once knew, the daughters of other industrialists, even some ladies of the landed gentry, perhaps, have largely chosen to let their acquaintance with you fade away. At the same time, because Inspector Treadles has been so sensitive about exposing his colleagues to his wealthy wife, you have been unable to make friends with the wives of those colleagues, who, under different circumstances, would have formed the bulk of your new social circle.

"You were already hungry for camaraderie and now you grew starved for support. Understandably enough, you mistook Mr. Sullivan's seeming lack of enmity for friendship. And he, sensing your vulnerability, exploited it to the utmost.

"What did you confess to him? Probably not too much directly. You are, after all, a sensible woman. But he was a clever man and deduced the rest for himself, didn't he? Did he make advances? Did he demand an affair?"

Mrs. Treadles, who had been shrinking farther and farther into her chair, flinched.

"He did, then. And when you refused, did he threaten to tell your husband lies that would have irreparably damaged your marriage?"

Inspector Brighton paused again, a craftsman studying his handiwork—in this case, the ashen pallor on Mrs. Treadles's face.

"You yourself are not inclined to lie," he mused. "Nor are you good at it. But you realized that Mr. Sullivan was a liar of a different caliber. You had believed him, when he'd feigned friendship. Why would your husband not believe him, were he to insinuate that you two had become closer than necessary?

"And *that* was why you were paralyzed by Mr. Sullivan's betrayal—and his threats. Your husband already faulted you for trying to carve out a place for yourself at Cousins. And now *this* happened. Even if Inspector Treadles were sympathetic, what would be his counsel? To give up trying to change things at Cousins and come home—which you were loath to do.

"Furthermore, you worried that Inspector Treadles, a good investigator, would soon unearth the grain of truth in Mr. Sullivan's story. You didn't *do* anything with him. But could you have denied that before you discovered his treachery, you had looked forward to seeing Mr. Sullivan, that he had become the one you thought you could rely on, when everyone else, including your husband, had turned their backs on you?"

Had he been on a stage, Inspector Brighton would probably have taken a bow. Certainly he sounded enormously pleased with himself.

"And how would your husband feel—he a son of laborers—to discover that you had formed an attachment, however innocent, to a man of your own class, the sort of man he could never be, no matter how successful he became as a police investigator?"

Mrs. Treadles rose abruptly. "Your conjectures are moot, Inspector. I never brought up Mr. Sullivan's name at home, nor did Mr. Sullivan ever seek an audience with Inspector Treadles."

The front door rang loudly and insistently. Inspector Brighton half turned his head, revealing a sharp, frowning profile. Mrs. Treadles fell back into her seat, set her elbows on an armrest, and buried her face in her hands.

The moment the door was answered, a woman's voice ordered, "Out of my way."

Footsteps stormed up the stairs, followed by the sound of the drawing room door bursting open.

"Is it true, Mrs. Treadles, what they are saying about your husband?" said the same woman.

"Eleanor, please, this isn't the best time." Mrs. Treadles made as if to lift up her head from her hands. She did not manage that, but sank more deeply into herself, a woman at the limits of her endurance. "Can you come back tomorrow instead? I still must answer questions for Scotland Yard."

A very pretty woman of about Mrs. Treadles's age, dressed in widow's weeds, appeared at her side. She set a hand on Mrs. Treadles's shoulder. Mrs. Treadles, after a moment, turned and pressed her face against the woman's stomach.

"Mrs. Treadles, I'm sorry!" Mrs. Graycott, the housekeeper, too, had arrived. "I didn't even have a chance to tell Mrs. Cousins that you aren't at home to visitors."

Mrs. Cousins, the wife of Mrs. Treadles's late brother?

Mrs. Cousins glared at the policemen. "And who are you barbarians?"

Inspector Brighton, who had already risen when the woman entered, bowed slightly. "Inspector Brighton of Scotland Yard at your service. And this is Sergeant Howe, also of Scotland Yard. Pleased to make your acquaintance, Mrs. Cousins."

Mrs. Cousins looked affronted at being addressed by him. She said stiffly, "Gentlemen, I am not usually so inhospitable, but I believe the time has come for you to leave. Mrs. Treadles has had a horrific day and she needs to rest. Immediately."

"Mrs. Cousins," Mrs. Treadles protested weakly, while holding on ever tighter to her sister-in-law, "the gentlemen are here on official business."

"And they can return for their official business tomorrow. They already have Inspector Treadles, do they not? He is not going anywhere. And the dead are still dead, so speed is of no essence whatsoever." She turned and glared again at the policemen. "You need not torment this good woman anymore on the worst day of her life. Such a small mercy is not beyond you, I hope?"

Silence.

Inspector Brighton laughed, the sound soft yet unpleasant. "You are right, Mrs. Cousins. Good night, ladies. Mrs. Treadles, I will see you first thing tomorrow."

———※———

"They are gone," said Mrs. Cousins, who had disappeared from view. She must be listening at the door.

Mrs. Treadles exhaled audibly. "Thank you, Eleanor. Thank goodness you came. I don't think I could have taken another minute of that interrogation."

Mrs. Cousins returned to the narrow slice of the drawing room visible in the private parlor's mirror. "I'm glad I was able to do something. At least have some rest before you must face the police again."

Mrs. Treadles shook her head. "I don't know how I shall sleep."

"So is it all true, what happened?"

"Eleanor, please don't believe what the papers are trying to imply about Mr. Sullivan and myself."

Mrs. Cousins tsked. "Why would I? I know the kind of man he was."

"I wish I'd listened to you better," said Mrs. Treadles weakly. "You don't believe Robert did it, do you?"

Mrs. Cousins rolled her eyes. "No. Even though I still don't think you should have married your Inspector Treadles, he never would have made such a hash of things if he really wanted to do away with Mr. Sullivan."

"Thank you. And please don't say that in front of him—the first part, that is."

"I make no promises. Unconscionable, the way he didn't even ask you a single question about Cousins for that long."

"Eleanor—"

"I know. I know now is not a good time to carry on a grudge against your husband."

Mrs. Treadles took her sister-in-law's hands in her own. "No, it's not just that, Eleanor. I hadn't wanted to tell you too much because I knew how Robert would feel, having private particulars of his life disseminated. But ever since he came back from Stern Hollow, he's been trying to change for the better. He took over menu planning and looked after most of the details when we invited the Longsteads for dinner. He had a glass of whisky waiting for me every evening, when I came back from work. He even invited me to join the policemen's caroling this Christmas. So please, please, don't think so badly of him!

"In fact, if anyone's at fault, it's me. I should have told him about Mr. Sullivan. But I was so afraid. Finally things were lovely again at home and I was just so afraid it would all go wrong again."

"Stop blaming yourself or I'll hate him again."

Mrs. Treadles wiped the corners of her eyes with the heels of her hands. "Please don't hate him. He really has been very sweet."

Mrs. Cousins sighed. "I'm glad he's seen the light—if that is indeed the case—even though he should never have been that blind to begin with."

She pulled Mrs. Treadles from her chair. "Now come, you look like you haven't slept for days. Let me take you to your bedroom. I'll tell Mrs. Graycott to bring some supper. After you eat, we'll count out a few drops of laudanum for you. Don't worry, I'll err on the side of caution. You'll be fully alert in the morning for your next interview with this evil-looking Inspector Brighton."

"All right," acquiesced Mrs. Treadles. "Thank you, Eleanor."

"Speak nothing of it. You did the same for me when your brother—" Mrs. Cousins paused. "Never mind that. Let's go."

Charlotte went to the door of the private parlor. From where she stood, she could see the two women ascend, Mrs. Treadles leaning on her sister-in-law. Not long after, she heard Mrs. Cousins speak to Mrs. Graycott, who must have gone up the service stairs after having been summoned.

Mrs. Cousins, after asking for a plate of supper for Mrs. Treadles, concluded with, "And also have the staff wait in the servants' hall for me. I will speak to them after I've seen to your mistress."

"Yes, mum," murmured Mrs. Graycott, and left.

Charlotte waited another minute, then slipped down the way she'd come. She found Mrs. Graycott in the basement, giving directions to a maid.

"You offer the supper plate to the mistress and the tea tray to Mrs. Cousins. And then you leave straight away. You don't look at anyone or anything, you understand?"

"Yes, Mrs. Graycott."

"Good girl. Now go." She turned around and saw Charlotte. "Ah, Miss Holmes. I'm sorry you didn't get to see Mrs. Treadles."

"That's all right. I will see her tomorrow. In the meanwhile"—she glanced toward the servants' hall, where the staff was having their supper—"may I speak to the staff? It's all part of the investigation Mrs. Treadles has asked my brother to conduct."

Mrs. Graycott hesitated a moment. "Yes, of course. Do please come in and have a seat. Let me get you a cup of tea."

The servants numbered six in total: Mrs. Graycott, two housemaids, the cook, a kitchen maid, and a man who served as both groom and coachman.

Mrs. Graycott confirmed the time of Sergeant MacDonald's arrival in the morning. "He was here for twenty, twenty-five minutes. The missus didn't look herself when he left, but she didn't tell us anything. She went out, taking the carriage, and the rest of us carried on with our duties. It wasn't until that Sergeant Howe showed up with a constable in the afternoon to question us that we first learned anything was amiss."

It made sense that Inspector Brighton would have first sent a lieutenant or two to the Treadleses' household, if he himself couldn't be spared right away.

"What did Sergeant Howe tell you?"

"That Inspector Treadles's recent movements are of interest to the police and that we should inform them of everything we knew. We didn't know much of the inspector's movements. Mrs. Treadles uses the coach to get about, but the inspector always prefers to go on foot. Once he leaves the house in the morning, we don't see him again until he returns from work in the evening."

"I understand he went out of town recently."

"Yes, but that's also not unusual."

"Was there anything unusual in his comings and goings recently?"

The question was for Mrs. Graycott but Charlotte looked at everyone in the servants' hall. They all shook their heads.

"Did the police ask about Mrs. Treadles's movements?"

They had, but only in passing, except to Cockerill the coachman, asking him in detail about the night before. But Cockerill saw little. Apparently there had been complaints on the part of Cold Street residents about guests at other parties blocking the lane with their carriages. He had been directed by Longstead's staff to park his vehicle several streets over, where older structures had been torn down to make room for new row houses. As a result, he'd been on Cold Street only to deposit his mistress and then to collect her again, but not at any point in between.

"What else did the police ask?" Charlotte's question was for the entire room.

No one spoke. After a while, Mrs. Graycott said, "They asked how the master and the mistress got along. Of course they get along. They are devoted to each other."

"Of course," Charlotte echoed. "Did they ask to see the house or any specific parts of the house?"

"They did ask to see the house but I said I must first have permission from either Inspector or Mrs. Treadles. They left then, but right after Mrs. Treadles came back, Sergeant Howe returned with Inspector Brighton and they did look over the house before sitting down to have tea with the missus."

"And that would have been shortly before my arrival?"

"Yes, miss."

"Do you know whether they found anything worth remarking on in the house?"

Everyone shook their heads.

A bell rang, probably Mrs. Cousins, wanting the dinner tray taken back down.

Mrs. Graycott dispatched the girl who'd carried it up.

Charlotte rose. "I will leave you all to your supper now."

As she expected, Mrs. Graycott came with her. "I'll see you out, Miss Holmes."

At the service door, where they were out of earshot of the other servants, Charlotte said, "No need to tell Mrs. Treadles tonight that

I've called—let her rest. But you can tell her tomorrow morning, if you'd like."

"Yes, miss."

"I also have a question or two for you, Mrs. Graycott. Do you know if the inspector took his service revolver with him on his latest trip?"

"I don't, miss. He wasn't to the manor born, the inspector, and he still prefers to do his own packing. Neat as a pin, too, he is," said Mrs. Graycott with pride that was threaded through with a hint of resignation.

Charlotte nodded. Theoretically, all she needed to do was wait for her appointment with Inspector Treadles tomorrow morning and ask him everything. But if Inspector Treadles had exculpatory evidence to offer, he would not be spending the night at Scotland Yard.

"Can you tell me whether anything strange or unusual happened in this household recently, Mrs. Graycott?"

Mrs. Graycott nodded immediately. "Before he left for this last trip, the inspector called me aside and asked if anything was missing from the house. That question nearly made me jump out of my skin. The thought that a theft might have taken place under my watch—it was abhorrent.

"I asked him what was missing but he wouldn't say; he only wanted to know whether I'd been aware of any items that had disappeared. I told him, even though I was shaken at the point, that I believed everyone who worked under me was honest and God-fearing. What other sort would work in the home of a police inspector?

"He said he trusted me. But he asked if there were any occasions when the house was empty. I told him that for a few hours on half days it might very well be, with Mrs. Treadles at Cousins and the staff out on their own errands.

"This morning, after Sergeant MacDonald had been, Mrs. Treadles asked me the same question you did just now, about whether

Inspector Treadles took his revolver with him on his trip. When Inspector Brighton's men came this afternoon, I told that Sergeant Howe that maybe Inspector Treadles's revolver had been gone since before he left. Maybe that was what he was asking about when he wanted to know if anything had been missing and if the house might have stood empty.

"Sergeant Howe didn't say anything. I had the feeling that . . . he didn't think what I told him mattered. But it has to matter, doesn't it, if the inspector never had the revolver? Unless, oh, goodness, unless . . ."

Unless the police believed it to have been an act on Inspector Treadles's part.

Briefly Mrs. Graycott covered her mouth with her hand, her eyes wide with fear. When she had herself under control again, she asked in a low voice, "Miss Holmes, we've heard of Sherlock Holmes in this household, of course. Will he be able to bring the inspector back home soon?"

"I don't know," said Charlotte.

Mrs. Graycott swallowed.

Charlotte briefly set a hand on her arm. "It is thus at the beginning of any new venture for Sherlock Holmes and company. We cannot predict outright that we will succeed, but we also have no reason to expect failure. And we are determined to be as thorough and enterprising as Inspector and Mrs. Treadles would wish us to be, and to get to the bottom of the case as soon as possible."

Which, of course, would be easier if Mrs. Treadles would tell the whole truth.

Seven

Papa, what are stars made of?" asked Carlisle, Lord Ingram's son. Lucinda, Carlisle's elder sister, was usually the one who stayed awake longer at bedtime and had more questions. But tonight she was already fast asleep. Carlisle, though his eyelids drooped, still persisted in curiosity.

"Stars are mostly hydrogen," said Lord Ingram.

Carlisle should have a fairly good idea what hydrogen was: Not long ago, Lucinda had asked what water was made of, which had necessitated a plunge into the basics of chemistry.

Lord Ingram wondered if he had better go fetch a volume of *Encyclopedia Britannica* in case his grasp of astronomical spectroscopy proved too shaky for Carlisle's ensuing questions, one of which was bound to be *"But how do you know?"*

Carlisle frowned. "Can you wish on hydrogen?"

Lord Ingram almost laughed out loud. "Well, why not?"

It had to be just as valid as wishing on chunks of rock and metal, the composition of falling stars.

"But how do you know stars are made of hydrogen?" asked Carlisle, yawning widely.

As his father was still recounting Newton's experiments with light and prisms, the boy fell asleep. Lord Ingram tucked his hands under the blanket and kissed him on the forehead. He then moved to the other bed and kissed his daughter on her cheek.

Outside the nursery, Miss Potter, who had once been his own governess, awaited.

"They are asleep now," he said. "I'll leave them in your care."

She smiled at him. "Very good, my lord. And good evening to you."

He arrived at Mrs. Watson's afternoon parlor, where the windows and the mantelpiece were now draped in garlands of spruce and red cedar—Mrs. Watson and Penelope worked fast—just before Holmes entered in her dinner gown.

She loved a frock, Holmes. He wouldn't say she loved her clothes as much as she loved her cake, but the love was just as sincere and unabashed. Her taste in clothes, well, he'd used to semi-dread what she might appear in; these days he rather looked forward to seeing her outfits, the way one didn't mind encounters with cherished old friends, even if they now communed with fairies via games of dominoes.

Had his retinas not been seared by the Christmas tree dress, her dinner gown would have been the most outlandish thing he witnessed today. It had a red redingote with enormous black dots, and the exposed skirt was black with small red dots.

A dress that would have swallowed its wearer whole, were it not for her evident enjoyment of its flamboyance.

"Hullo, Ash."

"Hullo, Holmes. New frock?"

"Indeed. The first I've commissioned since I left home—with money I made off you, in fact."

"I am delighted that my pounds sterling have gone on to support so worthy a cause, madam."

The other two ladies were also taken aback by the new dress. "A unique and sensational confection, my dear," declared Mrs. Watson diplomatically, after a moment of gaping. And Penelope, with evident relish, exclaimed, "It's a ladybird beetle dress!"

"It's actually a black widow spider dress, if we must discuss its entomological inspiration. Did you guess that, my lord?" Holmes glanced at him, looking very ravishing but not remotely arachnid.

"No, ladybird beetle for me also."

"I see. It evidently lacks menace. I wonder if the dressmaker can do something about that."

He thought not. No costume, however sinister on its own, could reduce the initial impression she gave of resolute darlingness. On the other hand, for those who knew her well, not even her most riotous dresses could completely alleviate the twinge of apprehension they felt in her presence.

They did not love her less, but they loved her knowing that they could keep no secrets from her.

Mr. Mears, Mrs. Watson's butler, arrived to announce that dinner was served. They descended together, Mrs. Watson on Lord Ingram's arm, the younger women as a pair.

All the dishes had been laid on the table. Mr. Mears ladled soup, filled wineglasses, and left, closing the door behind himself.

"Oh, Miss Charlotte, do please tell us how it was done," said Penelope immediately. "How was it that Inspector Treadles was locked in with the dead men?"

Holmes, who had been studying the dessert, a still-warm apple Charlotte to be served with sweet custard cream, lifted her gaze rather reluctantly. "Well, either he walked in on his own power or he was carried in and left there. As for how it was done . . . what do you mean by 'it,' Miss Redmayne? That the door was locked from inside? If there were only two dead men in that room, the question might prove somewhat curious. But Inspector Treadles was there and he was perfectly capable of locking the door."

"But why did he wish to lock himself in a room with two dead men?" Penelope continued with her question. "And why didn't he open the door even when the police came?"

Holmes took a sip of her soup. "I ask myself the same."

"And?"

"Lord Ingram and I see him tomorrow. I plan to pose these questions to him directly."

But if Inspector Treadles had satisfactory answers to those questions, his wife would not have enlisted Sherlock Holmes's help in a panic, would she?

Since Holmes appeared unwilling to discuss the case in much greater detail, Penelope's questions turned to their recent Parisian adventure, during which they had burgled a French château that turned out to be Moriarty's stronghold.

It was probably in anticipation of this very topic that Mrs. Watson had served her dinner à la française—placed on the table as if at a buffet—requiring no servants in the room.

"I still can't believe that you were all in Paris and didn't let me know," said Penelope with a mock pout.

"In the beginning, it was because I didn't want to disturb your studies. By the end, I could only be thankful that you weren't at all involved. And that because it was a fancy dress ball, we were all masked that night." Mrs. Watson sighed. "Perhaps it is still possible for those of us present tonight—and Miss Olivia—to spend the remainder of our lives having no further entanglements with Moriarty. But that is not an option for Mr. Marbleton. I hope he's well. I hope Moriarty treats his own son with some compassion."

"If he's a person capable of compassion," said Holmes.

A chill skidded down Lord Ingram's spine.

"Have you had news from Miss Olivia?" Penelope asked Holmes, after a small pause. "I understand that Mr. Marbleton gave her false reasons for his departure. Is she all right?"

Holmes paused between sips of soup—a barely noticeable interval, which nevertheless told Lord Ingram that the matter had been very much on her mind. "I haven't heard from my sister since she left. But Mrs. Watson did accompany her on her rail journey home, after Mr. Marbleton made his farewell."

"Well, I expected her to break down at some point during the journey but she never did." Mrs. Watson furrowed her brow—and hurriedly smoothed her forehead with a finger. "She was . . . oddly composed. She kept saying that she had prepared for this day. That she was grateful for all the laughter and understanding Mr. Marbleton had bestowed upon her. And that knowing their time together was finite had made her treasure every moment."

"That does not sound like Miss Olivia to me," said Lord Ingram.

As sensitive as she was, rejections, even those most kindly meant, would always be devastating.

"I suspect she is deliberately treating this as nothing more than a love affair that ended abruptly," said Holmes.

When it was something much more sinister and perilous.

"I can't say I blame her," said Penelope, "if this Moriarty is half as frightful as you say."

They fell silent, as though no one at the table wished to speak more on the oppressive subject of Moriarty. After an interlude of quiet soup consumption, Holmes turned to him and asked, "How did your visit with Scotland Yard go, my lord?"

"Profitably. We will have no problem viewing the bodies, the collected evidence, or the scene of the crime itself, provided we have an escort from Scotland Yard. We have also been granted permission for a short visit with Inspector Treadles tomorrow morning."

Holmes nodded.

Mrs. Watson, taking in the uncharacteristic tightness of her expression, said, "You do not expect to learn anything useful at Scotland Yard?"

"I very much do. Only not from Inspector Treadles himself."

Mrs. Watson rolled the stem of her wineglass between her fingers, back and forth, back and forth. "I've been wondering the same. If he cannot exonerate himself, he, an esteemed member of Scotland Yard . . ."

"Then we will do it for him," said Holmes simply. "Anything else from Scotland Yard, my lord?"

"They have given us leave to speak to those who might shed light on the case, but we will need to arrange those tête-à-têtes ourselves."

Holmes glanced toward Penelope. "Can I entrust that task to you, Miss Redmayne?"

"Certainly—" said Penelope.

"Surely—" exclaimed Mrs. Watson at the same time.

"I have a greater task for you, Mrs. Watson: You will be looking into Cousins Manufacturing," said Holmes. "Cousins is what links together Mr. Longstead, Mr. Sullivan, and Inspector Treadles. We have to know what is going on at Cousins, if we are to find out why two of the three men are dead and the other was locked in a room with them."

Mrs. Watson's hand stilled. "I'm honored by your request, Miss Charlotte, but are you sure I have enough wherewithal to take on such a large and possibly specialized portion of the investigation?"

"I have always been impressed by your financial acumen, ma'am. I am not mistaken in guessing that you know something of double-entry bookkeeping, am I?"

Mrs. Watson blinked—Lord Ingram had seen this expression a number of times on individuals who'd been told something about themselves by Holmes that they'd never shared with her. But Mrs. Watson, having been Holmes's partner for a while, needed only a fraction of a second to recover. "I did do bookkeeping for a small theatrical company. But in scale it cannot compare to Cousins."

"Perhaps not in scale, but in principle they should be comparable."

"And what am I to look for, exactly, at Cousins?" asked Mrs. Watson, her gaze anxious.

Holmes served herself a slice of venison. "The press enjoys the narrative involving Inspector Treadles in the narrative, because husbandly jealousy leading to murder is both titillating and easy to understand. But if we remove Inspector Treadles from consideration, then we are left with no apparent suspect and no apparent motive."

Lord Ingram hadn't thought of that, at least not in such unambiguous terms. As he glanced around at the other ladies, he saw that it was the same for them.

"I am not sure what we can do to produce a suspect," Holmes

went on. "So first we must see if we can find a motive—a different reason for someone, anyone at all, to want to kill Mr. Longstead and Mr. Sullivan. And that is what I have entrusted to you, Mrs. Watson, that motive—or at least, clues to that motive."

At the conclusion of the meal, they returned to the afternoon parlor, where they played a few hands of whist. Both Mrs. Watson and Penelope then pleaded fatigue and retired.

Lord Ingram wondered if he should come around less often, so as not to always cause his hostesses to rush off to hide in their rooms.

Holmes rose from the card table, took a seat on the settee, and shook out her skirts. He suspected that those skirts, laden with tiny jet beads, didn't need such elaborate arranging, but that she enjoyed hearing the tiny plinking sounds the beads made, when they struck one another with the movement of the brocaded satin.

When the other ladies had left, they had told them to keep playing, but it was obvious that the games had ended for the night. He began to gather up the cards and was about to ask after her sister Bernadine Holmes, who now lived with her, when she looked up and said, "Inspector Brighton was at Mrs. Treadles's house when I called."

He was immediately alert. "Oh?"

She recounted the interrogation she had overheard.

He didn't know at which point he abandoned the task of returning the playing cards to their case. He only realized, at the end of her recital, that he had deformed three cards in his left hand, so hard did he clutch them.

"He was *that* blunt and merciless? He went *that* far in his conjectures?"

"He was. And he went no further than I would have. In fact, I would have gone further—and I think he, too—had Mrs. Cousins not interrupted the proceedings."

He smoothed out the bent cards as best as he could, a hard weight over his lungs. He hated to think of Mrs. Treadles's plight, so desperately alone and in need of friends. He'd never held it against Inspector Treadles, when the police officer had grown distant from him. Nor had he thought ill of his friend on Holmes's behalf: Holmes needed no one's good opinion; her own was sufficient.

But he was angry on Mrs. Treadles's behalf, that the husband whom she'd loved so deeply and for whom she had given up so much had not treasured her as he ought to. Had abandoned her when she was most in need of warmth and support at home.

And yet he could not stoke that anger without remembering how proud Inspector Treadles had been of her, the last time they'd spoken, right after—if he wasn't mistaken about the chronology of events—the reconciliation between husband and wife. Nor could he entirely disregard what Holmes had related just now, of the efforts Inspector Treadles had put in since his return from Stern Hollow to become a better husband.

In the end his careening emotions coalesced into a sharp anxiety, a wedge of fear veined with the hope that the Treadleses should have that most precious of all commodities, time. Time enough to heal the wounds; time enough to begin anew; time enough to regrow trust and build something stronger and more resilient together.

But none of it would be possible if Inspector Treadles couldn't regain his freedom.

Lord Ingram forced himself to breathe deeply, to put away the cards, and to train his thoughts to settle back on the case at hand. Only to realize something that made his heart thump. With no small amount of reluctance he glanced at Holmes. "Mrs. Cousins arrived at an extremely fortuitous moment. I take it you think it had more to do with planning than with luck."

She looked at him a moment longer than necessary, as if assuring herself that he was all right, before saying, "When I walked past the servants' hall the first time, the coachman was not there. The second time he was, but he had a bit of rain on his clothes, just where a mackintosh might let some through. The basement of a house such as Mrs. Treadles's typically extends all the way to the mews. And even if there aren't steps inside the mews leading down into the basement, there should be a set of steps right outside."

Smoking bishop had been served just before Mrs. Watson and Penelope left. He picked up his still-warm cup. "So . . . unless he was in fact out driving a coach, he would not have become as wet coming from the mews to the servants' hall."

"Exactly. His master was in a jail cell at Scotland Yard, his mistress at home. Why did he go anywhere at all?"

Except to bring Mrs. Cousins at his mistress's command. Mrs. Cousins who, when she got there, would stop the interrogation.

The mulled wine had been steeped with roasted Seville oranges and cloves. He didn't mind cloves, normally; tonight, he found their taste overpowering. But still he cradled the cup in his hands, needing another source of warmth. "Mrs. Cousins performed her task well."

"And Mrs. Treadles's relief was such that she had to hide her face either in her own hands or against Mrs. Cousins's clothing, so as not to have it too plainly visible to Inspector Brighton."

"Which means that Inspector Brighton, however devastating his points, still hadn't reached the core of the matter." The weight on his lungs grew heavier. With even greater reluctance, his gaze landed on her again. "Was that why you went there? To get to the core of the matter?"

Her settee was next to a robust pot of fern. She reached out a hand and caressed a leaflet. "I wanted to speak to her before Inspector Brighton did. Because if he had what I believed he had, then Mrs. Treadles . . . I don't think she quite understands yet the inexorability of a murder investigation, how it grinds down all the edifices one puts up to protect the truth."

He felt himself winding tighter. "What did you think Inspector Brighton had on her?"

She folded her hands in her lap and looked back at him, her eyes clear, her tone inexorable. "Did you notice how many things Mrs. Treadles found in the wake of Sergeant MacDonald's visit? The letters from Inspector Treadles, recent and long ago, the absence of the service revolver from his dressing room, to name but the items that she actually mentioned to us.

"At the time it seemed as if she were intensely interested in Inspector Treadles's whereabouts in the days leading up to the murders. But what if that was a wrong assumption? What if she wasn't turning over her house for *him*, but only found those things because *she* was looking for something else altogether?"

"What?"

His question was barely audible.

"It's possible that last night, before she came home from the party, she went into 33 Cold Street, where Mr. Longstead and Mr. Sullivan were later found dead. It's also possible that she left behind evidence that she was there."

Her voice, too, had turned softer, but there was no way to soften the impact of her words. Lord Ingram felt as if he'd been gripped by the throat. If Mrs. Treadles had been there, in an empty house with either of the dead men—or, God forbid, both—it would have made the jealous-husband motive much stronger.

Incalculably stronger.

From the earliest moment, he'd sensed that Mrs. Treadles was afraid she'd further incriminate her husband. Was this why?

"Wait!" With a sudden surge of hope, he pushed aside the smoking bishop, crossed the room, and sat down on the settee next to Holmes. "You said, *if* Inspector Brighton 'had what you believed he had.' Do you no longer believe he has it?"

She let out a long sigh, which fluttered the delicate chiffon edging of her high collar. "He was forceful in his interrogation. Yet it was the force of personality and intellect, allied with the power of his position. However he tried to intimidate her into giving up the truth, he had only logic and inference on his side. He didn't produce actual evidence. Or at least he chose not to produce, or even mention, evidence in the nature of a personal item that would have attested, indubitably, to her presence at number 33 last night."

Her hand again reached out, this time tracing the entire length of a frond. "And for that reason, frightened as she was, she held on to her version of events and did not yield the confession he sought."

He slumped against the back of the settee, wrung out with relief.

Holmes studied him and almost smiled. "Since that was the case, I left Mrs. Treadles in her sister-in-law's care. But Mrs. Cousins's presence—and Mrs. Treadles's apparent reliance on her—surprised me: I was under the impression that Inspector Treadles had been less than fond of both Barnaby Cousins and his wife. But the two women did not appear to repulse each other at all."

He pushed off the settee and poured himself half a glass of cognac before coming back. "Now that you mention it, remember that I invited Inspector and Mrs. Treadles to the house party at Stern Hollow after Christmas?"

He'd invited her, too, to come in the guise of Sherrinford Holmes, but she had declined.

"Just before we left for our French adventure," he went on. "I received a letter from Inspector Treadles, asking me if it would be all right for him to bring Mrs. Cousins and put her up nearby. She was still in mourning and not moving in society but they thought a change of scenery would be good for her."

Holmes nodded, sliding the fern frond between her fingers.

"You are—interested in Mrs. Cousins," he said on a hunch.

He could not read anyone's mind. But he had been observing her for nearly half of his life, sometimes surreptitiously, often incredulously, but always keenly, especially when his attention was drawn to her in spite of himself. And as a longtime student of Charlotte Holmes, he had noticed that she was not frustrated about not having achieved what she'd hoped to accomplish this evening.

Which could only mean that she did learn something worthwhile.

"Good guess. Mrs. Cousins had a decidedly negative opinion of Mr. Sullivan. I plan to find out how she came about it." She finally let go of the fern and looked squarely at him. "And now you know exactly how things stand at the moment, as far as this case is concerned."

—⁂—

Wind roared outside. Sporadic drops of rain thudded against the windows. The man who shared Charlotte's seat nodded at her words and took a sip of his cognac. He leaned against his corner of the settee, one arm settled along its back, his long legs comfortably stretched out.

He was not going anywhere in a hurry.

This . . . was not like him.

This was not like *them*.

Their pattern had been set early, from their first encounter, when she saw him coming up the grand staircase of his uncle's house, a dark-haired, dark-gazed boy of fifteen.

Charlotte, then thirteen and on the premises to attend a children's party she was too old for, had been thinking of her tea. The previous afternoon's spread had included an array of little iced cakes, soft as pillows, with crumbs that stuck scrumptiously to the backs of her teeth.

As he ascended, taking two steps at a time, this unsmiling, sharp-featured boy with just a little too much dirt at the edges of his boots, she forgot about the possibly best cake she'd ever consumed in her life. Yes, it was how he looked and how he advanced, his physicality, the lupine dominance of his motion. But he also possessed an inner ferocity that she could not articulate, except to understand that it provoked in her a response almost analogous to what she felt for cake.

When he went past her without acknowledgment—not exactly unforgivable as they hadn't been introduced—she stopped where she was, turned, and watched the rest of his progress up the grand staircase.

At the top he sensed her attention and turned back. She continued to study him—it would take her years to stop openly scrutinizing those who piqued her interest. They stared at each other, he frowning, she with that near-cake-equivalent absorption.

He scowled and continued on his way.

In the years since, they had never truly deviated from that pattern.

She was the aggressor. She wanted things: his company, his letters, and later, his body. He kept his distance and withheld his body as if he were the city of Vienna and she the Mongol Horde just outside the gate.

She wouldn't say that it had been a good pattern, but it had become a familiar one. And had they continued to conduct themselves according to this pattern, right now, with everything that needed saying having already been said, he would be taking his leave.

To avoid handing her the sort of opening she could seize upon.

Tonight he continued to remain where he was—and even served himself a slice of Madame Gascoigne's holiday cake, from a plate Mr. Mears had brought and left on the occasional table near the settee.

She was astounded into speech. "I thought you didn't care for cake."

"I don't love it as you do and I don't seek it out, but I don't mind an occasional nibble. It's rather good, this one."

He ate without any hurry, as if entirely engrossed by the cake's taste and texture.

As always, she was aware of the coiled energy within him, the leashed sexuality—the very same quality that had left her utterly riveted on that staircase long ago, experiencing a different hunger than any she'd ever known.

"Are you planning to kiss me again?"

To her own ears, she sounded both a little angry and a little impatient.

He looked up. "Would you like me to?"

Yes.

No.

"I don't know."

"I thought so."

She blinked. "You did? Why?"

"I know what you are feeling."

How? *She* could barely make sense of what she was feeling.

"You are disoriented because I am not behaving the way I typically do," he said softly.

She was silent.

"You've been able to count on my restraint—or rather, my cowardice—for so long, its absence must feel unsettling. It occurs to you that now there is no reason that I wouldn't want more and more of you, so much so that you wouldn't be able to hold me back, not without injuring my feelings or damaging our friendship."

Would it not be so?

As if hearing her thought, he sighed. "You are assuming infinite time and infinite opportunities, but I have a less optimistic view of the future. Mr. Marbleton isn't the only one over whom Moriarty has leverage. The mother of my children has now taken up with those sworn to oppose him—I don't know when I will find myself drawn into his orbit again, if I am not already."

He gazed at her, a steady, calm contemplation. "We live in a precarious present, Holmes."

As the lead instigator of a large theft from Moriarty's stronghold, she could not disagree with his assessment, but she remained silent.

He set down his plate and turned it a few degrees on the occasional table. "Do you remember the first time you and Mrs. Watson came to visit Stern Hollow?"

She did recall the occasion. They hadn't seen each other for several months before that. He had shown her and Mrs. Watson the grounds and then he and Holmes had toured the kitchen garden, the part of his estate that most intrigued her.

"On that day, for the first time in a very long time, I felt something like happiness."

All at once she had a startlingly clear recollection in her head. The two of them had been walking side by side, under a golden, unseasonably warm sun, past a row of lovely espaliered fruit trees that promised to yield legendary jams and puddings. She had been cajoling him to call on her at the cottage she and Mrs. Watson had hired nearby, during Mrs. Watson's afternoon naps—in other words, investigating whether, with his wife out of the picture, he had become more receptive to the idea of sleeping with her.

You did not write for three months and you think I would be amenable to perform such services at your beck and call? he had answered in mock severity.

You *did not write for three months,* she had retorted. *And you think I would be mollified with anything less than such services at my beck and call?*

He had smiled at that. And she, who had not seen a true smile from him in years, had been transfixed by the luminosity in his eyes.

Was that when he first realized that he was no longer imprisoned by his marriage and could allow himself to be happy again?

"For too long I was fearful of getting too close to you," said the man in front of her. "But I wish to cast aside that fear. I don't want to look back and regret not being happier because I lacked courage."

He leaned forward, and took her hands in his. His hands were rougher than those of most gentlemen, the hands of someone who never hesitated to pick up a shovel and dig for artifacts. Who had intensified his self-defense training because he lived in a precarious present, its veneer of normalcy liable to shatter at any moment.

Without realizing it, she rubbed her thumb across a row of calluses and felt a tremor beneath his skin.

Lifting one hand, he traced the shell of her ear with a fingertip. She bit the inside of her cheek as heat careened through her. His eyes met hers, his gaze gentle yet resolute.

"Ages ago, in one of your letters, you said that you did not understand why people resisted change, as everything in life must invariably change. Perhaps you understand that resistance better now—it isn't change that we fear, but loss.

"Our friendship has never been a static entity. We have changed over the years and so has it. And it will continue to change in the coming days and years."

He kissed her on her forehead, her lips, and then, her eyelids, which she didn't realize she had closed. "But whatever happens, I will always be your friend."

Eight

I n the stark and starkly lit room, the dead looked stony, heavy.
The living, or one of them, at least, was scandalized.

The pathologist, a Dr. Caulfield, was whispering to Sergeant MacDonald, obviously about the prospect of letting a woman see two naked men without the latter's prior consent. His breaths vapored, a fog of offended masculinity. Sergeant MacDonald, who appeared no worse for wear after his own encounter with Inspector Brighton, seemed to be trying to convince him that the men, being already deceased, could not possibly mind.

The woman in question was very different from the vixen in the red-and-black dinner gown the evening before. She looked to be in her late thirties, stern and no-nonsense, with a steel-gray unadorned overcoat that matched her demeanor exactly.

If he himself were a dead man, mused Lord Ingram, he could not imagine being studied by a more respectable woman.

But the pathologist disagreed. Would he have been more amenable had Holmes appeared as her usual self? Or should she have come as a wizened old lady?

Or would he have accommodated her only if she'd shown up as Sherrinford Holmes?

Holmes's cheeks were turning red from the cold. He supposed he should be thankful that the viewing room, part of Scotland

Yard's mortuary, was unheated, and that the wintry air slowed the decomposition of the two men. Still, the interior, which reeked of formaldehyde and disinfectant, held a note of putrefaction, a stench that had burrowed into walls and floors, however bare, and could not be made to disappear unless the site itself was first demolished.

When Holmes stamped her feet against the floor, trying to keep warm, Lord Ingram decided that they'd waited long enough.

"Dr. Caulfield," he said to the pathologist, "pray cease thinking of Miss Holmes as first and foremost a woman. She is here solely as her brother's eyes, because Mr. Sherlock Holmes cannot be here himself."

"Surely, my lord, you could also—"

"I cannot. Miss Holmes has been especially trained and my powers of observation pale in comparison. I am touched by your concern for everyone's modesty, but I am sure these gentlemen here"—he indicated the bodies—"are more interested in receiving Sherlock Holmes's insight than in quibbling over etiquette at this late stage."

The pathologist hesitated.

"We also need to examine the scene of the crime and speak with family members—all before noon. Time flees, Dr. Caulfield. Let us have no more demurrals."

Reluctantly, the man acquiesced, but not without casting a disgruntled look in Holmes's direction. "As you wish, my lord."

"Miss Holmes."

"Thank you, my lord. Much obliged."

She observed first Mr. Longstead, who in life might have appeared younger with animation; but with his almost completely white hair, in death he looked every one of his sixty-seven years. The wound was through his chest. There were no other wounds on his person.

Mr. Sullivan, on the other hand, had a bruise on his right forearm, a cut on the back of his head, and was shot through the forehead.

Holmes leaned down and peered at the bullet hole.

Lord Ingram took the opportunity to satisfy his own curiosity. "What do you make of the cause of death, Dr. Caulfield?"

During the carriage ride to Scotland Yard, they had discussed the possibility that she, as a woman with professional inquiries, might not be welcome at the mortuary.

At least you won't need to ask questions. The pathologist probably won't be able to tell you anything you won't have deduced for yourself, he'd said.

She'd smiled slightly and answered, *Then you should ask a few. We wouldn't want him to feel completely superfluous.*

Indeed Dr. Caulfield puffed up at having his expertise sought. He rubbed his hands together. "The shot that killed Mr. Longstead was a contact shot—that was easy to see from the fabric of his clothes. The shot that killed Mr. Sullivan, on the other hand, was not fired from such close range. At least, there was no powder residue on his forehead."

"What do you make of the other injuries on Mr. Sullivan?"

"Hard to pin down exactly what caused the bruise on his forearm. The cut on the back of his head probably happened as he fell—he could have hit it on the windowsill."

"And the time of death?"

"Between one and three o'clock Tuesday morning, I would say, judging by the development of rigor mortis."

Dr. Caulfield seemed particularly pleased to offer up this particular morsel, although Lord Ingram was almost certain interviews could have yielded the same knowledge.

He thanked the pathologist gravely. Holmes indicated that she was finished. Sergeant MacDonald conducted them to the room where evidence collected from the scene of the crime was held.

Once they were alone, Holmes asked in a low voice, "How did your interview with Inspector Brighton go, Sergeant?"

Lord Ingram had wondered the same—he'd requested that Sergeant MacDonald be their liaison at Scotland Yard for that very reason. He hoped Inspector Brighton wouldn't have been as harsh to a fellow policeman. Then again, he'd thought that Mrs. Treadles would have been treated more gently, too.

A shadow crossed Sergeant MacDonald's otherwise open mien, but his voice was steady. "He was persistent, that man. But I told him I didn't know anything. Fortunately, that was mostly true—and I didn't let slip the part about Inspector Treadles looking over maps of Yorkshire."

Lord Ingram exhaled. "Thank you, Sergeant. I hope you won't be adversely affected by your loyalty."

Sergeant MacDonald smiled gamely. "Not if Sherlock Holmes proves the inspector's innocence."

Lord Ingram glanced at Holmes. The pressure on her must be enormous—even he felt it difficult to breathe sometimes, thinking of the possible consequences of *not* succeeding.

But she only nodded calmly. "Then we'd best get to work."

Sergeant MacDonald, too, nodded, if more grimly. He showed them two sets of men's evening attire, including a walking stick that he said belonged to Mr. Longstead. One otherwise snow-white shirt, Mr. Longstead's, judging by the bullet hole on the chest, was dark red in the front; the other had very little blood.

Holmes inspected all the pockets on the clothes. They'd already been emptied, but she turned out one particular pocket and sniffed at a white residue on her fingertips. To Lord Ingram's inquiring gaze she said, "I'm not going to taste it but it certainly smells like peppermint."

"And here's what Inspector Treadles was wearing that night," said Sergeant MacDonald, producing more items.

Lord Ingram almost gasped aloud. Inspector Treadles's clothes had a lot of blood. His boots looked as if they had sloshed through blood. The front of his trousers was blood-soaked from the knees down. His coat, jacket, and shirt were all slashed through and blood-stained at the same spot.

"I think he might have tripped in Mr. Longstead's blood," Sergeant MacDonald explained hurriedly, seeing Lord Ingram's reaction. "He doesn't have any injuries to his lower limbs."

But that didn't explain the cuts and blood on his upper garments.

"Was a blade of some kind found on the scene?" asked Holmes, fingering the sleeve of the coat.

"No, miss," said the sergeant.

Despite the severity of the situation, he seemed fascinated by Holmes's disguise. But Lord Ingram sensed in his gaze no greater interest in the woman, only in how she had been believably transformed.

Holmes now touched the coat where it was missing two buttons on the front. The ends of the threads left behind were jagged, indicating that the buttons had not been cut away, but ripped off.

"Were the missing buttons found at the scene?"

"No, miss."

Holmes lined up all three men's footwear side by side and, with her magnifying glass, scrutinized their soles.

"Inspector Treadles and Mr. Sullivan both have specks of glass in their soles, Sergeant. Was there broken glass on the scene?"

Sergeant MacDonald glanced at the reports in his hands. "In the attic of the house, yes."

"But the men were all found in a bedroom, weren't they?"

"Indeed they were, in a bedroom two floors down."

Lord Ingram suppressed a grimace. Knowing what he did now, it was difficult not to imagine a confrontation between Inspector Treadles and Mr. Sullivan, the would-be interloper in his marriage. But if they had indeed confronted each other, why in the attic? How had they then ended up in a different room? And where had Mr. Longstead been during that time?

Or Mrs. Treadles, for that matter.

Holmes returned to the formal evening clothes of the victims and scrutinized their gloves.

Mr. Longstead's white ball gloves were both bloody.

Mr. Sullivan's, on the other hand, were all but pristine.

"Was Mr. Sullivan wearing his gloves at the time of death, Sergeant?" she asked.

Sergeant MacDonald again consulted his reports. "No, Miss Holmes. His gloves were tucked into an inside pocket."

"Carefully?"

"The report does not say that."

She lifted the firearm that had been found at the scene of the crime and turned it before her eyes. Her fingers were long and delicate, but the backs of her hands were very slightly chubby, a sight that always made Lord Ingram want to smile. Even now, he allowed himself a small one.

"Official issue, I take it?" she asked.

The Webley revolver bore the emblem of the Metropolitan Police. It also had a personal embellishment: Inspector Treadles's initials were engraved underneath the emblem, possibly an addition undertaken by his devoted wife.

"That is correct."

Holmes popped out the chamber, which, when full, held five rounds. One round remained.

"Mr. Sullivan and Mr. Longstead were each killed with one shot," she mused. "Were there any other bullets or bullet holes found at the scene?"

"Yes, the report says that the door of the attic was shot at twice."

What was the significance of an attic in an unoccupied house? When they reached 33 Cold Street, would Holmes be able to glean from it the secrets of the night?

A pocket lantern had also been found at the scene, along with three spent matches. The dead men and Inspector Treadles all carried matches, but it was easy enough to judge from the stubs that they had come from Inspector Treadles's box. A fourth spent match, of a different make, had been found at the bottom of the staircase in number 33. But as Mr. Longstead and Mr. Sullivan used the same kind of matches, it was not clear which victim had lit that particular one.

They were last shown a scrap of black fabric, of decent but not luxurious wool, that had been found impaled on the fence surrounding the entrance into the service door in front of the house.

"What do you make of this, Sergeant MacDonald?" asked Holmes.

Sergeant MacDonald lowered his voice. "To be honest, I'm trying not to be too excited about this, Miss Holmes. Sergeant Howe, who works under Inspector Brighton, said that it's probably from a passerby's jacket, caught on a finial. But I've been to number 33. The fences in front are higher than my elbow. Unless I walked with one arm stuck out above the fence, I don't see how any part of my jacket could be caught. Much more likely that somebody—the real murderer, I'd say—jumped out from number 33 and got his coattail and whatnot speared by a finial."

Lord Ingram's pulse quickened. This was the most hopeful evidence that they'd come across.

Holmes dropped the scrap back into its envelope. "And now we've seen everything of interest found at number 33?"

"Everything," answered Sergeant MacDonald.

Everything except the item Holmes had deduced Mrs. Treadles must have left behind.

Where had it gone?

And who had taken it?

Alice Treadles smiled. She smiled so hard her cheeks hurt. "Robert, dear, are you all right?"

He was smiling as hard as she—his teeth were clenched together. "I'm quite all right. You, dear Alice?"

She stood by the door of the small room, and not within his embrace, because she still trembled from her second interview with Inspector Brighton, who had not taken kindly to being booted from her house the night before. She had wished to see Robert before she had to endure Inspector Brighton again, but Inspector Brighton had arranged for the opposite.

He wanted Robert to see her after he had browbeaten her for an entire hour, during which he came just short of labeling her a whore. She supposed she couldn't blame him. She'd lied to him and he'd smelled it.

She'd known that he would try to break her. That he would call her all the nasty names, ones that even Mr. Sullivan might have never heard of.

She'd steeled herself for it. Or at least she thought she had.

She had been wrong about the breadth of Inspector Brighton's vocabulary. He hadn't used any unfamiliar words, only the well-known ones. And she had been wrong about how much she could brace herself against such rhetoric.

The contempt inherent not just in Inspector Brighton's cold, cutting voice, but in those words themselves. The brutal disgust embedded in every syllable. The barely leashed violence of all those who had ever hurtled those words over the entire history of the English language.

She'd felt slapped, thrown, and kicked. All within a quarter hour of the beginning of her interrogation.

A battering not of the body, but of her belief in her right to exist.

She smiled even harder. "I'm all right. Everything is all right. Mrs. Cousins has been so very helpful. And Sherlock Holmes is on the case, too—and Lord Ingram as well."

He gazed at her. He was not in shackles, her Robert, but he looked so pale and worn. She wanted to rush forward and hold him tight, but she dared not. The moment he felt her shaking all over, he would know that she was lying, that nothing was all right and everything had gone horribly awry.

Her hard-fought smiles must be saying all the wrong things. His hands balled into fists. His throat moved. "I'm sorry, Alice. I'm terribly sorry."

"It's—it's all right." Her voice emerged as a croak. She forcibly blinked back her tears. "Are they treating you well? Do you have enough to eat and a decent place to sleep?"

Belated she noticed that he was in the clothes she'd sent. The room they were in was no cell, but a neat, book-lined room. She should be reassured; someone without knowledge of the case walking by would have guessed him to be simply another CID inspector, at another normal day of work.

But he held himself with such agitated tension, his breaths quick, his eyes wide with fear, as if he were a roebuck that had stumbled into the middle of a pack of wolves. Her own heart slammed frantically into her rib cage.

He lifted a hand, as if trying to stretch it out in her direction, before dropping it again. "I'm sorry. So sorry."

"It's—it's—"

She wanted to give more reassurances but nothing more emerged.

She dared not approach him because she trembled. Why did he not come to her and enfold her in his arms? There was a guard outside, but in here they were alone. Why was *he* frozen in place?

Was he keeping his distance because—because—

"No, I didn't kill them! I didn't!"

At the anguish in his voice, she fell against the doorjamb. "I believe you! I believe it wasn't you. Sherlock Holmes will find out who killed them. You just tell Inspector Brighton the truth so you can come home, Robert. Come home, please."

Her Robert only looked at her a long time and said, very softly, almost inaudibly, "I'm sorry, Alice. I'm sorry."

⁂

Mrs. Treadles did not immediately recognize Holmes in her disguise, Lord Ingram realized. She looked uncertainly from Holmes to him and back again.

She herself appeared almost unrecognizably drained, her deathly pallor made even more alarming by a sheen of sweat.

"Mrs. Treadles," he said quickly, "Miss Holmes and I have come to speak with Inspector Treadles. But we are glad to see you also."

Her lips parted. Her eyes had a glazed quality. He feared she would ask outright, in her confusion, where Miss Holmes was, but she blinked and said, "Indeed, how good to see you both again. May I present Inspector Brighton of Scotland Yard? Inspector, Miss Holmes and Lord Ingram Ashburton."

Lord Ingram immediately tensed. Mrs. Treadles's tormentor was around forty years of age, tall and slightly portly, with strong features and a wry countenance.

After a few exchanges of pleasantries, he said, rather ruefully, "I must say, this is not what I'd envisioned when I came to uphold truth and justice in London—that I would be immediately investigating one of my own colleagues."

If Mrs. Treadles didn't appear so wretched—and if Lord Ingram had never been through a police investigation himself—he might have been inclined to like Inspector Brighton. But now his façade of affability only made Lord Ingram's stomach twist: It was more difficult to gauge how much cruelty a man could wield, when that man happened to be charming.

"I'm sure everything will prove to be a misunderstanding, where Inspector Treadles is concerned," he said. "And then you can return to policing as usual."

"It was also my great hope. Alas, Inspector Treadles has been anything but informative." Inspector Brighton's expression turned calculating. "But as Sherlock Holmes is a great ally of his, perhaps you two will have better luck than I did."

"My brother's primary allegiance has always been to the truth. As his emissary, I hope I will not disappoint him," said Holmes.

"We have heard of his detective prowess in faraway Manchester," said Inspector Brighton with sharp-edged heartiness. "It will be an honor to witness his work."

"I will convey your compliment—I'm sure Sherlock will be tickled by the idea of his burgeoning fame," said Holmes. "In fact, let me do more than that. You must be extraordinarily busy at the moment, Inspector. Why not allow me to escort Mrs. Treadles out? I'm sure she could use the comforting presence of a woman right now."

"Yes, indeed," said Mrs. Treadles, a bit too fast. "You are much too kind, Miss Holmes."

Mrs. Treadles barely took her leave of Inspector Brighton before rushing off alongside Holmes, her desire to get away from him unmistakable. Inspector Brighton watched the departing women for a moment, then he turned to Lord Ingram.

"My lord, if I may say so, Inspector Treadles is in a perilous position. If he is charged with murder and tried, he stands a high chance of being convicted. He must know this. It is therefore even more incomprehensible that he chooses to keep silent about everything that happened the night of the murder—and also about his movements in the days and weeks beforehand.

"I do not know him well—the reason I've been chosen for this task, I imagine. But here at Scotland Yard he has an unimpeachable reputation, as a man who is both intelligent and hardworking, and who has remained humble despite his rise up the ranks. I would hate to see it all go to ruin."

Lord Ingram had the distinct sensation that Inspector Brighton would not hate to see that at all—that he might, in fact, derive a distinct pleasure from Inspector Treadles's downfall. His grip tightened on his walking stick.

"I wish we were only speaking of his career," continued Inspector Brighton. "His life is at stake, too. Yet, even with that being the case, I cannot needlessly prolong this investigation. All evidence points to his culpability—not circumstantial evidence, but direct evidence."

Inspector Brighton paused to let his words sink in.

Lord Ingram held his breath for what was coming next.

"If he is unwilling to speak on his own behalf, I see no reason not to formally charge him before Christmas and let the matter proceed to trial." With a small smile, Inspector Brighton glanced at the front door, through which Mrs. Treadles had left a minute ago. "As he won't think of himself, I beg that you ask him to think of his wife. She is already devastated. She will be that much more so were he to hang."

Alice Treadles collapsed onto the seat of her carriage.

"Here," said Miss Holmes, pushing a small flask into her hands.

Alice took a swallow, coughed, and took an even bigger swallow.

The whisky burned like sulfur on its way down. Her eyes watered. But at least she'd stopped shaking.

"Did Mrs. Graycott tell you that I called last night?" came Miss Holmes's cool voice from the opposite seat.

"Yes, she did, this morning."

"I would not have crossed Inspector Brighton by interrupting his interrogation."

"Lesson learned." Alice panted several times, from the lingering harshness of the whisky. And the memory of Inspector Brighton, garroting her with his inescapable logic. She returned the flask. "But just like last night, he didn't get anything from me."

"It must have been an enormous relief," said Miss Holmes blandly, "realizing that he doesn't have the thing you dropped in number 33."

Alice's fingers dug into the tufted seats. Had she been forced to disrobe in public, she could not have felt more exposed. "I—you—"

"You were looking for too many things in too many places, Mrs. Treadles, after being told of the murders at 33 Cold Street. What did you leave behind? An earbob? A hair ornament?"

Alice scooted back involuntarily, her body trying to shrink into a corner of the carriage.

"As I thought," said Miss Holmes, her voice coolly relentless. "Something the absence of which could easily go unnoticed until the next day, when you performed an inventory of your accessories. So it was a hair ornament then?"

"A jeweled comb," Alice heard herself admit.

"Do you not worry that someone else has it now? Someone who might not have your best interest at heart?"

Even though she'd made herself appear older and drabber, Sherlock Holmes's oracle still commanded attention, occupying her seat as if it were a throne.

Alice suppressed a shiver. "I can't care about that now. If someone besides the police has it, then they were also in that house that night. Let them come forward and explain why they were there in the first place."

"Inspector Brighton knows you are lying."

"Maybe. But that's not the same as having a confession."

She held on to that. Inspector Brighton had no confession from her and therefore she could not hurt Robert's chances . . . of survival.

"What *were* you doing in that house that night?" asked Miss Holmes quietly.

Alice clenched her jaw. Did Lord Ingram have to submit to such a grinding before he was helped? "Does Mr. Sherlock Holmes not already know, he who knows everything from a glance?"

Miss Holmes looked directly at her and Alice immediately regretted her question. But it was too late.

"He does have an idea," said Miss Holmes calmly. "You were raised a lady. You are also an attractive woman. You have no good reason to leave a safe, well-lit house to venture into a dark, empty one at night. He thinks it's likely you only went into number 33 because you saw your husband enter."

Alice gripped her hands together so they wouldn't shake. "No wonder my husband had qualms about working with Sherlock Holmes. He really is terrifying."

No reaction crossed Miss Holmes's face at this assessment. "Why hire us to help you find the truth when you will not even tell us what truths you already know?"

"Because what I can tell you does not matter and would only muddy the waters. Because my husband did not kill those men. Therefore whatever you learn about me will only be incidental. Fool's gold—all glittering to make you think you've got something valuable when it's completely worthless!"

Alice was panting again.

She hoped she was right about Robert. Sometimes, much of the time, she simply didn't know anymore. She was defending him to the utmost of her ability—and she would continue to defend him as long as she had a shred of strength left. But what if she was wrong?

What if she was wrong and Inspector Brighton was right?

She felt sick at the thought even darkening her mind. But trust was a most fragile thing. She had never imagined it possible that he would abandon her within their marriage, but he had, for months and months, as if she had become a complete stranger.

Did she really know him?

Had she ever known him at all?

Miss Holmes was still watching her, with neither the pity Alice dreaded nor the understanding she craved. Miss Holmes simply watched, as if hers were the eyes of God.

"Fortunately for you, Mrs. Treadles, I agree with you."

Alice was stunned into momentary paralysis; then her eyes filled with abrupt, grateful tears. "You *do*?"

"Yes, I do agree that the role you played that particular night was a minor one. Which is why, instead of scolding you, I am going to introduce you to another of Sherlock Holmes's associates. And the two of you will head to Cousins."

This instruction was so unexpected, Alice barely noticed that she was wiping away her tears. "We will?"

"You've suspected for a while that not all is well at Cousins, haven't you?" said Miss Holmes, with that same impervious neutrality. "In the beginning, you thought that the resistance of your directors and managers was only due to you being a woman. Then you began to realize it was too strong, too persistent. But you couldn't find out anything, since those men stood in your way at every turn. Now is your chance to bring to light everything they've kept hidden."

Alice felt a little faint. Cousins had been a locked door. She'd been desperate to pry that door open. But now that a proper crowbar had been thrust into her hands, did she really want to know what lay beyond?

"Not to mention—if you want Sherlock to help Inspector Treadles, then my brother needs a motive for the murders, a motive other than your husband's jealousy, real or imagined. Cousins, which links together all of you, is the best possible place to look for this motive."

Alice's fingers shook. Her innards quailed, too. But she raised her chin and looked Miss Holmes in the eye. "All right, then."

"Excellent," said the magisterial Miss Holmes. "You've long wished to take matters into your own hands, and now you can."

———※———

Holmes did not return until the exact appointed hour of their meeting with Inspector Treadles. To Lord Ingram's inquiring look, she only gave a small nod.

They were taken into a room that appeared to be a small library, its shelves lined with law books and annual police reports. Inspector Treadles sat to one side of a large desk, handsomely attired in a gray Newmarket coat.

Lord Ingram recalled the observations Holmes had made about Inspector Treadles, upon the latter's first visit to 18 Upper Baker Street, concerning his clothes: excellent material and equally excellent workmanship, yet two years behind fashion, with buttons replaced and cuffs rewoven.

From that Holmes had inferred that Mrs. Treadles's income had reduced: Instead of a generous father, she now had a much less generous brother. She'd further deduced that Mrs. Treadles had done everything in her power to make sure that her husband was still impeccably turned out, that he felt as little of the lessening of their circumstances as possible.

The Newmarket coat that he wore now, perfectly cut and subtly stylish, was most certainly a new acquisition: Despite her husband's obvious displeasure at her taking over Cousins Manufacturing, Mrs. Treadles had used her newly inherited wealth to arrange for a new wardrobe for him.

And Inspector Treadles had continued not to inquire into her work.

Lord Ingram would have liked to think that he himself would have been satisfied with much less from his own wife. But he knew that had not been the case. He, too, had wanted to be everything to his wife. He, too, had not thought that was too much to ask for, even though he never would have asked for it aloud.

Perhaps another man could more easily condemn Inspector Treadles, but that man was not he.

At Holmes's entrance, Inspector Treadles had risen, though he blinked a time or two before recognizing her. "Miss Holmes, my lord, thank you for coming."

The Inspector Treadles that Lord Ingram had known was a man of energy and confidence. He might have preferred to be known for his courtesy, but no doubt he had been an assertive man, an expansive presence.

This man, however, seemed to want to occupy as little space as possible. He wasn't hunched over or otherwise physically pulling into himself, and yet he emanated a desire for minimization.

For invisibility.

"Have you been well?" asked Holmes. "Has your arm been tended to?"

"Yes, and yes. Thank you," answered Inspector Treadles, his tone soft and . . . uninformative.

"I'm glad to see that you are not in a cell," said Lord Ingram.

"I have one," replied Inspector Treadles. "But Inspector Brighton prefers more elegant surroundings for himself so I've been brought here for my questioning."

Lord Ingram recalled what Inspector Brighton had said to him. After he and Holmes left, would Inspector Treadles be subject to another round of interrogation?

"May I offer you some seats?" said Inspector Treadles. "I apologize that I don't have tea or biscuits."

Did he know that Inspector Brighton planned to formally charge him very soon? Lord Ingram could not imagine Inspector Brighton hadn't relayed the threat in person. What did it cost Inspector Treadles, then, to be so calm, almost withdrawn?

Or was he, in fact, completely overwhelmed?

They all sat down. Lord Ingram scanned the room. They were alone inside, but he wasn't sure that they wouldn't be overheard.

He looked to Inspector Treadles, hoping the latter might give some indication as to whether these walls had ears. But the policeman sat with his eyes downcast and his hands in his lap, obscured by the desk.

A silence fell.

Lord Ingram glanced at Holmes. She studied Inspector Treadles for a minute, then asked, briskly, "Inspector, has Mrs. Treadles ever mentioned either of the dead men to you?"

Was Inspector Treadles surprised by this sudden transition? His speech remained uninflected. "Mr. Longstead, yes. Mr. Sullivan, no."

"Why do you suppose she never did so, with regard to Mr. Sullivan?"

Inspector Brighton wouldn't have inflicted his hypothesis only on Mrs. Treadles. Even if Inspector Treadles hadn't intuited anything before the fateful night, he most assuredly had been told by now that at one point, isolated and beleaguered, his wife had depended on Mr. Sullivan more than she had on him.

"I do not have any good conjectures," said Inspector Treadles.

Lord Ingram knew now beyond a shadow of doubt that his friend spoke to them as he had spoken to Inspector Brighton: He did not trust that the information exchanged in this room wouldn't be overheard. But what about Mrs. Treadles? Had he been just as detached and uninformative with his own wife?

"Mrs. Treadles thought you were investigating a case in the Kentish countryside, when in fact, for the fortnight before the murders, you were on leave from Scotland Yard. Why did you lie to your wife, Inspector?"

Holmes, with her measured tone, was as inexorably forceful in her questioning as any police inspector.

Inspector Treadles's brow furrowed, but he radiated no anger or annoyance, only an almost fatalistic forbearance. "I prefer not to discuss that."

But we are your friends! If you don't tell us anything, how are we to help you?

Holmes remained unaffected. "Where were you in truth, when she thought you away for work?"

"I would rather not discuss that either."

"When did you return to London?"

A muscle leaped at Inspector Treadles's jaw, the only indication that he wasn't as composed as he let on. "I cannot tell you."

"Cannot because you do not know, or because you choose not to share that with us?" Lord Ingram couldn't help adding this question of his own.

Inspector Treadles closed his eyes for a moment. "I choose not to answer."

Do you not know the impossible position your wife has been put in? Do you not understand that your own neck is in palpable danger?

Lord Ingram plunged his fingers into his hair, so as not to shout these questions aloud.

Holmes, undeterred, carried on. "What were you doing at 33 Cold Street on the night of the murders, Inspector?"

"I have nothing to say about it."

"Is there anything you do have something to say about, Inspector? Your injury, perhaps?"

Coming from anyone else, the question would have dripped with sarcasm—or burned with frustration. But Holmes managed to imbue it with nothing more than professional curiosity.

Inspector Treadles raised his head for the first time. "I can assure you that I did not kill either Mr. Longstead or Mr. Sullivan."

Holmes nodded. "Thank you. I have no more questions. My lord?"

Lord Ingram rubbed his temple. "It behooves me to pass on Inspector Brighton's message that he does not mean to wait long, Inspector, even though I'm sure he has already related it in person."

"He has indeed informed me that he intends to charge me on Christmas Eve. But thank you anyway, my lord," said Inspector Treadles quietly.

Holmes, who had not been privy to the conversation between Lord Ingram and Inspector Brighton, did not appear remotely surprised.

Lord Ingram regarded his gently uncooperative friend. "I very much hope that you and Mrs. Treadles can still come to the gathering at Stern Hollow, Inspector."

"It is my fond hope, too."

"If there is anything I or Sherlock Holmes can do . . ."

"What Sherlock Holmes typically does should be good enough for me. Please convey my deep gratitude," said Inspector Treadles, looking directly at Holmes.

Holmes nodded and rose. "Good day, Inspector."

Inspector Treadles got to his feet. "Good day, Miss Holmes. Good day, my lord. And thank you. You are both the finest of friends."

Greater Scotland Yard was receding from the carriage window when Lord Ingram asked, "You don't think Inspector Treadles conveyed anything in code, do you, Holmes?"

Charlotte, who had been absently patting her wig, feeling the unfamiliar texture of hair that had once been the crowning glory of another woman, shook her head. "No, not via blinking or any facial twitching."

"Did you expect him to?"

She shook her head again. "He's no specialist and wouldn't have been able to manage anything more complicated than a variant of the Morse code. If what he needs to keep secret is that important, then it was wise of him not to gamble on a primitive cipher that others might see and decode."

"Why do you think he would rather keep his silence, knowing very well that it puts his wife in a state of terrified suspense?"

"You have a fairly good idea, do you not?"

He exhaled. "I wish I didn't."

One possibility was that Inspector Treadles had committed such atrocities that he would be getting off lightly, being accused of only two murders. But having already eliminated this possibility at the onset, they had to contend with the likelihood that Inspector Treadles *knew* something. And this something was so highly danger-ous that he would rather take his chances with a trial—and the hangman's noose—than to let it be known that he was in fact in possession of this knowledge.

Lord Ingram tapped his fingers a few times against the head of his walking stick, not bothering to hide his agitation. "He believes that what he knows endangers not only himself, but his wife, doesn't he?"

Charlotte wondered whether they would be better acquainted with Inspector Treadles's troubles if they hadn't been in France for most of the preceding weeks. But they had been in France and could only guess at the nature of what Inspector Treadles had unhappily learned.

Rain fell, striking solidly against the top of the carriage. It had snowed the previous week, raising hopes of a white Christmas. Now the specter of a wet Christmas loomed far larger, though the precip-itation did not diminish the enthusiasm of three street musicians they drove past, playing "Joy to the World" loudly on two accordions and a violin.

"Thinking of a cup of hot cocoa and a slice of plum cake?" came his voice.

He had on a midnight blue greatcoat. She remembered this coat. Several years ago, at a winter country house party, she had emerged from the library to the sight of him striding across the cavernous entry of the stately home.

His had always been a striking physical presence, but it had never simply been a matter of height, build, or even athleticism. There was something in his skeletal alignment, a fortuitous combination of posture and fluidity, so that when he stood, he was straight yet loose-limbed, and when he moved, he did so with the lightness and muscularity of a Thoroughbred.

Standing in the shadows of a row of great pillars, she had been transfixed by the balance and mechanics of his gait, the drama of him doing something as unremarkable as traversing a large indoor space. He did not see her. She was at first glad that she could stare for as long as she liked, and imagine running her hands all over the coat. But after he left via the front door, she had spent the rest of her day in a state of unhappy listlessness, knowing that he would always remain out of her reach.

So was she wise, or completely mad, not to fall upon him now as she would a plate of cake after she had at last vanquished Maximum Tolerable Chins? Goodness knew she still wanted to touch the coat, this once forbidden garment.

She became aware that he was still waiting for an answer to his question about whether she was thinking of hot cocoa and plum cake.

"I was thinking of your children." She was not entirely lying. She *had* thought of his children several times since last night. "You were on your way back to Stern Hollow. They don't mind staying longer in London?"

"They enjoy London. They've never been in London so close to Christmas and are still ecstatic to spy yet another Christmas tree through a window," he answered, smiling a little.

She loved that smile—and almost didn't ask her next question. "I don't suppose you've told them about your divorce yet?"

His smile fading, he shook his head. "No. I've decided to speak to them after the New Year."

"How do you think they will react?"

"As children do, I hope, with great sorrow and outrage." He looked at her. "This is more interest than you usually display in my children."

He was no longer tapping the top of his walking stick, but was instead passing the handle from one hand to the next, almost as if he were tossing a ball back and forth to himself. It was performed with a magician's dexterity, but still, for him, this was fidgeting.

"I suppose it's because I wonder whether you'll expect me to play a larger role in their lives."

He went still. "Did you get that impression from what I said last night?"

"No. But recall that at Stern Hollow we became lovers out of necessity."

One corner of his lips lifted. "How can I forget?"

Her heart thudded. She pushed on. "At the end of the case, when I asked you why we couldn't continue on as lovers, you said that perhaps your body in bed was enough for me, but the reverse wasn't true. You'd already endured years of unhappiness because you wanted more than what a woman could give. You would not put yourself through that again—especially not with me.

"That was your position not long ago. But now you are willing to put yourself through exactly that?"

He looked fully at her, his answer businesslike, almost stern. "Recall that at Stern Hollow I was forced to admit, to a pair of police investigators, that I loved you, with you right there in disguise. I did not enjoy making that confession and would never have done so, were I not under duress. Having done that, I didn't want to make any further concessions. If you couldn't love me the way I loved you, I'd have rather we not be lovers at all.

"But now . . ." His voice softened. "I suppose I've become less precious about it. Now I'll be happy for you to love me however you would."

She felt as if she'd been caught next to a fifty-foot-tall gong struck at full force, the shock of the vibration pushing all her organs out of place. "You presume a great deal! You presume that I love you."

"You don't?" he countered calmly.

She looked down at her hands and said nothing.

He picked up his walking stick and knocked it lightly against the floor. "As I said, however you love me will be fine."

Nine

Cold Street was in a relatively new district. Thirty years ago, it had still been agricultural land. But these days, its location, south of Hyde Park, was considered convenient enough. And the stone and white stucco houses, their façades assiduously maintained against London's grimy air, were suitably grand.

Here the attraction was not just bigger houses, but a feature that the older row houses of the more aristocratic areas did not possess. Lord Ingram's town house in Belgravia, like many others in his district, was built around a garden square, and enjoyed a view of greenery out of the front windows.

The houses on and around Cold Street, on the other hand, were erected with their backs to a long green space, thus serving as the fences around it. And where gaps opened between stretches of houses, wrought iron gates were installed to keep the large garden private.

It was before one such gate that they alit. A young bobby named Lamb, standing guard, read the letter Lord Ingram produced from Scotland Yard, and was about to open the gate for them when Holmes said, "Lord Ingram and I will first walk around the outside of the garden."

At the moment, it was not raining in this part of London. The temperature had risen a few degrees, but along with that slight increase in warmth came fiercer winds. Lord Ingram had to press a hand on his hat to prevent it from flying away. "Yesterday I hoped the Serpentine would be frozen soon, but that seems less likely today."

She scanned their surroundings. "Your children like skating, don't they?"

He looked at her a moment, enjoying the sight of her on the hunt. He'd once considered it intolerable, to tell her that he loved her, and then wait for a verdict. Now that he'd actually taken that step, it felt oddly freeing. He'd laid all his cards on the table; he didn't need to worry about how or whether to play them anymore.

"They adore skating. So does Miss Olivia, if I recall correctly."

"Livia is a good skater. She tried to teach me to skate. Alas, I balanced about as well as a sack of flour would on skates."

He chortled.

"Looking back," she continued, "I marvel at her patience with me. I didn't like anything she wanted me to try; and she wasn't interested in cake."

It's because she was certain of your love. Because she knew she was safe with you. I didn't understand for the longest time that I, too, have always been safe with you.

They stopped at nearly the same moment, she looking toward the base of a small bush next to a house, and he to the edge of the curb. Buttons. Buttons that looked exactly like the remaining buttons on Inspector Treadles's coat.

The enclosed garden's length of approximately 700 feet far exceeded its width, at about 150 feet. Both 31 and 33 Cold Street were near the middle of its long western side. Lord Ingram and Holmes currently stood on the pavement along its shorter southern edge, just outside another garden gate. If this was where Inspector Treadles had been attacked, there would have been drops of blood on the street in the immediate aftermath. But it had rained enough since the night of the party to wash away all traces of blood, leaving only the buttons.

Holmes took out a pair of tweezers from her reticule, picked up the buttons, and packed them away in a handkerchief. They kept walking and finished the round, but did not encounter anything else of note.

Back at the spot between 31 and 33 Cold Street, Constable Lamb opened the gate and let them through. Inside they found an expansive stretch of smoothly clipped lawn, the grass still green, though a paler, yellower shade. Large plane trees were scattered throughout, their bare forms, though somewhat forlorn-looking, still shapely. Here and there clusters of smaller trees or larger bushes formed, almost like the parkland of a country estate, if one ignored the houses that delineated the edges of this parkland.

A pebbled path wound through the lawn. Holmes stepped on the path and walked some thirty feet toward the interior of the lawn before turning around to inspect the two houses in question.

"You can actually see into number 31 from number 33," she said. "And vice versa."

Because of the gap between the two houses—and because the architects for both had decided to take advantage of that and put in windows.

Constable Lamb, who had gone off to unlock number 33, now stood at its back door, beckoning them to come in.

"Constable Lamb, was the back door open, when the police got here?" asked Holmes.

"No, miss, it wasn't. Only the front door."

She examined the rear entrance. "This house is otherwise unoccupied, I understand?"

"No tenants now, miss," confirmed the young constable. "None since summer."

She raised a brow. "This doormat looks rather new though."

When she wished to encourage someone to keep talking, Lord Ingram noticed, her expressions grew more animated. Conversely, when she wanted someone to stop lying, her face became more and more opaque.

After they'd left Scotland Yard, where there was a greater chance someone would recognize her, she'd taken off the makeup and devices that made her appear different and older. He enjoyed seeing her real face in a state of vivacity, a change rather akin to a dramatic haircut.

The eager-to-help Constable Lamb did not disappoint her. "That's because Miss Longstead, from number 31, uses the house from time to time."

"Did Mr. Longstead also own number 33?"

"Yes, miss."

This was not a terribly unusual arrangement. Mrs. Watson, for example, owned several houses near her own, including the property at 18 Upper Baker Street. If one already lived in a district, then one understood its characteristics and would be quicker to spot a good deal. And it was easier to keep an eye on one's investment properties if they were close by.

She tapped a gloved finger against her chin. "What does Miss Longstead use number 33 for?"

"The attic was made into a painting studio by the previous tenants. I hear Miss Longstead used it to make extracts and whatnot." Constable Lamb shook his head. "A shame it was turned upside down. The servants from number 31 cleaned it up after Inspector Brighton and the photographers had been there, but before that it was full of broken glass."

And its door had been shot at, twice.

Lord Ingram's fingertips tingled. Holmes tsked in suitable disapproval.

They entered the town house via the dining room, which was often found on the ground floor, toward the rear. The furnishings were covered in large protective cloths, the dining table and its chairs in one huddle, the sideboards in another. The floor, too, was spread with dust sheets.

"I understand that the policemen who first discovered the bodies entered from the front door. What about those who've come here since?"

"The front door, too, miss, as far as I know."

Constable Lamb sauntered forward deeper into the house, no doubt expecting them to follow in his wake. Holmes, however, knelt down to examine the dust sheets.

The dining room had three windows, two facing the garden, one in the direction of number 31, and only the curtains on this last had been pulled back, admitting the watery light of a rainy morning and a view of a tightly shut number 31, a house in mourning.

Lord Ingram drew back all the remaining curtains.

Now there was enough light for him to see a tangle of footprints, none terribly muddy or pronounced, but enough to distinguish that most were left by men's boots—the police, heading out the back door to take a look at the garden and then coming back in.

He held his breath, hoping not to see any prints of a lady's— Mrs. Treadles's—delicate evening slippers. He didn't, but he did remark a few dark red drops marking a straight line toward the interior of the house.

Inspector Treadles, passing through?

Holmes crouched down at a spot not too far from the dining table huddle and took out her magnifying glass, which he had given to her a few years ago for her birthday. When he crouched down beside her, she handed him the magnifying glass.

His first glance at the dust sheet did not reveal anything out of the ordinary. Even looking through the magnifying glass yielded no unusual details. It was only by lowering his face nearly to the floor, while making sure he didn't block any light, that he saw what she wanted him to see.

Several filaments of long, light brown hair, otherwise almost invisible against the dun-colored dust sheet.

Mrs. Treadles had light brown hair.

They exchanged a look as they rose. She took the magnifying glass back from him and went to a spot of what he presumed to be bloodstains. They followed the bloodstains out of the dining room, to the central staircase, where they were met by the sight of bloody boot prints coming down.

He remembered Inspector Treadles's boots, which had looked as if they'd sloshed through blood.

"It's a bit like this up to the attic—the blood drops, not so much the boot prints, that is," called Constable Lamb from above. "Do you want to see the murder scene first?"

At the bedroom two floors up where the murders had taken place, she spent a moment on the door, which still bore signs of having been violently kicked in, before turning her attention to the chalk outlines on the dust sheets.

"Those outlines—do they mark where the victims lay?"

"That's right, Miss Holmes. Mr. Longstead here and Mr. Sullivan here."

Mr. Longstead's outline was closer to the door. A large pool of dried blood stained the dust sheet underneath him. A smaller pool marked where Mr. Sullivan had been shot in the forehead, at the foot of the covered-up bed, his head under a window that looked toward number 31.

A trail of dark red boot prints led to two windows on the far side of the bed, facing the street outside. Inspector Treadles's blood-soaked soles again came to mind.

"Were you by any chance on the scene yesterday, Constable?"

"Yes, miss. I didn't discover the bodies but I was among the men brought back from the station by Constable Wells."

Holmes cradled her chin in the space between the thumb and forefinger of her right hand—her gestures, too, became more numerous, when she was in a mood to encourage the flow of information. "So you saw how they lay, the dead men, before they were moved?"

"Helped move them, too, after the photographer had been."

She asked Constable Lamb to demonstrate for them how the men lay. He did, stretching himself out on the dust sheets, but not on the outlines themselves, for fear that the blood still hadn't fully dried.

His imitation of Mr. Longstead in the latter's final pose had Mr. Longstead lying faceup, one arm stretched out, the other over the wound on his chest. Mr. Sullivan, several feet away, had been more crumpled up, his legs folded, one arm caught under his body, his face almost but not entirely buried in a dust sheet.

"A pocket lantern was sitting nicely right here," supplied Constable Lamb, patting the sill of the window under which Mr. Sullivan had lain, the one that looked toward number 31.

All this struck Lord Ingram as rather inexplicable. Judging from the way Mr. Longstead had fallen, the killer should have stood facing the door. But if he was to believe the pathologist, then for Mr. Sullivan to have staggered backward and hit the back of his head on the windowsill on his way down, the shot that killed him should have been fired *from* the direction of the door.

If Mr. Longstead had been murdered first, and if Mr. Sullivan had been in the room at the same time, wouldn't he have run toward the door and been shot in the back, rather than in the forehead?

If Mr. Sullivan had been fired on first, then why had Mr. Longstead subsequently allowed the killer to march straight up to him and place the tip of the gun right against his chest? Or did Mr. Longstead arrive late enough not to witness the death of his nephew?

"Where was Inspector Treadles?" asked Holmes.

The bobby pointed at the windows facing the street. "They said he was crouched behind the bed, with his weapon drawn and aimed at the constables."

Holmes went around the bed and lifted the sash of one of those windows. Her hands on the sill, she leaned out for a look.

"You are a little more agile than me, my lord," she said, yielding her place. "Do you think you could have left the house via this window?"

They were three floors up, but the house had an ornate façade; below and above the windows protruded architraves that wended along the length of the entire row.

Without too much difficulty, he could hang on to the architrave just outside this window and drop himself onto the small balcony one floor below. From there, to reach the pavement walkway, he would need to leap clear of the fenced area in front of the house, which enclosed the descent to the basement service entrance. But that would not have posed too great a challenge.

Under normal circumstances.

"If I could see—not a problem. But wasn't it all fogged up that night?"

Was that why Inspector Treadles had been at the window but had never left? Because it had been too dark and foggy to see his way down?

When Lord Ingram turned around, Holmes was inspecting the dust sheet that covered the bed. "Can I trouble you gentlemen to lift this cloth so I can have a look underneath?"

The men obliged.

He had to give her credit. She positioned the young constable on the far side of the bed, holding up the cloth with both arms above his head and therefore having no idea that she was going over the mattress with her magnifying glass.

He refrained from asking, as he and the bobby put the cloth back, what she'd been looking for.

Or whether she'd found it.

"May I make a quick sketch of this room?" she asked the bobby.

"I don't see why not, miss."

She was not what one would consider an accomplished artist; certainly she hadn't the output of one. In an age when almost every lady could manage *something* with watercolor, he'd never seen her render as rudimentary a subject as a vase of flowers or a country landscape.

But she had the makings of a draftsman. When other tourists at the beach painted seascapes, she made blueprint-like drawings of sailing vessels and changing cabins. Once she'd sent him a sketch of a cross section of a nautilus shell, a beautiful image, at once organic and profoundly architectural. He still had it in a portfolio in the back of his dressing room at Stern Hollow, along with most of the letters he'd ever received from her.

Within a few minutes, Holmes had a decent diagram of the room, along with the location of the windows and the positions of the dead men. She put her sketchbook back into her large handbag. They walked out of the room and Constable Lamb began to go down the stairs.

"What of the attic, Constable?"

"Oh, that's been locked again. Mrs. Coltrane, the housekeeper at number 31, asked Inspector Brighton if they could lock it up again. She said she felt too awful with it open and she was sure Miss Longstead would feel even worse. So Inspector Brighton said yes."

"Well, then," said Holmes, "I guess it's time for Lord Ingram and I to visit number 31."

—❧—

Their hostess at number 31 was exceptionally beautiful.

Her African ancestry was evident in the light brown of her skin and the texture of her hair. Her European ancestry was equally evident in the color of her skin, and her golden green eyes.

Eyes that were puffy and red-rimmed from crying.

"Do please forgive us for intruding on your grief, Miss Longstead," said Lord Ingram.

Miss Longstead gripped her handkerchief, black-bordered but still stark white against the black parramatta silk of her mourning gown. "I wish I were better able to master my emotions, but it's been a terrible shock losing my uncle. I can't believe he's gone."

"We are very sorry," said Holmes.

"Today I walked all the way to the door of his study—to say something to him—before I remembered that he is no longer with us. Even now I expect him to walk in and demand to know what is all this ridiculousness."

By "ridiculousness" she no doubt referred to the black drapes that now covered windows and mirrors, making the drawing room look not only somber, but slightly macabre. The woodsy scent of fresh evergreens still lingered in the air, but the Christmas tree—and all other decorations put up for either Christmas or her coming-out party—had disappeared.

Miss Longstead wiped away fresh tears. "I'm sorry. I'm not typically so useless."

"Please, Miss Longstead, you must not apologize for your sorrow," said Holmes. "Someone you loved has been taken from you most cruelly and yours is the most natural reaction possible."

"Thank you, Miss Holmes."

A servant brought in a tea tray. Miss Longstead poured for everyone.

As Holmes added milk and sugar to her own, Miss Longstead tucked her handkerchief into her cuff and said, "I agreed to meeting with you at this time, Miss Holmes, because of the name Sherlock Holmes. We've been in town since summer and I was absolutely fascinated by his brilliant detection in the Sackville case—from afar, no less. So even though at the moment I shouldn't be receiving anyone, I still wish to hear what the great sage has to say about what happened."

Lord Ingram was grateful that Miss Longstead was diplomatic enough to omit any mention of the Stern Hollow case, which had been no less a feather in Sherlock Holmes's cap.

"You may wish to know, Miss Longstead," said Holmes, "that the great sage, as you call him, has been engaged by *Mrs. Treadles* to find out the truth of what happened."

"I have been told that. But I trust that when Sherlock Holmes is engaged in finding out the truth, the truth is in fact what he will unearth. His reputation precedes him."

"Sherlock will be gratified by your assessment of his professional good name, Miss Longstead," said Holmes, smiling a little at the young woman's genuine admiration. "I understand that the unfortunate events took place on the night of your coming-out party."

Miss Longstead sighed. "Initially I was not in favor of the party. Looking as I do, I am stared at anytime I leave the house. To set aside an entire evening for people to look their fill at me—there was nothing I wanted less.

"But Uncle was adamant. I found his insistence baffling. One reason we lived together in such harmony was that we both preferred a quiet life, spending our time in the search of knowledge and innovation, rather than out in the world among others.

"And he announced it all of a sudden. That also wasn't like him. He was not dictatorial by nature and usually would ask for my opinion. But this time he'd made up his mind and that was it."

Miss Longstead picked up the sugar tongs, then regarded them uncertainly.

"You already added two sugar cubes to your tea," said Holmes.

"Thank you. That is good to know," said Miss Longstead with an embarrassed half smile, setting down the sugar tongs again. "Now where was I? Right. The rush unnerved me, too. If I was going to be looked at all night long, then it seemed to make sense that I should have some time to prepare myself, to acquire a suitably impressive dress, and just as importantly, to spend some time with a dancing master."

"I understand you looked sensational."

Miss Longstead's expression was something between a smile and a grimace—the memory of her triumphant debut forever tainted by the murders. "We were able to commission a lovely gown. And Uncle taught me to dance himself."

A wistful look came into her eyes. "I never knew he was such a good dancer. He told me, for the first time, that he'd learned to dance to woo a particular young lady who loved a good soiree. And he'd won her hand, too. But she died of illness before they could be married. He said it affected him deeply, to see someone so full of life—and love of life—be taken away so soon.

"I wish I'd paid better attention and relished those hours. I mean, I did, but I was also worried over the party, about whether I'd be able to withstand the scrutiny, or conversely, about whether anyone would show up and whether any gentlemen would invite me to dance."

She took a sip of her tea—and shook her head. "In retrospect my worries were completely inconsequential, but at the time they loomed like avalanches. Had I known he'd be gone so soon . . . but I hadn't the least idea. I thought we'd live quietly and uneventfully together until some distant ripe old age for him."

Holmes let a few seconds pass. "Other than this sudden insistence on your debut, was there anything else different about him in the days and weeks leading up to the party?"

Miss Longstead winced. "I didn't see very much of him in that time, Miss Holmes."

"No?"

"My uncle had a number of patents to his name. He had been teaching me for years, mathematics, physics, especially thermal dynamics, principles of engineering, etc. But my true love has always been chemistry, which he rather lamented because he disliked the smells produced by chemical experiments. At our place in the country, he had an outbuilding converted into a laboratory for me. Here in the city, I have turned to making essential oils and other extracts, and have found that I dearly adore this more fragrant side of chemistry. Of late I've been thinking of scaling up my production, so in the studio of the spare house—"

"Number 33, you mean?" murmured Holmes.

"Yes, number 33. That was another reason I was against my debut: I was consumed with designing new equipment and experimenting with temperatures and proportions."

Through her grief, Lord Ingram heard an echo of the excitement she must have felt for her enterprise, her pride in its progress.

"If anything, the approach of the party made me want to escape even more to number 33 and the studio. As a result, I didn't see much of my uncle in those days, except for our dance practices— and even then I was only half paying attention."

Tears welled up in Miss Longstead's eyes again. She brushed them away with the tips of her fingers. "I'm sorry."

"Please don't apologize for living your life as both you and Mr. Longstead wished you to live," said Holmes, with greater gentleness than Lord Ingram was accustomed to seeing from her. "If you can't tell us about the days leading up to the soiree, can you tell us whether you noticed anything unusual while it took place?"

"Unfortunately I'm almost blind without my glasses—you would have seen me in them today except I've been crying and taking them on and off, and at the moment I'm not sure where they are." Miss Longstead smiled ruefully. "And of course, I was firmly overridden on wearing glasses to the party, by every single woman in the house. Even my uncle thought it would be best if I were to leave them alone for a night.

"I can see a person's face, if he or she is standing right before me. But five feet out features begin to blur. If someone is standing ten feet away, I can distinguish whether it's a man or a woman by their attire and the shape of their hair. And if I'd paid attention earlier on, I might be able to tell the women apart by the color and cut of their dresses. But men are nearly indistinguishable to me from that distance, especially if they are of a similar build and attire—as they are usually all wearing the exact same things at an evening function."

"You didn't notice what your uncle, Mr. Sullivan, or Mrs. Treadles were doing at all?"

"My uncle I can sometimes find by his mop of white hair. And his girth—he'd put on a bit of a paunch in recent years. Mrs. Treadles was wearing a very conservatively cut gown almost entirely in black, except for a band of lavender around the wrists, I think—she is still in mourning for her brother and probably wouldn't have come except to support my uncle and me, knowing that I worried about attendance.

"The two of them both checked on me from time to time, or at least Mrs. Treadles did so until she left, because of a headache exacerbated by the brightness of all the candles. As for Mr. Sullivan, our paths crossed very little during the night. He was not seated next to me at the dinner, nor did he ask me to dance. And I couldn't have differentiated him from the other gentlemen at any distance, so I really do not know what he was doing during the party."

Her voice turned a few degrees cooler as she spoke of her cousin. Lord Ingram wondered how Mr. Sullivan had earned her dislike. Surely not in the exact same way he had turned Mrs. Treadles's opinion against him.

The change in her tone could not have escaped Holmes's attention but she only asked, "How did your uncle seem to you?"

"Both apprehensive and excited—exactly how I felt." Miss Longstead's thumb rubbed over the delicate handle of her bone china cup. "I was asked similar questions yesterday by Scotland Yard, about whether there was anything to note during the party. The only thing out of ordinary I could think of then, and the only one I can think of now, was that I saw someone enter number 33 from the back."

Holmes, who had been studying the array of biscuits on offer, looked up. "Do please tell more. Did you notice the time, by any chance?"

Miss Longstead shook her head. "There was no place on my dress for a pocket watch and I couldn't see the time on the grandfather clock in the corner."

"What about your dance card? If we know which dance you left blank, we might be able to estimate the time."

"We didn't have dance cards printed. Since we entertained so little, we didn't think of dance cards until much too late. Mrs. Treadles assured us then that it was not entirely necessary for a smaller gathering. She said she would have a word with the matrons present— they would let the gentlemen know what to do. She also said that the musicians could decide what to play next. So without a dance card filled ahead of time, I didn't need to worry about keeping my appointments throughout the evening. At one point I simply excused myself and slipped out to the garden to cool off."

"Do you remember what music was playing while you were in the garden?"

"No, I'm sorry. I don't have a good memory for tunes."

Large balls often had a set sequence for the dances, this many quadrilles, that many waltzes, a smattering of galops and polkas. But with musicians left to their own devices, even if Miss Longstead remembered the melody that had wafted out of the house, the musicians might not be able to recall when they'd played it.

Holmes did not appear concerned about this additional difficulty. "Was it not cold in the garden?"

"Quite, but it was *very* warm inside the house and I was glad for a minute in fresh air. I was standing somewhere in the middle of the lawn, looking up at the sky, when I turned around and saw someone go into the house next door."

"How far were you from the house?"

"About forty feet."

"You can see from that distance?"

"Movements and such. My night vision isn't bad. These houses are white stucco. A dark shape going up to a white wall, I can distinguish that, with the light spilling out from the party."

"Do you have any idea who it was?"

"Not at all, except to think that it was a woman—something about that silhouette."

"Did you not think that it was alarming, that someone went into number 33?"

Miss Longstead cleared her throat. "I am twenty-four, Miss

Holmes, not exactly in the first blush of youth. Mrs. Coltrane had told me that sometimes things happen at social gatherings. Obviously questionable conduct is much more likely in country manors where guests stay for days, and not truly expected at a town house dance. Still, before the ball started, we locked the bedrooms in the house—number 31—for precisely that reason.

"So when I saw the woman going into number 33, that was where my thought went—that it would be illicit, not criminal. There wasn't anything worth stealing in the house—nothing, in any case, that could have easily been taken out. With the exception of the door between the dining room and the staircase hall, unlocked to allow me passage to the attic, all the other rooms in the house were locked, the attic double-locked."

Thus explaining why the attic door had been shot at twice?

"In fact, my main thought, when I saw the woman going into number 33, was that I shouldn't call any attention to it, lest it erupt into some sort of acute embarrassment, perhaps even a scandal. To that end I returned to the party immediately, in case anyone came outside looking for me and witnessed more than they needed to.

"I did, however, want to let somebody know about it. I looked for my uncle, but before I found him, I was swept again into several dances. Then I spoke for a bit with my friend Miss Yates, and only afterwards did I manage to locate him and tell him about the person who went into the house next door."

"The person? Not the woman?"

"It felt a bit slanderous to state that it was a woman, even though I was sure it was."

"How did Mr. Longstead react?"

"He was . . . he didn't seem to be as concerned about it as I'd expected him to be. He told me not to worry about what I saw. That I should go back to being the belle of the ball and let him look after such a minor matter. And that was the last I thought of it until . . . everything else happened."

She looked down at her hands, now tightly gripped together in her lap. Holmes picked up a plate of biscuits and extended it toward her. To Lord Ingram's surprise—his own appetite diminished with emotional distress—Miss Longstead accepted a biscuit, ate it, and appeared more in charge of herself.

"Thank you, Miss Holmes," she said.

"Nothing like a good coconut biscuit to help one carry on." Holmes selected a biscuit herself and took a bite. "When you came back to the house, did you see either Mrs. Treadles or Mr. Sullivan?"

"Neither—I was swept up in the next dance." Miss Longstead smiled a little. "It *was* rather fun to dance, provided one's partner didn't steer one into other couples. And in any case, I couldn't see beyond my immediate vicinity."

"How much time do you estimate passed between when you saw the woman enter number 33 and when guests started to leave because of the fog rolling in?"

Miss Longstead frowned slightly. "I apologize. I'm terrible at estimating the passage of time. When I'm bored, I'll think an hour has passed when only twenty minutes have, and vice versa when I'm thoroughly absorbed."

"Please don't worry about that," said Holmes, sounding very reassuring. "Tell me instead what Mr. Sullivan was doing, the last time you saw him—and the same for your uncle."

"I think I saw Mr. Sullivan speaking to Mrs. Treadles at one point, before one particular dance. But at the end of the dance when I saw her again, she was in the company of another woman.

"The last time I saw my uncle was when I told him someone had entered number 33. He asked me if I was having a good time and I said that I was, far more than I expected to. At which he grinned and said, 'See, I told you it would all go off splendidly.' And—and that was the last I saw him alive."

"You didn't have need of him the rest of the party?"

"Before the party began he told Mrs. Coltrane and me he was going to stay up as late as he could but that he might not be able to last the entire length of the gathering. So when I didn't see him at the end of the night, I simply assumed that he'd gone to bed."

Holmes let some time pass, before asking very softly, "And then came the knock on the door?"

Miss Longstead reached toward her temple, as if wanting to adjust the position of her glasses. Belatedly she remembered she wasn't wearing them and dropped her hand. "I'd gone to bed but couldn't sleep. It had been an exciting night. A surprising night. I was astonished at how well it had gone. I'd felt—I'm sure it's a shallow thing to say, but I'd felt . . . not accepted, per se, but that I had exceeded the expectations of those who'd met me and that acceptance was now a possibility.

"It was a very small thing to be so excited about, but one reason I had been content not to socialize much was because I understood that I was sheltered, that in this house my uncle's acceptance protected me. I didn't know how I would fare elsewhere. So the party was the first time I thought perhaps I might be able to negotiate the outside world on my own—and not too shabbily either."

Her yearning for a place for herself struck a chord deep inside Lord Ingram. Looking back, so many of the wrong choices he'd made in life had been in search of that acceptance. And she had far greater hurdles to clear than he had faced.

"I finally fell asleep," she went on, "and it seemed right away the commotion began. I was groggy and confused when I opened my eyes to see it was still dark. Mrs. Coltrane, our housekeeper, was by my bedside, telling me things that I couldn't believe then and still can't believe now.

"I stared at her awhile after she said that the police had requested someone from the household to identify the victims next door. She said she would go, but I told her that no, if anyone was to go, it had to be me. And then I walked to my uncle's room and knocked on the door—and opened it to see that his bed was empty . . . and still perfectly made."

He could only imagine how she'd held on to her disbelief and marched to her uncle's room, intending to show Mrs. Coltrane that Mr. Longstead was fast asleep in his own bed and that all was well with him. With this little world that had existed peacefully under his aegis.

But her disbelief must have cracked at the sight of the empty and still perfectly made bed.

"I went back to my own room, dressed, and took my keys—not realizing that I wouldn't need them at all as all the doors that required those keys were already open," said Miss Longstead, her face blank, her voice disembodied, as if she were narrating the experience of a stranger—as if that was the one way she could get through her account. "And then Mrs. Coltrane and I went together to number 33. When we got there, we were asked if we knew anything about the attic of that house. I told them what I did in the studio. They said that it had been destroyed.

"I—" She passed a hand over her face. "I couldn't care at all about the studio. And then somebody pointed out Inspector Treadles and asked if I knew him. I just nodded. I was in such a state of shock that I didn't ask myself what he was doing there. Even after I'd identified my uncle and Mr. Sullivan for the police, and come down and seen him again, it still didn't occur to me that he might have had anything to do with it. I even asked him if he knew what had happened. He shook his head."

Holmes gave her time to drink tea and eat another half biscuit. "Why do you think anyone would have wanted to kill your uncle?"

"I cannot understand it. My uncle is—was a wonderful man, a truly kind, generous, loving soul. I find it mind-boggling to even contemplate the possibility that it might have been Inspector Treadles, of all people, who might have done it."

She leaned forward. "You see, my uncle wanted very much for Mrs. Treadles to succeed. He saw it as patently unfair that the managers and directors stood in her way. Their task should have been to assist her, not to keep her from the company that was rightfully hers."

"He spoke of the goings-on at Cousins to you?"

"Not too much. But sometimes, after a meeting, he would be in a rather disheartened mood. When I asked him, that was what he would tell me, that he didn't like what was happening to Mrs. Treadles."

"Is there any chance that he was pretending to be Mrs. Treadles's ally, but was in fact opposed to her presence?"

The incredulity on Miss Longstead's face was complete. "No, that wouldn't be like him at all. If he didn't think Mrs. Treadles should be at Cousins, he would have told her so himself."

At least Mrs. Treadles had been correct in thinking of him as an ally.

Lord Ingram exhaled. The relief he felt seemed out of all proportion with the confirmation he'd received. But Mrs. Treadles had already been cruelly disappointed by the men in her life and he desperately did not want Mr. Longstead to be yet another such man.

"He saw in her something of her late father," said Miss Longstead with great conviction. "He thought the world of Mr. Cousins, who, even though he'd been a man of commerce, had possessed a generosity of spirit that he'd greatly admired. He felt that Mr. Cousins's son hadn't inherited those traits, but that Mrs. Treadles had in her an abundance of intelligence, sensitivity, and nobility of character, everything that was needed both to succeed in commerce and to not lose one's soul along the way.

"He was very pleased when she asked him to be her adviser. He considered her a true heir to her father and looked forward to a renaissance at Cousins." Tears once again filled her eyes. "Perhaps it will yet happen. Perhaps I will witness it for him."

—❦—

Mrs. Coltrane, the Longsteads' housekeeper, showed Holmes and Lord Ingram the rest of 33 Cold Street, with Constable Lamb trailing in their wake, but keeping a respectful distance.

As Miss Longstead had said, all the other rooms in the house had been locked during the night of the murders. Mrs. Coltrane herself had unlocked them, when Inspector Brighton had come through to inspect the scene of the crime from top to bottom.

"Would you happen to know, Mrs. Coltrane, who all has keys to number 33?" asked Holmes.

"I have the entire set," said Mrs. Coltrane, rattling the ring of keys in her hand. "Miss Longstead has keys to the front and back doors and the studio, as did Mr. Longstead."

Holmes looked inside each room, to satisfy herself that the police hadn't overlooked anything significant. As there were a number of rooms, the process took some time. Lord Ingram sometimes watched her work, and sometimes spoke to the others present. Constable Lamb was grateful that number 31 kept him supplied with tea, biscuits, and sandwiches. And Mrs. Coltrane told him that despite her own grief, Miss Longstead had gathered the staff, comforted them, and assured them that they didn't need to fear for their employment.

When Holmes was finished with the last room on the floor just beneath the attic, she said to Mrs. Coltrane, "I understand that the police found the front door open. And Miss Longstead saw someone enter the house from the back at some point during the party."

Mrs. Coltrane groaned. "Oh, dear. I won't mind admitting it, Miss Holmes: That is mortifying. *Mortifying.* I don't know how either instance could have happened. For number 33, I check the doors every day before dinner, after Miss Longstead comes home. Yesterday she never left home because there was so much to do, but still at about half past six I came and checked the doors here. They were all locked, front, back, and the service entrance, too."

"You, Miss Longstead, and Mr. Longstead were the only ones with keys to number 33?"

"We were the only ones."

"Do you have any thoughts as to why the door to the chief bedroom should have been open, when the other rooms remained locked?"

The chief bedroom was where the murders had taken place. If Mrs. Coltrane was the only one who could access the individual rooms, then even Mr. Longstead shouldn't have been able to get into that bedroom.

Mrs. Coltrane groaned again. "It's an absolute mystery to me, Miss Holmes. Miss Longstead walked past that bedroom every time she went to the top floor and she said that the door always appeared properly closed to her. I check the entire house once every week and can attest that I've had to unlock the room every single time."

Holmes nodded. She was not the most energetic person, but could muster a great deal of stamina, if necessary. Lord Ingram, however, worried that she'd barely had any rest after their return from France.

Even a Sherlock-ian must weary from time to time.

The stairs that led to the highest floor were narrow and steep.

"Oh, I am getting old," mumbled Mrs. Coltrane, even as she ascended easily.

The air here nearly bounced with the pungency of essential oils in too great a concentration. Rosemary, rose, lavender, quintessentially English. But also, wormwood, spikenard, and myrrh, an olfactory tour of the Song of Songs.

And more than a hint of alcohol.

The low, narrow attic door probably could have been kicked in, except the stair landing was too small for such a maneuver. Instead, an irregular hole gaped where the in-door lock had once been. The old hasp and stable—for the padlock that had also been blown off—were blackened and twisted with the force of impact, the wood behind them splintered and blackened.

A new set of hasp and stable had been put in for a new padlock. Mrs. Coltrane unlocked the unprepossessing door.

An unexpectedly large space opened up before them.

It was raining again. And yet, the studio was not at all dim, thanks to the glazed skylights and several large mirrors. Mrs. Coltrane explained that the house was not currently connected for gas, then lit several tapers and placed them in wall sconces set before those large mirrors. All at once, the interior was bathed in a warm golden glow.

The studio was shaped somewhat like a dumbbell, with the portion immediately next to the door, having to accommodate for the space taken up by the staircase, being the narrowest, like a corridor that connected two larger spaces at either end.

Several worktables were lined up along the length of this corridor. They must have once held Miss Longstead's equipment; but now stood sadly empty.

Holmes wandered toward the larger area in the direction of the garden, which had been set up as a sitting area. Not long ago it might have been a comfortable spot, with books on low shelves and a writing desk that would have given its occupant an excellent view of the garden.

Lord Ingram imagined his children in this studio. Come summer, with the trees outside in full foliage, they might easily believe that they were in the midst of a forest, perched high above.

But now the shelves were in pieces. The books, many of which appeared damaged from having been thrown about, stood in desolate piles on the floor. The writing desk looked as if it had been gouged—someone had wielded a poker with great force.

"It was such a charming space," lamented Mrs. Coltrane. "I don't think Miss Longstead can comprehend what happened here and I don't blame her. I don't either. You cannot imagine how much glass we swept up."

The smells inside were weaker than in the stairwell, possibly because the windows had been opened: It was as cold as an ice well inside the studio, and everyone's breaths vapored.

"The previous tenants didn't leave behind the furniture, did they?" asked Holmes, testing with a fingertip the depth of a particularly large gouge mark on the desk.

"No, indeed, they didn't. Once it was decided not to put the house up for let again, Miss Longstead had things brought over from the other house."

Lord Ingram made his way to the other end of the studio, near the windows that looked down on the street. Here a different work area had been set up, with an ironing board placed next to a chair. Mrs. Coltrane explained that those were for Miss Longstead's maid, who stayed with her while she worked and used the time to perform some of her own duties. And that there had been a sewing basket and a knitting basket, but the baskets were destroyed, and their contents mixed up with too much debris to salvage.

"Miss Longstead didn't need the company but it was an empty house, after all. Both Mr. Longstead and I insisted that she not be alone here."

The studio had been formed by removing thin walls that would have separated the space into small rooms for the servants. Not all the partitions had been removed. Near the maid's station, one such room remained.

"It was used as a storage closet by the previous tenant. I do believe he left behind a few boxes of old art magazines. They were strewn all about yesterday morning, the boxes thrown against the walls," said Mrs. Coltrane, opening the closet to show its empty inside to Lord Ingram and Holmes, who had by now repaired to this side of the studio. "Miss Longstead's Christmas present from her uncle, too, was smashed to pieces. And it was such a magnificent pearl necklace. It would have looked stunning against her complexion."

Holmes turned toward her, her hand over her heart, her brow raised. "Mr. Longstead had already given Miss Longstead her Christmas present?"

Both a noticeable expression and a noticeable, indeed, exaggerated gesture. Holmes didn't just want the housekeeper to keep talking; her curiosity was truly piqued.

"She and Mr. Longstead had this tradition, you see. They hid each other's gifts around the house, quite often in a corner of the other person's rooms. New places every year, too; they don't reuse old locations. Usually by mid-December Miss Longstead starts looking around for her present, but this year, what with the soiree, she was distracted.

"And then, the same morning after she'd had to identify his body, to come here, see this swathe of destruction, and catch sight of the necklace's fragments strewn all about . . . She did very well, Miss Longstead—she didn't shed a single tear before the police. But I did. I was with her and I couldn't stop myself from crying."

Mrs. Coltrane dabbed at her eyes again. Lord Ingram felt his own eyes sting.

Holmes took another look inside the empty closet. "May I inquire about the smell of alcohol?"

"Oh, that." Mrs. Coltrane smiled sadly. "Mr. Longstead enjoyed a good brandy and Miss Longstead wanted to see whether she couldn't distill something decent for him herself. All her efforts were destroyed last night, of course."

Two sets of Christmas presents, razed in one paroxysm of violence. For Miss Longstead, other Christmases would come, and other presents. But for her uncle, stowed away in a mortuary that smelled of formaldehyde and decay, there would never again be anything else.

———— ❊ ————

Outside of number 33, after assuring Charlotte that he would meet her later for their interview with Mrs. Cousins, Lord Ingram bade everyone good day—it fell to him to speak to the guests who had been at the party. He left swiftly, his greatcoat streaming in the wind.

"Well, there goes a man who knows how to cross a street," said Mrs. Coltrane, not immune to the allure of his lordship in motion.

Charlotte could not disagree. "You should see him cross a marble hall."

And he's mine, rose the words, unbidden.

He was hers—they both knew that. But was she his—and to the same degree?

She feasted her eyes on him another moment, then followed Mrs. Coltrane back to number 31.

Back to the case at hand.

"You probably know Mr. Longstead's daily habits better than anyone, Mrs. Coltrane. Could you give me an idea of them?"

The housekeeper was conducting Charlotte around the ground floor, which had been used for the party. She opened the door to a small, book-lined study that did not look much used. "I know this will sound odd but Mr. Longstead was not a person of regular habits. He rose between six to nine o'clock in the morning, depending on what hour he had retired the night before. Often he would only decide on his schedule after he had risen. He might ask Miss Longstead if she would care for a lesson, or a walk, and she would either oblige him or tell him that she already had other plans for the day."

This seemed to Charlotte a lovely way to live. But . . . "Did that complicate matters for the staff?"

"No, we didn't need to have his shaving water sent up the moment he opened his eyes or anything of the sort." Mrs. Coltrane led the way across the stairwell hall to the dining room at the rear—number 31 and number 33 shared a remarkably similar floor plan. It was possible this entire row of houses utilized the same scheme of interior arrangement. "He was happy to wait or to do things out of order. And since his breakfast tended to be simple, it didn't fluster the kitchen to fry him an egg at seven one day and half past eight the next. Dinner was always at eight in town and seven in the country—

it would have inconvenienced the staff to move dinner about and he never inconvenienced anyone if he could help it."

Charlotte looked at the black-draped windows of the dining room and felt a small pang in her heart for this much-beloved man. "So he got up when he pleased and took his dinner at eight. In between he might take a walk or tutor Miss Longstead in thermodynamics. Anything else?"

Mrs. Coltrane straightened dining chairs that appeared perfectly placed to Charlotte. "He read. He looked at the small notices—after he met Mr. Charles Babbage a good twenty years ago he took up an interest in ciphers. He sometimes visited the Reading Room at the British Museum. He and Miss Longstead went to lectures and exhibits. From time to time they went to the theater. He took himself to various shops around town, to see what new and interesting items they might have. Occasionally he met with old friends."

She spoke slower and slower, as if with every recollection his loss became more difficult to bear.

For her benefit, Charlotte moved to the window that faced number 33 and lifted the curtains, ostensibly to check on the line of sight between the dining rooms of the two houses—when she'd already looked out each window of number 33 and gauged how it gave onto number 31. "And this irregular pattern continued up until his death?"

"Well," said Mrs. Coltrane after a minute, "this was the slightly peculiar thing. His habits became rather regular in the weeks preceding his death. We'd become accustomed to a leisurely pace in the morning. We were surprised when suddenly he was up at half past six every day."

Charlotte dropped the curtains and turned around, a flutter of excitement in her stomach. "Was there any reason you could think of for this change?"

Mrs. Coltrane, who had moved to rearrange bric-a-brac on the mantel, frowned. "Not really. It just happened one day and went on happening. He would have his breakfast, get ready, and then walk to the Reading Room. Whenever he went to the Reading Room he'd be back only at teatime. After the first two days, we thought surely he wouldn't make a habit of it. But he did for a good three and a half weeks."

"Until his untimely death."

"Until that."

The flutter in Charlotte's stomach only grew stronger. "Did he have an appointment book?"

"Scotland Yard has it now. They said they'd give it back when they've made a proper study."

Drat it. She would much rather see it this minute. "Do please let me know when you have it back."

They continued the tour. After the ground floor, they went up to the first floor, which had also been used for the party. And then came the true objective of the tour: Mr. Longstead's rooms, which, according to Mrs. Coltrane, had been left as they were, when he descended the stairs to host his niece's coming-out soiree.

The master of the house had a floor to himself—as did Miss Longstead, who occupied the floor above his. His bedroom was tidy enough, but his study . . .

Charlotte was not particularly neat in terms of her possessions. The canopy rails of her bed usually had a petticoat or a chemise thrown over them. An empty plate or two typically graced her desk, as a woman at work required sustenance. And her nightstand always bore a jumble of items, because when she was already in bed at night, comfortably ensconced, she didn't want to have to scramble off again for a dictionary, a pair of scissors, or the nice bonbons Miss Redmayne had brought back from Paris.

Mr. Longstead's study, however, made Charlotte feel that she herself must be as meticulous as those servants who assured uniform distance between plates and water goblets with a measuring tape.

On his shelves, the space between the tops of the books and the bottom of the next shelf were stuffed with more books. When there was still room left, it was crammed with notebooks and dossiers.

And the overcrowding was not limited to one or two areas; entire walls of shelves were packed, jammed, and wedged this way.

But at least those items had been packed, jammed, and wedged to conform to the general shape of the shelves. The desk, however, had been eaten.

At least that was one explanation for the mountainous entity that stood at the center of the study, with teeth made of lawyerly letters and thick volumes on ornithology and chemical analysis for feet.

"Mr. Longstead had his own way of organizing his papers," Mrs. Coltrane hastened to explain. "He knew what he had and where everything was to be found."

Minds worked very differently—Charlotte knew that better than most. But even so she found it a little difficult to credit Mrs. Coltrane's assertions. She cleared her throat. "Do you know where anything is in here, Mrs. Coltrane?"

"I'm afraid I don't," said Mrs. Coltrane apologetically. "No one else was to touch anything on or within three feet of his desk. Even if something had fallen off, we were to leave it alone."

And so many things had fallen off they hid the desk from every direction.

"Well," said Charlotte, "he is no more and I must go through his things."

She rolled up her sleeves. Mrs. Coltrane, after a moment of astonished paralysis, joined her.

There were newspapers, some recent, some from the summer. There were communications with solicitors and agents. Personal correspondences. A number of books. There was even a photographic album, featuring a much younger Mr. Longstead, posing before a factory in various stages of completion, often alongside another young man, whom Mrs. Coltrane confirmed to be Mr. Mortimer Cousins, Mrs. Treadles's late father.

"Are these the items typically found on his desk?" Charlotte asked

Mrs. Coltrane, gesturing at this immense multiplicity, now spread on the floor, taking up almost all the room in the study.

Mrs. Coltrane was still a little glassy-eyed from the endeavor. "I'm afraid I can't be sure, since we aren't permitted to tidy the desk itself. And there were always several layers of everything, so I haven't the slightest idea what was in the bottom layers."

"What if he left some half-eaten food on his desk? No one could touch that either?"

"Oh, he would never do that to us," said Mrs. Coltrane fervently. "He never ate in here."

No small mercy, that.

The first desk drawer Charlotte opened was just as stuffed. Stationery, engraved pens, pencils, more letters, coins and pound notes, among dozens of other categories.

"Good gracious," exclaimed Mrs. Coltrane. "I'm glad I never saw the insides of his drawers. It would have given me palpitations of anxiety."

Even Charlotte felt the urge to flee. She'd seen Lord Ingram's private spaces, when she'd investigated the case at Stern Hollow. They'd been uncluttered and exceptionally shipshape. She would like to lie on the carpet of his dressing room, and do nothing but wallow in its orderliness for a span of twelve hours, at least.

In the next drawer, Charlotte unearthed lug nuts, a handful of acorns in a yellowed envelope, and a silk drawstring pouch filled with smoothly tumbled pebbles of agate and tourmaline.

Stowed with the semiprecious stones she found a brooch made of gold-mounted jet, polished and gleaming. At its center was a glass-covered cavity that held a lock of hair, the individual filaments tied together with golden thread.

A piece of mourning jewelry.

The back of the brooch, which should have had the name and the dates of birth and death of the departed, or at least initials and the date of death, had been filed to remove the identifying information.

Charlotte handed the brooch to the housekeeper. "Have you ever seen this item before, Mrs. Coltrane?"

Mrs. Coltrane turned it over in her hands. "No, I've never seen it. I have seen this pouch of stones before—I believe Miss Longstead gave it to him quite some time ago."

At Charlotte's request, Mrs. Coltrane took the brooch to Miss Longstead, only to return shaking her head. "Miss Longstead says this is the first time she has ever come across this brooch."

"Have you any idea who this might belong to?"

Mrs. Coltrane shook her head again. "The hair inside is dark blond. Of those close enough to Mr. Longstead in life that he would have wanted to keep a lock of their hair after death, I can only think of old Mr. Cousins as having had hair like this. But that was when he was young. His hair, or what remained of it, turned white years before he died."

They persevered through the rest of the drawers. Afterward, as they escaped Mr. Longstead's study at an unladylike speed, Charlotte asked Mrs. Coltrane whether she knew where Mr. Longstead kept his set of keys to number 33, which Charlotte had not seen either in his desk or as part of the evidence collected by the police. Mrs. Coltrane didn't.

She also didn't know whether Miss Longstead would know, but implored Charlotte not to trouble her mistress again so soon. "Please let her have a little respite from all this talk of the murders."

It seemed unlikely to Charlotte that Miss Longstead's mind could stray far from thoughts of the murders, but she acceded to Mrs. Coltrane's wish and followed the housekeeper to her small, trim office in the basement of the house for tea, coconut biscuits, and Mrs. Coltrane's account of the night of the party.

As the senior servant in charge, Mrs. Coltrane had been terribly busy, making sure that everything went off properly and that the footmen hired especially for the evening knew what they were supposed to do. She, like Miss Longstead, had thought Mr. Longstead had gone to bed—he'd told her that he might not last the entire night.

"The main thing I remember feeling, after the guests had departed, was that I was both relieved the fog came in, forcing everyone to leave, and truly sorry that it happened. The party could have been legendary, the kind where people still dance at five o'clock in the morning. That would have been rough on the staff, as we still had to get up in the morning for the next day's duties, but I would have liked that for Miss Longstead. I would have liked for everyone to always remember that on the night of her debut, the guests were so taken with her that they made merry as if there was no tomorrow."

Charlotte gazed at her a moment. Mrs. Coltrane was not a handsome woman, but her kindness made her lovely. How much better Charlotte would feel about Livia being stuck at home if she had a Mrs. Coltrane in the household, looking after her.

"So you barely slept that night," she said softly.

"I'd just lain down, in fact, when I heard the doorbell ring. I was peeved when I got to the door and couldn't believe a word the policeman was saying. In fact, I marched right up to Mr. Longstead's room and banged on the door, convinced that he would be just as vexed as I'd been to be woken up. But I had to drag him downstairs to show him to the copper.

"My knocking brought no response. And when I opened the door and saw that there was no one inside—my blood congealed. Miss Longstead, when I woke her up, had precisely the same reaction. She didn't believe me and rushed to her uncle's room.

"In the end we went together to the next house. The horror of it. The carnage." Mrs. Coltrane inhaled deeply. "Afterward, in the entrance hall of number 33, I saw Inspector Treadles. I almost lunged at him. We hosted him. We respected him. I couldn't believe he would do this to Mr. Longstead. To his wife."

After her interview with Mrs. Coltrane, Charlotte also spoke to the other servants, one by one, in the servants' hall. All had been run to ground the night of the party, and none had had enough interactions with the master of the house to tell her anything useful.

The one exception was Miss Longstead's maid, Owens, who was also black. Unlike her spectacular mistress, Owens was rather plain looking and shy of demeanor. But she declared firmly that in the days leading up to the ball Mr. Longstead had been more silent than usual.

On edge, it felt to her.

"He wasn't an aloof gentleman," Owens said, looking up from a stocking she was mending—her mistress's stockings, Charlotte assumed. "He didn't need the servants to keep their eyes down and be quiet as ghosts. If he saw you, he'd ask how your family was getting on, or if you'd done anything interesting on your half day. He knew that I'd been sitting with Miss Longstead in her studio and that Miss Longstead's been having me learn some algebra, so he'd ask if I'd learned how to solve for equations with two variables. Once, we talked about factoring polynomials and I told him that I didn't mind factoring them—I liked when I got them correct. But I couldn't see for the life of me what they were for. He had a right old laugh at that.

"But in the last few weeks, it felt as if he never even saw me. As if he even had to make an effort to see Miss Longstead—and he'd always been wonderful attentive to her."

"I see," murmured Charlotte.

What exactly had Mr. Longstead been doing with his new routine, that he'd been too distracted to pay attention to his beloved niece?

Owens bit her lower lip. "Please don't tell Mrs. Coltrane I said that. She wouldn't have us speculate about the master."

"Did she say this to you after he died?"

"No, no, she didn't. She just doesn't like us to gossip in the servants' hall."

"I won't tell her anything," Charlotte promised. "And you did the right thing. If nobody gave us any information, my brother and

I wouldn't be able to be of any use, as we are strangers and only come in after disasters have taken place."

"Will you—" Owens hesitated. "Will Mr. Sherlock Holmes really be able to find out who killed Mr. Longstead, if it's not Inspector Treadles?"

Mrs. Graycott, the Treadleses's housekeeper, had asked Charlotte whether Sherlock Holmes would be able to bring Inspector Treadles back home soon. Charlotte had given a noncommittal answer, as she sincerely had no idea whether she could do anything for Inspector Treadles.

Owens, however, asked a very different question.

"Yes," said Charlotte. "Sherlock Holmes will find out who killed Mr. Longstead. And when he does, it will be thanks in part to your help, Miss Owens."

Ten

Alice Treadles was more than a little afraid of Miss Holmes. The young lady might be only conveying her brother's insights, but her seemingly artless gaze made Alice's gut tighten. She was sure Miss Holmes not only detected lies and omissions, but perceived the slightest bending of the truth.

She had, therefore, warily—and wearily—braced herself for this other associate of Sherlock Holmes's.

Someone similarly omniscient, similarly cool and removed.

Miss Holmes had left to fetch Mrs. Watson from the latter's own carriage. Alice sat with her face in her hands. Despite a full night's sleep, she was already exhausted again by the impossibility of the situation. Yes, she would keep putting one foot down in front of the other, but what was the use of it all?

Miss Holmes returned with a woman in a jewel-blue cape. At her entrance, the interior of the carriage brightened, as if lit by an invisible halo.

"Mrs. Treadles," said Miss Holmes, "may I present my colleague Mrs. Watson? Mrs. Watson, Mrs. Treadles, our client. I must call on

Inspector Treadles now and will leave you ladies to be better acquainted. Good day, Mrs. Treadles. Good day, Mrs. Watson."

After Miss Holmes left, Mrs. Watson sighed softly and looked at Alice. "It has just been awful, hasn't it, my dear?"

With Miss Holmes, Alice felt as if every single one of her mistakes and shortcomings, accumulated over her twenty-eight years on earth, had been laid bare, with no place to hide and all defenses crumbled.

But with Mrs. Watson, her bewilderment, loneliness, and pain—her entire self—was seen. And not just seen, but gently, and ever so kindly, embraced.

Tears immediately stung the backs of her eyes. She covered her mouth with her handkerchief, as if by doing so she could dam the flood of need.

"I'm—I'm so besieged."

Sympathy radiated from the older woman. "Of course you have been, my dear. It has fallen on you and you alone to preserve your marriage and look after a large enterprise—and now, to save your husband's life. But you mustn't despair. You are not alone anymore. We are here to help. And if I may boast a little, Mrs. Treadles, we are *formidable* help."

Not just sympathy. Mrs. Watson also radiated *confidence.*

Alice had always known that Miss Holmes—that Sherlock Holmes would be formidable help. But not until this moment did relief wash over her, an avalanche she was glad to be buried under.

More words gushed out of her. "Ever since Sergeant MacDonald showed up at my house, I've felt as if I'm walking on a high wire suspended over a bottomless abyss. One false step and it would be the dreadful end."

Mrs. Watson took her hands. They both wore gloves, yet Alice's ice-cold fingers instantly felt warmer. "You are all right now, my dear. We are your safety net. Even if you take a wrong step, we will still catch you. We won't let you fall."

No one had reassured her like this in a very long time.

A nightmarish high-wire act described her life for the past few days. Before that, ever since summer, it had been as if she'd been trapped inside a large maze, with the walls closing in all around her, until she must move sideways, squeezed so tight she could barely breathe. All the while knowing that as much work as she put into each step, she was no closer to putting the struggle behind her.

Her voice broke. "I don't know what to do anymore."

"You don't need to know everything, my dear. Together we will find a way out."

Mrs. Watson moved to Alice's seat and enfolded her in an embrace. And the tears Alice had been holding back, today, yesterday, and for months and months, fell down her cheeks into Mrs. Watson's velvet-soft cape.

"Inspector Brighton will not let up. He's convinced of impropriety between Mr. Sullivan and myself. And he is convinced I was there at number 33 the night of the murders."

"I believe that there was nothing between you and Mr. Sullivan."

Alice's conscience burned. "I can say that nothing *happened* between Mr. Sullivan and myself."

Mrs. Watson rubbed her back, the contact light yet fortifying. "My child, your husband was a fool for an extended period of time. He was so involved in his own abraded pride that he, an investigator by profession, could not perceive that you were embattled at Cousins. Was it any wonder that, however briefly, you looked forward more to seeing Mr. Sullivan than to seeing Inspector Treadles? Was it any wonder that you imagined, once or twice, how different your life would have been had you married a more broad-minded man, such as Mr. Sullivan gave every appearance of being?"

More of Alice's tears soaked into Mrs. Watson's cape—was there any possibility that she could keep this wonderful cape, to hold tight when she needed comfort and understanding? "It might have been little wonder, but I feel deeply disloyal for having had those thoughts."

Mrs. Watson sighed. "And do you think, during all the time your husband had himself that long, silent tantrum, that he never looked at someone else's wife and wished that he'd married a meeker, more deferential woman? Do you think he never considered how different his life would be if he had a wife who depended solely on him and thought solely of him?"

"I'm sure he must have, but—"

Her hands on Alice's arms, Mrs. Watson straightened Alice and looked into her eyes. "But you don't think it was disloyal of him. In fact, you are downright grateful that he only thought—and didn't *do* anything with anyone else. But he isn't particularly noble for not doing what he should not have done, and you, my dear, are not at all faithless for having had a thought you never would have acted on. Since you understand why he had such thoughts, please, extend the same understanding to yourself."

But she didn't know how. She didn't even know, until Mrs. Watson pointed out the discrepancy, that she held herself to a far more stringent set of standards. "I wish I'd had you in my life sooner."

"Well, I didn't arrive too late, I don't think—I arrived when I was meant to."

Mrs. Watson dabbed at Alice's still-wet face with a handkerchief that smelled of orange blossoms. "Now tell me about the night of the party. Tell me what really happened."

Logically Alice knew that whatever she told Mrs. Watson, Miss Holmes would know, too, but it was the difference between confessing a mistake to a strict headmistress and admitting the same to a loving mother from whom she needed fear no recriminations.

Mrs. Watson had placed the handkerchief in Alice's palm. Alice wiped her face some more, feeling a little stronger, a little braver. "It was an excruciating night. I'm not entirely out of mourning for my brother and went only because Miss Longstead worried that the party would be thinly attended. She need not have fretted. The attendance was most gratifying. Yet in all that crowd, I could not seem to get away from Mr. Sullivan, who was always appearing at my elbow, looking solicitous but with a snide comment under his breath. Around half past midnight I could bear it no more and went out into the garden behind the house.

"There I saw a man enter the house next door. From the back, he looked very much like my husband, who was supposed to be away from London. Mr. Longstead's house was brightly lit. The house next door, not so much. And I was far away enough that I couldn't be sure my eyes weren't playing tricks.

"Then I had a horrible thought. Mr. Sullivan had threatened to go to my husband and tell him lies. What if he had done so after all? What if my husband had told me that he would be out of town so he could observe me in secret? Was that why Mr. Sullivan kept coming near me, to give an impression of intimacy where none existed?

"Without another thought, I ran across to number 33. The folly of my action didn't occur to me. The most important thing, the only important thing, was that my marriage must not fall prey to a pack of lies.

"It wasn't until I was inside number 33 that I began to feel apprehensive. What if the person who'd entered the house was not my husband, but a squatter or a night burglar?

"The house was cold and silent. I stood where I was, not daring to move farther into its interior. I could see a little—whoever had come in before me had opened the curtains on the window facing Mr. Longstead's. But it was the kind of light that made the dark corners even darker.

"I thought I heard something higher up in the house. My heart thumped. By this point I was thoroughly regretting my rash entry. My feet started moving toward the back door.

"That's when Mr. Sullivan came in. 'Well, well,' he sneered. 'We could have had our assignation in a warm room with a proper bed, my dear Mrs. Treadles. But how like you to delight in uncomfortable thrills.'

"My lips must have flapped a few times before any protests emerged. 'Mr. Sullivan, I will have you know—'"

She broke off, and covered her face. She wanted to deliver her account with aplomb, but her gut churned at the memory, and both shame and anger burned in her throat.

Mrs. Watson pressed a small flask into her hands. "Here, have some."

Alice took a healthy swallow, breathed hard for a few seconds, and steeled herself to continue. "Before I could finish my sentence, he forcibly grabbed me and kissed me. I struggled, my head full of both revulsion and panic.

"And then, there came a loud crashing sound. Or at least what sounded like a loud crashing sound. Startled, Mr. Sullivan let go of me. I ran. Back into Mr. Longstead's house, into a cloakroom where I could hide—and retch.

"You can scarcely imagine my frame of mind. Horror. Relief. Fury. Sheer self-vilification. I vaguely remember checking in a mirror to see that my hair didn't look too disarrayed. I might have absentmindedly re-pinned my coiffure. But really my attention was elsewhere.

"When I finally emerged from the cloakroom, I decided that I couldn't stay a moment longer at the party. In any case, it was going beautifully and my presence made no difference to anyone. I left as soon as I could."

Mrs. Watson patted her on the back of her hand, a gesture of reassurance, as if Alice had done well simply to reach this point in her narrative.

She supposed she had. She supposed, in a way, that she had done well enough to be still standing. But she'd done so much trudging of late, half-buried in mud and sinking ever deeper. How she wished she were high up in the sky instead, her wings spread, soaring.

She shook her head a little and went on. "After I reached home, I couldn't sleep—and began to wonder again if it was really my husband I saw entering number 33. What was he doing in London when he was supposed to be out in the Kentish countryside, not expected home for another day? And why, if he had come back, had he not said anything to me?

"This is where Miss Holmes—or maybe I should say Mr. Holmes—was somewhat incorrect. I pulled out my husband's recent letters to me at that moment—not after I learned of the murders, but right then. The discrepancy between where he said he was and what the postmarks on the envelope attested to, and the possibility of his unannounced presence in London—that was what led me into his dressing room. I didn't really know what to look for so I rooted around in his clothes for some time and left.

"In the morning, I saw at last that my jeweled comb was missing. Almost immediately Sergeant MacDonald was announced. It occurred to me, after he left, that if my jeweled comb had dropped down inside number 33, it would be nearly impossible to convince anyone that my husband hadn't killed Mr. Sullivan in a fit of jealousy.

"I ran about the house, hoping desperately that the comb had instead fallen off after I came home, as I was moving about, still half-dazed from the events of the night. And that was when I saw that my husband's service revolver was missing from his dressing room."

Her fingertips shook with the memory of her overwhelming panic. Her throat was tight. Her heart pounded.

She made herself look Mrs. Watson in the eye. "And now I've told you everything I know about that night."

<hr>

Somewhere an organ grinder played a tinny rendition of "Hark! The Herald Angels Sing." Two passing pedestrians complained loudly about the overabundance of organ grinders in London. And it was raining again, the rain beating steadily on top of the carriage, still parked two streets over from Scotland Yard.

Alice felt drained, but at least she no longer needed to hide any-thing from those she wished to trust. But what they would think of her, now that—

"Remember, Mrs. Treadles, that you did nothing wrong," said Mrs. Watson firmly.

It was exactly what she'd hoped she would hear, yet words of objection left her lips on their own. "But I—"

"Stop blaming yourself for not having done everything per-fectly. You did nothing wrong. Now you say it."

Alice had no idea the extraordinarily kind Mrs. Watson could speak with such authority. In her bright blue cape, her gaze level, her back ramrod straight, she was no less queenly a figure than Miss Holmes had been.

"I—I did nothing wrong."

"Precisely. And Miss Holmes would have been the first to tell you so, had you trusted her sooner."

Alice's face burned. "I'm sorry."

"On this, you do owe her an apology. It hampers our ability to help you when you withhold important information. But that's be-hind us now. We need to turn our attention to the matter at hand. Miss Holmes has entrusted me to look into Cousins Manufactur-ing. I should very much like to hear what you can tell me."

Alice exhaled. "I wish I could tell you exactly what the matter is, but all I have are insufficient documentation and indirect evidence."

"That is often how an investigation begins." Mrs. Watson gave her an encouraging smile. "Please, go ahead."

Alice needed a moment to pull her thoughts together, to turn her mind from Robert's peril to a subject that had receded to a place of secondary importance since his arrest. "My brother helmed Cous-ins for four years. He began when our father was still alive. He'd never been terribly interested in the day-to-day operations of the com-pany, and Father wanted to ease him in over time, rather than thrust the entire responsibility on him all at once.

"I tried to distance myself from concerns about Cousins—my father didn't want me to be involved and my brother Barnaby certainly wouldn't have appreciated unsolicited advice. But sometimes an uneasiness gnawed at me: Barnaby didn't like to learn; he resented being corrected; and he despised any insinuation that he wasn't quite the man his father had been. And he loved flattery—he needed to be told that he possessed all the cleverness and discernment in the world."

"In other words," mused Mrs. Watson, "it wouldn't have taken much to pull the wool over his eyes."

"Unfortunately so. It also didn't reassure me that he didn't boast about his successes. Barnaby loved feeling superior. If the firm had been doing as well under him as it had under my father, we'd have known. That he never said anything to that effect could only mean that such wasn't the case."

"So you were prepared for problems," said Mrs. Watson, with approval in her voice.

Alice wallowed in her approval. She felt like a child who'd been given a much-longed-for bonbon, luxuriating in that glorious sweetness.

But she was also a grown woman who knew that confections, however delightful, could not sustain her.

Yes, she'd had enough foresight to anticipate problems. But what had she done once she'd run into those problems?

"I wanted to see the accounts. I wanted to visit the factories. I wanted to speak to suppliers and customers. I wanted a full audit of the firm conducted at the earliest opportunity. Instead I got a roomful of men who, when they didn't treat me like an infant who'd somehow escaped her bassinet, took great offense that I dared to imply that they hadn't done brilliantly and perfectly at their positions. They even tried to persuade my solicitors that it would be in *their* interest to get me to leave things alone, because that would give my solicitors more work and therefore more money—and I'm not sure they hadn't succeeded, at least halfway, in their attempt."

She could no longer quite look Mrs. Watson in the eye. Or maybe it was her younger self she couldn't bear to face, the girl whose only dream was to be part of this great enterprise that made train engines—train engines! How disappointed that girl would have been to know that her grown-up self had allowed that dream to turn into a nightmare.

"The only things I could get my hands on were some abbreviated reports I'd found in my brother's study. And bank statements that showed the movement of funds—though in aggregate, which does not give me a detailed picture of what is happening inside the company. Still it seems to me that the company suffers from a shortage of cash."

As she spoke those words aloud, she again felt the same sinking sensation that had assailed her the day she'd come to that realization. Cash was the vital blood of a going concern. A company chronically strapped for cash was as sick as a man suffering from severe cardiac disease.

Mrs. Watson's expression, too, turned somber.

"My brother purchased a number of older factories to be modernized and refitted to our specifications. I concluded that too much money was spent on the endeavor and the returns have not been impressive. Needless to say, the men who oversaw the acquisition and renovation of those factories vehemently objected to that conclusion. They spouted all kinds of accounting reasons, amortization costs, and whatnot to justify why incomes have stagnated.

"I know what amortization costs are. I am familiar with the practice of writing off costs over time. I also understand the advantages of having amortization costs so that we may pay less to Inland Revenue. But cash flow affects operations in the here and now, and cash flow is a problem that no amount of accounting wizardry can explain away.

"The funny thing is, I'd been tentative about my conclusion, since I had so little data. I would have been perfectly happy to be shown otherwise. But instead of concrete evidence, I was given only obstruction, complaints, and temper tantrums. I am now convinced that something is wrong. Very wrong. Had that not been the case, my managers would still have been condescending and patronizing, I don't doubt that, but not to this appalling extent."

She realized, only after she'd finished speaking, that she had crushed Mrs. Watson's delicate handkerchief in her grip.

Mrs. Watson, however, did not seem to mind at all. "Shall we put an end to all that appalling condescension?"

Miss Holmes had said the same, that it was time to take matters into her own hands. And Alice wanted to. How she wanted to. But . . .

"H—how?"

"How else, my dear? You need to present yourself at Cousins and stop this nonsense."

Alice's stomach quivered. Many a morning she'd regarded herself in the mirror and told her reflection that this was the day she would stop this nonsense. That this was the day she truly became the owner of Cousins.

Yet that day had kept receding into the future.

"So . . . tomorrow?"

"No, not tomorrow," said Mrs. Watson decisively. "Today. Right now."

"But right now I must look a fright!"

"Given the events of recent days, no one will expect you to look your best."

How could she make Mrs. Watson understand? "They'll be able to tell that I've been crying."

Her managers already disdained her so, when she was put together smartly. How could she go before them with puffy eyes and splotchy cheeks?

Mrs. Watson tilted her head a little. "Did looking perfectly self-possessed ever help you in your cause?"

Had it *not* helped? "I don't think I was ever perfectly self-possessed. I was probably nervous, impatient, and frustrated."

"And why is perfect self-possession so important now?"

"If they don't think I look and act the part, how can they take me seriously?"

Mrs. Watson raised a brow. "Was your father never impatient or frustrated when he presided over the company?"

Alice was startled. But why was she startled by a perfectly reasonable question? "Ah . . . he was impatient at times."

"He did not suffer fools gladly, you mean."

"He was never cruel or crude, but he did speak his mind."

"And why was it all right for him to speak his mind but not for you?"

At least this question she could easily answer. "He built the company from nothing. Of course he was entitled to speak his mind to those he hired."

"What about your brother? He did not build the company. Was he a beacon of tact or diplomacy?"

Again, Alice was startled. Enough to draw back in the carriage seat. "No, but . . ."

She trailed off.

Mrs. Watson leaned forward. "He was put into place by the terms of your father's will. You were also installed by the terms of your father's will. Do you believe you have less right to be there than your brother did?"

"No, of course not."

Mrs. Watson regarded Alice, her gaze at once sympathetic and penetrating. "May I speak bluntly, Mrs. Treadles?"

Had she not been speaking bluntly all along? Alice's stomach clenched. "Yes, of course."

"You may issue denials, my dear, and you may believe sincerely in those denials. But your misgivings tell me something else altogether. They tell me that having been told early and often that you had no place at Cousins, that judgment has seeped into your marrow."

A loud noise went off in Alice's head, followed by an awful silence. She'd felt this way once before, a long time ago, when she'd learned that her mother had a fatal tumor.

This time, the diagnosis was about *her*.

"But I never agreed with it," she implored Mrs. Watson, not wanting it to be true.

It could not be true. It couldn't. Helming Cousins had been her *dream*.

"Few are truly impervious to the opinions of others; fewer women still. Miss Holmes, perhaps, but the rest of us must make a conscious effort not to let our own judgment be preempted by outside forces."

Alice had always been proud to follow her own judgment. But if Mrs. Watson was right, then whose judgment had she been following?

"Remember what I said about you having done nothing wrong with regard to your husband? Alas, with regard to Cousins, you *have* done something wrong, my dear."

Alice's heart quaked with dread. Yet she yearned to hear the older woman tell her how she'd erred—she had no one else to teach her. "Please, I'm listening."

Mrs. Watson smiled a little, as if relieved that Alice hadn't taken umbrage at her words. "Many in this world have little or no power. That is not your predicament. Your circumstances gave you power. Your birthright gave you power. But you, my dear, have acted as a powerless supplicant in front of your subordinates, hoping that if you appear good enough for long enough, the men who already have a place at Cousins would come to accept you."

Alice squirmed. She would have looked away, but Mrs. Watson's gaze held hers, refusing to let go.

"Were nothing the matter with Cousins, you might have eventually garnered that acceptance—perhaps. I'm not confident of that. We women have been taught since birth that virtue is our greatest asset. I have nothing against virtues—I'd like to think that there are many virtues I practice assiduously. But power does not yield to virtue. Power yields only to power.

"Over time your virtue might have gathered you enough support to translate into power. But you don't have time now. Today, when you walk into Cousins, it won't be to convince anyone of your fitness to hold power, but to exercise the power you already have as the lawful owner of Cousins Manufacturing.

"Therefore, you will not mind your appearance. You look fine. The red rims around your eyes are of no consequence whatsoever. It doesn't matter even if you walk in with tears still streaming down your face. Do you understand that, Mrs. Treadles?"

Alice's breaths came in short. Her stomach was already in a knot. Mrs. Watson spoke in such muscular, declarative sentences, but Alice was the one who would need to face the men at Cousins who had been dismissive of her for months on end. "I—I think so."

"That will not do, my dear. Do you understand that you are not going to plead for power today, but to wield it?"

Alice's hands shook—she was crushing Mrs. Watson's handkerchief again. Yes, she was afraid to wield that power. But she was also apprehensive of power itself. *Power.* To hear Mrs. Watson label it so plainly and openly—it seemed that she, a very ordinary woman, ought not to want it, let alone have it.

The rest of us must make a conscious effort not to let our own judgment be preempted by outside forces.

Was this what was happening here? She'd absorbed the verdict of so many other people that it now spoke to her in her own voice?

She squared her shoulders. With her hands still shaking, she said, "Yes, Mrs. Watson, I understand. I am the owner of Cousins Manufacturing. It is time I acted the part."

———— ❧ ————

Alice perspired.

The room was warm, flames blazing in two large fireplaces. It was crowded—every single supervisor with some responsibility, it seemed, had filed into the room. The large table held sixteen. But there must have been twice that many men in the room.

But also twice the usual number of women.

All eyes had converged on Mrs. Watson when she walked in. She was no longer a young woman, but she remained a stunning woman, with an almost elemental charisma. She wore an unadorned gown in a muted russet shade, yet the fabric was luxurious and the cut sublime. Without smiling, she calmly surveyed the gathered men, taking their measure.

Alice had supplied her with a quick analysis of what they faced. Her opponents were not a unified pack. Two unequal factions existed. One, formerly led by Mr. Sullivan, consisted mostly of men who had joined the firm after her brother took over. A smaller group comprised the old guard, men who had served under her father. There also remained a collection of those who were not openly allied with either of the other two factions; they were not cohesive enough to be considered a coterie, but not so insignificant in number that they could be ignored altogether.

Alice took the seat at the head of the table. Directly opposite her on the far end was Mr. White, Mr. Sullivan's chief lieutenant. She was accustomed to seeing Mr. White in that position: When Mr. Sullivan had pretended to be her friend, he'd sat somewhere toward the middle of the table, allowing her to think that Mr. White was her greatest opponent.

Which he would be today.

Mrs. Watson occupied the chair to her right, the place that had once been reserved for Mr. Longstead. Behind Mrs. Watson stood two burly men. They were dressed appropriately, but still gave the impression that they had perhaps participated in a boxing match the night before—or in something a great deal more illicit.

Mrs. Watson nodded at her. Alice took a deep breath.

"Thank you all for being here." Her voice emerged squeaky, but she forced herself to keep speaking. "Mrs. Watson, may I present my managers and supervisors. Gentlemen, this is Mrs. Watson, who will serve as my adviser today."

Still not smiling, but with a gracious expression, Mrs. Watson inclined her head at the assembled men, who nodded or half bowed in return.

"A great tragedy has befallen Cousins," Alice continued, willing the hands that she'd placed on the table, loosely held together, not to shake. "Mr. Longstead and Mr. Sullivan are no more. Many of you have worked for years with Mr. Sullivan. Some of you have worked even longer with Mr. Longstead. We are all the poorer for the loss of these captains of men. But the work of Cousins must go on.

"Our first order of business must be a thorough audit of the company's finances and operations. No audit has been performed in six years, which is in grave contradiction of the company's policy of conducting one every four years. The acquisition of factories under my esteemed late brother, though increasing production capacity in an admirable manner, has left us—"

"Mrs. Treadles!"

Mr. White's interruption came exactly when she expected it to. *And so it begins.*

"Yes, Mr. White?" she said coolly, even as her throat turned dry.

"I confess I cannot believe what I am hearing, Mrs. Treadles. Mr. Sullivan and Mr. Longstead were murdered *by your husband*, and you sit here as if nothing has happened."

There was a collective intake of breath, including her own. The men's faces swiveled from Alice to Mr. White and back again.

She felt the force of his words in her solar plexus, but she would not let him see it—or hear any change in her tone. The projection of power mattered almost as much as power itself. Mrs. Watson, for all that she had told Alice not to worry about her appearance, had then proceeded to make sure that she looked as well as possible under the circumstances.

"Mr. White, Inspector Treadles has been temporarily detained by Scotland Yard for questioning. The investigation is still very much ongoing and I caution you not to assign guilt prematurely, especially when he could be released at any moment."

Mr. White looked as if he wished to throw something. At her. "He was caught with the murder weapon in his hand."

Members of his clique appeared excited by his aggressiveness. Several other men shifted uncomfortably.

"Appearances can be deceiving," said Alice. "Men who are caught with murder weapons in their hands may simply be in the wrong place at the wrong time. Much as men who appear friendly and helpful may be nothing of the sort."

An unsubtle reference to Mr. Sullivan. She was speaking ill of the dead when he was barely cold. Granted, he had been a despicable man, but she had never expected to trot out the truth before his cohorts.

A muscle worked in Mr. White's jaw. He, too, had not expected such a thinly veiled dig. "Nevertheless, Mrs. Treadles, I had expected you to announce that you would recuse yourself from Cousins."

She placed a hand on the notebook she had brought with her. Mrs. Watson had counseled having one or two props to give her hands something to do. "Why, pray tell?"

"Because your husband has been arrested on suspicion of murdering two of our finest!"

She wanted to shout, too. Instead, she made her reply softer, more unhurried. "And that makes Cousins Manufacturing a lesser concern for me? Or does it somehow make the firm less mine?"

Mr. White's face flushed with anger. "Have you no sense of propriety, Mrs. Treadles, to be abroad at such a time?"

Her hand moved to the fountain pen that lay beside the notebook. The notebook was from a stock in her office, but the pen had been given to her by Robert, the day before he had left to the "Kentish" countryside.

They had yet to speak openly of their estrangement. She knew she dared not disturb the fragile sweetness of their recent reconciliation by dredging up the pain and mistrust of the only slightly less recent past. Perhaps he feared the same. Which had made his gift of the pen, engraved with the Cousins crest and her initials, an even more poignant gesture.

I have an engraved service revolver, he'd told her, *you should have something similar.*

And it had not escaped her that by saying so, he'd equated her work with his.

She rubbed a thumb over the engraving. "My sense of propriety is dictated by my sense of duty, Mr. White. Wherever I have duty, there my presence is appropriate. Given that I am ultimately responsible for its well-being, I have every duty to Cousins."

"It is an insult to Mr. Sullivan's memory, to have the wife of his murderer here."

A bead of perspiration rolled down her back. She made her voice cold. "*Mr. White,* kindly remember that you are speaking to the late Mr. Sullivan's employer. Your employer, too, I'll remind you."

With a loud scraping of chair legs, Mr. White rose to his feet. "That is a travesty! Mr. Sullivan did more for this company than anyone except its founders. And he was a kinsman of Mr. Longstead's. It is an injustice that the company did not belong to him."

Another bead of perspiration rolled down her back. Inside her boots, her toes clenched hard. And her heart pounded as if she were Philippides, sprinting from Marathon to Athens.

She smoothed a finger along the edges of her notebook. "Mr. Longstead sold his stock in the company to my father when he left. He chose not to give it to his kinsman. It matters not at all what you think of that decision, Mr. White. Mr. Sullivan was not a stockholder but an employee. As such he was well compensated, and there was nothing noteworthy about his status as an employee while the company remained in my family's hands."

Mr. White gritted his teeth. "I hope what I say doesn't surprise you, but you don't deserve to be here."

Despite everything—all that Mrs. Watson had told her, all of dear Mr. Longstead's encouragement, and all she knew to be true— she almost agreed with him.

So much contempt in his face, so much dismissal.

"I remind you one last time, Mr. White, that you speak to your employer. You serve at my pleasure, sir, not the other way round."

Mr. White laughed, the sound full of derision and impatience. "And what would you do without me? I am an indispensable member of this firm. You are but a woman who doesn't know her place."

For so long she had feared this, open enmity, open confrontation, an irreversible rupture. Yet now that it was at last here, she found that she didn't fear it anymore. No, she wanted it. More than anyone else in the room, more than the belligerent Mr. White could even imagine. "You are wrong, Mr. White. I do know my place. My place is here, at the head of this table, whereas your place . . . is no longer at Cousins."

Silence, then an eruption of startled speech, men turning to one another around the table to make sure their ears hadn't deceived them.

Alice turned slightly. "Mrs. Watson, kindly have your men escort Mr. White out."

She did not raise her voice, yet it carried, silencing the men.

Mr. White pounded a meaty fist on the table. "You can't do this, you harpy!"

After what she had been through with Inspector Brighton, Mr. White's insult barely registered. She regarded him coldly. "Let me repeat: You serve at my pleasure, Mr. White, and I have decided that for your insubordination and other derelictions of duty, including but not limited to the failure to conduct a company-wide audit in more than five years, you have proved that you have neither my nor Cousins's best interest at heart. Your employment has been terminated. Mrs. Watson's men will show you out."

"If he goes, then I go, too!" roared a man by the name of Kingford as he rose. He was one of Cousins's lead engineers—and an entrenched member of Mr. Sullivan's clique.

"Mrs. Treadles, this is not how we do things here!" cried Mr. Pollard, the leader of the old guard.

Aha, the old fox was at last out of his hole, happy to let his rival be sacked before he piped up to garner some advantages for himself.

"Mr. Pollard, this is indeed not how we do things here. Since when did it become acceptable for a mere manager to be openly hostile and disparaging to the owner of the enterprise—and expect to keep his position? Since when did it become acceptable for a man not to do his work, offer a myriad of excuses, and hide evidence that might show that indeed his work has been shoddy? And since when did it become acceptable for those entrusted with the well-being of this company to condone such conduct, to speak up not at its proliferation, but only when one of its worst perpetrators has been shown the door—and then only to defend said perpetrator?"

Mr. Pollard, who had not expected such a direct offensive, flapped his lips a few times. "Mrs. Treadles, why, your father would not have acted this way!"

"And would anyone here have acted as he had *to* my father?"

"But—but that's because your father wouldn't have wanted you here," said the wily old fox.

An insidious answer that pierced her straight through the heart. It would always hurt, at least a little, that her father had excluded her from Cousins and that it would never have come to her had Barnaby not died childless. But that was between a daughter and her father's memory.

"I happen to believe that my father would have been greatly angered by the way I have been treated," she said firmly. "My father, however, is not here to settle this dispute. And therefore, *I* am the arbiter of how things are done at this great enterprise."

She looked around the table, meeting each and every gaze. "Gentlemen, this is a good time to join the exodus. For too long I have tolerated ill conduct in and out of this room. No more. If your loyalty is more to Mr. White and Mr. Kingford than to Cousins, leave now. I will not keep any here who do not know their places."

A deathly silence.

Mr. Pollard blinked. Two men, Mr. Ferguson the chief accountant and Mr. Adams the lead cashier, pushed back their chairs and rose. Mr. Hadley, another lead engineer, almost lifted his behind off his chair, but then went no farther.

Alice leaned back in her chair. "You mustn't hesitate, gentlemen. You must let your convictions guide you. Were you to stay, I would take it to mean that you have understood that mine is the only tenure here guaranteed by law."

"Mrs. Treadles, this is no way to speak to the men," protested Mr. Pollard, this time with a hint of real fear in his voice. "You will suffer a catastrophic loss of talent."

Her stomach twisted with the exact same fear, but she could not back down now. She would not. "Talent is replaceable, Mr. Pollard. A man might be invaluable to his loved ones, but on a battlefield the war continues even when the general falls. Someone else will take the responsibility. Someone else will do the work—often surprisingly well. And that new person would be more grateful, too, for having been given the opportunity."

She looked around again. "Does anyone else wish to leave?"

No one said—or did—anything.

Alice turned to the men Mrs. Watson had brought. "Gentlemen, you may escort Messrs. White, Kingford, Ferguson, and Adams from the premises."

"Not so unceremoniously!" moaned Mr. Pollard.

Alice stared at him. "These men will have their wages and their belongings sent to them. I note again, Mr. Pollard, that you showed no concern for *my* dignity when it was being trampled upon, but are now fretting over the dignity of the men who did the trampling most enthusiastically. Am I going to face such inequitable applications of your solicitude on a regular basis in the future?"

"I . . . why . . . that is . . . no, Mrs. Treadles, you will not."

"Thank you, Mr. Pollard," she said coldly.

The entire room watched as the four men made their way out. At the door, Mr. White turned and snarled at Alice, "Your husband will hang and you will never be able to show your face here again."

Her fingers tightened around her fountain pen; her thumb slid over the engraving. "My husband will be exonerated and I will preside over this company, in person, until my dying day."

The exiled men left. The room fell silent again. An eerie, blessed silence. She was exhausted, utterly exhausted. But she sat up straighter. "And now, gentlemen. We have work to do."

Eleven

"O livia, why do you persist in contorting your hand in that most unattractive manner?" grumbled Lady Holmes. "Do stop."

Livia, who was trying to work out the stiffness in her fingers, flattened her lips but complied. Or at least she made sure she appeared to by dropping her hands into her lap, so her mother, seated on the other side of the tea table, would not be able to see them beneath the tablecloth.

It was only tea time, but twilight was already fading. These were the darkest days of the year; the sun seemed to barely rise in the sky before fleeing again beneath the horizon. Livia often experienced melancholy and lethargy when she was too long deprived of sunlight. This year the doldrums hadn't set in yet because she'd had a glorious fortnight in France with Charlotte. And since her return, she had been copying out her story with dogged resolve.

This morning she'd got up early and once again put in long hours at her desk, the reason she'd needed to bend her hand this direction and that to relieve the cramping in her fingers. But at the rate she was going, she'd be done with the task in a day or two, at most. What would she do then? What else did she have to occupy herself?

"My goodness but the world and everything in it is deteriorating at a rapid pace," said Lady Holmes in disgust, tossing down the newspaper in her hand. "Read it for yourself, Olivia. A Scotland Yard police inspector has murdered two people who worked for his wife."

Livia had hoped to hide from her mother for the entire duration of her father's callous absence. But Lady Holmes, bored and restless, needed someone to listen to her at tea. Livia had thought long and hard about pretending to be unwell, but in the end she wasn't cruel enough to deny her mother half an hour, even if they had never enjoyed being in proximity to each other.

Whereas it had been so wonderfully easy to be in Stephen Marbleton's company. Charlotte made Livia feel that being herself was enough. Mr. Marbleton made being herself feel *glorious*.

A nameless distress shadowed her heart at the thought of him.

No, she'd already told herself not to remember him anymore. Their acquaintance had ended. He was probably in bright, warm Andalusia, drinking Spanish wine. Or else on the Côte d'Azur, walking on a long sandy beach with aquamarine waters lapping at his heels. And she . . . she was on a cold, wet island in the North Atlantic, with no prospect of sunshine in the near future.

She grabbed the newspaper—maybe the scandal in London would distract her—and nearly gasped aloud. The murderous policeman was none other than the despicable Inspector Treadles! Why, she couldn't have come up with a more fitting downfall for him had she been standing behind the Almighty's heavenly throne, whispering vengeful suggestions.

As she finished the article, however, she frowned. Charlotte wouldn't be involved in this, would she?

"What?" cried Lady Holmes. "What in the world is *this*?"

There was news more startling than Inspector Treadles's sensational disgrace?

Wide-eyed, slack-jawed, Lady Holmes turned to Livia. "There is a cheque of fifty pounds for me. From *Charlotte*."

❖

When Charlotte reached Mrs. Cousins's house a little after tea time, Lord Ingram was already waiting in front, an umbrella in one hand, his face dramatically contoured and shadowed in the light of a nearby street lamp.

"How do you do, my lord?" she murmured as he helped her descend.

He extended the umbrella over her. It had a large canopy, enough for them to maintain several inches of distance, but sharing the space underneath still felt intimate, almost cocoon-like.

"I'm trying to remember when was the last time I spoke to so many people in a row," he said wryly. "I'm profoundly grateful that Miss Longstead's party was only a dance and not a ball."

After she had left the Longsteads', she, too, had called on some of the guests. But he had a far larger list. "Have you learned anything interesting?"

"There was a discrepancy but I don't know if it means anything. Miss Longstead has a friend named Miss Yates. She mentioned that during the party she'd conversed with Miss Longstead's cousin Mr. Proctor. But when I called on Mr. Proctor, he was certain she hadn't—said he spent most of the night trying to work up the courage to speak to another young lady."

They were now under the portico in front of the house and he was closing the umbrella, his motion graceful and efficient. She had to resist the urge to reach out, close her hand over his upper arm, and feel the movement of his sinews as he continued with his mundane task.

She adjusted her hat ribbon instead. "Thank you for meeting me for this."

He looked back at her and smiled. "Do I need to tell you, Holmes, that the pleasure is entirely mine?"

He was different. More relaxed. She'd seen him at rest but never truly relaxed—always before he'd carried this tension, a man trying his best to fit into a norm he didn't entirely believe in. But now that he'd made his choice . . .

Now that *she* was the one holding out from an abundance of caution . . .

She looked away and rang the doorbell.

The address of Mrs. Cousins's house told Charlotte that it was unlikely to have been Mrs. Cousins's marital home, during her union with a scion of industry. Now, having seen the inside of the house, Charlotte was sure that it wasn't.

A great deal of thought had gone into making the interior look more spacious: mirrors, chairs with openwork backs, fretwork doors on cabinets and sideboards. But there was no disguising the fact that the house was small.

Still, the drawing room, with its delicate furnishing, its pale green and soft gold wallpaper, was elegant. Mrs. Cousins was more elegant still. Widow's weeds could overwhelm some women, washing them out entirely. On Mrs. Cousins, however, Charlotte was reminded of an old Dutch portrait, an arresting, starkly lit face staring out from a shadowy background.

"How can I help you?" she asked simply.

Charlotte felt a bit of uncharacteristic embarrassment.

She knew that Inspector Treadles used to think of Barnaby and Eleanor Cousins as snobs—certainly they would not have chosen him, a man from a working-class background, for an in-law. So she'd used that thin excuse to request that Lord Ingram accompany her for this interview, in case his high birth could be used to disarm Mrs. Cousins into being more cooperative.

Mrs. Cousins, alas, was not at all recalcitrant. Which made it obvious, to Charlotte at least, that she simply wanted her friend nearby.

She didn't look at him, except with a glance toward a mirror on the opposite wall. Inside the mirror his reflection smiled a little, as if to himself. Amused. But also, pleased.

Charlotte cleared her throat. "Thank you, Mrs. Cousins. I must have been under a mistaken impression that you and Inspector Treadles did not get along."

"We don't and I don't expect we shall. My sister-in-law, however, is an exceptionally good person. I didn't always appreciate her sterling character—more fool me. But she has proved herself a true friend—the sister I've never had—and I will do everything in my power to help her."

Charlotte had deduced as much from Mrs. Treadles's reliance on Mrs. Cousins the other night—that a true rapport had developed between the two women. Alas Charlotte had related what she'd observed to Lord Ingram, so he knew as much as she did. And yet he had nodded with great gravitas when she had said she might need him.

This time, she couldn't even look at his reflection in the mirror.

She took a sip of tea and bit into a random biscuit from the selection on offer. "In that case I'll begin. Were you acquainted with both victims?"

"Yes, although I won't be able to tell you much about Mr. Longstead. He and my late father-in-law were great friends. Soul mates, almost. But I'm afraid he found my late husband a disappointment, and my husband did not take kindly to that. So we didn't see him often—or much at all. He did, however, call on me to offer his condolences, which greatly surprised me. In fact—"

Loud cries erupted in the street outside, along with startled neighing and the metallic screeching of brakes. Mrs. Cousins leaped up, her hands clutched over her heart. Lord Ingram rose, too, crossed to the window, and looked out. "It's all right," he reported. "A child ran out into the street but the carriage stopped in time."

Mrs. Cousins approached the window gingerly, to reassure herself that indeed nothing tragic had happened. "Thank goodness!"

She returned to her seat, her breaths still uneven. "I'm sorry. When I was a child, my family was in a bad carriage accident that severely injured my brother. I'm afraid to this day similar noises still have me in a lather."

"It's highly understandable," said Lord Ingram. "Shall we ring for a fresh pot of tea for you?"

"Yes, please. Thank you," said Mrs. Cousins, smiling weakly.

Fresh tea was brought. After a cup, Mrs. Cousins rallied, apologized again, and said, "We were on the subject of Mr. Longstead, weren't we? Mrs. Treadles spoke of him often. She was inordinately grateful that he was kind to her—the only person at Cousins who could be said to be kind. I'm very sorry that he is no more."

Charlotte waited to see if she had more to say about Mr. Longstead, but Mrs. Cousins only looked down at her hands, one clutched onto her skirts, the other opening and closing with nervous energy.

Charlotte moved on to the subject she had come for. "I was at Mrs. Treadles's house the other night, when she had her interview with Inspector Brighton. From your exchange, I gathered that you knew something of her dilemma concerning Mr. Sullivan. When did she tell you?"

Mrs. Cousins seemed more surprised by Charlotte's knowledge of Mr. Sullivan than her presence at Mrs. Treadles's. "What is it that you know, Miss Holmes?" she asked warily.

Before she called on Mrs. Cousins, Charlotte had gone back home briefly and had encountered Mrs. Watson returning from Cousins with boxes upon boxes of accounts. And Mrs. Watson had told Charlotte of Mrs. Treadles's confession. "Everything," she said. "I know that she was being threatened by Mr. Sullivan and I know what she encountered at number 33 the night of the party."

"All right, then. If she's told you, then I suppose I can talk about Mr. Sullivan." Still Mrs. Cousins cast an uncertain glance in Lord Ingram's direction. "Alice—Mrs. Treadles told me about Mr. Sullivan a week or so before the murders. She didn't want to burden me with the knowledge, but eventually it became too heavy to carry all by herself. And of course, there was the fact that I'd warned her about Mr. Sullivan and she hadn't paid sufficient attention to my warning."

Her lips curved in a derisive smile—Charlotte had the feeling that the derision was directed at herself. "I don't blame her. In the time she'd known me, I had probably displayed very little sound judgment. But even a clock that stands still is right about the time once every twelve hours—and I was right about Mr. Sullivan."

"And may I ask how you learned of Mr. Sullivan's character deficiencies, Mrs. Cousins?"

Mrs. Cousins glanced again at Lord Ingram. She hesitated. "My apologies, my lord, but I would feel more comfortable if I were to discuss this with only Miss Holmes."

He rose immediately. "I'll wait in the carriage. Good day, Mrs. Cousins."

If Charlotte could blush, she would have. She'd made him come join her on the flimsiest of excuses *and* without considering that she would be inquiring into a highly sensitive subject.

But he had a house party to host after Christmas and must leave London soon. And after that, she didn't know when she would see him again . . .

After he had closed the door behind himself, Charlotte gathered herself and said, "Mrs. Cousins, it behooves me to inform you that Lord Ingram is an integral part of this investigation. What you tell me today, I will most likely share with him, at least in the abstract."

"I understand," said Mrs. Cousins, her hand sliding back and forth across her skirts. "Given that you are an emissary of Mr. Sherlock Holmes, I do not expect that no masculine ears will ever hear my story—the pretense that we are alone is good enough."

"Thank you, Mrs. Cousins."

Mrs. Cousins bowed her head. Abruptly, she sprang to her feet, marched to the window, then to the opposite wall, then back to the window again. Her hand over her forehead, she said, "I'm sorry. Ever since I learned of Inspector Treadles's arrest, I haven't been able to sit still."

She paced furiously another minute before she stopped behind her own chair, her hands gripping its top. "I'm so angry at him—I nearly marched down to Scotland Yard to give him a good whack.

I'm so afraid for her. And I'm scared that she might have to watch him hang."

Charlotte glanced around the room, crossed to the sideboard, and poured two fingers of a bright red liquid from a decanter—cherry brandy, by its heady aroma. She went to Mrs. Cousins and pressed the glass into her hand. "Here, have some."

"Thank you," said Mrs. Cousins, her voice slightly hoarse. She took a good swallow, followed by another. "A month ago, I might have said good riddance. But since he returned from Stern Hollow, she's been so—perilously happy. Do you know what I'm talking about, Miss Holmes?"

Charlotte shook her head.

"There was so much fear mixed into her happiness, fear that it would all go away again in an instant. Still, even I, who had already stopped believing in love, began to feel that perhaps they had indeed righted the ship. That they could now weather storms together and sail into safe harbor."

She gazed beseechingly at Charlotte. "Will he be all right? Will *they* be all right?"

Charlotte had to give the same answer she'd given to Mrs. Graycott. "I'm afraid I can't answer that at the moment, Mrs. Cousins."

She had theories. But theories would not prevail, when the police had caught Inspector Treadles standing over the dead men, murder weapon in hand.

Mrs. Cousins's free hand balled into a fist. "Then I had better tell you everything I know about Mr. Sullivan, in case it's any help at all."

She set down her glass and started pacing again, her fingers massaging her temples. "My husband rarely spoke to me about Cousins Manufacturing or the men under him—he didn't think women should be involved in such things. But since Mr. Sullivan was Mr. Longstead's nephew, he had more of a claim of closeness with the Cousinses.

"We dined with him and his wife a few times over the years. The first time, after they left, my husband said something along the lines of 'A toady, that man, but a pleasant toady to have around.' And that was what I thought of him, until the beginning of this year.

"My husband and I were never truly close. He wanted a handsome, well-bred wife; I wanted a wealthy husband. It seemed a good enough foundation for a marriage."

A shadow crossed her face. She dropped her hands from her temples and stopped in the middle of the room. "And it might have been but for the fact that I kept miscarrying."

"I'm very sorry," murmured Charlotte.

"As was I," said Mrs. Cousins quietly. "Mr. Cousins, on the other hand, was vexed by what he saw as my great failure. I, already unhappy, became angry at being blamed. We had not reached the stage where we detested each other. But looking back, it would only have been a matter of time."

She stood stock still for another second, then resumed her pacing. "Into this increasingly tense picture came Mr. Sullivan. It was at a dinner in March that he first spoke to me in a familiar manner. And by familiar, I mean that he seemed to know my private torment. You cannot imagine my astonishment at hearing my secret struggles referred to, however obliquely. He sounded so very understanding, so very sympathetic and conspiratorial. Of course none of it was my fault, he whispered. One had but to look at my husband to know that he must be the cause of the problems. And to think that I had to bear his displeasure and his lectures, that I had no defense against such unkindness."

She came to a halt beside a small upright piano, her expression half-dazed, as if again struck by how brazenly Mr. Sullivan had sown discord. "*Mr. Cousins* and I barely touched the subject. To hear Mr. Sullivan talk of it was shocking. Yet even as I was agog at his presumption, and deeply mortified no less, I couldn't help but feel a sense of spiteful pleasure to hear Mr. Cousins spoken of as a fool."

She shook her head. "That I neither defended my husband nor demanded that he stop must have emboldened Mr. Sullivan. The next time we met, he again made a point to speak ill of my husband and I again enjoyed it. Some poisons have a sweet taste, don't they?

"The third time this happened, he—" She bit her lower lip. "The third time this happened, he added to his repertoire by propositioning me. Did I not want to punish my husband? Then let him be my instrument of vengeance."

Charlotte was not shocked, only saddened for Mrs. Cousins's loneliness, which had left her vulnerable to Mr. Sullivan's predation.

Mrs. Cousins gave a dry, humorless laugh. "*That* finally shocked me out of my complacency. I didn't love my husband but I understood my obligations. I rejected Mr. Sullivan's advances categorically and he became nasty. Called me all sorts of names. And then immediately went to speak to my husband. Nearly gave me an apoplectic attack, thinking of what he might have said to Mr. Cousins.

"As far as I could tell, he didn't say anything. And then my husband passed away and his solicitors had to tell me that he left me a very small dower portion, not wanting me to have a bigger dower—and then go on to marry some other rich man."

She lifted and lowered the piano's lid, lifted and lowered it, the chagrin on her face changing to bewilderment, then resignation. Walking slowly, she returned to her chair and took a seat. "After the reading of Mr. Cousins's will, I received an unsigned typed note that said, *Do you not wish that you had cuckolded him when I gave you the chance? I am laughing at you both.*

Her eyes flashed with anger. "I hated him for that, his gleeful pleasure at my pain. When I realized Mrs. Treadles would be working with him, I begged her to beware of him. I was beginning to be very grateful to her, but we weren't close yet, and it was such a personal and deeply humiliating story that I couldn't bring myself to give the details. Perhaps if I had told her everything in full, she would have been more careful. But you can see it, can't you, how he would have done it? Pretending to understand her difficulties to gain her trust, but only so that he could better prey on her."

She drained the rest of the cherry brandy and drew a shaky breath. "I shouldn't say this, but I'm not at all sorry that Mr. Sullivan is dead. Whoever killed him did us all a service."

—❧—

As Charlotte came out of Mrs. Cousins's house, Lord Ingram descended from their waiting carriage.

She did not blush or otherwise react, but in her throat and chest she felt the heat of the same embarrassment. It certainly didn't help that he was smiling. The brim of his hat cast a shadow on his face, which only made the curvature of his lips more striking.

She was not accustomed to such full, unguarded smiles from him. Or the undisguised pleasure in his expression.

Perhaps the heat she felt, which seemed to expand everywhere, wasn't only embarrassment.

As he handed her up, his hand held hers a moment longer than necessary.

For two people who had been lovers, and who had kissed rather lavishly only the day before, a slightly prolonged handhold, with both parties sturdily gloved, really shouldn't matter all that much. But a new scalding heat surged up from her fingers directly into the socket of her shoulder.

"I'm sorry to have wasted your time," she said in a rush, before he had even sat down across from her.

"I was at the home of some party guests not far from here," he said, knocking on the roof of the vehicle to signal the coachman to start. "And Mrs. Cousins's is on the way to the next house I need to call on. So it's no inconvenience at all."

"Still—"

"And I'm happy to see you again."

It wasn't so much the words—he'd said similar things to her before—but the ease in his voice, the unreserved candor.

And she had no idea how to respond, either in speech or in sentiment. He did not compel her but he had changed, and that change . . . it was as if she were a seed of many winters set in warm soil and generously watered. Something swelled and burgeoned inside her. And that put stress on her, a great pressure from within.

She gave him an account of what Mrs. Treadles had told Mrs. Watson in the morning, as well as what she'd learned from Mrs. Cousins just now.

He was silent, a grave silence. "I have met such men in my life. But that I am a man of a certain station in life makes me nearly immune from the worst they can do. Not so much the Mrs. Cousins and Mrs. Treadles of the world. And it pains me to think of all the women who have far less wealth and standing than they do, and all the Mr. Sullivans they must face."

She gazed at him. To him, power was synonymous not with the subjugation of others, but with care and responsibility. He looked after those in his life, sometimes to the detriment of himself.

"You don't think of Mrs. Cousins as having encouraged Mr. Sullivan?"

He shook his head firmly. "She is human and displayed foibles. But foibles are not the same thing as ill will. I can fault her for having made questionable choices, if I must, but I will not use her mistake to justify Mr. Sullivan's predation."

"I'm glad you think so."

He glanced outside the carriage window, a pensive expression on his face, and looked back at her. "I have said this to you before: You are the reason I have questioned many things that I would otherwise have happily accepted as given. But I have not told you that I'm glad of it. I would have been a different man, a lesser one, were it not for you."

It took Charlotte a moment to understand the strange, expansive, yet somewhat uncomfortable feeling in her heart. She was *humbled*.

Their gazes held. The carriage turned. The light from its lan-

terns swung. Somewhere on the street a hawker loudly advertised his
fresh, fragrant Christmas wreaths.

She felt as if she ought to say something. But what did one say to
such a monumental confession? She moistened her lips, opened her
mouth, and out came, "I . . . I wonder what manner of woman is
Mrs. Sullivan."

———✖———

Mrs. Sullivan was a small, plump woman who gave the impression
of being easily startled, with her large, darting eyes and fingers that
kept lacing and unlacing in her lap.

Mourning attire did swallow her whole. In the ornate padded
chair she occupied, she seemed less like a widow than a bundle of
clothes left behind.

In fact, the entire drawing room overwhelmed her, packed as it was
with grandiose furnishing. Not an inch of the walls could be seen for
the paintings, large and small, that had been fitted onto them like pieces
of an ambitious mosaic. Nor was much of the wood used in the construction of the furniture visible, obscured by the ivory inlay, ormolu
motifs, and gilded caryatids that had been heaped onto all the surfaces.

Charlotte had seen a more wildly outfitted house, which Livia
had described as both "a brothel *and* a circus." Mrs. Sullivan's drawing room did not make one think of a bordello with greater aspira-
tions, but rather the warehouse of an auction house, on the night
before its biggest public sale, packed pell-mell and stuffed to the gills.

Charlotte liked it, this room, the gaudiness of which could not
be entirely muted even by the black crape draped over windows and
mirrors. And she could not help but think of the smile that would
have animated Lord Ingram's lips, had he been on hand to intuit her
enjoyment of the décor.

Alas he had not accompanied her to this house but gone on to
the next set of guests he needed to speak to, though he'd said he'd meet
her on Cold Street, where she would have her last scheduled appointment of the day, if he finished soon enough.

"Thank you for seeing me, Mrs. Sullivan," Charlotte said. "I apologize for taking up your time in your hour of grief."

"It's quite all right," answered Mrs. Sullivan. She must have been in her late twenties, but her voice sounded girlish, almost childish. "They don't let new widows do much. My sister has taken charge of my children, my mother handles the callers, and Mr. Sullivan's cousins will be making all the arrangements for the funeral. Other than mourning—and being fitted for more mourning attire—I have no other duties in my moment of grief."

Charlotte raised a brow—people who were this candid to strangers usually wished for a reaction. "I see," she said, calibrating her tone to make it sound as if she was trying not to betray how taken aback she was.

Hers seemed to be the correct reaction. Mrs. Sullivan leaned forward. "So what can I do for you, Miss Holmes?"

"Ah . . . right. I am here as a representative of Mr. Sherlock Holmes, my brother, who has agreed to help Mrs. Treadles find out the truth of the case."

"Yes, I know that. The note Mr. Holmes sent around made that very clear. I hope you will be more thorough in your work than the police. That Sergeant Howe who came barely asked any questions of anyone in the house, me least of all, as I didn't attend the party."

As Charlotte had thought, here was a woman who needed attention. And given her husband's interest in other people's wives, it seemed reasonable to assume that he hadn't paid his own wife as much mind as she would have liked.

"Perhaps Sergeant Howe didn't want to be indelicate at a time such as this."

"Pfft." Mrs. Sullivan waved a dismissive hand. "He wasn't considerate. He was uninterested. And he only asked questions I couldn't answer, such as when Mr. Sullivan left that night and whether he knew Inspector Treadles."

Interesting. "You didn't know when Mr. Sullivan left that night for the party?"

"He didn't come home that evening, so he must have gone directly from work."

"Was that a common occurence?"

Mrs. Sullivan shrugged. "It wasn't unusual for him to socialize without me. He found me too gauche, I'd guess, not suitable for the kind of crowd he wanted to be associated with."

Gauche was not exactly the word Charlotte would have used for Mrs. Sullivan, but she could see how Mr. Sullivan might have been disdainful of her need for attention, when she wasn't beautiful enough to draw all eyes.

"Mrs. Sullivan, you said you didn't know whether Mr. Sullivan had met Inspector Treadles?"

"He never mentioned meeting the man. But my husband didn't tell me much," said Mrs. Sullivan plaintively. "If I'm already gauche, you'd think he'd at least want me to be less ignorant, wouldn't you?"

Charlotte was considering how she ought to respond when Mrs. Sullivan sighed dramatically. "Then again, maybe Sergeant Howe didn't ask any questions because it was perfectly obvious my husband was killed for coveting another man's wife."

Charlotte had been generating varying expressions of astonishment and dismay at Mrs. Sullivan's remarks. Now she let her jaw drop.

It was not so easy to hold other people's attention. If Mrs. Sullivan meant to do so with personal confessions, then naturally she needed to give away details of an increasingly private nature. Still Charlotte was a little surprised at how quickly they had arrived at this point.

She made small noises of distress for Mrs. Sullivan to feel that her declaration had had its intended effect. "Surely—surely Mr. Sullivan didn't tell you himself that he 'coveted another man's wife'?"

"Oh, yes, he did," said Mrs. Sullivan, as unexceptionally as another woman would confirm that indeed her husband had brought home a bouquet of flowers the evening before. She picked up an embroidery frame and jabbed a needle through the white handkerchief it held. "He was a very sinful man, my husband. And extraordinarily proud of his sins, no less."

Charlotte pulled at the cameo brooch at her collar and cleared her throat. "And by 'another man's wife,' we are speaking of Mrs. Treadles, yes?"

"That is correct. But she didn't want him, so he told her that he would bear false testimony before her husband." From the other direction, Mrs. Sullivan again jabbed her needle through the handkerchief. "I always did tell him that he would get himself killed one of these days, because he wouldn't leave well enough alone. Wouldn't remain within the boundaries of holy matrimony, his or anyone else's. I told him that God would punish him in the form of a wrathful husband that he had wronged."

Despite the pathos of the scene, Charlotte did not believe that the relationship between the Sullivans was as simple as that of a helpless wife wringing her hands at her husband's rapacious misdeeds. How was it that Mrs. Sullivan had not had her energy and sense of self destroyed by a man so skilled at preying on the vulnerability of others?

She cleared her throat again. "Did you not think, Mrs. Sullivan, that perhaps you ought to have warned Mrs. Treadles that your husband did not mean her well?"

"But he doesn't mean anyone well. Should I have warned the whole world?"

Charlotte widened her eyes to what must have been a comical extent.

Satisfied, Mrs. Sullivan carried on. "Not to mention, he lied. Whenever he met an attractive married woman, he always told me that he was going to have an affair with her. It took me years to realize that it amused him to see my reaction. Sometimes he tried to have that affair; sometimes he didn't. And seldom did he succeed. So whom should I have warned ahead of time, before I myself knew for certain whether he was acting in malice or only speaking so?"

Charlotte had seen her share of bad marriages, but none remotely similar to the Sullivans', at once repellent and riveting.

She made her tone tentative. "Mrs. Sullivan, are you not concerned that what you say will damage Mr. Sullivan's reputation?"

Mrs. Sullivan snorted. Her needle stabbed. "My husband did not have a wonderful reputation. I almost laughed out loud when I read what the papers wrote about him. Handsome and popular, eh? He might have been handsome once, when he was still in school. And he was popular only if you mean people disliked him but feared what he might do, so they didn't dare cross him openly."

Charlotte made another face, feeling the muscles of her cheeks tiring. "If I may ask, Mrs. Sullivan, was your 'gaucheness' the only reason your husband didn't want you at the party?"

"He said that Mrs. Treadles would be there without her husband, so my presence would only hinder him in his quest to drive a wedge between Mrs. Treadles and her husband."

A black geometric border was beginning to take shape on the white cloth in the embroidery frame—Mrs. Sullivan was making a mourning handkerchief.

"When did you realize he hadn't come home?"

"I don't sleep very well without laudanum. With laudanum . . . I sleep a little too well. There wasn't much for me to do that evening. He was gone. The children had been bathed and put to bed. I had a plate of supper in my room, read for a while, and took my laudanum—no point staying awake on a night like that and tormenting myself with thoughts of what he might or might not be up to. He would tell me soon enough, when he came home.

"But instead I woke up to my maid banging on the door of my bedchamber because the police were below, asking to speak with me."

"Did you tell the police any of what you told me?"

Charlotte would have dearly loved to see Sergeant Howe's expression. Then again, being an experienced officer of the law, he might have barely batted an eyelash.

"Only that my husband didn't like Mrs. Treadles, which is all I know for certain, in any case. He didn't care for her and said she shouldn't have been at Cousins, trying to run things."

A calculating look crossed Mrs. Sullivan's face as she gave her answer—Mr. Sullivan might have considered his wife gauche, but she knew how to choose her audience.

And now they came to a question that Charlotte was beginning to be highly curious about. "Mrs. Sullivan, are you grieved by your husband's passing?"

The new widow's eyes shone. "I feel no sorrow that he's gone. Maybe grief will come later, but for now I'm only shocked. I thought wicked men such as my husband always lived to ripe old ages, their malice somehow acting as their lucky charm in life. That he has been cut down in his prime? Perhaps God has been paying attention after all. Perhaps all wicked men should be afraid."

Twelve

C harlotte's next appointment—thankfully, her last of the day—
was at 31 Cold Street to test Miss Longstead's vision. But after
she left Mrs. Sullivan's house, she still had some time. So she called
on Mrs. Treadles.

Mrs. Treadles was not home, but Mrs. Graycott, her housekeeper,
pointed Charlotte to a nearby park. The park was a small green space,
enclosed by a wrought iron fence. At this hour, in the intermittent
rain, Mrs. Treadles was the only person inside, clad in a mackintosh,
walking on a narrow path. Cockerill, her groom and coachman, stood
beside a gate in the fence to keep an eye out for her safety.

"Miss Holmes!" she cried, startled, when she saw Charlotte. "Is
everything all right?"

"Nothing is amiss," said Charlotte, falling into step beside her.
It felt good to move, for a change, after having spent so much of her
day sitting either in carriages or in drawing rooms. "Congratula-
tions on your decisive action today at Cousins."

The light from nearby street lamps was just enough to illuminate Mrs. Treadles's slightly tremulous smile. "I will not deny that
it was a relief to at last wield some authority. I can't thank you enough
for sending Mrs. Watson my way. In fact, it was she who told me
that I ought to have a vigorous walk after reaching home. She said

my body would need the exercise to properly expel the tension of the day."

"Mrs. Watson is an invaluable ally indeed," said Charlotte wholeheartedly. "When I left her this afternoon, she had already begun a preliminary review of the Cousins accounts she'd brought back."

Mrs. Treadles's pace increased, as if propelled by a surge of inner turmoil. "Will she have enough time? Inspector Brighton told me that—that he planned to formally charge Inspector Treadles before Christmas."

"We are working as fast as we can." Charlotte briefly rested a hand on Mrs. Treadles's arm. "Would you show me a few items from your house?"

Mrs. Treadles breathed heavily a few times. "Shall we head back there then?"

They left the park, Cockerill trailing a respectful distance behind.

"I also need to ask you a few more questions about the night of the party," said Charlotte. "I understand that it is an unpleasant subject, but can you recount for me what exactly facilitated your escape from number 33 that night, after Mr. Sullivan accosted you?"

Mrs. Treadles coughed. She glanced back at Cockerill, who was out of earshot. Still she lowered her voice. "There was a loud noise, which startled Mr. Sullivan. That was how I got away."

"What kind of noise? Can you be more specific?"

"Ah . . . if I must guess—please remember that I was completely distraught at the time—but if I must guess, I would say that it sounded more like a door slamming on an upper floor than anything else. The house very nearly shook with it."

"You are certain of it?"

"As certain as I could be of anything under those circumstances." Mrs. Treadles's brow creased. "I have wondered more than once what—or who—could have made that noise. I do ask myself if it was my husband, as I'd gone into the house in the first place because of him. But I . . . I . . ."

"But you don't want it to have been your husband, because that would give further credence to Inspector Brighton's hypothesis that he killed Mr. Sullivan in a rage."

Mrs. Treadles pulled her mackintosh tighter about her body, as if she felt cold. But her voice was firm. "In the end I don't believe it was him. Had it been him, and had he known that it was me, he would have come and found me at Mr. Longstead's house to make sure that I was all right."

She was capable of great faith, this woman.

As was Lord Ingram.

Charlotte hadn't realized this before, because she was not accustomed to thinking in such terms, but he had placed his faith in her, who did not always understand the full spectrum of human emotions.

"I'll keep that in mind," she said. "Was that the last you saw of Mr. Sullivan?"

"Yes."

The relief was evident in Mrs. Treadles's voice, even though Mr. Sullivan would never be able to prey on her again.

"And Mr. Longstead—when did you last see him?"

"After I returned to his house I came across him speaking to Mrs. Coltrane, his housekeeper—they were near the cloakroom where I hid for some time."

"Before or after you went into the cloakroom?"

"Before. I remember thinking that I didn't want them to see me, and they didn't. Or at least Mr. Longstead didn't."

Silence fell. The heels of their boots clicked on wet pavement. A gust blew, shaking bare branches all along the street. As they walked past a house with a blazing Christmas tree by the window, someone inside began to play "Silent Night" on a piano, the notes faint yet crystalline.

Mrs. Treadles worried her upper lip, her apprehension warring with her need to know. "May I ask what your questions are about, Miss Holmes?"

"I wonder whether it was possible that the loud noise had been produced by none other than Mr. Longstead. If that were the case, I could see he and Mr. Sullivan getting into a heated argument after your departure."

"*What?*" The volume of Mrs. Treadles's voice shot up.

Hastily she glanced around before asking, in a vehement whisper, "Surely you aren't implying that Mr. Sullivan then killed Mr. Longstead with my husband's service revolver?"

"If Inspector Treadles didn't kill them, and as there is no trace of anyone else who did, then we must consider that possibility," Charlotte pointed out.

There was, of course, the scrap of fabric that had been found on the fence outside 33 Cold Street, which could have been left by the escaped murderer. But they would have a difficult time persuading Scotland Yard of that.

"But then how did Mr. Sullivan die?" Mrs. Treadles demanded, her eyes full of doubt and incomprehension.

"He could have shot himself."

"No, not him," said Mrs. Treadles decisively. "If he had shot Mr. Longstead, he would have tried his best to wriggle out of it, not kill himself. There was too much spite and vanity in him to let a moment's panic bring him to suicide."

Despite Charlotte's assertion, the facts were on Mrs. Treadles's side. The shot that had killed Mr. Sullivan hadn't been a contact shot. That meant the tip of the revolver had *not* been pressed against his forehead, which argued much more strongly in favor of homicide.

They were now behind Mrs. Treadles's house. She opened the back door and asked, in a low, anxious voice, "Have you other theories, Miss Holmes?"

Charlotte shook her head. "None worth mentioning, I'm afraid."

Mrs. Treadles smiled gamely. "Well, there's still time. We are still three days away from Christmas."

She led Charlotte to Inspector Treadles's dressing room, a neat and well-organized space, so Charlotte could see where his service revolver was usually kept.

Holmes looked down into the drawer. The only item it contained was an unopened box of cartridges, the edges of its wrapping paper still glued together.

"Mrs. Graycott said she told you about Inspector Treadles asking about items missing from the house," said Mrs. Treadles. "I believe, as she does, that the revolver was missing from before he left on this last trip. As you can see, he didn't take any rounds. A man intending on using a revolver would have taken rounds."

There was a note of pleading in her voice, even though she must know that Scotland Yard would simply say he had acquired cartridges elsewhere.

Charlotte closed the drawer. "May I have the letters that he sent you when he was away recently?"

When Mrs. Treadles realized that Charlotte was not going to comment on the cartridges, her eyes dimmed, but she kept her voice even. "Inspector Brighton took the letters. I can give you the envelopes though—I'd already removed the envelopes because I didn't want the police to see that the locations on the postmarks didn't agree with what he'd written on the letters themselves."

Charlotte was by the door, putting on her overcoat—she needed to leave for 31 Cold Street immediately to keep her appointment—when Mrs. Treadles came down with the envelopes. She placed them into her pocket. "Mrs. Treadles, when I spoke with Inspector Treadles this morning at Scotland Yard, he said that Sherlock Holmes would be able to help him by doing what Sherlock Holmes typically did. Would you happen to know what he meant?"

Mrs. Treadles blinked. "Surely, just that Mr. Holmes's brilliance would prevail yet again?"

They said their goodbyes. Charlotte already had her hand on the door when she turned around and looked Mrs. Treadles in the eye. "I know the situation appears dire, Mrs. Treadles, and time is running out. But much can happen in a few days. Could you have imagined yesterday, or even this morning, when you woke up, that before the end of the day you would have at last gained control over Cousins?

"Similarly, exculpatory evidence is scant now, but it may very well be forthcoming. I may not have a viable theory today, but that doesn't mean I won't have one tomorrow. So I ask that you do not torment yourself with worst-case scenarios, but place your faith in those of us working to clear Inspector Treadles's name. I never promise results ahead of time, but I have always delivered on those results."

She inclined her head. "A good evening to you, Mrs. Treadles."

———※———

Livia closed the door of her bedroom and leaned against it, breathing hard.

After Lady Holmes recovered from her stupefaction at having received fifty pounds from Charlotte, of all people, she'd paced in the parlor for a good half hour, pulling her hair out, convinced that Charlotte was under the protection of a man and was, sin of sins, trading her body for pin money.

But half an hour was as long as her moral quandary lasted. After that, her mind made the resolute turn toward how she ought to spend the money and enjoy herself. Dozens of ideas spouted forth from her lips, some dumbfounding Livia.

Wintering in Nice? Did Lady Holmes have any idea how much that would cost? Neither did Livia, to be sure, but she would be amazed if on that gilded aristocratic playground fifty pounds lasted longer than a two bob bit did in their little village.

She said nothing—it was not wise to puncture her mother's daydreams at their frothiest. But eventually, Lady Holmes's fanciful notions collapsed under their own weight. She slumped back into her chair. "But I can't go anywhere, can I? You are still unmarried, still home, and that means I, the responsible mother, am stuck at home with you."

Livia shot to her feet. A long tirade against her was on its way, waiting only for Lady Holmes's resentment to escalate to anger. "I still haven't written a Christmas card to the Openshaws. I'd best go do that right now!" she cried.

And fled.

Livia sighed, her back still against the door of the bedroom, her head in her heads. She'd escaped, for now. But tomorrow the anvil of her mother's wrath would still fall.

Perhaps she should write a letter to Charlotte. But she didn't want to tell Charlotte about the disharmony at home that had been brought on by her kindly meant funds.

Not knowing what else to do, she crossed the room and reached into her hiding place for the notebook that contained the last quarter of her story. As she lifted it, a photograph floated down from between the pages.

It was a picture of her, one she'd never seen before. She was seated at a table with glasses of wine and a basket of sliced baguette, her face turned to the side. The lighting was insufficient, yet enough to illuminate the delight on her face.

Her heart clenched.

The week before, in Paris, she and Mr. Marbleton had been able to spend a few hours by themselves, exploring the Jardin des Tuileries and the Sacré-Coeur. He'd carried with him his detective camera, disguised as a thick but not very large book, and used it to take photographs of her.

Afterwards, they'd stopped to refresh themselves at a bistro, its air redolent with the aroma of herbs and warm, bubbling stew. She'd gazed at the crowd outside, rushing to and fro on their own business, and imagined how the boulevard would look come summer, with all the great elms along its length in their full leafy glory.

Life always seemed to abound with possibilities when he was near.

But he was no longer in her life.

His had been the passage of a legendary comet, lighting up entire skies. But comets, however brilliant and extraordinary, are only visitors. They arrive from some mysterious region in the heavens, and disappear there again, leaving behind only dazzling memories.

Yes, she should drown in woe and wistfulness, for what she'd had all too briefly. Yet as she gazed upon her own image, and remembered his mischievous laughter after he'd taken the picture, what she felt was not sadness, but a cold dread that seeped from her heart to her lungs.

Why did she need to be afraid for him? He was a comet, for goodness' sake.

She put the photograph away and sat down at her desk. But it was a quarter of an hour before she managed to pull herself together enough to resume copying.

This time, when Miss Longstead received Charlotte, she had on her glasses, wire rimmed with tortoiseshell temples. But the glasses were quickly put into her pocket: Charlotte had come to test her vision under conditions similar to the night of the dance.

Number 31, which in mourning had shut down tightly, now had all the windows on the two lower floors ablaze with light, their curtains drawn apart. Miss Longstead, wrapped in a great black cape, stood in the garden, at the spot where she believed she had been.

Charlotte would ask her to close her eyes. When she opened her eyes again, Charlotte would have a trial ready for her. Sometimes Charlotte sent a manservant to stand before the back door of number 33, sometimes a maid, sometimes no one, and sometimes two servants at once. Miss Longstead squinted but correctly identified the gender of the person or persons at the back door, except once, when a maid and a manservant stood in a line and she thought only the maid was there, because her dress had a bigger silhouette. She also said so when no one had been sent to stand before the door.

After Charlotte was satisfied that she could trust Miss Long-stead to be right about what she'd seen that night—a woman going into number 33 from the back—she thanked the servants. Mrs. Coltrane, on hand to observe the proceedings, shepherded them back into the house. Charlotte marched farther into the garden to thank Miss Longstead.

"No, Miss Holmes, I should thank you for being so thorough," she answered. And then, with her voice lowered, even though there was no one else within earshot, "Have you made any progress?"

There was no mistaking the anxiety in her question. "You are worried for Inspector Treadles."

Miss Longstead nodded tightly. "Mrs. Treadles is a lovely woman—I really don't want the murderer to be her husband. And the inspector himself has been very kind, too. When we dined to-gether, he took the time to ask about my experiments in depth."

And if Inspector Treadles hanged for Mr. Longstead's murder, would the two women ever be able to see each other again?

"I've learned some things," said Charlotte. "But I'm not sure how they fit together. Perhaps you could help me. Do you have time to take a round in the garden?"

Miss Longstead set her hands over her heart. "Oh, I was hoping you'd say that. It has been awful, staring at the four walls of my room. I don't know why being grief-stricken has to equate to being house-bound, but Mrs. Coltrane said it wouldn't do for me to be abroad so soon after my uncle's passing, even if it was only to walk in the park by myself."

Charlotte thought the young woman might have a difficult time of it, especially with her laboratory, where she had spent significant hours of the day, destroyed on that same night. Charlotte herself, amazingly enough, had had enough tea and biscuits and needed some exercise before she felt virtuous enough for dessert at dinner.

The garden grew darker—the curtains of number 31 were again drawn, the lights in the unoccupied rooms dimming one by one.

"Miss Longstead, in your view, is there any chance that your uncle was killed *because of* his support for Mrs. Treadles?" asked Charlotte, as Miss Longstead guided her onto a garden path.

Miss Longstead reached inside her pocket, pulled out her glasses, and put them back on. "I can see Mr. Sullivan killed for such a reason, perhaps. But my uncle didn't know how to play games."

"He didn't need to have been playing games. He could have been killed for the sincerity of his support with regard to Mrs. Treadles."

They passed near a brilliantly lit house, its light reflecting in the lenses of Miss Longstead's glasses. "I—I don't think so."

"Why not?"

"I don't doubt the depth of his sympathy for Mrs. Treadles's plight. Nor do I doubt the integrity of his character—he would never have supported her to her face and then stabbed her in the back. But—" She exhaled. "If I were Mrs. Treadles, I would have found his support—"

Miss Longstead's pace slowed. Her gloved hands, held before her diaphragm, twisted together. "I don't know how to say it without sounding as if I disapprove in some way of this wonderful man who raised me with all the diligence and attention I could have asked of a father. But you see, my uncle, he was a very successful man. He worked hard and was properly rewarded for his hard work. Life was fair for him and so he believed that it is fair for everyone—that if they would do as he did, they would achieve the same satisfying results.

"*Persist*, he told Mrs. Treadles. *Have patience. Good things will come.* His advice was not wrong. But he failed to consider that when he'd worked hard, he'd had old Mr. Cousins for his partner, old Mr. Cousins who had been a vigorously honorable man, keen on making sure my uncle received his rightful share of the profits. Mrs. Treadles, on the other hand, had to work with Mr. Sullivan and his cohorts."

She said this last sentence in the same tone another person might have used to say, *Mrs. Treadles, on the other hand, fell into a pit of vipers.* Charlotte was already under the impression that she didn't care for this cousin.

But it seemed that Miss Longstead didn't merely dislike Mr. Sullivan—she despised him.

"So, in your opinion, Mr. Longstead's support of Mrs. Treadles, while genuine, was insufficient," said Charlotte.

"Yes, but not by intention." Miss Longstead rearranged her cape around her shoulders, as if it was causing her to be uncomfortable. "He didn't understand his own position of power—the reverence with which he was regarded both inside and outside of Cousins. Mrs. Treadles didn't want to dismiss all the men who opposed her, because she was worried about what that would do to the company, especially given that she is a woman. But if he'd stood by her and done the sacking with her, she would have been shielded from most of the consequences.

"That didn't happen because he saw himself only as an old retiree who no longer had shares in the company, someone who ought not to agitate for major changes. He was genuinely kind to Mrs. Treadles, but he never gave her the kind of support that would get him killed."

She tried to keep her voice uninflected, but Charlotte heard the frustration she must have felt. Charlotte recalled that the Longsteads had dined with the Treadleses twice in the past month. It would appear that after dinner, when the ladies customarily withdrew to the drawing room, leaving the gentlemen behind to enjoy a glass of port, the two women had engaged in discussions having to do with Mrs. Treadles's situation.

The path wended around a cluster of trees. "There!" said Miss Longstead. "That's my uncle's favorite spot in the garden."

Charlotte could make out the ground swelling into a small knoll.

"You probably can't see it," continued Miss Longstead, "but there is a bench on top of the rise, and he loved to sit on it in summer. Some of our neighbors were equally keen to occupy that seat. And there was eventually a meeting held among its devotees on how to equitably divide time on the bench.

"That was seven years ago. Afterwards I called the gathering the bench conclave. My uncle enjoyed that name so much that he adopted it, too, and we began to refer to the bench conclave as if it were a watershed event in our lives. 'Do you remember when that happened?' I'd ask him about something. And he'd say, 'Oh, that was a good fifteen years before the bench conclave.'"

She laughed softly to herself, but the last note of her laughter sounded like a sob.

Charlotte looked down at the path and waited until it turned. "Mrs. Treadles has told me that Mr. Sullivan was a false friend to her. He pretended to be sympathetic, but was in fact actively undermining her efforts at taking control of her own company. Do you think it was possible that your uncle learned about this, and confronted Mr. Sullivan?"

"And *Mr. Sullivan* killed him?"

"Let's set aside who killed whom for now. We are still trying to find an understandable motive for why your uncle and his nephew have both been shot dead. Are you aware of any tension between Mr. Sullivan and Mr. Longstead, old or new?"

"My uncle was indifferent to Mr. Sullivan," said Miss Longstead, still sounding mystified at the direction of Charlotte's inquiries. "I believe Mr. Sullivan resented him for that, but that had long been the case."

"Why did Mr. Longstead not like Mr. Sullivan?"

"Mr. Sullivan, as a young man, tried to flatter my uncle. My uncle did not care for flattery; he considered it an offshoot of chicanery."

Charlotte pressed her point. "Since your uncle already did not like Mr. Sullivan, what was to prevent that casual dislike from sharpening into loathing, should he learn of what happened between Mr. Sullivan and Mrs. Treadles?"

Miss Longstead stopped. "Did Mrs. Treadles tell my uncle anything?"

"No, she said that she never told anyone anything until the police started asking questions. But your uncle could have perceived it, no?"

Miss Longstead shook her head vigorously. "My uncle was a simple man. It was his great virtue. But it was also . . . his great limitation. He was such a decent man, and life had been so decent to him, that he often did not perceive things, even if they were blindingly obvious to others."

"Such as?"

Miss Longstead resumed walking, but did not answer Charlotte's question. They covered nearly half the length of the garden before Miss Longstead said, "I think—I think I can trust you, Miss Holmes. I don't know you very well but I feel that you are not a person given to . . . preconceived notions."

Charlotte liked to think so herself, but she'd never been evaluated in this manner by someone she interviewed in the course of a case. "Thank you."

Her answer sounded more like a question than a statement.

Miss Longstead drew an audible breath. "You asked me what my uncle did not perceive. Whenever we were in town, we always dined with Mr. Sullivan and his wife. But in all these years, my uncle never grasped that I hated to be anywhere near Mr. Sullivan. He continued to see this nephew for whom he had no affection, because Mr. Sullivan was the son of his favorite sister, and it was the right thing to do."

Charlotte began to understand why Miss Longstead had hesitated for so long—and why she broached the subject only after she'd decided that Charlotte could be trusted not to hold certain views.

"My father was my uncle's youngest brother. On my mother's side, her father was an Anglican missionary, and her mother, a Sierra Leone Creole. My mother was born in Freetown, but spent most of her life in London. This was where she met my father, where they were married, and where they are buried.

"My mother was a keen reader of history. Although she died when

I was very young, I remember her telling me that I must know history, personal, tribal, national, and preferably that of the entire world.

"As I grew up, I dutifully read history. In recent centuries the history of black people has not been a happy one. So I turned to accounts of the abolition of slavery throughout the British Empire. It seemed such a grand, jubilant event, such a triumph of justice and humanity. A fairy-tale ending, almost.

"But in life, there are no happily-ever-afters, are there? Instead there was a backlash, one that gathered force as the decades went by. First came that essay by Thomas Carlyle, questioning the ability of those of African descent to handle freedom. Then, a disconcerting amount of support here in Britain for the South in the American Civil War. And in recent years, this circus of lecturers who go about expressing views that would have been unacceptable in the years just after abolition."

Earlier, Miss Longstead, in conversation with Charlotte, had frequently looked toward Charlotte. But after the long silence, she'd spoken with her face set resolutely forward, as if she wasn't entirely sure on her choice to trust Charlotte.

Or perhaps that was the only way she could contain the pain her words brought her.

"It was part of the reason I turned resolutely toward the sciences," she went on. "The molecules and the forces of the universe do not care about my heritage, nor would they speculate in public forums whether I have brains enough to understand them."

Charlotte had experienced plenty of such speculations because she was a woman, but never for her ancestry. If she had Miss Longstead's ancestry, would she have successfully convinced the public that her unseen brother was a genius and that she herself could undertake all manners of investigative tasks on his behalf?

At last Miss Longstead turned again toward her, her beautiful visage earnest yet strained. "I don't want you to think that my life hasn't been a happy one. It has been a blessed, privileged existence, and I wake up thankful every day to have been given so much and loved so well. But it is impossible to remove myself entirely from the tides of history. Impossible not to feel, in spite of the cushioning of my own comfortable life, an anxiety over how much further attitudes will slide. I don't believe slavery will be brought back, but I don't think it is out of the realm of possibility that a new designation of inferiority might arise for people like me, either in my lifetime or my children's lifetime."

Her tone remained even, but her distress was palpable. Charlotte, not prone to strong emotions, felt a stab of horror. She, too, could not declare with complete certainty that what Miss Longstead feared would not come to pass.

"Mr. Sullivan, when he lived, made a point of never sitting down at our dinner table without bringing up the latest theories on African inferiority. He never presented it as his own opinion, but always as that of someone else. 'Why, Uncle, have you heard of this lecture in Birmingham in which so-and-so, a professor of this-or-that-ology, stated that evidence points to a closer link between Africans and animals than between Africans and Europeans?'

"Perhaps at every dinner he attended he brought up the same subject, but somehow I don't think so. It might have been presented as an intellectual debate for my uncle, but I never doubted that his true purpose was to rile and humiliate me.

"My uncle always immediately refuted the claims Mr. Sullivan brought up. Mr. Sullivan would spout more 'evidence' his 'scholar' du jour had presented. My uncle would dismiss that, too, and then advise him to be more critical in his thinking and not pay attention to every crack-brained theory raised by every quack who gets up behind a lectern.

"And he would not notice that I sat there white-knuckled, torn between throwing a goblet at Mr. Sullivan and running away to my room."

Her voice had become very quiet. With the flapping of her cape in the rising wind and the grinding of carriage wheels on the streets outside, Charlotte had to strain to hear her.

"I asked him once, my uncle, why he supposed that Mr. Sullivan was so interested in this subject. 'We all are, aren't we?' was his puzzled answer. 'It's a debate of monumental importance. Already too much misery and injustice have been committed in the exploitation of Africans. So now the right views must prevail.'

"Afterwards I didn't bring up the subject again. He did not understand that it stained my soul, each time Mr. Sullivan was allowed to mimic some supposed expert's views that my ancestors are subhuman. My uncle did not understand that it was not curiosity or concern that drove Mr. Sullivan, but malice.

"Mr. Sullivan despised my uncle because my uncle did not care for him. He despised me because I lived the life of a lady while he must still work for a living, albeit a very good living. He could do nothing about my uncle, but he had power over me. And he could flex that power and denigrate me anytime he liked, because my uncle never put a stop to his antics."

She turned once more toward Charlotte, her gaze beseeching. "Please, please do not think that my uncle didn't care how others treated me. He cared deeply. Any servants disrespectful to me were immediately let go. And he gave the cut direct once, to a family who was snide about my presence at a country party.

"But as I said, he had his limitations in understanding. Sometimes the evils among us are not less perfidious, but less obvious, and he did not recognize some of those less obvious evils.

"So no, I do not believe he would have been aware of Mrs. Treadles's dilemma. He did not see what Mr. Sullivan openly did to me in front of him. He would not have perceived that Mr. Sullivan was covertly threatening to destroy Mrs. Treadles's marriage."

Thirteen

Charlotte did not immediately instruct her carriage to depart. Miss Longstead's words still weighed on her. Murders are ugly things; and even those that end up neatly solved still expose decades of cruelty and wrongdoing. But murders, the killing of individuals by individuals, are not yet the ugliest things in the world.

Evil exists on a far greater scale, so great that it can penetrate an empire from top to bottom, and integrate itself into the very fabric of society. So great that when its worst incarnation had been eradicated, its imprint still remained, more than half a century later.

And an echo of that imprint had been powerful enough to slash a chasm between Miss Longstead and her uncle.

A knock came at the carriage door. She started.

"You cannot believe how many vehicles are on the road," said Lord Ingram cheerfully as he climbed in, took his seat, and lightly struck the top of the carriage with his walking stick. "I got out of my hansom cab half a mile away to walk. I was hoping you might take a little more time, or I would have missed you."

His expression changed once his gaze settled on her. "Are you all right, Holmes?"

She told him of what she'd learned from Miss Longstead.

He was silent for some time. His natural father had been Jewish.

Was he thinking of how he himself had been denigrated for that heritage?

She waited for him to speak, but he only leaned forward and took her hands.

They were both gloved, yet after a while, she felt his warmth. His warmth. His strength. His courage. She lifted her gaze from their hands to his face, half lit, half in shadows, and altogether beautiful.

Before she could say anything, he let go of her. "Is that Miss Redmayne?"

She half turned. Indeed it was Miss Redmayne, running after the carriage, one hand holding up her skirts.

He signaled the coachman to halt, then descended to help her up.

"I thought this was Aunt Jo's coach!" said Miss Redmayne happily, panting a little.

"We are delighted to be able to ferry you home," replied Lord Ingram, "after everything you have done this day."

Miss Redmayne had volunteered to distribute Sherlock Holmes's cards to all the houses that surrounded the garden, and in the row of houses opposite 33 Cold Street.

Abovestairs *and* belowstairs.

Miss Redmayne blew out a breath. "At least that's done."

"Thank you," said Charlotte sincerely.

Miss Redmayne grinned. "Indeed I do believe I ought to be thanked. But before I tell you what I've learned, let me ask you two a question. Have we come to a conclusion yet about how many people went in and out of number 33 that night, before the police discovered Inspector Treadles in a room with the dead men?"

All eyes landed on Charlotte, who said, looking across to Lord Ingram, "What do you think, my lord?"

She wanted to hear his voice.

Lord Ingram raised a brow, but proceeded to say, "I'll confess myself also puzzled by *how* everyone got into number 33. Besides Mr. Longstead, that is—he could have let himself in. But for the others, we must assume either the doors of number 33 were left open, accidentally or deliberately, or many more people had keys than we know about."

Charlotte had been thinking of the same thing, especially of Mr. Longstead's set of keys. She had meant to ask Miss Longstead this evening whether she knew where they were to be found but had forgotten to in the wake of Miss Longstead's sobering disclosure.

"As for how many individuals visited number 33 that night," continued Lord Ingram, "Inspector Treadles, Mr. Longstead, and Mr. Sullivan were there, by irrefutable physical evidence. Mrs. Treadles, too, by her own admission. These four we can be sure of.

"Miss Longstead saw a woman enter number 33 from the garden that night. Our problem with her account is that although we can trust her vision—as verified by Miss Holmes just now—she couldn't tell us with any precision at what time she saw this woman. If it wasn't Mrs. Treadles, then we have a fifth person on our hands."

Lord Ingram paused, glanced at Charlotte, and then at Miss Redmayne. "How much do you know about Mrs. Treadles's movements that night?"

"I went back home for a short time in the afternoon and saw my aunt. She told me what Mrs. Treadles told her this morning," said Miss Redmayne, her tone matter-of-fact.

"In that case you know we also must think about the person who slammed a door and startled Mr. Sullivan into letting go of Mrs. Treadles. Holmes, what do you think of the chances that person was either Inspector Treadles or Mr. Longstead?"

"I thought it more likely than not," Charlotte replied. "But I spoke to Mrs. Treadles this evening before I called at Cold Street, and Mrs. Treadles, at least, did not believe it was either. And now I'm not sure what to think."

Lord Ingram waited for her to continue. When she didn't, he said, "Moreover there was the person who leaped out of the window and had a scrap of a coat caught on a wrought iron fence finial below—

that scrap is now in police custody. And last, but by no means least, the person who picked up Mrs. Treadles's jeweled comb."

Miss Redmayne made a tally on her fingers. "So four people, potentially, in addition to the victims and the Treadleses."

Lord Ingram rubbed the pad of his thumb across his chin. "But since we don't know when most of these events took place, it's possible that the woman Miss Longstead saw enter the house made away with Mrs. Treadles's ornament. It's even possible, though somewhat improbable, that this same woman also slammed the door and jumped out of the window."

In the bouncing light of the carriage lanterns, Miss Redmayne's eyes gleamed. "What do you think, Miss Holmes?"

Lord Ingram shifted forward, as if to better hear Charlotte's answer. A warm pleasure buoyed her. From the very beginning, he had listened to her—closely.

"According to Mrs. Treadles, the door-slammer was higher up in number 33, when he or she made that great noise. At that moment, Mrs. Treadles and her jeweled comb were both in the dining room, on the ground floor. She ran out, but we don't know what Mr. Sullivan decided to do. If he went after her, then our door-slammer stood a reasonable chance of going down to investigate and coming across the jeweled comb.

"But if Mr. Sullivan instead headed upstairs to look into the source of the noise, forcing the door-slammer to leap to the pavement— it seems a desperate enough departure that I find it unlikely that this person would come back to the house again, let alone come back to find Mrs. Treadles's jeweled comb in the dark."

"Well," said Miss Redmayne, rocking a little with excitement, "here's something you may find relevant, Miss Holmes. Across the street and two houses down from number 33 lives an old lady named Mrs. Styles, a very spry, very superior woman. She told me that she would have had greater dealings with her neighbors if she didn't find them so vapid."

Miss Redmayne nodded, as if again amused by Mrs. Styles's condescension. "In any case, apparently her health isn't as good as it appears and she must take a remedy four times a day without fail. She goes to bed at nine. Her night dose, at eleven, is administered by her grandson Mr. Bosworth, who lives with her and is, according to her, a young man of unimpeachable virtues.

"The night of the party, Mr. Bosworth roused her for her eleven o'clock dose. Then he kissed her on the forehead, turned off the light, and left. Mrs. Styles normally goes back to sleep fairly easily, but that night she didn't. So she got up and used the water closet. Upon returning to her room she realized that there was a party going on— some guests at Mr. Longstead's had opened a window for air, and music was temporarily audible from where she stood. She pulled back the curtains for a look and indulged in fond recollections of the dances of her own youth.

"And then, just as she was drawing the curtain shut again, a movement caught her eye. She thought she saw someone leap from number 33."

Lord Ingram sucked in a breath. Even Charlotte sat up straighter. Satisfied with their reactions, Miss Redmaye carried on. "The sight startled Mrs. Styles so much that she shut the curtains, then stood for a moment before opening the curtains again to make sure that she hadn't been imagining things. But of course by that time the street below was empty again."

Lord Ingram frowned. "She is positive that this happened shortly after eleven?"

"She declared her grandson unfailingly punctual in the matter of her night dose. He always waves a small alarm clock before her when he comes to give her that medicine. And that night was no exception. She had no doubt that she saw the man jump from the house within a quarter hour afterwards."

Charlotte remembered what Mrs. Treadles's groom had said about having berthed his carriage several streets over. She looked to Lord

Ingram. "My lord, when you spoke with the guests, did you also speak with their coachmen?"

"I did, but they were directed to park their vehicles on Cascade Lane, so none of them would have been on Cold Street at that time to corroborate Mrs. Styles's account."

Charlotte turned toward Miss Redmayne. "Did Mrs. Styles notice anything about the man?"

"She said he seemed like a ruffian." Miss Redmayne chortled. "It seems to me that she saw him for only a fraction of a second. It also seems to me that Mrs. Styles is the sort to consider a large segment of the male population to be ruffians."

"At half past twelve, Mr. Sullivan and Mr. Longstead were still very much alive." Lord Ingram set his knuckles against his chin. "I was sure the jumper was the murderer. But if he leaped off more than an hour before the men were killed, then—"

He slapped a hand on his seat. "I've been so taken with the thought that the person whose jacket was caught on the finial was the murderer, that I've failed to ask myself why Inspector Treadles voluntarily locked himself in a room with the two dead men. He must have felt himself in danger—and of course the sleeve of his coat had been slashed through by a sharp implement. In which case, it's possible, perhaps even highly likely, that the person who wounded him was also in the house."

Silence. It was raining again. The streets felt quieter, emptier. Their town coach drove by a household receiving its Christmas fir, much to the joy of children crowded at the door. Past the next intersection, Charlotte's nose twitched at the unmistakable scent of a great many freshly baked gingerbread biscuits coming out of ovens.

"Poor Inspector Treadles," murmured Miss Redmayne. "I do wonder what he was doing in that house in the first place."

❈

Lord Ingram parted ways from the ladies to see his children to bed. When he had done that and arrived once again at Mrs. Watson's, he encountered Holmes and Penelope returning from Fleet Street, where they had each visited the offices of three newspapers.

Their objective had been twofold: to inquire into the identity of the person who placed the roses-are-red-violets-are-blue message, and to place small notices of their own. The second goal had been easily enough achieved, but alas, no one had come in person to place the malicious message in question. Its text had been sent in by post and paid for with a postal order.

They found Mrs. Watson in the dining room, moving papers from the dining table, where she'd spread out the Cousins accounts, to make room for dinner.

With all the dishes again served à la française, and Mr. Mears off to his own dinner in the servants' hall, Penelope asked, "Did you spot any nefarious malfeasance, Auntie Jo?"

"Unfortunately, nothing so obvious," said Mrs. Watson, frowning slightly—only to remember herself and smooth her brow.

For as long as Lord Ingram had known Mrs. Watson, the lady had been on a not terribly serious, but also not entirely facetious quest not to add to her collection of wrinkles. She never prevented herself from laughing, but she did from time to time stop mid-frown.

Penelope reached over and pretended to iron out Mrs. Watson's forehead. "There now. Taken care of."

"Thank you, my dear." Mrs. Watson chortled, before her expression once again turned somber. "Nothing obviously wrong at Cousins, but nothing, if I were Mrs. Treadles perusing these accounts, that would set my mind at ease either. In fact, I must say that Mrs. Treadles has an excellent sense about these things. She is almost exactly right about the firm's financial position.

"But for a company created a generation ago, the founders of which are no longer involved with its operations, and which for some years was run by an heir who was neither as brilliant nor as interested— are we looking at a natural state of decay?

"The reputation of Cousins products seems to have diminished since old Mr. Cousins's passing. Sales and income have become stagnant, while there are large loans to service, loans taken on to renovate and modernize some of the firm's older factories. So it isn't doing terribly well, but not so badly that one would question—yet—whether it would continue to be a going concern."

Lord Ingram hadn't expected Mrs. Watson to find instances of glaring fraud in a matter of mere hours. Still he was disappointed. "Do the accounts seem genuine to you?"

"I'm not the best judge of that, but the age of the documents feels correct. Documents dating from the beginning of the decade are yellower and more brittle than more recent ones, and the ink on them has faded more. And the spines of sewn volumes also seem to have come by their creases naturally, from having been consulted over time."

"But why," asked Miss Redmayne, "if everything seems aboveboard, did Mrs. Treadles have so much trouble accessing this information?"

"Why indeed?" murmured Holmes, cutting into an oyster patty. "Her brother was neither competent nor attentive. The managers could have blamed everything on him."

"But since everyone knew that he was an inept heir, wouldn't the blame then fall on those who should have known better?" asked Lord Ingram.

"You mean they tried to keep their failure from Mrs. Treadles because they were loath to look bad before her?" mused Penelope.

"I'm not saying these men did," said Lord Ingram. "But I've seen men do far more stupid things for the sake of their pride."

Mrs. Watson and Miss Redmaye nodded in contemplation. Holmes glanced at him from across the table. The other ladies did not know him as she did. They thought he was merely relating his observations from a life lived among boys and men. They did not think that he, too, had needed to appear invulnerable and infallible. Or that he, too, had done very stupid things for the sake of his fragile pride.

But Holmes knew—and still loved him, in her way.

He smiled at her.

She speared a piece of oyster patty and put it into her mouth. After a moment, the corners of her lips lifted.

His heart floated.

The topic soon moved on to other facets of the investigation, as the true health of Cousins was not a debate that could be resolved by mere discussion. After dinner was put away, the accounts were again spread on the dining table, and everyone joined in the search for potential irregularities.

As a man with some expertise in archaeology, over the years Lord Ingram had been presented with a number of old letters purported to have been written by notable historical figures, from Charlemagne to Shakespeare.

He was no true paleographist, but he did happen to have made a close study of handwriting, was able to write a number of scripts fluently, and could credibly imitate the penmanship of others on short notice. Out of curiosity he had also inquired into historical paper-making.

He set aside yet another box of documents he'd riffled through. Mrs. Watson moaned and rubbed her temple. "My poor head. And my poor old eyes. Any luck on your part, my lord?"

He shook his head. "Upon closer examination I might come to a different conclusion, but a cursory look has not revealed any flagrant instances of fraud."

Nothing particularly suspicious, even.

Holmes, at the other end of the table, was no longer looking through the accounts but at the envelopes she'd brought back from Mrs. Treadles's house, the ones upon which the postal marks were at variance with the addresses listed inside.

A kettle of water had been brought in, as well as a spirit burner. While the water heated, she looked over every inch of the envelopes. And then, as steam began issuing, she held the envelopes over the spout of the kettle, reliquefying the glue that held them together. She even steamed the stamps to come off.

But the envelopes, when spread open, revealed no secret communication along seams where flaps had gummed over one another. There was nothing written on either the back of the stamps or underneath them. The stamps themselves, too, proved absolutely ordinary, penny stamps featuring the stiff visage of the queen.

Mrs. Watson sighed. "It's been a long day for everyone. I say we turn in, get a good night's sleep, and carry on with the work tomorrow."

Everyone rose.

"I will see you out, my lord," said Holmes.

He paused in the gathering of the papers before him. She had not seen him out the evening before and he couldn't think what she wanted to say to him. "Certainly," he said. "Thank you."

As it turned out, she didn't simply see him to the door. She got into a hackney coach *with* him and gave a Cold Street address.

When they arrived, Holmes rang several times before the door was opened by a bespectacled and round-faced young man.

"Mr. Bosworth?" she asked.

Mr. Bosworth regarded them with a mixture of curiosity and alarm. "Yes?"

"I am Miss Holmes," said Holmes. "And this is Lord Ingram Ashburton. My colleague Miss Hudson called on Mrs. Styles this afternoon."

Mrs. Watson, when she was in disguise as Sherlock Holmes's landlady or housekeeper, went by Mrs. Hudson. Miss Redmayne similarly referred to herself as Miss Hudson when she was out and about on Sherlockian business.

"Ah, yes, my grandmother mentioned it at dinner. About the . . . events next door. Miss Hudson was making inquiries for Sherlock Holmes, the detective."

"For my brother, yes."

"A pleasure to meet you both, but my grandmother is already abed."

"We came to speak not to Mrs. Styles, but to you, Mr. Bosworth," said Holmes. "May we come in for a minute?"

Mr. Bosworth hesitated another moment. "Ah, yes, of course. Do forgive me."

He started toward the staircase that would lead them up to a drawing room, but Holmes said, "Your study would be good enough."

Mr. Bosworth turned around in surprise. "But the study lacks sufficient chairs for all of us."

"That would be quite all right," Holmes reassured him. "We will not be long."

Mr. Bosworth gazed at her, puzzled. He turned to Lord Ingram, as if looking for clarification.

"I'm only here as Miss Holmes's assistant," he said cheerfully.

Mr. Bosworth must have come to the conclusion that it was best not to argue with strangers who called late at night. "This way then."

"You are a barrister," said Holmes, after a look at the study, its lights already on. "And a very busy one at that."

These were not mind-boggling inferences: Lord Ingram could have said the same thing. Law books lined the shelves. The desk was covered by papers and more law books, its inkwell uncapped. A half-eaten plate of biscuits and a mostly empty teacup sat on the book-shelf next to the desk.

"I see even assistants to the famed Sherlock Holmes are skilled practitioners in the art of deduction," said Mr. Bosworth politely. "I would offer you tea but the staff have retired for the night and I am strictly forbidden even to light a cigar for myself, as I have been deemed a permanent fire hazard."

Holmes chuckled. "Please take no trouble. We didn't come for tea."

"Then I'm afraid I can't tell you much of anything. I didn't even know about the murders until I came home the next evening and heard a paperboy shouting about murders on Cold Street."

"I didn't come to ask you about the night of the Longsteads' party,

Mr. Bosworth," replied Holmes gravely, "but to see your two alarm clocks."

Mr. Bosworth blinked. As did Lord Ingram. He recalled that Miss Longstead had said something about Mr. Bosworth waving an alarm clock before his grandmother to let the latter know that it was time for her dose.

In the shelf above the teacup and the plate of biscuits there were indeed two small alarm clocks, one facing out, the other facing the back of the bookshelf. The one facing out said twenty to eleven, more or less the correct time.

"May I see the other one?" asked Holmes.

Mr. Bosworth hesitated.

"If I'm not mistaken, that one says eleven o'clock—all the time. Because it isn't wound daily. Or ever."

Mr. Bosworth hesitated a little more, before handing the other alarm clock over. Lord Ingram took it. As Holmes said, it registered eleven o'clock. He put it to his ear; no ticking whatsoever.

Mr. Bosworth cleared his throat. "Normally I go to bed a little past eleven, so it was easy enough to wake up my grandmother for her dose before I make my preparations for bed. But recently I've worked late every night.

"It's not that I don't wish to be punctual. The first night I knew that I would work late, I set the alarm clock to go off at eleven. But when I slammed my hand over it, intending to stop working in the next minute or so, my attention was pulled back into the work and by the time I looked up again it was a quarter past twelve."

He looked at them, his fingers fiddling with the other alarm clock.

"That is quite understandable," said Holmes charitably. "We have all lost track of time while deep in concentration."

"So I was late attending to her. She always asks for the time when I wake her up. In the past I'd shown her the time on the alarm clock on her night stand. That night I was ashamed of my lateness and didn't want her to know. So instead of showing her alarm clock to her, I changed the time on mine and showed her that instead.

"The next day I borrowed her alarm clock, so that I would have two sets of reminders. But I was so absorbed in my work that I slammed my hand on both alarm clocks and still ended up being more than an hour late. I repeated my trick with that alarm clock to show her eleven o'clock."

He again looked at them, as if hoping for absolution.

But Holmes only said, "Since Mrs. Styles doesn't have much use for her alarm clock, you decided to keep it. You stopped winding it and set it to eleven once it had fully stopped."

"True," said Mr. Bosworth slowly, the bottom of his shoe scuffing against the thick carpet that covered most of the study.

"And now the alarm clock, the one that still keeps the right time, rings only to let you know that whenever you remember next, you should go up and give your grandmother her medicine."

Mr. Bosworth passed the alarm clock in his hand one palm to the other, and then back again. "That's—also true."

He must have been several years senior to her, closer to Lord Ingram's age. Yet as he fidgeted under her gaze, Lord Ingram was reminded of a misbehaving little boy having to account for himself before a much older sister.

"Can you recall, Mr. Bosworth, at what time you gave your grandmother her dose on the night in question?"

"Not specifically, I'm afraid. But typically it has been after midnight. And these days I usually go to sleep around two. So it had to have been somewhere in between."

Which restored the possibility that the jumper might be the murderer.

Lord Ingram exhaled.

Mr. Bosworth continued to regard Holmes with both apprehension and admiration. Lord Ingram, who often regarded Holmes in exactly the same manner, felt a surge of pleasure, the delight in seeing a master at her craft.

Holmes inclined her head. "Thank you, Mr. Bosworth. You said earlier that you didn't see much of anything the night of Miss Longstead's party. I said that my aim was only to see your alarm clocks. But since Lord Ingram and I are already here, I would like to ask you to please examine your recollections of that night. We are not looking for something as extraordinary as witnessing someone leap to the street below. If you noticed anything at all out of the ordinary, we'd be pleased to hear it."

"I would dearly love to be able to be of help," said Mr. Bosworth. "Let me think."

He again reminded Lord Ingram of a little brother, one trying to better his sister's opinion of him.

"Ah! Now that I look back, I remember feeling particularly annoyed at myself that night, because at some point between eleven and twelve, I actually left my desk and stood in front of this window for a minute or two."

"This window," behind Holmes and Lord Ingram, looked across the street.

"When I stood there, a brougham came by and stopped next to the garden gate," continued Mr. Bosworth, "an unusual-looking brougham painted with white and black stripes. I didn't wait to see who emerged from within, because something about the case I was working on occurred to me and I hastened back to my desk.

"At midnight, the grandfather clock in the entrance hall strikes. I don't always hear it as it strikes, but I will later realize that it has already struck. And that realization usually marks the moment I leap up from my desk to give my grandmother her medicine.

"As I said, that day I was particularly peeved at myself, because if I'd never left the desk after the alarm went off, that would have been one thing. But I had; I'd gone to the window and then returned to my desk, until I realized that midnight had already come and gone.

"Anyway, before I went to bed that night, I stood in front of the window in my bedroom, still thinking about my case. And that was when the brougham came back again. A fog was rolling in then, and the street was already rather scantly lit, but still, it was hard to miss a horizontally striped carriage. I thought it was simply there to pick up the same guests it had dropped off earlier. It never stopped; then a few minutes later it came back again from the other direction."

Lord Ingram and Holmes exchanged a look. A carriage that was easily identifiable even at night? They could find this vehicle.

"What colors were the stripes?"

"They were black and white," said Mr. Bosworth, looking with hope toward Holmes. "Is that—at all helpful?"

His hope did not go unrewarded. "We will not know until we look into the carriage," said Holmes. "But we are most grateful to you, Mr. Bosworth, for a new avenue of inquiry."

Mr. Bosworth smiled with relief. "That's wonderful!"

"Thank you," said Holmes. And then, with one last elder-sister look, "I hope you will do the right thing."

Mr. Bosworth reddened. "You are right, Miss Holmes. I will be sure to rise the moment the alarm rings tonight. And I will apologize to my grandmother tomorrow for having failed to properly discharge my obligation earlier."

——✻——

As soon as their waiting hackney had pulled away from the curb, Lord Ingram turned to Charlotte and kissed her.

"What was that for?" she asked after several minutes, breathing unsteadily.

"Nothing. Just that I've spent a fair portion of today in your company and I'm happy about that. Also you looked ravishing when you demanded that Mr. Bosworth produce his two alarm clocks."

She felt a smile rising up. She was vain enough to be thoroughly delighted at being called ravishing.

"Come to think of it," he went on, "I've always thought you especially handsome in such moments. Do you remember when you showed up at the Roman villa at my uncle's place that very first time?"

"Of course." That would be the occasion on which she'd blackmailed him into kissing her.

"I demanded to know how you found my remote site, and you explained that you'd checked the debris on my Wellington boots, which had been left at a side entrance to the manor, against the results of a geological survey that had been done on the estate."

She remembered. Very well. She'd "borrowed" the detailed survey from the office of the estate manager. And with that in hand, it had been easy to determine the only path he could have taken that would have accounted for both the red clay on the bottom of his boots and the fact that those boots had been in water almost high enough to submerge them.

"I'd noticed you before, of course—you were the girl who was always staring at me. Openly," he murmured, tracing one gloved fingertip across her lower lip. "But that moment . . . that moment I was a bit stunned, and not only by your impeccable logic."

Her heart thudded. She curved her own gloved hand behind his nape. "Are you saying, Ash, that you didn't kiss me solely because I threatened to bring a horde of rowdy children to your site?"

He leaned in. His breath on the shell of her ear sent pleasure pulsing along her nerve endings. "Please, Holmes, I was excavating the site with the blessing of my uncle. I was his favorite nephew and you were a somewhat insignificant guest. Had I been merely concerned about the preservation of my site, I'd have reported you to him and had you expelled from the estate."

The smile that had been rising and rising at last burst onto her face. "Oh, my."

And before he could kiss her again, she pulled him to her and kissed him.

Fourteen

Robert Treadles had paced for miles.

In the narrow space between the desk and the bookshelves, he had walked and walked. And turned so many times to avoid colliding with one wall or the other that he was faintly vertiginous.

One single word thumped in his head.

Alice. Alice. Alice.

Judging by how mercilessly he himself had been interrogated—and skewered in places where he was most vulnerable and helpless—he could only imagine the accusations that had been brought to bear on her.

He hurt for her distress. But it was the pincushion sensation of guilt that kept him hurtling from one end of the room to the other, a windup toy gone mad.

There was so much that he didn't know, so much that she didn't feel that she could tell him. So much she'd never told him because she understood him better than he'd understood himself.

He had always wanted to give her everything. But it had been an everything that revolved around him. He'd never known what she wanted. And how could he have, when he firmly believed that he knew enough for both of them?

A key turned in the door. He stilled, his heart pounding. He hoped he was being taken back to his cell. He'd rather face a day of jeers from drunks and miscreants in neighboring cells—and their combined stench—than an hour of Inspector Brighton's face in his own, his stomach churning at the caraway smell of the man's shaving soap.

The door opened.

"Alice!"

She was thinner. Shadows bloomed under her eyes, as if she hadn't slept in days. And yet she didn't look nearly as crushed as she had the morning before. As soon as the door shut behind her, he rushed over and pulled her into his arms.

He was sure that he could be seen and heard in this room, even with the door closed. The first time she'd visited he had deliberately stayed away from her, but now he could no longer. He buried his face in the crook of her shoulder, needing her, needing the solace of their embrace.

She trembled, but her back was straight and her arms around his back strong.

"Robert, are you all right?"

"I'm fine. You . . . you seem better."

There was a smile in her voice. "I sacked four of Mr. Sullivan's most staunch allies yesterday. Thank goodness for Mrs. Watson, who gave me enough spine for it."

Mrs. Watson? Charlotte Holmes's Mrs. Watson? The woman who had been a stage actress and goodness knows what else?

But those filaments of dismay were buried under an avalanche of relief. Every single person who aided Alice now would forever have his gratitude.

He pulled back to look at her.

She set her palm on his cheek. "Now I finally have all the Cousins accounts. Miss Holmes says that they are important because if you didn't do it, then it's most likely because of something at Cousins and—"

His entire body shaking, he stopped her words with his lips on hers.

She must have sensed his tremors. She pushed against him, trying for enough distance to see his face. "Robert, what's the—"

"Alice, listen to me." He spoke directly into her ear, an urgent whisper that he prayed would not be overheard. "Be very, very careful about inquiring into the doings at Cousins. Don't, in fact. Don't look into it at all!"

Silence.

He let go of her.

"Why?" she mouthed, her face ashen, her eyes fear-stricken.

He shook his head. He dared not tell her. He dared not breathe a word of the reasons. He could only take her hand and place it over his madly beating heart. "Please, Alice, trust me. And please, proceed no further!"

"I don't think I'll need any makeup today to look ten years older," said Charlotte sadly, over her third cup of tea.

Livia possessed the ability to stay awake—and alert—for two entire days. Charlotte was almost as fond of her beauty rest as she was of cake. When she'd returned the night before, after having clarified matters with Mr. Bosworth, instead of finding a somnolent household, she'd come across Mrs. Watson and Miss Redmayne still bent over the loot from Cousins.

Apparently, during Charlotte's outing, Mrs. Watson had realized that there was no proper summary of how much the renovation and modernization at each factory cost. Despite the hour, she had immediately proceeded to sort through hundreds of invoices and receipts, as well as to audit all the accounts for relevant entries, in order that she could arrive at her own rough estimate.

At one o'clock Miss Redmayne had shooed her aunt off to bed—Mrs. Watson had an early train to catch in the morning to Reading. The rest of the work fell on the younger women, with Charlotte not leaving her station until well past four o'clock, after she had completed a neatly written overview, accompanied by supporting documents.

And now she and Miss Redmayne were reviewing, at a somewhat sluggish pace, the notes the latter had taken while speaking to all the Longsteads' neighbors.

"Miss Hendricks to see Mrs. Hudson," announced Mr. Mears, with a clearing of his throat.

Charlotte and Miss Redmayne exchanged a look.

The previous evening, while arranging for small notices in the papers that invited members of the public to write to Sherlock Holmes should they possess information about the events at 33 Cold Street, Charlotte and Miss Redmayne had also placed a different small notice, this one promising a significant reward for the return of a jeweled comb bearing the inscription, *To my beloved R.*

The claimant, a woman in her late forties, had not come alone. With her were two girls of around eight and six, respectively. They looked about the morning parlor, Mrs. Watson's seldom-used formal drawing room, curious at this change of scenery but also appearing a little disappointed that it was only another room. The woman, on the other hand, studied everything with a wretched intensity, as if she found herself in a crime scene where those she loved had met their end.

"Miss Hendricks?" said Charlotte. "Good morning. I am Mrs. Hudson and this is my sister-in-law, Miss Hudson."

At her appearance, a wave of pure misery crested upon Miss Hendricks's face. But she rallied, greeted her hosts courteously, and introduced the girls as her charges, though without giving the girls' names.

Miss Hendricks's reaction intrigued Charlotte. She was dressed for another day out and about as Sherlock Holmes's sister in a dowdy brown dress and the same brunette wig she'd worn the day before. Her appearance was lackluster, certainly, but hardly revolting.

"I love having young guests in the house!" enthused Miss Redmayne to the girls. "Alas, I have no idea where my childhood books and toys are to be found, but I do have some bonbons I recently brought back from Paris. What say you, ladies, that we open a tin of those bonbons and demolish them? With your governess's permission, of course."

Miss Hendricks tensed at the suggestion that her charges be parted from her, but Miss Redmayne's guileless request was difficult to refuse. And—thought Charlotte—the woman really wanted to speak to Charlotte alone.

And so Miss Redmayne made away with the children. Mr. Mears delivered a tea tray and poured the remaining women each a cup.

As soon as he had withdrawn, Miss Hendricks pulled out a bundled handkerchief and untied its corners to reveal a sparkling jeweled comb.

Charlotte examined the comb. Only half of the inscription had been given in the small notice, so as to make authentication easier. The one on the comb read, *To my beloved R, from your faithful M.*

Rebecca and Mortimer Cousins, Mrs. Treadles's parents.

"Is this the item you are looking for, Mrs. Hudson?" came Miss Hendricks's anxious and unhappy question.

Charlotte set the comb down on the tea table. "May I ask, Miss Hendricks, where you came upon it?"

"At the park."

"Oh? Which park?"

"A small park in our neighborhood, ma'am. I'm sure you wouldn't know."

The comb glittered amidst plates of biscuits and sliced cake. Miss Hendricks regarded it without a single shred of covetousness. And yet she stared. Stared and stared.

And then she looked at Charlotte, gazed at her full on for the first time since Charlotte came into the room. After a second or two, her expression, that of a similarly all-encompassing heartbreak, took on a hint of bafflement.

"This is a beautiful house," she said tentatively. "Wonderful address, too. Is it yours, ma'am?"

"It is."

The confusion in her eyes deepened. "Is . . . is the comb yours, ma'am?"

Charlotte took a leisurely sip of her tea. "Indeed it is not. I am only an intermediary, seeking it on behalf of its owner."

"Oh," said Miss Hendricks. She relaxed slightly, only to tense again. "May I ask—may I ask . . ."

Her voice trailed off. "No. Of course I shouldn't ask anything about its owner."

Charlotte set down her teacup. "But *I* have been asked to verify the time the comb was found, as well as its precise location, as it was lost under rather perplexing circumstances."

Miss Hendricks clutched at her now empty handkerchief. "Surely it wasn't stolen?"

"I am not at liberty to disclose that. But I must have the information before I may dispense with the reward."

Miss Hendricks looked down at her lap with an air of defeat. "I found it in a park on Rosmere Road, not far from where my charges and I live. And I found it three days ago, when I took the girls out for their morning constitutional."

Three days ago. In the morning. The day of the party, but *before* it had taken place.

Charlotte had brought a pocket map of London with her to the morning parlor. She opened it to an already-familiar page: Rosmere Road was four streets to the east of Cold Street.

"This park?" She pointed to a spot of green.

"Yes, that one."

Charlotte wrote down the information on a piece of paper, as if she really were making the inquiry for someone else. "Is there anything else you can tell me about the finding of the comb, Miss Hendricks?"

Miss Hendricks shook her head.

Charlotte looked at her a moment, then handed over the ten

pounds promised in the small notice. Miss Hendricks stared at the banknote for a while. Again, with no covetousness, only pain.

She murmured a quiet thank you and bade Charlotte a pleasant day.

—❋—

When Miss Redmayne returned to the morning parlor, Charlotte was standing before a window, watching Miss Hendricks and her charges squeeze into a hansom cab.

"Did you find out the children's address?"

"Yes," answered Miss Redmayne. "They live on Rengate Street."

Rengate Street was one of the four streets that enclosed the private garden 31 and 33 Cold Street backed onto. Houses on Rengate were across the garden from houses on Cold Street. Depending on where on Rengate Street Miss Hendricks lived, she might have a decent view across the garden to number 31 and number 33.

Charlotte handed over Mrs. Treadles's jeweled comb to Miss Redmayne, who turned it around in her hand. "But what could this Miss Hendricks possibly have been doing at number 33 that night? She doesn't appear to be the sort to sneak out after dark."

"Mr. Longstead and Mr. Sullivan died in a bedroom," said Charlotte. "I examined the bed. Or rather, the mattress. It bore signs of having been repeatedly used for coitus."

"*Miss Hendricks?*" Miss Redmayne caught the comb as it slipped from her fingers. "But aren't governesses expected to be entirely abstemious? And if she had been caught, wouldn't it have led to her dismissal?"

"It would have. But sometimes that isn't enough of a deterrent," said Charlotte, whose current occupation stemmed directly from her own dismissal from society, due to having been caught while not being abstemious.

"But surely it was reckless to hold an assignation next door to a party in full swing."

"Quite so," said Charlotte.

Miss Redmayne held the jeweled comb up to the light. "Why do you think Miss Hendricks gave it back? Ten pounds is a nice sum but she could have pawned this for significantly more money."

Charlotte stretched her arms over her head—all the hours hunched over the accounts the night before had left her shoulders sore. "Perhaps she had no rendezvous with her lover that night. Let's suppose that she lived in a room with direct sight to number 33 and that she happened to look out of her window. At least four men, if we count the one who leaped to the street, went into the house that night. What if she saw one of those men enter the house? From the back, from that distance, might it not be reasonable to conclude she assumed that man to be her lover?

"If this was *your* lover, going into *your* place of assignation, without having alerted *you* ahead of time, what would you do? Go back to sleep?"

Miss Redmayne chewed her lower lip. "So the poor dear went to investigate and, as she was feeling her way across the dining room, kicked the comb, crouched down, and felt around for this object, only to close her hand around something that she could immediately ascertain, even in the dark, to be an item of female ornamentation, something that did not belong to her."

"And stumbled out, back to her place, convinced that she'd been played for a fool." Charlotte pulled her right arm across her chest—ah, that felt better in her shoulder blades. "Miss Hendricks came today not for the reward, but to see the woman the comb belonged to."

Charlotte pulled her other arm across. "What I don't understand is, why wasn't she at all concerned about the murders?"

"I can answer that," said Miss Redmayne eagerly. "The children went to their cousin's birthday party in Cambridge recently. They left early in the morning after the murder and started their return trip only this morning. They reported that Miss Hendricks purchased a paper at the train station in Oxford and was reading the small notices on the way back. And, once in London, she hailed a cab to take them not home but here to this house."

"So she doesn't know yet?" murmured Charlotte. "She has a shock waiting for her then."

Miss Redmayne emitted a whistle. Not at all a ladylike action, but Charlotte enjoyed it precisely for that reason.

"Do you think we'll ever be able to get the truth out of Miss Hendricks?" asked Miss Redmayne, giving the jeweled comb back to Charlotte.

"We may not need to. We may already know enough to find out the identity of her lover," answered Charlotte, rising to her feet. "Cold Street beckons. I must be off."

Miss Redmayne stood up, too. "And I should head out to the British Museum."

They still needed to check whether Mr. Longstead had spent as much time at the Reading Room in the days and weeks before his passing as his household believed he had.

The doorbell rang, loudly and insistently. The two women glanced at each other. Had Miss Hendricks returned?

The caller Mr. Mears showed in was Mrs. Treadles, looking even worse than she had upon emerging from her interrogation with Inspector Brighton the day before. As soon as Mr. Mears left, closing the door behind himself, she blurted out, "I don't know why, Miss Holmes—Inspector Treadles wouldn't give me a reason—but he has begged me to please not look too deeply into the accounts at Cousins. He's—he's frightened."

Charlotte poured a glass of cognac and pressed it into Mrs. Treadles's hands. "I imagine he must be. That's the reason he's said nothing to anyone."

"But—"

"Besides," said Charlotte calmly, "it's too late. Mrs. Watson and Lord Ingram are already looking into the matter."

Fifteen

Livia climbed over a stile, careful to avoid a puddle as she set her Wellington boot down. It had stopped raining, but the ground remained muddy in places. She crossed the empty pasture, breathing in the cold, pure air.

The sky was a pale blue. The sun was out, a sight that usually lifted her spirits. But today her spirits refused to buoy, her heart as heavy as an anvil.

Last night she'd dreamed of Mr. Marbleton—without being able to see his face. Instead he was endlessly walking away into an all-obliterating fog. Her dream self had run after him, calling his name, except she'd been running as if in a vat of glue and her cries, too, had been stuck inside her larynx, silenced, never emerging.

She shook her head. It was just a dream. He was fine—of course he must be.

She made her way over another stile. Now she was on a lane not too far from the Holmes house—and her mother trampled toward her!

Livia had left the house when she'd heard her mother stirring, for the express purpose of avoiding Lady Holmes as long as possible. Experience had taught her that, deprived of a target for her ire yesterday, Lady Holmes would not let Livia escape so easily today.

Panic swamped her. Her steps faltered. She wished she could

turn around and flee in the opposite direction—at least she would have no problem outpacing her mother.

And then where would she go, in her old coat and muddy boots, without even a coin in her pocket for buying a cup of tea at the village pub?

Lady Holmes stomped nearer, her face screwed in displeasure. Livia stood paralyzed.

"Where have you been, Olivia Holmes?" shouted Lady Holmes. "Is it not enough that I am stuck here in this godforsaken village. Now I have to go outside on a cold day to see my own daughter?"

This was but the overture to the operatic diatribe to come. No, not even that, this was the orchestra barely warming up.

Of the three Holmes girls Lady Holmes deigned to speak to, Henrietta, the eldest, had been clever enough to flatter her—and had escaped home via marriage more than a dozen years ago. Charlotte, the youngest, had possessed the fortitude and detachment not to let Lady Holmes's tirades bother her.

Livia, however, had always been both too proud to get along with her mother and too sensitive not to be hurt.

"Mamma, I'm terribly sorry for your ordeal," she blurted out. "I really am."

Her mother stopped mid-step, blinking.

A confounded Lady Holmes was better than an angry one.

"I mean, I can see how dull it is for you here," Livia hastened to add. "And there are so many unpleasant memories. Why wouldn't you wish to be somewhere else, anywhere else? And I'm sorry that I'm still here, a burden to you, an albatross around your neck."

A trace of real sorrow wended through her words. She did, in fact, understand her mother's plight. She did understand what it was like to live with a man who thought so contemptuously of his womenfolk. They could all have been allies together, Lady Holmes, Livia, Charlotte—and what a formidable ally Charlotte would have been. But Lady Holmes had valued her daughters as little as Sir

Henry had, had demeaned them to make herself feel more power-ful, and had ended up as unloved as her husband.

Lady Holmes was still blinking, her brows drawn together.

It abruptly occurred to Livia why Charlotte had sent fifty pounds to Lady Holmes the day after Sir Henry, having received his one hundred pounds, had flounced off. It was not only to be fair to their mother, but to create an opportunity for *Livia*.

One that was not yet too late for Livia to exploit.

She walked forward to Lady Holmes. "But you *don't* need to stay here, Mamma, afflicted and joyless. You *can* go wherever you like—provided you take me with you."

Her mother scowled, unimpressed by the idea of holidaying with her.

With a deep breath, Livia took Lady Holmes by the arm, turned her in the direction of home, and started walking, half pulling Lady Holmes along. "If you take me with you, then nobody can question your fitness as a mother. Mothers and daughters travel together all the time; it is the perfectly done thing. And you don't even need to pay for me: I have some money saved up and should be able to spon-sor my own railway ticket, as well as my own food and lodging.

"And once we are away, I won't ask you to take me out anywhere, or to buy me anything. You won't even have to see me if you don't want to—I'll stay in my room and read and have my meals there, too."

Livia glanced at her mother. Lady Holmes trudged on, her breaths already a little heavy. But she didn't look galled. In fact, her expres-sion was . . . speculative. She was *tempted*.

Livia's heart trilled. "Think about it, Mamma. Between being unable to go at all, and doing almost exactly as you wish, what would you choose?"

Goodness gracious, who knew she had it in her to be so convinc-ing? In front of her mother, no less.

Lady Holmes frowned again, as if sensing that there was some-thing too good to be true about Livia's proposal.

Livia did not allow time for her misgivings to gather. "There are very reputable places in London that cater exclusively to lady travelers. I have a list of them in a magazine in my room." Bless Charlotte for having collected a wealth of such information when she'd still hoped to go to school and become headmistress at a girls' school. "If you want to leave soon, say, on the morrow—and why would you want to stay here any longer than necessary?—then you can cable a few of those establishments and we'll have their responses by the end of the day, or at the latest with the first post in the morning."

"London?" Lady Holmes spoke for the first time since Livia had begun weaving her web of persuasion.

She sounded doubtful. But then again, she often sounded that way when it came to ideas that weren't her own.

"I know London isn't a new destination for you—or a particularly lovely one. But London is a perfect place for diversion. And shopping, of course—imagine everything that would be on hand on Bond Street. Not to mention, from London you can go anywhere in the blink of an eye. Overnight to Paris. Overnight to Edinburgh. The possibilities are myriad. And you don't need to take me on any of *those* trips. If you leave me behind here, everyone will know you got on a train by yourself and they will talk. But if you leave me behind in London, who will know?"

Her mother's eyes grew rounder, a rare inner exhilaration coming through. Then her face fell and she pursed her lips. "Abbotts will know."

Abbotts was her maid and Lady Holmes wouldn't think of traveling without her. Not only did she need Abbotts to "do" for her, but she wouldn't feel like a proper baroness without a servant trailing in her wake.

"You can tell Abbotts that I went to stay with Henrietta for a few days."

Henrietta, of course, had never invited her younger sisters to stay with her, but Lady Holmes had not complained greatly about that, given that Henrietta remained her favorite.

"Hmm," said Lady Holmes, walking faster as if her excitement grew.

"And what is Abbotts going to do?" Livia struck while the iron was hot. "Question your word? Write to Henrietta to ask if I indeed stayed with her?"

"And what am *I* going to do about it? Actually leave you in London by yourself?"

"You'll be leaving me at a reputable, respectable establishment for ladies, remember? And nobody will know. That's the best part. Once we are away from this village where everyone's nose is always in somebody else's business, no one will know or care what you do or where I am."

"But—"

"Do you really think I will get into any trouble, Mamma? I'm not Charlotte. I don't like people and I have no gentlemen friends. And what have I ever done in life, except reading and taking long walks?"

"I—I need to think about it."

They were almost at the house. Livia let out a breath. Maybe, if she was lucky, she and her mother might in fact head for London. But at least she'd managed to neutralize Lady Holmes's anger and set her mind on a different course. Which was not badly done of her at all!

"There'll be no Society in London, this time of the year," mused Lady Holmes as they entered the front door. "But I do wonder if the Openshaws might be there. Where did you say they were going to be on Christmas?"

Livia stilled. Openshaw was the name the Marbletons had used, when they'd come to visit the Holmeses. Or rather, when they had come to see Livia for themselves, because Stephen Marbleton had been that serious about her.

And he'd severed all ties with her, a mere fortnight later.

Despite the warmth inside the house, Livia felt cold. Not because of what Mr. Marbleton had done, but because the questions she hadn't allowed herself to ask had at last surfaced.

Why had he lied to her? What was the real reason he had cast her out of his life? What had happened to make him come to that terrible decision?

"Did you not hear me, Olivia?" said Lady Holmes, a little peeved.

"Sorry, Mamma." Livia squeezed out a smile. "The Openshaws, my word, they are going somewhere wonderful."

———※———

Cousins Manufacturing was best known for its production of locomotive engines. The Cousins factory in Reading did not make locomotive engines, but specialized in steam boilers and conical boiler tubes. Before Mrs. Treadles had gained control of her own company, when she had come to see the works, the foreman had turned her away, telling her firmly that it was no place for a lady and that she ought to send her agents instead.

Mrs. Treadles had now sent her agents, which included Lord Ingram; Mr. Bloom, an expert Lord Ingram had engaged; and Mrs. Watson, once again a woman.

Mrs. Watson had come dressed in dark gray, though she remained eye-catching for her aura of warmth and vivacity. The same foreman, a broad man with salt-and-pepper hair named Fogerty, was clearly wary of her. But the sacking of Messrs. White, Kingford, Ferguson, and Adams seemed to have had a dampening effect on his own enthusiasm for keeping out interfering women. He received his three callers with cautious civility and made no mention of Mrs. Watson's gender.

Lord Ingram might have found his wariness amusing, were it not for the fact that the same wariness had led to Mrs. Treadles's inability to enter her own property.

He addressed the matter directly. "Mr. Fogerty, I understand that earlier you refused Mrs. Treadles entry."

Mr. Fogerty nearly choked on his tea. He coughed. "It was . . . it was an unfortunate misunderstanding."

"Do please elucidate us on how the misunderstanding arose," said Lord Ingram coolly.

"We, ah, we acted out of concern for Mrs. Treadles, of course."

Lord Ingram raised a brow. "And who would be this 'we' you speak of, Mr. Fogerty?"

"That would be myself and the late Mr. Sullivan."

"Do you mean to say Mr. Sullivan specifically told you that you should, out of concern for Mrs. Treadles, refuse her entry?"

Mr. Fogerty's eyes didn't quite meet Lord Ingram's. "Y—yes. It really is no place for a lady, the inside of a factory, grease, soot, and noisy machines everywhere."

As if trying to underscore his point, a great din erupted on the factory floor, its volume only partially muted by the walls of Mr. Fogerty's cramped office.

Lord Ingram was unmoved. "Mr. Fogerty, will you swear in a court of law that what passed between you and Mr. Sullivan was exactly as you described?"

Mr. Fogerty's teacup paused on its way to his lips. "But why would I need to give evidence on oath? I had nothing to do with Mr. Sullivan's death at all."

"The inspector in charge of the case thinks Inspector Treadles killed Mr. Sullivan because of Mrs. Treadles. Should the case proceed to trial, counsel for the defense has cause to call anyone who has interacted with both Mr. Sullivan and Mrs. Treadles. Will you stand up before a judge, with your hand on a Bible, and give the same account?"

Mr. Fogerty fidgeted in his seat. "Ah . . ."

"Then pray do not try to pawn me off with a cheap imitation of the truth. I will accept that you acted on Mr. Sullivan's order, but I do not believe that either of you were remotely motivated by chivalry."

Before his severity, Mr. Fogerty seemed to wilt. "My lord, you must please understand, Mr. Sullivan was the one who brought me in to run this factory. I'm qualified and I do good work but there are many who are qualified and do good work. He brought me here to be loyal to him."

Lord Ingram's breaths quickened, but he kept his tone clipped. "Mr. Sullivan didn't own this place."

"I understand that, but he ran it, my lord. In all the time I worked here, I never heard from the younger Mr. Cousins, only Mr. Sullivan, Mr. White, and their secretaries. Mr. Sullivan said that Mrs. Treadles's interest would wear off soon, if we but put a few obstacles in her way. And then things could go back to the way they were before and my position would be safe."

Lord Ingram and Mrs. Watson exchanged a look. Would they at last hear something useful?

"Why did you think that your position wouldn't be safe were Mrs. Treadles to see this factory?"

Mr. Fogerty's nose and forehead beaded with perspiration. "It's nothing like what you're thinking, my lord. I've looked after this factory as if it were my own child. But I'm Mr. Sullivan's man, you see. And Mr. Sullivan said that if he were to go, then there would be no one to protect me from axes falling from above."

"And why did he think he might be let go?"

Mr. Fogerty looked uncomfortably toward Mrs. Watson, who gazed at him with grave interest.

"You need not worry that the lady might turn light-headed," said Lord Ingram, with a touch of impatience. "She investigates alongside Sherlock Holmes. The things she has seen would make you need smelling salts."

Still Mr. Fogerty looked down at the floor, as if by not seeing Mrs. Watson he could pretend she wasn't there. "Well, Mr. Sullivan told me that Mrs. Treadles fancied him. But as he didn't fancy her back, she was highly vexed—hell hath no fury and whatnot. He said that she was looking for excuses to get rid of him and that I mustn't give her one."

Lord Ingram had to marvel at Mr. Sullivan's monumental lack of decency. "You believed him?"

"I . . . I didn't think to question Mr. Sullivan. But I daresay after I saw Mrs. Treadles myself, well, I don't wish to speak ill of the dead but Mr. Sullivan never struck me as all that particular about the company he kept—company of the female persuasion that is. I couldn't imagine he'd have turned Mrs. Treadles down if she'd actually fancied him. You see what I mean?"

"I do, very much."

"But Mr. Sullivan said she would be interfering and would want to change things and give lots of orders, and he wasn't lying about that. She did seem to want to do all those things."

Lord Ingram held on to his temper. "She owns the company, Mr. Fogerty."

"Still, my lord . . ."

When he received no word of agreement from anyone else, Mr. Fogerty took to drinking his tea with great speed and concentration.

Lord Ingram sighed inwardly. He turned to those who had come with him. "Mrs. Watson, Mr. Bloom, if you are sufficiently refreshed, I believe Mr. Fogerty can show us around."

The factory sat on two acres but most of the manufacturing was concentrated in a great brick-and-iron shed building measuring three hundred feet in length and two hundred and fifty feet in width, with a high roof partially made of glass. Inside a number of furnaces roared. In summer, they might have made the place unbearably hot. But in the dead of winter, on a day in which the temperature hovered near freezing, the heat, which smelled of burnt oil and molten metal, was only stifling and no worse.

The noises, however, could drive a man to distraction: the grinding, clashing, screeching, and above all, the thunderous clangs of plates being riveted both manually and by steam riveters. Perspiring workers, their faces darkened with soot, swarmed like bees around large, unfinished boilers. They glanced up as Lord Ingram, Mr. Bloom, and Mrs. Watson walked by, accompanied by Mr. Fogerty, but their attention quickly returned to their tasks.

Lord Ingram's natural father had been one of the country's wealthiest, most successful bankers. His banks had made—and continued to make—numerous industrial loans for the construction and modernization of factories. Consequently the banks had, at their disposal, individuals capable of judging whether that money had been put to good use.

Mr. Bloom, a rail-thin man with a large mustache, was one such highly regarded individual. Lord Ingram noticed that whereas his and Mrs. Watson's eyes were quickly drawn to the hive-like activity, Mr. Bloom perused the physical assets, from the shed building itself, to the vertiginous pyramidal framework surrounding each steam riveting machine.

During the inspection, his few questions quickly revealed Mr. Fogerty's ignorance of the factory's prior incarnation. His subsequent request for documents and photographs only made the latter more discomfited.

"I'm afraid I wasn't given anything of the sort," answered the foreman, mopping his face with a large handkerchief. "The place when Mr. Sullivan entrusted it to me was fresh and spanking. Awful pretty. It never occurred to me to ask how it was before."

Mr. Bloom made no comment. He didn't say anything until they were in a carriage, driving away, and then he asked to see the rough estimate Mrs. Watson had brought, of the cost of renovating and refurbishing this particular factory.

He studied the one-page summary, written in Holmes's hand, for long minutes, so long that Lord Ingram and Mrs. Watson looked at each other several times, Mrs. Watson's expression growing more tense with each iteration.

"How accurate do you consider this estimate, Mrs. Watson?" asked Mr. Bloom at last, his voice disconcertingly quiet.

Mrs. Watson swallowed. "I'll admit that of the three people involved in its preparation, there is not a single professional accountant. But we can trace every one of the major payments used to arrive at this sum. If anything, I'd say we've been conservative in our approximation."

Mr. Bloom was again silent. Lord Ingram and Mrs. Watson exchanged another look and asked no questions.

They took a quick luncheon at the railway inn across the street from the station. And it was only after the plates had been cleared that Mr. Bloom said, "It behooves me to be prudent before making pronouncements. May I examine the accounts myself after we return to London?"

Lord Ingram felt his heartbeat suspend. What pronouncements? "I will need to obtain permission from Mrs. Treadles but I believe that will be readily granted. In fact, I will send a cable now, so that you may see the accounts as soon as possible."

Before he could rise, Mrs. Watson, her face drawn, asked, "Mr. Bloom, I know you don't wish to rush to judgment. But surely, you have some ideas now. Some very concrete ideas."

Beneath the table, Lord Ingram's nails dug into the palm of his hand.

"I do," answered Mr. Bloom, frowning. "And unfortunately, if I must speak at the moment, I will say that at most two thirds of the money supposedly spent on this factory actually went into it. Likely only a half."

❖

"No," said Mrs. Coltrane decisively. "The locks on the exterior doors of number 33 were changed after the previous tenants left.

They'd been there for years and there was no telling how many copies of the keys might be lying about; it was safer to change the locks."

She and Charlotte sat in her small office in the basement of 31 Cold Street, where Charlotte had just received the item she had officially come for, Mr. Longstead's appointment book, freshly returned by Scotland Yard. "What about the letting agent? I assume you had one for number 33 to find new tenants?"

"We did have one. After the previous tenants left, maintenance work was done—a thorough cleaning of the flues, a changing of the wallpapers, etc. It was during that period Miss Longstead discovered the attic and fell in love.

"When the work on number 33 was nearly finished, she asked Mr. Longstead whether she couldn't read in the studio in the interval before a new tenant moved in. She didn't make many requests of him and he said yes immediately. The letting agent was told to give advance notice, so that Miss Longstead had time to make her way out of number 33, ahead of any prospective tenants being shown around.

"Then Mr. Longstead saw how much she enjoyed her new space and instructed me to have a word with Mr. Cornwall, our letting agent. He wanted Miss Longstead to have free use of the studio, for as long as we were in London. So his solicitor told Mr. Cornwall that we wouldn't be putting the house up for let until we decamped to the countryside. We asked for the keys back at the same time. Mr. Cornwall is a trustworthy man, but we preferred not to take any risks."

Mrs. Coltrane leaned forward, her expression earnest. "You see, Miss Holmes, we do have all the keys here."

Do you? "Miss Longstead's set is with her, true," said Charlotte. "But we still haven't seen Mr. Longstead's."

"I'm sure they must be in his study somewhere," said Mrs. Coltrane. "In the meanwhile, I can show you the keys in my keeping."

She rose and opened a locked key cabinet on the wall. Inside, among a congregation of keys, all carefully labeled, were the two sets for number 33, one large and one small.

"Have these keys ever left your keeping?"

Mrs. Coltrane began to shake her head but stopped. "Now that I think about it, in September, Mrs. Norwich, who lives on Rengate Street, called on Mr. Longstead in a rush. She is a widow, you see. A good woman, but a bit of a penny-pincher, as all she has is her house and her annuity.

"She'd ordered coal. But with the coal wagon standing there, it was discovered that her coal hatch couldn't be opened. The coal company said that she would need to pay them the delivery fee and then the same fee again after the coal hatch was repaired, because they'd made their delivery and it wasn't their fault that her coal hatch wouldn't open.

"As I said, a bit of a penny-pincher, Mrs. Norwich. She asked Mr. Longstead if he wouldn't mind taking delivery of this coal. Except we'd just had a delivery ourselves and our coal cellar was full. Mrs. Norwich proceeded to ask after the cellar at number 33, which was empty, so we took her coal after all—and paid for it, too, as the coal was now ours.

"I had a fever that day and stayed in bed. Miss Longstead came herself to get the key for the key cabinet from me—since the big ring of keys was needed to get to the coal cellar. I thought she would go and open the doors for Mrs. Norwich, but later, when she came to return the cabinet key and to let me know everything was back in its proper place, she told me that she'd given the keys to Mrs. Norwich instead. And Mrs. Norwich had her butler handle everything."

Charlotte's heart leaped. "How long were those keys in Mrs. Norwich's hands?"

"An hour or so, I'd guess." Mrs. Coltrane's expression turned a little uneasy. "But she couldn't possibly have done anything with them, could she have?"

"No, I dare say she wouldn't have," said Charlotte.

But what about her butler?

———※———

Charlotte would have liked to speak with Miss Longstead, but her aunt, Mr. Longstead's last surviving sibling, had arrived in London and she had gone to condole with that lady. Charlotte returned to Mrs. Watson's carriage. There, after consulting Miss Redmayne's notes from her many interviews the day before, she asked Lawson, Mrs. Watson's coachman, to drive to a nearby street. And then she composed a message and entrusted it to Lawson to deliver.

> Dear Mr. Woodhollow,
>
> I have reason to believe you were at 33 Cold Street on the night of Mr. Longstead's death. Pray discuss the matter with my representative in the town coach parked before 48 Miniver Lane.
>
> Yours,
> Sherlock Holmes

As she waited, Charlotte closed all the curtains inside the carriage, extracted a piece of fruitcake from her handbag, and took a meditative bite. She was perfectly capable of thinking without cake, but having one in hand was like adding a splash of kerosene to the grate. And on a day when she'd had less than four hours of sleep, a few splashes of kerosene might prove necessary to keep the fire going.

She'd finished her first slice and was debating whether a second one was called for immediately—or better deferred to later in the day—when she heard footsteps coming to a stop outside the carriage.

An entire minute passed before two rapid, agitated knocks came at the door.

"Come in."

The man who opened the carriage door was in his midthirties, tall, well-built, and remarkably handsome. He wore the black garments of a butler, crisp and well-ironed. Were he in more fashionable attire, a casual observer might have believed him a gentleman. But he was without the assertiveness and assurance of those accustomed to deference from others. Instead, he blinked a great deal and stood with his shoulders hunched, exuding dread and diffidence.

"You're—you're not Miss Hudson."

He would have remembered Miss Redmayne, who, as Miss Hudson, had called on all the nearby houses the day before, abovestairs and belowstairs.

"No, indeed, I'm Miss Holmes, Sherlock Holmes's sister. Pray come in and close the door, Mr. Woodhollow."

He glanced about warily and then, with surprising speed, did as Charlotte asked. "I don't know why you sent me the message, Miss Holmes, but I've never—"

"Miss Hendricks, from 36 Rengate Street, went into 33 Cold Street that night, because she thought she saw you enter."

Mr. Woodhollow recoiled, as if Charlotte had slapped him. "Miss Hendricks would never have—she—she wouldn't—"

"Indeed she wouldn't have discussed this matter with a stranger. But when she entered number 33, she discovered an item on the floor of the dining room, a lady's jeweled comb. There could be dozens of explanations for the presence of that ornament in an empty house, but the only conclusion she came to was that you must have been meeting someone else."

Mr. Woodhollow stared at Charlotte. "That's preposterous. Miss Hendricks is kind and patient and terribly learned. That she deigns to spend time with me—I have no words to express my gratitude. How could she possibly think I would arrange to meet anyone else in a place that belonged to us?"

The words left him in a surge. And then, realizing what he'd said, he flushed scarlet.

"Perhaps Miss Hendricks believed you to be meeting someone

else because she doesn't consider herself as young or as handsome as you."

"And I can never be as clever or as erudite as she." He bit his lower lip. "I hope I have not got Miss Hendricks in trouble with my admission."

"Not with me. I do not believe you and Miss Hendricks had anything to do with the murders and therefore I do not intend to involve either of you in the official inquiry. But I would like you to tell me what happened that night, because what you might think of as irrelevant to the case could very well contain what I need for my investigation to proceed in the right direction."

The butler's voice trembled. "I have your word that none of this will get out?"

"You have my word."

He panted a few times, eventually bringing his breathing under control. "Very well. I had some trouble falling asleep that night. So I went out for a cigarette. Mrs. Norwich wouldn't have liked it if I'd been seen loitering outside the front door, so I stood by the back door, a few steps into the garden. When I was done, I was about to go inside when I saw a woman going into number 33."

"A woman, you say?"

Mrs. Treadles?

"Yes, a woman. There was enough light from the side windows of number 31 that I couldn't have made a mistake about her silhouette."

"And what time was this?"

"Five minutes to midnight. I looked at my watch when I saw the woman."

Excitement shot through Charlotte. "You are certain about that?"

Mr. Woodhollow nodded. "Mrs. Norwich is very particular about punctuality and my watch is the same kind carried by railway guards."

He pulled out his pocket watch to show Charlotte. She checked the time it displayed against that on her own, even as her mind leaped in all directions.

Five minutes to midnight. The woman Mr. Woodhollow saw couldn't have been Mrs. Treadles, who went inside 33 Cold Street at half past twelve. Nor could she have been Miss Hendricks, who entered only after Mrs. Treadles had left.

"Could you tell the woman's identity?"

Mr. Woodhollow returned the watch to a pocket on his waistcoat. "She was already halfway in when I saw her, so I didn't see her face, and her movement was too quick for me to discern what she was wearing, except that it was dark in color, which was what Miss Hendricks usually wears.

"I was confused. Miss Hendricks didn't have any keys to that house; only I did, one to the back door, and one to the chief bedroom. I didn't know how she was able to open the door—or why she was going there without first setting up a rendezvous with me. Yet who else could it have been, going into that particular house at night?

"I meant to cross the garden right away to check, but just then Mr. Eldridge from 60 Rengate Street decided to take a stroll in the garden with his friend. They often do that, debating all sorts of topics at all hours. Except this time, instead of strolling, they planted themselves directly in the middle of the garden, and I wouldn't have been able to go from my house to 33 Cold Street without being seen."

Mr. Woodhollow's fingers knotted together. "It's always been my fear that one day Miss Hendricks would realize that I'm just an uneducated man from Camden who's probably risen as high in the world as he will, someone who'll spend the rest of his life in someone else's basement. I thought that moment had come. That she'd already put me aside.

"As I was about to give up and go back inside, the philosophers left at last. I rushed to number 33. The door was closed but unlocked. I climbed up the stairs to the room where Miss Hendricks and I normally met. And——" He reddened again. "And I stood outside listening for a bit before I unlocked the door."

"It was locked?" This was the chief bedroom, the site of the murders.

"Yes, it was locked. I always make sure to lock it after——after we've used it. Anyway my heart pounded with relief when I saw that the room was empty. And then I heard two people talking below, a man and a woman. I couldn't hear every word they said but the man sounded smug and the woman, panicked. Then they stopped talking."

"Miss Hendricks told me that she'd had such an employer once, a man she could not afford to be caught alone with. For an entire year under his roof she'd felt like a fugitive, with pursuers always only one step behind and around every bend."

A look of unhappy guilt crossed his features, as if he blamed himself for Miss Hendricks's erstwhile distress.

"I wanted to do something but I didn't dare show my face. The idea came to me to make a loud noise. I slammed the door hard. And when I opened it again, as quietly as I could, I heard the woman shout, 'Out of my way!' followed by footsteps running off.

"I was ever so relieved. And then I heard someone coming up the stairs." He swallowed. "All the other doors in the house were locked. The only way I could avoid being seen was by leaving through a window. So I did that.

"Thankfully the façade of the house offered plenty of footing and there was no one else on the street. My coat got caught on a finial as I jumped from the small balcony one level below to the street, but luckily I wasn't hurt. I yanked my coat free and ran down the street until I came to the next gap between the houses, where there was another gate. There I climbed into the garden and went back to Mrs. Norwich's house, shaking all the way."

His hands trembled in his lap, even though he clamped them together tightly.

Charlotte gave him a moment to recover from the fright that assailed him anew. "I take it you didn't say anything to the police?"

He shook his head. "I would have lost my position if I'd admitted to the police that I'd been in number 33 that night. It's the only position I've got and I need to save for at least another ten or twelve years before I'll have enough to . . . Well, besides, I did hear the names of those two people in the dining room when they spoke to each other. Mrs. Treadles's husband already punished the man who would have assaulted her, didn't he?"

Not an answer Inspector Treadles would have wanted to hear.

As for what Charlotte wanted to hear, Mr. Woodhollow had already revealed himself to be both the person who slammed the door and the one who left from the window and had his coat caught on the finial. Would the keys in his hands lead to any clues?

"If I understand correctly, the problem with Mrs. Norwich's coal hatch happened because you realized that number 33 wouldn't be let for a while and that if you could get your hands on those keys, you'd have access to a place where you and Miss Hendricks could meet in relative safety."

Mr. Woodhollow shifted on his seat. "Please, Miss Holmes, I know what I've done wasn't right, but please don't think of me as a criminal. I've been in service since I was twelve, starting as a hallboy, and I've never taken so much as a spoon from any employer."

Charlotte looked at him. "But you made duplicates of keys that didn't belong to you."

He lowered his gaze. "When I left home, I meant to also leave behind everything *about* that home. But I guess I still know how to take impressions of keys and where to get duplicates made without questions asked."

"Did you ever let anyone else have the keys?"

"Absolutely not. Never."

"And you have the keys still?"

"I can surrender them now if you'd like," he said glumly. "I don't imagine Miss Hendricks will wish to go back to number 33 again."

Charlotte sighed. "Mr. Woodhollow, I assume you have not spoken to Miss Hendricks since that night. You left number 33 believing that she had not betrayed your trust. She, on the other hand—"

"But I'm saving up money so that someday I may have enough to ask her to marry me!"

"Does she know that?"

He twisted his fingers. "I'm afraid she'll say no. She comes from a respectable stock. No one from my family, men or women, have ever been respectable enough to be entrusted with the education of other people's children."

"Surely, Mr. Woodhollow, you understand why Miss Hendricks might also have doubts?"

"She shouldn't," he said stubbornly.

"But she does. Very few people think better of themselves than the world thinks of them. You feel undeserving because you are not a man of means. She feels undeserving because she is no longer a young woman. Tell her what you feel. Tell her that it is not merely her learning or the novelty of your affair that interests you. Do not assume anything that is self-evident to you must be equally self-evident to her."

Perhaps her words at last made sense to him. Or perhaps he heard and understood her desire for there to be no more misunderstandings between him and his beloved. He raised his face and said solemnly, "I will tell her, Miss Holmes. Thank you."

She scribbled a note and gave it to him to pass on to Miss Hendricks. "Good luck, Mr. Woodhollow."

The butler left, still thanking her.

Charlotte sighed again. She was actually rather sincere in wishing the man luck. She must be getting soft with age—or from Lord Ingram's influence.

At the thought of him, she smiled to herself.

Sixteen

Lord Ingram had sent his cables. Mr. Bloom was on his train back to London. And Mrs. Watson at last permitted herself to whisper, "At most two thirds. And likely only a half!"

She and Lord Ingram were in a hired town coach, driving away from Reading's crowded railway station. Trains whistled. Street musicians pulled tirelessly at accordions. Hawkers, huddled around fires in metal bins, cried mince pies and roasted chestnuts.

Against this racket, their coachman, perched on the driver's box in front, his head covered by a thick woolen cap, couldn't possibly overhear any words exchanged inside the vehicle.

Yet Mrs. Watson dared not speak at her normal volume.

Lord Ingram moved to sit beside her, one arm around her shoulders.

His proximity allowed her anxious thoughts to at last pour out. "If we are accurate in our figures and Mr. Bloom correct in his assessment—and I have a sinking feeling he might very well be—then where did the rest of the money go? That is a *lot* of money. And this is only one factory!"

Under the younger Mr. Cousins's tenure, the firm had acquired and modernized multiple factories.

"Is this why Mr. Sullivan did his best to obstruct Mrs. Treadles from learning about the inner workings of the company? He was diverting funds from the company to line his own pockets, wasn't he? Did Miss Holmes not say that his drawing room was filled top to bottom with show pieces?"

"An excess of furniture does not a man indict," said Lord Ingram slowly. "But I do agree with you otherwise. With the younger Mr. Cousins having been an ineffective chief, and with Mr. Sullivan and his cabal having arrogated most of the decision-making power to themselves, I'd be surprised if the hostility he directed at Mrs. Treadles *wasn't* part of a concerted effort to prevent his crimes from coming to light."

An awful thought struck Mrs. Watson. She turned toward Lord Ingram and gripped his arm. "The rumors that have been flying— so many of them have been about Inspector Treadles as a jealous husband. But—what if instead he'd been investigating this very matter and had learned about Mr. Sullivan stealing tens, possibly hundreds of thousands of pounds from his wife's family? That would be sufficient cause to make anyone extremely—"

She stopped. Her hand dropped away from Lord Ingram's arm—to cover her own mouth.

They were trying to exonerate Inspector Treadles, not to discover more plausible motives for him to have killed Mr. Sullivan.

Lord Ingram, who no doubt understood that her latest line of reasoning did Inspector Treadles no favors, frowned. "What I don't understand—what I've never understood from the beginning—is why Mr. Sullivan and Mr. Longstead were killed *together*."

An even more awful idea clobbered Mrs. Watson.

"What if—" she said from behind her hand, "what if Mr. Longstead wasn't who we thought he was? What if instead of being grateful to old Mr. Cousins for buying out his shares, he resented old Mr. Cousins all these years? Could he have felt that old Mr. Cousins had forcibly separated him from his one great achievement in life? Remember he never offered Mrs. Treadles any substantive help. It couldn't have cost him much to be kind to Mrs. Treadles to her face, especially if he'd been directing his nephew to siphon away her fortune. A man who is wonderful to his niece and solicitous of his servants can still be a monster to others."

Lord Ingram looked pained. He gently pulled Mrs. Watson's hand away from her face and held it in his own. "Unfortunately, this theory also places Inspector Treadles at the very center of the murders—and gives him every motivation."

Mrs. Watson slumped against the back of the carriage seat. "Poor Mrs. Treadles. If I were her, I'd probably be stark raving mad by now. I am not her and still I feel the hangman's noose tightening."

Unexpectedly, Lord Ingram smiled. "I felt that distinct sensation not too long ago, when I was the prime suspect in the case at Stern Hollow. Have I ever told you what Miss Charlotte said to me when she came to visit me in my jail cell?"

Mrs. Watson not only straightened. She leaned forward and took hold of his other hand. "Tell me."

"I let her know that I was terrified and she said, 'Don't forget, sir, that I am a queen upon this board, and I do not play to lose.'"

He held Mrs. Watson's gaze, his eyes deep yet clear. "I had her in my corner then. Inspector Treadles has her in his corner now. She will not let him down."

Mrs. Watson felt a smile rising to her own lips. But—"I thought that at Stern Hollow Miss Charlotte had a strong idea from the very beginning as to who was responsible for the body in the icehouse. Here she must be in the dark, the same as the rest of us."

Lord Ingram pitched a brow, a hint of mischief to his expression. "*We* are in the dark, absolutely, my dearest lady. But Miss Charlotte? She most likely has a clear idea *what* happened and is only looking to find out why."

—❖—

After Mr. Woodhollow left her town coach, Charlotte made a close study of Mr. Longstead's appointment book, which recorded, beginning from the final week of November, numerous instances at the

British Museum, several meetings at Cousins, two trips to the chemist's, and one encounter with his physician.

As Charlotte was already in the neighborhood, she asked her way to Sealy and Worcester, the nearest establishment of pharmaceutical chemists. Both Mr. Sealy and Mr. Worcester knew Mr. Longstead, and had considered him a friend as well as a faithful customer, who, when in town, could be expected to frequent the shop weekly.

"Was there anything he bought on a regular basis?" asked Charlotte.

"I believe those kept him coming back." Mr. Sealy gestured to a row of large, clear glass jars that contained vividly colored sweets. "My sister is a talented confectioner and Miss Longstead is very fond of our gummy-textured sweets. Mr. Longstead could usually be counted on to buy a packet of her favorite flavors, a packet of my sister's newer creations, some household items entrusted to him by his housekeeper, and one or two things that simply caught his attention."

"Mr. Sealy is correct," said Mr. Worcester, emerging from the back room to join his partner behind the counter. "It was really the sweets he came for. But we flattered ourselves in thinking that perhaps once in a while he enjoyed conversation with others who've had some scientific training."

"May I have a penny's worth of this lemon-flavored gummy sweet?" Charlotte pointed to a glass jar. "And may I ask what conversational topics interested Mr. Longstead?"

"Oh, many," said Mr. Worcester. "When his niece grew interested in the making of abstracts and absolutes, he consulted Mr. Sealy, who has broad experience with tinctures."

"We did speak for a while on that," concurred Mr. Sealy as he scooped bright yellow sweets into a small paper packet. "And then there was the time you and he discussed remedies for cancer."

"Which we do not sell," Mr. Worcester hastened to assure Charlotte. "Mr. Longstead and I agreed they exist solely to extort money from the already desperate."

Charlotte also asked for a packet of peppermint sticks—it was almost Christmas, after all.

"Mr. Longstead liked a peppermint lozenge once in a while," said Mr. Sealy. He weighed and closed the packets carefully. "And Mr. Worcester and I both participated in a conversation with him about the days before the regulations of '68. I made my own fireworks back then. Alas, Miss Longstead won't be able to."

His partner patted him on the arm. "But you did give Mr. Longstead a recipe in case his niece wished to prepare her own photographic solution. The practice of chemistry didn't stop being enjoyable with the regulation of explosives."

"True, true." Mr. Sealy chuckled. "Likely I'm missing being young, rather than being able to make fireworks."

Charlotte let the reminiscences continue for a few more exchanges, enjoying their camaraderie, and then she asked, "Do you gentlemen remember when Mr. Longstead last came in?"

"That would be the Tuesday before he passed away," said Mr. Worcester. "Mr. Sealy was feeling poorly that day so it was only me in the shop."

"And before that?"

"Before that he came in two days in a row, which was rather unusual," answered Mr. Sealy. "He told me it was because the first day he was so busy talking he forgot to make his purchases, and realized only when he got home."

He smiled, only to have that smile fade into sadness.

Mr. Worcester again gave him a reassuring pat on the arm. "And those two days would have been the Monday and Tuesday of the week before," he told Charlotte.

To thank the pharmaceutical chemists, in addition to the sweets, Charlotte also bought a bar of rose soap and a tin of lip salve, both again made by Mr. Sealy's talented sister. As she paid for her purchases, she asked, "You wouldn't happen to know the address of Dr. Ralston, Mr. Longstead's physician, would you?"

—⋇—

Dr. Ralston lived nearby. A few minutes later, Charlotte was knocking on his door.

The physician did not appear to be in the best of health. As Charlotte was shown into his drawing room, he coughed into a monogrammed handkerchief and, in a raspy voice, begged Charlotte for her forgiveness.

After a brief inquiry into his health—he'd caught a cold several days ago—Charlotte explained the purpose of her visit. "I understand that Mr. Longstead died of a gunshot wound, and not from any illnesses. But is there any light you can shed on his health?"

Dr. Ralston added two spoonfuls of honey and a twist of lemon into his tea, took several swallows, and sounded less hoarse when he spoke again. "What ailed Mr. Longstead was a combination of actual problems alongside a mental incapacity to restrain himself. In a different man, such health issues as he had wouldn't have been enough to force an early retirement. But he couldn't not overwork. If there was a problem, he wouldn't eat or sleep until he'd solved it. That temperament was terrific for a man with many engineering difficulties to solve, but terrible for someone whose body needed to be properly fed, rested, and otherwise cared for.

"Perhaps if he'd married, his wife might have been able to regulate his schedule. But he remained a bachelor who didn't understand the meaning of moderation. And so it was that he nearly killed himself twice through sheer carelessness and overwork, before old Mr. Cousins, of all people, made the decision that he absolutely must stop."

"Mr. Mortimer Cousins?"

"Yes, a truly excellent man, old Mr. Cousins. Mr. Longstead's innovations were the lifeblood of the company, but for Mr. Longstead's health, Mr. Cousins gave up untold future profits. The first time Mr. Longstead nearly ruined his health, he said he would retire, but he still had shares in the company and couldn't help getting involved. The second time, Mr. Cousins bought out his shares on terms highly advantageous to Mr. Longstead. Mr. Longstead separated himself thoroughly from the company, and rusticated for some years. Lo and behold he was fine. Mind you, he was never as hale and robust as me—my normal self, that is—but speaking as his physician, his was a perfectly tolerable state of health."

Charlotte had always been open to the possibility that the partnership between Mr. Longstead and old Mr. Cousins *hadn't* been as robust and mutually affectionate as those around them preferred to believe. Yet here another person had added his voice to the chorus and attested to the very solidity of that friendship and alliance.

"Did Mr. Longstead have any recent health issues?" she asked.

"None that I was aware of, and we saw each other regularly. In fact, I would have been there that night at his niece's party, if I hadn't caught this accursed cold the day before." Dr. Ralston coughed again. "And this tragedy has not helped my recovery."

It was rather warm in the room for Charlotte, but Dr. Ralston gazed with some longing at a thick, knitted shawl draped over the back of a chair. Charlotte rose, retrieved the shawl, and handed it to him. "When you say you saw each other regularly, do you mean in a professional capacity?"

"Thank you, Miss Holmes," said Dr. Ralston gratefully, spreading the shawl over his lap. "Mr. Longstead and I saw each other more as two bored old men—I am three quarters retired myself. When he was in town, we attended lectures together about once a month. Once a month I also host a whist game, to which he had a standing invitation.

"And when he came to my card games, either before or after, I would serve as his physician for a quarter of an hour: take his pulse, look him over, and ask him about his health. Sometimes I think his niece was the best thing to ever happen to his health. He very much wanted to be sure that he didn't orphan her—not before she found a good man to marry, in any case."

But despite her uncle's intentions to the contrary, Miss Longstead was now once again an orphan.

Dr. Ralston fell silent.

Charlotte took out Mr. Longstead's appointment book. The dates of Mr. Longstead's last few visits to the pharmaceutical chemists, at least according to Messrs. Sealy and Worcester, had *not* agreed with the ones recorded inside. *Those* took place at the beginning of December. She opened the appointment book to the page on which the word "physician" had been jotted down, and showed it to Dr. Ralston. "Does this appear to be the correct date and time for your card games?"

"Yes, I always have them on the second Thursday of the month, in the afternoon."

"And he played on that day?"

Dr. Ralston put a lozenge in his mouth. "No, Mr. Longstead didn't play on that day. Eight of us should have been there but two bowed out at the last minute. We were going to take turns, but Mr. Longstead entered into a conversation with Dr. Motley and they seemed to enjoy themselves. They even went for a walk together."

The name was familiar to Charlotte from an earlier case. "Dr. Motley, Mrs. Treadles's family physician?"

"Indeed, the very same."

"Did they know each other well?"

"They most certainly knew *of* each other but I don't believe their paths crossed very often."

Charlotte looked again at the word "physician," scrawled on the still open page of the appointment book. "Were you surprised that they took so well to each other?"

Dr. Ralston drank more of his honey lemon tea, his eyes taking on a faraway look. "The day before the whist game I ran into Miss Longstead. She confessed herself nervous about her coming-out party. When Mr. Longstead came the next day, he appeared unusually grave. I attributed his sober mood to worries about his niece.

But then he and Dr. Motley began chatting and he seemed fascinated by everything Dr. Motley had to say.

"Perhaps I was surprised, too. But my most prominent feeling, both as his friend and his host, was one of relief, to see him keen and animated. After that I allowed myself to be absorbed in the game."

He rubbed a hand over his face. "But now I look back, and wonder whether I shouldn't have paid closer attention."

On her way back to Mrs. Watson's house, Charlotte read Mr. Longstead's appointment book one more time, beginning on the first of January, commemorated with an instance of sledge driving with his niece in newly fallen snow.

By the time she arrived home, she had the distinct sensation that something was missing from Mr. Longstead's records—and that she should have already realized what it was. Yet the realization refused to drop into her lap.

She blamed her sluggish brain on the fact that she still hadn't had her luncheon—how could she expect to think properly, being underfed on a day when she was already underslept?—and repaired immediately to the dining room.

As she was tucking into an excellent roast beef sandwich, Miss Redmayne returned, bringing with her a large pile of letters that she had retrieved from the general post office: Sherlock Holmes had called for the public to write with information about the murders and the public had responded.

She joined Charlotte at the table—though not for the meal, as she had already eaten at the proper hour. They spoke of their respective findings and Charlotte learned that at least according to the register of admissions, Mr. Longstead hadn't been anywhere near the Reading Room of the British Museum in recent weeks, despite what he had told his niece and his housekeeper—and written down in his appointment book.

"The clerk at the Reading Room was terribly helpful, and looked up instances of Mr. Longstead's visits going several months back," said Miss Redmayne with an approving nod. "We compiled a record of his attendance from August onward. I'll set it here for you."

She left the dining room shortly thereafter, as Lord Ingram had sent a cable and she had to prepare for the imminent arrival of Mr. Bloom, the expert who had inspected Mrs. Treadles's factory in Reading and now wished to see the Cousins accounts.

Charlotte wiped her hands with a napkin and perused Mr. Longstead's attendance record. Prior to the last week of November, the dates accorded with the instances noted down in Mr. Longstead's appointment book. But after that, outings documented as visits to the Reading Room had turned out not to be visits to the Reading Room.

She picked up her sandwich again. The same problem existed with regard to forays to the chemist's that had been logged in the appointment book. Only his trip to Dr. Ralston's house was recorded correctly.

If she asked for verification from Mrs. Treadles, would she find that his documented visits to Cousins also hadn't taken place? Or took place at entirely different times than what he wrote down?

Charlotte stopped eating. The roast beef sandwich had not only filled her stomach; it had revitalized her poor, tired brain. She knew now exactly what had been missing from Mr. Longstead's appointment book.

He had never mentioned his call of condolence to Mrs. Cousins.

Seventeen

Mrs. Cousins shook Charlotte's hand warmly. "Miss Holmes, please, have a seat. And please allow me to thank you for introducing Mrs. Watson to my sister-in-law. When I called on her yesterday evening, she was enormously relieved that at last someone gave her the courage to do what she should have done long ago."

"That courage was Mrs. Treadles's own," answered Charlotte, sitting down.

"Very true, but sometimes we need a nudge—or even a strong kick—onto the right path."

Charlotte inclined her head. "We are but doing what Mrs. Treadles engaged us to do."

Although she would not deny, if pressed, that she'd been a little harsher on Mrs. Treadles than absolutely necessary, so that when the latter encountered Mrs. Watson, she would open up that much more readily.

"May I trouble you to answer a few more questions, Mrs. Cousins?" continued Charlotte. "I should have been more thorough at our prior meeting."

Mrs. Cousins poured tea for Charlotte. "Oddly enough, after you left yesterday, I kept feeling that there was something I should have told you. My mother has been faring poorly of late. Between her health and my sister-in-law's troubles, I haven't been able to think, let alone think clearly. But I should dearly love to help if at all I could."

She raised her head. The day before she had doggedly answered questions because Charlotte had been Mrs. Treadles's emissary. Now her gaze held a gleam of hope and excitement.

Charlotte inquired after her mother's health, then said, "Perhaps you can begin by telling me when Mr. Longstead called on you to offer his condolences."

Mrs. Cousins gasped. "But that's just it! I remember now. I was about to speak more on his call when a carriage almost struck a child outside—and I was so unsettled that I forgot what I was going to say."

Charlotte considered herself equally responsible for the lapse. Even if her goal had been to learn about Mr. Sullivan, she should have left no stone unturned.

"He came at the beginning of December, a most unexpected visit," continued Mrs. Cousins. "He and Miss Longstead had sent a substantial wreath *and* attended the funeral. They had also sent a note of condolence. Wouldn't you agree, Miss Holmes, that Mr. Longstead had already done everything and more required by etiquette, given that he was never a personal friend to my husband?"

"Yes, I would agree," answered Charlotte.

"So you can imagine my surprise when he called to condole with me, more than four months after Mr. Cousins died."

Many things had changed for Mr. Longstead in the weeks before his death, and some of those changes had led him to call on Mrs. Cousins, with whom he'd rarely had any dealings. Charlotte let out a long, controlled breath. "Please give me all the details you can remember."

"Well, he didn't stay for much time, twenty minutes perhaps. We spent at least five of those minutes on the weather and another five on his niece. He lamented that she'd still not had a proper debut and took responsibility for the delay. I said I hoped it would happen soon but that alas, if it did, I would not be able to attend, given that I was still in first mourning.

"Eventually the topic turned to my husband. Mr. Longstead said he very much wished that in his younger years, instead of always locking himself in his workshop to tinker with prototypes, he'd had the wisdom to help my father-in-law guide my husband as he came of age. He wondered whether, if he'd done that, in later years we wouldn't have been better friends and allies."

She sighed. Framed against both the dark crape of her attire and the gold-and-green of the wallpaper beyond, she formed a near-perfect pre-Raphaelite tableau.

"I've been struggling to come to terms with the reality of the man I married. And for some reason, this wishful thinking on Mr. Longstead's part, this vision of a reality that never was—it touched me. My husband had many faults, but did I have any fewer? Had I known he was going to die so young, would I have been a different wife and would we have had a better marriage?"

She fell silent; her face turned toward the window.

Outside the sun was setting. The hour Inspector Treadles would be formally charged drew ever nearer.

Charlotte pressed on. "Did Mr. Longstead by any chance mention Cousins Manufacturing or Mr. Sullivan?"

"No, but he did bring up Inspector and Mrs. Treadles during our chat about the weather. They'd dined together shortly before and would dine together again in a few days. I was still vexed at Inspector Treadles's conduct, so I didn't say much in response."

And now the question Charlotte had come for. "Did he take anything from this household?"

Mrs. Cousins started. "How did you know?"

With a solid smack, Charlotte's heart fell back into place—she hadn't realized how much she needed her theory to be correct. "I saw a mourning brooch among his things."

"That was it. Near the end of his visit, we were both a little teary. He asked if I had any memento for him to remember Mr. Cousins by, a piece of mourning jewelry, perhaps. So I gave him the brooch."

Mrs. Cousins sighed and set a slender hand upon the column of her throat. "I've heard that some people can sense their own impending demise. I wonder . . . if Mr. Longstead wasn't one. A reconciliation of sorts with my late husband, a belated debut party for his niece—he seemed to be tying up all the loose ends of his life. Could he have sensed that his eternal rest was near?"

—❈—

The problem with growing closer to one's once-and-future lover in the midst of an urgent murder investigation was that one did not have time to proceed to the logical next step.

Or rather, that was Charlotte's problem. She doubted that Lord Ingram would have allowed "logical next steps" even otherwise: He had strict ideas about what being a married man entailed and even an impending divorce did not relax all of those standards.

Which was why, after some lovely and increasingly ardent kisses the night before, instead of tumbling into a nice feather mattress to enjoy being young and libidinous together, they had made rounds at the newspaper offices. The hour had been late, but that had been immaterial, as most morning editions did not finalize composition until the small hours.

Their purpose had been to disseminate yet another small notice, this time in a simple Caesar cipher, which, when decoded, read, *Would the owner of the most beautiful striped black-and-white town coach meet a sincere admirer outside the Dog and Duck in Bywater this evening at half past five o'clock?*

Charlotte and Miss Redmayne, driven by Charlotte, arrived at the rendezvous spot shortly after five. After circling the neighborhood for a few minutes, Charlotte was able to berth Mrs. Watson's carriage almost directly across the narrow street from the Dog and Duck, a pub doing a brisk business. At a quarter after five, Miss Redmayne emerged from the town coach in men's attire.

Her figure lent itself much more easily to the effort than did Charlotte's—no counterfeit paunch required to disguise the presence of a substantial bosom. Instead she looked lithe and rather rakish, sauntering off on the pavement.

With three minutes to go she reappeared, this time just to the side of the Dog and Duck's entrance, and, with a perfect degree of charming disreputableness, struck a match and lit a cheroot. Charlotte supposed she should have expected that of a Parisian student, even though she'd never smelled tobacco on Miss Redmayne's hair or clothes. She smiled slightly. Even a young woman with as understanding a parental figure as Mrs. Watson preferred to keep some of her vices hidden.

The street became more crowded. Did any of the carriages ferry passengers intent on taking a look at the "sincere admirer"? Several slowed as they passed the Dog and Duck. But none featured horizontal stripes in two highly contrasting colors.

Yet another vehicle slowed, a common hackney that could be hailed from any thoroughfare. This time, however, someone got out, a woman, thickly wrapped, her face obscured by a large, fur-fringed hood. With very little hesitation she headed for Miss Redmayne and said something, her voice too low for Charlotte to catch.

Miss Redmayne, flicking ashes from the tip of her cheroot, shouted, "Sorry, ma'am, I'm a little hard of hearing. Could you repeat yourself?"

Under her own enormous hood, Charlotte nodded in approval. Miss Redmayne was not remotely hard of hearing, but she had enough presence of mind to play a trick.

"I said, sir," the woman raised her voice, "would you mind pointing me to St. Barnabus's?"

Her voice!

Charlotte's hands tightened on the reins.

"Certainly, ma'am," Miss Redmayne hollered. "You'll find it three streets to the east, and then a little farther south."

The woman thanked Miss Redmayne. As she pivoted around to return to her hackney, Charlotte had a brief glimpse of her face.

Indeed, Mrs. Sullivan.

---※---

Mrs. Sullivan's hired vehicle disgorged her two streets away from her home. She wrapped herself tightly in her fur-lined mantle and trudged along, nearly tripping once on a crack in the pavement.

Charlotte, who had followed her at a discreet distance, parked her own carriage several houses down from the Sullivan residence. Within two minutes, a hansom cab drew up alongside and Miss Redmayne alit. Charlotte got down from the driver's perch that she'd been occupying for far too long, and gave her heavy coat to Miss Redmayne.

She also handed over the vulcanized hot water bottle that had been keeping her warm.

Miss Redmayne chortled. "I've come to greatly enjoy the sight of these hot water bottle cozies that you make."

Charlotte, too, greatly enjoyed her cozies. This one was meant to resemble a Christmas pudding: variegated brown on the bottom, representing the boiled pudding itself, creamy white on the shoulders for the brandy sauce, and at the very top, a sprig of red-and-green holly, the whole nearly sculptural, for having been crocheted in layers of small scales.

She almost said something about the anatomical cozy she was making for Miss Redmayne's Christmas present, but restrained herself. "I'll change now."

As Miss Redmayne shrugged into the gigantic coat and climbed onto the driver's box, Charlotte slipped inside the coach and made sure all the curtains were securely down. Two foot-warmers radiated heat from the floor; still she shivered as she peeled off her rough woolen coat and trousers.

When she re-emerged, she was once again dressed as Sherlock Holmes's sister, ready to call on Mrs. Sullivan.

Mrs. Sullivan, almost invisible amidst the glittery congestion of her drawing room, looked both apprehensive and excited at Charlotte's entrance, but mostly excited. "Miss Holmes, how unexpected! What brings you back here?"

"We've unearthed enough information in our investigation that I thought it best for me to speak with you again."

"Oh?"

Mrs. Sullivan's eyes shone. Did she also shiver?

"Indeed. Mrs. Sullivan, you told me, when I called yesterday, that on the night of Miss Longstead's party, your husband did not come home before he went to Cold Street. You said that he must have gone directly from work. Am I correct in my summary?"

"Y—yes," said Mrs. Sullivan, a hint of wariness to her reply.

"But it would have been a nuisance to go directly from Cousins, wouldn't it? Mr. Sullivan would have had to take his evening attire with him to work that morning. He would have had to make sure that nothing became wrinkled during the day. And he would have had to leave his work clothes behind in his office when he left." As she spoke, Charlotte counted her reasons on her fingers, in an exaggerated fashion. She then looked to Mrs. Sullivan. "Not exactly a reasonable course of action, was it, when everything would have been so much easier if he'd first come home?"

"Ah . . ." Mrs. Sullivan smoothed her skirts in a rather jerky motion. "I didn't see him leave in the morning. So I can't tell you whether he took his evening clothes with him."

Charlotte tilted her head. "I think it's much more likely that Mr. Sullivan had a secondary residence in town. You labeled him a proudly sinful man. How remiss of me not to take into account the possibility that he might have kept a mistress."

Mrs. Sullivan's mouth compressed. Then she rolled her eyes in an expression of resigned annoyance. "That's not exactly unheard of."

As Charlotte had thought, Mrs. Sullivan knew of the existence of this secondary residence.

"So you agree that he most likely didn't change at work, but instead at his mistress's place, where he already had evening attire waiting, and where he would have been able to bathe and shave and make himself properly presentable?"

Mrs. Sullivan's tone turned peevish. "As I said, I didn't see him at home and I don't know where he changed exactly. Cousins seemed as good a place as any."

Charlotte regarded Mrs. Sullivan. At first Mrs. Sullivan stared back defiantly, then bit by bit her gaze slid away.

"Mrs. Sullivan, you have not been very forthcoming with us," said Charlotte sternly.

The corners of Mrs. Sullivan's lips trembled, as if she were sincerely hurt by this accusation. "How could you say that, Miss Holmes? I've told you a shocking amount."

"You have also elided over many things. Going by what you said earlier, that you were awakened the next morning by the arrival of the police, I must conclude that no carriage from this house left to pick up Mr. Sullivan from the party or you would have known much sooner that something was amiss. How did he expect to reach home at the end of the party? Hail a hansom cab at two o'clock in the morning on a residential street?"

"He always managed just fine on the evenings when he didn't take me anywhere."

"And you knew not to worry because you knew that he had a mistress, set up in a household with its own conveyance. He went to the party in that carriage and he would have gone back to his mistress's in that same carriage."

Mrs. Sullivan gave a righteous toss of her head. "Well, you could scarcely expect me to speak of *that*."

"Why not? You already spoke of him lusting after other men's wives."

Mrs. Sullivan sputtered.

"Allow me to make a conjecture," continued Charlotte. "You didn't mention the mistress, her household, or her carriage, because you wished to omit them from the narrative. You wanted to be able to gratify yourself by speaking of your husband's terrible sins, but still keep your own part of the night away from investigators."

Mrs. Sullivan jerked. Her fingers dug into the padded armrests of her chair. "My part? I did absolutely nothing. I was here all night."

Charlotte smiled slightly. "It will not be difficult for me to discover where the mistress resides. Mr. Sullivan's solicitor is certain to know it, as he would have been expected to deal with the expenses associated with that household. And once I have the mistress's address, I will be able to question her coachman. What do you think he would tell me, if I were to ask him what he did that night?"

Mrs. Sullivan, eyes large, face white, said nothing.

"He would tell me that after he dropped off Mr. Sullivan, instead of waiting for him all night somewhere nearby, he made himself a few extra coins by coming here—discreetly, of course, not directly outside the front door—to take you to Cold Street."

Mrs. Sullivan grabbed a round embroidery frame from a side table next to her chair; it still held the mourning handkerchief Charlotte remembered from the evening before. "And what would I possibly do there?"

"Spy on your husband, of course. Except you quickly realized that almost all the rooms in number 33, except the dining room and the entrance hall on the ground floor, were locked and you didn't have much of a vantage point into number 31, given that the dancing in that adjacent house happened on the floor above."

"That is—ridiculous!"

"You probably do think so, but still you weren't able to stop yourself from doing just that. A rather distinct-looking carriage was seen arriving on Cold Street between eleven and twelve that night. Did it disgorge you? How long did you stay?"

Mrs. Sullivan gripped her embroidery frame as if it were a shield. "I refuse to answer such ludicrous questions."

Charlotte folded her hands primly in her lap. "I do wonder where you went afterward, Mrs. Sullivan. Did you go home directly? Or did you go somewhere else in that carriage?"

"Your imagination is getting the best of you, Miss Holmes!"

"Is it? Yet my imagination hasn't come up with answers for questions such as, how did you get into number 33? Did you make a habit of going where your husband didn't want your company? Also, did he know this about you?"

Mrs. Sullivan shoved aside the embroidery frame. "Miss Holmes, I think—"

Charlotte rose. "Indeed, Mrs. Sullivan, it would behoove you to think carefully. For, shall we say, twenty-four hours? After that, my brother will have me call on Inspector Brighton with our deductions and ask for Mr. Sullivan's other household to be looked into."

Eighteen

A s Charlotte expected, Mrs. Sullivan left soon, slipping out of the front door while glancing about, as if she were a maid neglecting her duties to meet with a follower, and not the only authority figure remaining in the household, able to come and go as she wished.

Miss Redmayne, now in the role of the coachman, followed. Unlike Charlotte, who'd learned to handle a vehicle in the country, Miss Redmayne had learned to drive in the city. *On Aunt Jo's phaeton, first in the parks, then mostly in quieter districts,* she'd told Charlotte.

Her relative lack of experience on thoroughfares did not bother Charlotte. Her attention was on the direction they were headed: into a *more* fashionable district, with more abundant gardens, and large, freestanding houses.

Would they be passing through or were they approaching Mrs. Sullivan's destination?

It was the destination.

And Mrs. Sullivan alit before a house both bigger and more opulent than her own.

Charlotte hesitated. This was not how one set up a mistress. Mistresses were usually kept in modest houses, described as *bijou* to give them an air of elegance. Was Mrs. Sullivan by some chance visiting a social superior?

Well past normal visiting hours and in a hired carriage?

Charlotte decided to try her luck. The maid who opened the door was at first disinclined to allow her to see the mistress of the house, but when Charlotte informed her that she was Mr. Sullivan's *other* mistress, here to discuss arrangements, she was promptly, if with great curtness, shown into the drawing room.

This drawing room, while still plentifully gilded, might in some circles have been accepted as elegant enough—in certain nouveau riche circles, that was. As a further point in its favor, it was not stuffed to the gills, but had enough space that each piece of furniture could be individually appreciated for its design and placement. Charlotte walked past large pots of ferns that added splashes of soothing green-ery, and mentally tallied the vases of fresh flowers that adorned every horizontal surface.

Mrs. Sullivan, seated on a white-and-gold settee, leaped up. "Miss Holmes, you—you—"

"Hullo again, Mrs. Sullivan. Will you perform the introductions?" murmured Charlotte, inclining her head toward the other woman in the room.

She appeared to be in her early thirties, pretty but not remarkably so, attired becomingly in a tea gown with an emerald-green open redin-gote, worn over a loose white underdress.

Charlotte aspired to own a tea gown, which had a racy reputa-tion as what married ladies wore when their lovers came by for an afternoon tryst. Perhaps now that Lord Ingram was at last willing, it was time to make such an investment?

"May I present Mrs. Portwine, Miss Holmes?" mumbled Mrs. Sullivan. "Mrs. Portwine, this is Miss Holmes, who is looking into the murders on behalf of Sherlock Holmes, the private detective."

Mrs. Portwine, obviously a woman of the world, did not appear too surprised or dismayed. She rose and offered Charlotte her hand to shake. "Miss Holmes, I can assure you that I had nothing to do

with the murders. Killing off my protector harms my livelihood—
and I guard my livelihood jealously."

"I believe you, Mrs. Portwine," said Charlotte. "I am here only
because Mrs. Sullivan has refused to answer questions as to her whereabouts that night. I decided to pose those questions to you instead."

"You said you would give me twenty-four hours to think!" said
Mrs. Sullivan plaintively.

"And you may still choose to tell me more at the end of those
twenty-four hours," said Charlotte. "I did not, however, give any promises as to how I would or wouldn't use those twenty-four hours."

Mrs. Sullivan pouted. "I didn't mean to bring her to your doorstep," she said, even more plaintively, to the woman with whom she'd
shared her husband.

"And yet here we all are," said Mrs. Portwine, addressing Mrs.
Sullivan, only a few years younger than she, as if the latter were a way-
ward niece. "We might as well sit down and have a cup of tea, like
civilized people."

The tea tray, which must have been already ordered for Mrs.
Sullivan, materialized that moment, carried in by the still incredulous-
looking maid.

Charlotte selected a small iced cake, reminiscent of the ones
her thirteen-year-old self had been thinking about when she saw
Lord Ingram for the first time. "This is a delightful house, Mrs.
Portwine."

Mrs. Sullivan wrinkled her nose, but made no comment about
how her husband did not buy this house for her.

"Thank you," said Mrs. Portwine. "It isn't mine, of course, and
I don't know how much longer I'll be able to stay here, now that Mr.
Sullivan is no more."

"Were you saddened by his passing?"

The corners of Mrs. Portwine's lips lifted in an ironic smile.
"Ours was a business arrangement. I would say Mrs. Sullivan has

been far more affected. She was . . . interested in her husband in a way I could never be."

Mrs. Sullivan, so loquacious in her first meeting with Charlotte, said nothing.

"Oh?" said Charlotte. "Would you like to tell me more, Mrs. Sullivan?"

Mrs. Sullivan stared at her own lap. "You might as well ask Mrs. Portwine. This is her drawing room, after all."

"Temporarily," said Mrs. Portwine politely. "It was always only mine temporarily."

Charlotte enjoyed Mrs. Portwine's wry, cynical, but not unkind presence. "Please, go ahead, tell me more about Mrs. Sullivan's interest in her husband."

Mrs. Portwine gave Charlotte a long look, as if wondering what sort of ostensibly respectable woman could be so at ease in the drawing room of a loose female. "Mr. Sullivan bought this house not too long ago. A new mistress seemed an appropriate inauguration for a new house. It so happens that I am good friends with Mrs. Calloway, his previous mistress. Mrs. Calloway wished to part ways from Mr. Sullivan. I was between protectors. She appealed to me for help and I took over from her, so to speak."

"Mrs. Calloway didn't want to go anywhere; Mr. Sullivan was the one who tired of her," claimed Mrs. Sullivan in all seriousness.

Mrs. Portwine smiled slightly, took a sip of her tea, and did not reply to Mrs. Sullivan, but instead said to Charlotte, "When I moved in, Mr. Sullivan told me that I may expect Mrs. Sullivan to call. He said to shut the door in her face, as Mrs. Calloway and his other mistresses had over the years.

"But I was curious about Mrs. Sullivan. She sounded . . . tenacious, to say the least, and I wanted to see what she was like in person. When I did meet her, I realized that for her, Mr. Sullivan was an obsession. Not an obsession that arose out of too much affection, I don't think. More as if—as if she only felt alive when he paid attention to her."

Mrs. Sullivan swallowed. She opened her mouth, but after a moment, shut it again.

Mrs. Portwine cast a glance in her direction, not a look of scorn, but more as a taxonomist might puzzle before a hitherto unknown subspecies. "Mr. Sullivan by no means returned the same strength of feelings, yet neither was he indifferent to this idée fixe of hers. In fact, a part of him *depended* on it. He was not a man who inspired devotion. At work he could make men fall in line because he had Mr. Barnaby Cousins's ear and he was mean-spirited to those below him. And for women, he could buy the likes of Mrs. Calloway and myself. But I don't believe he'd ever been terribly successful with ladies.

"So it meant something to him, his wife's sincere fixation, even if he didn't like that she was the only one to find him interesting or important."

Without looking at anyone, Mrs. Sullivan turned her face from one side to the other, as if there was something uncomfortable about the fit of her collar.

"What I've said now, Miss Holmes, is essentially what Mrs. Sullivan told me, not long after we met," Mrs. Portwine went on. "But you know how it is that mothers can complain bitterly about their own progeny, yet bristle with anger the moment anyone else dares to criticize those same darlings? So it was with Mrs. Sullivan, where her husband was concerned. She was allowed to brand him as morally corrupt and sexually degenerate, but I could only listen and never voice similar opinions."

What did Mrs. Sullivan truly feel for her husband? Or was it something too complex to be described by any single emotion? "It sounds as if you met with Mrs. Sullivan more than once," said Charlotte.

Mrs. Portwine adjusted her lapels, another ironic smile on her face. "Mrs. Sullivan became a regular caller."

"You charged me!" cried her regular caller.

"I charged your husband for my time; there was no reason to allot it to you gratis," said Mrs. Portwine patiently. "Beyond the initial titillation, I wasn't *that* interested in what passed between the two of you. But you wished for an audience and I was willing to listen for a price."

This "friendship" between the two women did not particularly surprise Charlotte. After all, while Mr. Sullivan yet lived, to whom else could Mrs. Sullivan speak truthfully about her husband? "Did Mr. Sullivan know of your meetings?"

"Eventually," answered Mrs. Portwine. "One day when Mrs. Sullivan left, my coachman, Whitmer, happened to see her. The indoor staff I hired, but Whitmer has always been Mr. Sullivan's man. He informed Mr. Sullivan and Mr. Sullivan was displeased. Not about his wife's visits—if I could tolerate them then he had no problem—but because I hadn't told him.

"'That woman pokes her nose into everything,' he said. 'I can't keep anything important at home because she would get her hands on it. And now you tell me she's been coming here?'

"It's true that Mrs. Sullivan is curious. Highly curious. The first time she came she inspected this entire house, including below-stairs. And on each subsequent visit she wanted to see if additions or changes had been made since her previous call.

"I didn't mind her curiosity so Mr. Sullivan's reaction seemed disproportionate to me. But he thundered that Mrs. Sullivan always found a way to open locks, whether they were on doors or drawers. He'd thought this house beyond her reach. But now he was not to have any safe haven at all."

Charlotte turned her little iced cake on its plate and considered Mrs. Portwine's words. "Did Mr. Sullivan forbid Mrs. Sullivan from calling here again?"

Mrs. Portwine glanced at Mrs. Sullivan. "Perhaps he did speak to her to that purpose, but Mrs. Sullivan is not without her own powers of persuasion. All I know is that in the end, she was not only not forbidden to come to this house; she was allowed to watch Mr. Sullivan and me in the bedroom, via a two-way mirror. I imagine that when they reunited afterward, things were . . . interesting enough that Mr. Sullivan went along with the new arrangement."

Mrs. Sullivan did not blush, but merely bristled in mutinous silence.

Charlotte felt an uncharacteristic urge to laugh—even she could not have anticipated all the salacious details erupting forth this evening. "How often did this happen?"

"Mostly on evenings when Mr. Sullivan attended a social function by himself. Whitmer would pick up Mrs. Sullivan from the back of her house. They might make a stop outside the function, for Mrs. Sullivan to catch a glimpse of her husband, if she could, before coming here. And then Whitmer would go back and bring Mr. Sullivan when he was done."

"Mr. Sullivan no longer worried about his wife's presence in this house?"

"He told me to keep her in sight. And not to allow her near the study, which he kept locked at all times."

"What about when you and Mr. Sullivan were engaged in . . . what he kept you for?"

A corner of Mrs. Portwine's lips turned up. "Interesting that you should ask. One time, some minutes after we were finished, Mr. Sullivan swore and leaped up. I followed him out and found him downstairs before the door of the study. Mrs. Sullivan was there, too. I judged from their interaction that he'd caught her trying to pick the lock with her hairpin."

Charlotte turned to Mrs. Sullivan. "Do you know how?"

She tilted her chin up. "I've succeeded once or twice."

Charlotte turned back to Mrs. Portwine again. "Surely it would have been a bother to disengage oneself every time, *post coitum*, to rush out and check whether one's wife was picking locks again."

Mrs. Portwine looked as if she was holding back laughter. "I agree. I did wonder what he would do the next time she was in the house. But the next time he was in no hurry. And when he left, I heard him say to Mrs. Sullivan, 'Are you still trying to unlock that door with your hairpin, you stupid woman? I'm going home now. Are you coming or not?'"

Mrs. Sullivan had become completely still, as if she were made of stone.

Charlotte sighed inwardly. "How would you describe his tone, Mrs. Portwine?"

"More amusement than irritation, though there was definitely irritation, too."

"And they left together?"

"They left together."

"When did this particular incident take place?"

Mrs. Portwine thought for a moment. "August. Early August."

"And the previous lock-picking incident?"

"A month before that, I'd say."

Charlotte rose. "With your permission, Mrs. Portwine, I would like to speak to your coachman."

Mrs. Portwine would have summoned Whitmer, but Charlotte said that she'd prefer to speak to him in the coach house, where he would be more comfortable.

As soon as the door of the coach house opened, the horizontally striped carriage was visible. It was, in fact, blue and white, but the blue was deep. Little wonder that in the middle of the night Mr. Bosworth had thought it black and white.

Rather warily, Whitmer confirmed for Charlotte that on the night of Miss Longstead's party, he had driven Mr. Sullivan to 31 Cold Street, and then picked up Mrs. Sullivan and brought her to the same spot.

"And then?"

Whitmer hesitated.

"You may answer Miss Holmes truthfully," said Mrs. Portwine.

Whitmer hesitated one more moment. "Mrs. Sullivan got out. She tried the front door of number 33, then she climbed over the garden gate between number 31 and number 33."

Tenacious, to say the least, Mrs. Portwine had said of Mrs. Sullivan. What did Mrs. Sullivan herself think of all the time and energy she had expended on her husband, a man no one else cared for? "Do you recall what time that was?"

"I can't be sure. Quarter to midnight, maybe."

With a small beckoning gesture of her hand, Charlotte indicated for him to continue.

Whitmer scratched the side of his neck. "After she went in, I drove twice around the garden. When I came around the second time, she came out of number 33 from the front door."

Which she hadn't been able to get into earlier.

"She asked me to bring her back here," continued Whitmer. "So I did."

Charlotte glanced at Mrs. Portwine, who nodded in confirmation. "I can't remember what time Mrs. Sullivan got here, but it would have been before one in the morning."

"Pray carry on, Mr. Whitmer," said Charlotte.

Whitmer scratched the other side of his neck. "I drove back to Cascade Lane, a few streets over from Cold Street. A little before two someone from the house came and said carriages had been called because the fog was getting bad. I went behind the others so I could park farther away on the street: Mr. Sullivan didn't mind being seen occasionally in this carriage, but he didn't want to be too obvious about it either.

"I waited. But all the other carriages drove off and he never did come out of the house. I didn't know what to make of it. I waited until the lights shut off in number 31 and then I drove round the garden a few times, looking for him. When I still didn't see him, I came back here, thinking maybe he went back to his own house in someone else's carriage."

He glanced at Mrs. Portwine again.

"You may carry on," she said.

"Yes, mum. When I reported this to Mrs. Portwine, she shrugged, but Mrs. Sullivan was worried. She said we ought to go back to Cold Street. Mrs. Portwine said that was rubbish. She said that Mrs. Sullivan should go home because if she went any later, she'd get lost in that fog.

"Mrs. Sullivan, after she got into the carriage, still wanted to go to Cold Street. I was worried about Mr. Sullivan myself, but the fog was getting too thick and no one ought to be abroad. So I said I had to do what Mrs. Portwine told me and took her home. And that was all I did that night."

I told him that God would punish him in the form of a wrathful husband that he had wronged, Mrs. Sullivan had said to Charlotte at their first meeting. But had she ever truly believed that anything would happen to him? Despite his disappearance in the wake of the party, when the police had come knocking the next morning, had she been any less dumbfounded?

As the two women traversed the rear garden in the direction of the house, Charlotte said, with a backward glance, "Your carriage is very distinctive, Mrs. Portwine. Did you wish it painted like that?"

Mrs. Portwine snorted, but there was barely a ripple to her voice as she said, "Mr. Sullivan enjoyed small cruelties. The carriage was painted according to, or I should say, against the preference of his incumbent mistress. If she was the sort who preferred to flaunt the fact that she was a rich man's mistress, then she received a staid black carriage, without even a bit of gold trimming. If she, like me, would rather not be known, upon first glance, as a kept woman, a flamboyant pattern it was then.

"Because of my friendship with Mrs. Calloway, his previous mistress, I was acquainted with his inclination to inflict such humiliations. Since I couldn't completely disguise the fact that I preferred not to advertise my fallen-woman status, I made it known to him that I disliked blue stripes intensely. Lo and behold I got blue-and-white stripes."

With great force, Mrs. Portwine kicked a pebble out of her way. "I like blue stripes. I especially like blue-and-white stripes. But still I would have given anything to scrub them off that carriage."

Back in Mrs. Portwine's drawing room, Mrs. Sullivan was still in the same chair, hunkered low, a bundle of gloomy black crape.

"Mrs. Sullivan, may I ask you a few more questions?" said Charlotte.

"I believe there's something that needs my attention in the kitchen," said Mrs. Portwine, her sense of discretion unimpeachable. "Do please excuse me for a minute."

"Surely, Miss Holmes," said Mrs. Sullivan dully, "your prurient curiosity should have been more than satisfied."

Mrs. Portwine's tea gown had a sack back that floated most elegantly behind her. Charlotte followed its progress, planning a dazzling tea gown of her own. The wrapper would need to be red or bright purple. No, even better, pink. She'd look wonderful in pink.

Only after Mrs. Portwine had gone did she turn to Mrs. Sullivan. "I remain curious about less prurient matters. For example, I am very interested in seeing you work the lock on the study in this house."

"You—what?"

"Your husband is no more. Who is to stop you from trying your lock-picking talents on that particular door?"

Mrs. Sullivan sat up straighter, only to slump again. "But he must have already removed whatever he didn't want me to see."

"Maybe, but you might find other things in there."

Mrs. Sullivan blinked—and shot out of her chair.

The study was on the ground floor. Its door had a solid brass knob with oriental motifs in bas-relief and a keyhole underneath, the whole mounted on a heavy-looking backplate. But the door was also secured with a substantial padlock.

Mrs. Sullivan pulled a few pins out of her coiffure and set to work on the padlock.

"You've had plenty of experience," said Charlotte after a moment. She herself had spent significant hours at this exact activity, albeit with better tools and under the guidance of a master practitioner.

"The books he allowed me to read were too tedious—much more fun to try to find out what he's hiding from me," said Mrs. Sullivan with two pins held between her lips, her syllables somewhat squashed. "But maybe if I'd read those books, his soul wouldn't be headed straight for, well, you know where."

Charlotte was not interested in Mr. Sullivan's fate in the afterlife, if such a thing indeed existed. "What do you enjoy reading?"

Mrs. Sullivan shrugged. "Many things. At one point we had every published volume of the ninth edition of the Britannica. And then one day he cleared them all out of the house, while I was still in the middle of the entry about Madame de la Live d'Épinay."

Charlotte's attention perked up. "Why do you suppose that was the case?"

"He said too much education wasn't good for a woman." Mrs. Sullivan made a dismissive sound. "I think he just wanted to frustrate me. He put locks on things for the same reason."

"You don't think he had anything to hide?"

Mrs. Sullivan went completely still. Then, she pulled a different pin from her lips and went on with her lock-picking, as if that moment had never happened. "Of course he had something to hide. I'd rather believe that he was playing lovers' games with me, but I doubt he cared enough to put that much effort into foiling me."

"Did you take up reading the small notices because he had an interest in them?"

"You were the one who put the notice about the carriage in the paper, weren't you?" Mrs. Sullivan put her ear on the padlock. "They don't offer much challenge anymore, the small notices. Hardly anyone thinks to devise real ciphers. One can only decode so many Caesar ciphers before they become as tasteless as old bread."

The padlock popped open.

"Well done," said Charlotte.

Mrs. Sullivan turned around, looking surprised—almost flustered—at the compliment. She cleared her throat. "That's the easy part—Mr. Sullivan liked padlocks. I'm not sure I can work the lock mechanism on the door itself."

"You don't need to. Mrs. Portwine graciously allowed me to borrow something from the housekeeper," said Charlotte, taking out a ring of keys from her reticule.

Mrs. Sullivan stared at them as if they were the best Christmas present she would ever receive.

Charlotte opened the door. Mrs. Sullivan rushed in and immediately began to open drawers on the large mahogany desk. Her face fell to find them unlocked—and mostly empty.

The leather-bound volume Charlotte took off the shelf did not have any of its pages cut. She checked a different book from a different shelf, the same. A third book, still uncut.

Mrs. Sullivan, meanwhile, had discovered an unopened box of Cuban cigars, as well as a loaded revolver and a box of cartridges. Charlotte pulled open the glass door on the top half of a display cabinet and inspected the decanter of whisky that had been thoughtfully placed inside.

"Did Mr. Sullivan enjoy his cigars and whisky?"

"As much as any other man," muttered Mrs. Sullivan, who was now on her knees, peering at the drawers.

Charlotte felt under the shelves, examined the cabinets, and even looked inside the grate. When she was satisfied that these locations held no other secrets, she approached the desk, the top of which held a marble inkstand, a blotting paper holder, and a copy of *Paradise Lost* by John Milton.

Unlike the books on the shelves, the pages of this volume had been cut, every last one.

"Was Mr. Sullivan interested in poetry? Or metaphysics?"

"One time I saw him read Shakespeare—First Folio," said Mrs. Sullivan, as she perused every square inch of the desk. "But when I asked him about his favorite plays, he said Shakespeare made his head ache. I even came across him with an open Bible in his hand on a few occasions—and he grew no closer to God. So who knows why he read Milton."

A movement outside the window caught Charlotte's eye. She had told Miss Redmayne to go home, as it was cold and she didn't want the young woman perched on the driver's box for too long. But now Mrs. Watson's carriage was back, driven by her coachman, Lawson.

And there was a passenger inside.

She turned back to Mrs. Sullivan. "Allow me."

She removed all the drawers for a closer look. None had false bottoms. She lit a pocket lantern and shone its light inside the gaping cavities where the drawers had been.

On the right side of the desk, at the very back, the bottom seemed a little thicker. She reached in. Her hand discerned a piece of wood a quarter inch thick, placed along the back panel. It was little more than an inch in width, and exactly as long as the cavity was wide.

She tried to move it, but it remained firmly in place. A few seconds later, she felt a depression on top of this small plank. Hooking two fingers inside the depression, she pulled.

A thudding noise came from the other side of the desk.

The small plank must have been dovetailed into the bottom of the back panel. With the plank removed, the back panel had dropped down.

Mrs. Sullivan, who had been crouched beside Charlotte, leaped up for a look. Charlotte followed her.

On the other side of the desk, a hidden drawer had been revealed. Mrs. Sullivan pulled it open.

Only the left side of the drawer was occupied: four thick envelopes. Mrs. Sullivan's eyes rounded as she opened one envelope. "This must be—this must be—"

Charlotte took it from her and fanned out the crisp banknotes. "A thousand pounds."

The next envelope held five thousand dollars, the near equivalent of one thousand pounds. And the remaining two envelopes proved to contain a thousand pounds in francs and marks, respectively.

"Is . . . is this why he didn't want me to come in here?"

Charlotte did not answer, but took the hidden drawer's dimensions with a measuring tape.

"What am I to do with all this money?" murmured Mrs. Sullivan.

"Leave what you owe Mrs. Portwine for today's visit on the desk and take the rest, of course—I doubt this money will be mentioned in Mr. Sullivan's will."

Mrs. Sullivan hesitated only slightly before doing as Charlotte suggested, setting a generous amount on the desk—likely far more than Mrs. Portwine's fees—before tucking the envelopes into her reticule.

Charlotte examined the desk again. Only when she was sure it had given up all its secrets did she and Mrs. Sullivan return it to its original state.

Mrs. Sullivan peered at Charlotte, her expression unusually diffident. "Will you accompany me back to my house, Miss Holmes? I don't know that I feel safe traveling across London with this much cash."

"My carriage is outside; I will see you home. But before that, I have a few more questions."

Mrs. Sullivan sighed. "I'll tell you what I did that night. Mr. Sullivan told me that Miss Longstead's coming-out party would be a circus. He said that he'd sent a note to Inspector Treadles and that the inspector would go into number 33, see how his wife conducts herself in his absence, and fly into a rage. But it wouldn't stop there. Mr. Sullivan anticipated that Inspector Treadles would then march into the party, make a nasty scene, ruin Miss Longstead's night, and forever rupture relations not just between himself and his wife but between his wife and Mr. Longstead.

"Mr. Sullivan lied as easily as he breathed and I didn't really believe him. But such was what passed for excitement in my life." Mrs. Sullivan pushed her lips to one side, an expression of forlorn resignation. "Besides, he'd never promised anything of the sort before, an actual scandal. I went to Cold Street with bloomers underneath my skirt, so I could climb over the garden gate if I had to.

"Which I did, when the front door of number 33 proved to be locked. But the back door was open. It was dark inside the house. I groped my way from floor to floor, hoping for an open room with windows that would give me a good vantage point.

"All the rooms were locked. I came back down to the ground floor, where the windows didn't face those of number 31 directly. But even with an oblique view, I saw that Mr. Sullivan had lied to me again. He said Mrs. Treadles fancied him. But when he approached her, she couldn't get away fast enough."

The toe of her boot dug into the large Aubusson carpet that covered most of the study. Her voice became barely audible. "He was an awful person. But I still wanted someone, besides me, to care about him. To like him a little, at least."

Her fingers plucked at the black crape of her mourning reticule. "I left via the front door, because I wasn't going to climb the gate again. Whitmer drove me here. But later, well past two o'clock, when Whitmer came back alone, I wondered whether Mr. Sullivan hadn't told me *some* truth after all. What if he had indeed summoned Inspector Treadles? What if, instead of turning his wrath on his wife or Mr. Longstead, Inspector Treadles had gone after the true culprit?

"I wanted to go back to Cold Street but Whitmer said it was too dangerous and took me home. I fretted and paced. I never imagined that my husband would be dead—I thought he'd be lying on a pavement, hurt and bleeding, after a solid beating from Inspector Treadles. But I couldn't go out and get him in the fog, so I took some laudanum and went to sleep. And, well, you know the rest."

She tried to give an insouciant toss of her head, but only looked like a child pretending not to care.

"If I may ask," said Charlotte, "as you left number 33, did you close the front door behind you or did you leave it open?"

"I closed it. Carefully pulled it shut." She plucked at her reticule some more. "Can we leave now? Or do you still have other questions?"

Charlotte gazed at her a moment. "Are you all right, Mrs. Sullivan?"

Mrs. Sullivan laughed as her eyes filled with tears. "I don't know. Even with all his lies and cruelty—perhaps particularly because of them—he was the center of gravity in my life. I revolved around him as the moon does around the Earth. What happens to the moon when the Earth is no more?"

Charlotte closed the distance between them and pulled the drawstring of Mrs. Sullivan's reticule into a tight knot. "My understanding of physics is very shallow, but I imagine the moon will continue to fly through space, and eventually settle into its own orbit around the sun. Now shall we find our hostess and bid her good night? It's time we delivered you home, Mrs. Sullivan."

Nineteen

Charlotte had expected to see Lord Ingram. Still, her heart leaped at the sight of him standing beside Mrs. Watson's town coach, his posture straight and perfect, a slight smile about his lips. He did not let his hand linger on hers as he helped her into the carriage; all the same, heat vaulted up from her gloved fingers.

They had been apart for less than twenty-four hours. There was, therefore, no reason for her to react so extravagantly. But how could she mind, when those extravagant reactions were also so pleasurable?

The ride, beyond initial introductions between Mrs. Sullivan and Lord Ingram, and the latter's murmurs of condolences, was silent.

At her own front door, Mrs. Sullivan turned around and waved to Charlotte, still in the carriage, and Lord Ingram, who stood by the carriage door, having helped Mrs. Sullivan descend a moment earlier. They both inclined their heads.

When he climbed back inside, he did not immediately approach Charlotte—not with the carriage curtains still open.

The coach left the curb. He closed one curtain. And Charlotte's heart leaped again.

But she did not let herself get carried away. "What was marriage like for you?"

He stilled, obviously not having expected that question. "You observed it, didn't you?"

"I have made my observations, yes. But I've never heard your thoughts on the matter, except once, shortly after your honeymoon."

"Ah, when I was still in thrall to the wondrous newness of it all—and even recommended marriage to you, of all people." He had been reaching toward the other curtain, but now he dropped his hand to his seat. "Why are you asking the question *now*?"

She had delved too deeply into Mrs. Sullivan's marriage today. Yet with regard to his, she had often felt as if she stood on the street in front of a shuttered house, not getting any glimpses inside except on the rarest of occasions, when a window was accidentally left open.

"I have—" She stopped, surprised by how reluctant she was to make this confession. "I have long wished to know. But it's only recently that you've become forthcoming."

His brow lifted, as if he, too, was taken aback by her admission. His thumb slid back and forth across the dark velvet of the carriage seat.

It was an intrusive question. He would be within his rights not to answer. And yet, as seconds dripped past, she felt her stomach tighten at the prospect of his refusal.

"In those years when my wife and I were estranged, I thought very little of our marriage," he said quietly. "What was the point? The mistake had already been made. The situation was permanent. My main concern was for the children, who needed to be shielded from the worst aspects of a marriage gone bitter.

"But after Lady Ingram left, after I learned the full extent of what she did while we still lived under the same roof . . ." He looked at her. "You can probably guess where my mind went."

She exhaled, relieved that he chose to trust her, after all. And she did indeed know where his mind had gone. "To your own culpability in the matter."

"To how much damage I'd inadvertently inflicted upon her." He turned his face to the window. "For a long time, I saw myself as her knight in shining armor. But given that her parents allowed her no choice except to marry a rich man, to her I was but her buyer and everything that happened between us, a transaction. Even after the rupture of our marriage, when I no longer demanded her affection, she remained dependent on my support, entirely aware that I was seen as a saint, and she, a heartless opportunist."

Silence. But in the silence she heard something else. A tentativeness approaching nerves.

"What is it?" she asked.

He turned back to face her, but his gaze was in the vicinity of her knees. He raised it slowly, as if with difficulty. "Have I—have I ever inflicted damage on you?"

She stared at him—the question was entirely unforeseen. *Had* he inflicted damage upon her?

"No," she said after a minute. "You were an education in humanity, not a source of damage."

He blinked—and laughed. "I was *what?*"

"I'd always thought that a quintessential aspect of being human—possibly the most quintessential aspect—lay in dealing with what one wanted but could not have. For years I believed I would not have that problem, because all I wanted was independence and I saw a clear path to it.

"Then you asked for Lady Ingram's hand and married her. And I became human. Now I, too, wanted something I couldn't have. It was . . . an instruction in pain. But that was merely the pain of being alive and being human."

They passed a street lamp, and its light traveled across the wonder and compassion on his face. She remembered that she had never brought up the subject before with anyone, least of all him.

She looked out the window at the approach of another lamppost. "I should ask the same question of you—perhaps I should have asked it long ago. Have I inflicted damage on *you?*"

He laughed softly. "I used to believe so. I had a great fear of being wrong, especially before others. And more than anyone else, you pointed out my errors. It took me years to learn that the burning sensation I used to feel was not my soul being crushed, but simply the abrasion of my overweening pride."

Silence. A silence like snowfall, pure and crystalline.

She pulled down the remaining carriage curtains and patted the spot next to her.

He placed his hand over his heart. "My, a Christmas miracle."

And came to sit beside her.

As Charlotte alit before 31 Cold Street, someone pushed open the garden gate and stepped onto the pavement.

Miss Hendricks.

Who noticed Charlotte and stopped dead.

Charlotte indicated to Lord Ingram that he should wait for her and approached Miss Hendricks, who glanced apprehensively toward Lord Ingram, even though he took himself a good thirty feet away.

"Miss Hendricks," said Charlotte in a low voice. "You must never worry that we would put your reputation or your employment at risk. Our sole aim is to find out what happened to Mr. Longstead, not to disrupt anyone else's life."

"Thank you," said Miss Hendricks in a small voice.

"I hope that a certain misunderstanding has been cleared up between you and a certain someone."

At this, Miss Hendricks bit her lower lip, as if trying to stop herself from smiling. "Yes, thank you very much. In fact—in fact, I was on my way to the postbox at the corner. I've written you a note. I'll give it to you now."

When she had disappeared back into the garden, presumably to make her way back to her employer's house, Charlotte opened the envelope and read it in the light of the lantern hanging from Mrs. Watson's carriage.

Dear Miss Holmes,

At the request of a friend, I am writing with information that I hope will be helpful.

On the night in question, I did step into the house in question. Perhaps I was awakened by the sound of fireworks, which have been a sporadic nuisance in the district of late. Perhaps it was simply my own nerves—I was due to take my charges to their cousin's birthday party fifty miles away and I have never been a confident traveler.

In any case, by the time I got up to have a drink of water and take a look outside—my bedroom faces the garden—it was half past one. My eyes fell on a certain house diagonally opposite. To my astonishment I saw someone enter.

You know enough of my circumstances to guess at my dismay. I am not sure what made me decide to have a look myself, despite the danger presented by a party in full swing in the house next door. But I dressed, slipped out, and crossed the garden.

Upon my arrival I found the door of that house unlocked. I was in the middle of the dining room when I kicked something. I knelt down and found it by feel. There was no mistaking the shape of a decorative comb, one studded with what I thought at the time to be paste gems.

I need not describe for you everything that went through my mind. I stood in place for a minute or two, my ears ringing. And then I left as quickly as I could.

Thanks to your intercession, I learned earlier this afternoon that the truth was not the catastrophe I had feared. Our mutual acquaintance asked me to tell you what I could of that night, which account I already gave above.

I am afraid it is a very meager narrative, but the discovery of the jeweled comb was such a shock that I did not notice anything else amiss with the house. But perhaps it might be useful for you to know, though I am almost certain you would have already heard it from other sources, of Mr. Sullivan's interest in number 33.

My late father served under the governor-in-chief of British West Africa, and I was born in Freetown and lived there until I was orphaned here—cold, wet England—to live with distant relations.

Not long after I came to work in my current position, I met Miss Longstead, sitting on a bench in the garden, reading a travelogue of West Africa. We struck up a conversation and were astonished to realize that her mother and I had once known each other, as her mother, the daughter of a missionary, had also spent her childhood in Freetown.

For that reason I know Miss Longstead rather better than the average governess might know the young lady of a neighboring house. And for that reason I paid attention, when I happened to be letting myself into the garden gate on a Sunday afternoon either late in July or early in August of this past summer and saw the Sullivans leaving the Longstead house.

Having had to fend for myself since I was seventeen, I developed a keen sense of self-preservation. I did not know Mr. Sullivan, but I immediately recognized him as the sort of man who would have tried to take advantage of me, had I been younger.

Later that same afternoon I came across Miss Longstead in the communal garden and asked her about this man, as the Longsteads did not entertain often or receive many callers. She told me that he was a cousin, one whom thankfully she only had to see a few times a year.

I felt better knowing that she need not be subject to a great deal of this man's company. Which made me all the more alarmed when I saw him the very next day, walking into the garden from the back door of number 33, in the company of someone who appeared to be a letting agent.

Miss Longstead was away at a lecture that afternoon. When I saw her again, she told me that her uncle would no longer put up number 33 for let. I was relieved and decided not to say anything about what I had seen. It was good enough for me, as long as Mr. Sullivan did not move in next door.

I do not know whether there is any connection between Mr. Sullivan's visit to number 33 and his eventual death there. It seems terribly tenuous, yet also too much of a coincidence.

I hope it will be of some use to you.

> *Yours truly,*
> *Ada Hendricks*

P.S. When I began this letter, I was determined to make it anonymous and to refer to everything only in the most vague terms. But that obviously changed in the writing. There is so much to identify me there is no use withholding my name. Do please burn after reading.

P.P.S. It still frightens me how close my friend and I both came to danger that night.

P.P.P.S. I hope you will find the true culprit. Mr. Longstead was a good man.

Miss Longstead and Charlotte held each other's hands for a brief moment. Sometimes friendship needed years to establish; and sometimes the bond took hold in an instant of great trust, as it had the evening before, between the two young women. Miss Longstead then turned and greeted Lord Ingram more formally.

Charlotte explained that Lord Ingram needed to leave soon and asked that he be allowed to take with him the mourning brooch from Mr. Longstead's study. Miss Longstead, nonplussed by her request, nevertheless granted it. She took Charlotte, who knew the exact location of the item, up to the study. A few minutes later they were back in the drawing room.

Lord Ingram, the brooch in hand, looked toward Charlotte. She inclined her head. The investigation had entered dangerous waters, but they had to sail full speed ahead—and avoid both Charybdis and Scylla. He returned the nod, bade Miss Longstead good night, and saw himself out.

Miss Longstead gazed another moment at the door through which he had disappeared, as if still puzzled by the speed with which the mourning brooch had been gathered and handed over, before she shifted her attention to Charlotte. "Miss Holmes, please don't tell me you've been working since when Mrs. Coltrane saw you this morning."

Charlotte blew out a breath. "I started my day well before that and I'm afraid my work still isn't done yet."

The hours had fled all too quickly. She still didn't have her hands on any evidence that could change Inspector Treadles's fate. But she hoped to change that. Very soon.

"You must be hungry and tired," said Miss Longstead. Behind her glasses, her green eyes were bloodshot but kind. "Let me ring for a plate of sandwiches for you. And please, sit down."

Charlotte took her seat but Miss Longstead didn't. "I just remembered that there is something I wanted to show you. Let me go fetch it."

She returned as the food she had asked for was brought in. Charlotte, though her stomach nearly gurgled at the sight of the sandwiches, took the letter Miss Longstead handed her.

"Last night, when I came across a condolence letter from my friend Miss Yates, I remembered that I had spoken to her exactly four dances after I returned to the house," explained Miss Longstead. "Since I felt bad about not being able to supply you even an approximation of the time I saw the woman enter number 33, and since Miss Yates always seems to know exactly when something happens, I wrote her and asked if *she* remembered when I spoke to her. This is her reply."

The letter read:

My Dear Louise,

It is no bother at all. In fact, I do remember when we spoke as someone behind me had just asked for the time. It was five to one. I hope that will be of some use.

I'm afraid I wept when I read what you wrote about finding the Christmas present from your uncle among the detritus in the studio at number 33. It made me remember that at the party I had in fact jokingly asked him whether he'd already done the gift-hiding this year. He had answered, with a twinkle in his eyes, that of course he had.

I wanted to know if it was a clever hiding place. He chuckled and said that it would either be the last place you looked—or the first. But that I was, of course, not to breathe a word to you. I further inquired whether there would be a cipher waiting when you did find your present and he declared ruefully that alas, he'd given up on making you adore cryptography as he did and would henceforth only give presents that furnished you undiluted pleasure.

Again, I'm sorry that such a horrible thing happened. And that you were robbed of the joy of discovering your present under better circumstances. Do remember his love for you always and the happiness he derived from your companionship all these years.

Yours faithfully,
Eliza

"This is helpful indeed," said Charlotte.

Though perhaps not for the reason that Miss Longstead had originally intended, solely to establish the time she saw the woman— Mrs. Treadles—enter number 33.

Charlotte gave the letter back to Miss Longstead and picked up a prawn salad finger sandwich. "I believe you mentioned the intruder to your uncle *after* you spoke with Miss Yates?"

"That is correct."

The sandwich was refreshing and slightly piquant. Charlotte allowed herself a moment to enjoy the very great pleasure of eating something delicious while she was hungry. "Miss Longstead, are you acquainted with Miss Hendricks, who lives and works at 48 Rengate Street?"

Miss Longstead's eyes widened with both surprise and pleasure.

"Do you also know her? Lovely woman. She and my mother had known each other when they were young girls in Freetown, in Sierra Leone."

"I learned from her that she had seen Mr. Sullivan tour number 33 in the company of a letting agent in the later parts of last summer, a day after the Sullivans called on this house. Before she could speak to you about it, you told her that the house was no longer for let, so she didn't mention Mr. Sullivan's visit, knowing that for you he was a distasteful subject."

The bafflement on Miss Longstead's face turned into unease. "That is strange. He never expressed any interest in number 33. Is Miss Hendricks sure that she saw him and not a different man?"

Charlotte nodded and picked up another finger sandwich, this one with a filling of potted chicken, the paste smooth and buttery.

"Do excuse me for a second." Miss Longstead left and returned shortly with a diary. She riffled through it. "I'm not the most consistent diarist. But——" Her page-turning came to a halt. "I see I did put down an entry toward the very end of July. Ah, I remember now, my uncle issued an invitation to all his nephews who were in London at the time. He never said so but it was not long after young Mr. Cousins's passing and I believe he was more affected than he'd thought he would be, seeing his best friend's only son cut down in the prime of life."

She moved her index finger down the page, her eyes searching. "Yes, the subject did come up. Mrs. Sullivan mentioned that she'd heard our tenants had moved out. She wanted to know if we would let the house out again. And my uncle said no, he'd decided against it, and was in fact about to instruct his solicitor to relate that decision to the letting agent."

She looked up. "And Miss Hendricks said Mr. Sullivan was there the very next day?"

"She was very certain about that. Did he know of your love for the attic studio, by any chance?"

"I should say not—neither Uncle nor I ever brought it up in front of him." Slowly, Miss Longstead closed her diary. "What could he have *possibly* wanted with the place?"

"Not to live there, that we can be sure of," said Charlotte. "Would you mind showing me to Mr. Longstead's study again? I still need to locate his keys."

The mountainous miscellany that used to be on top of Mr. Longstead's desk were still spread out on old newspaper on the floor.

Miss Longstead tapped an index finger on her temple. "I used to know where he kept everything, but it has been a good few years since I dug through this study for unexpected treasures. Let me think. No, he never did keep keys in the desk. They were usually . . ."

She picked her way to the shelves and carefully extracted an unused vase—it must have once marked the end of a row of books, but was now nearly swallowed by surrounding volumes, reminding Charlotte of a half-exposed fossil in a slab of a coastal shale. Miss Longstead shook it. It made no sound. Taking care not to step on the vast archaeological proliferation on the floor, she tiptoed along the shelves and excavated another vase. It, too, was empty.

The fifth vase she found clanged with her motion. She tipped it over and a set of keys dropped into her palm. "Here they are."

She weaved back to the door and handed the lot to Charlotte. Charlotte inspected the four keys, especially the two brass ones with long shanks and elaborate bows: There were bits of white powder stuck on them. She took a sniff. Peppermint?

Mr. Sealy, the chemist, had said that Mr. Longstead enjoyed peppermint lozenges once in a while. And when Charlotte had examined the physical evidence the police had gathered, one pocket of his evening coat had contained a residue that smelled of peppermint.

"Do you remember whether your uncle carried those keys on his person on the night of the dance?"

Miss Longstead took off her glasses and wiped the lenses with a handkerchief. "He checked on me when I was getting ready. Mrs.

Coltrane was with me at the time. She took one look at him and cried, 'Good gracious, Mr. Longstead, whatever have you got in your pocket? It's making your jacket appear lumpy.' And he chuckled and said that he would get rid of it presently."

They rang for Mrs. Coltrane. When the housekeeper arrived outside the study, she confirmed Miss Longstead's account. "Yes, that did happen, but I can't tell you what was in his pocket. He was standing half in the passage, which wasn't lit as brightly as Miss Longstead's room."

Mrs. Coltrane returned to her duties. Charlotte said to her hostess, "I have one more request to make of you, Miss Longstead. Would you show me the places in this house where you and Mr. Longstead have hidden Christmas presents in the past?"

Miss Longstead's eyes widened behind the glasses she'd just put on again. "All of them? Whatever for?"

"There is a chance that your uncle hid something in this house. Given that he expected you to search the house top to bottom for your present, what are the only places where you wouldn't have searched?"

"The places we already used before! Because we were supposed to find new hiding places every year and he always played fair." Miss Longstead's eyes lit. But just as quickly, excitement faded from her beautiful face, replaced by a fearful dismay. "But what could he have hidden? Do you think . . . do you believe . . . ?"

"Fortunately or unfortunately, I do think the item he hid had something to do with his murder. How directly the two were related, I don't know. But if we find it, I'd like to take it with me for closer study."

Miss Longstead braced a hand on the wall, but she needed only a moment to master herself. Opening her diary to a blank page at the back, she took out a pencil from a pocket, and wrote quickly.

"We spent three Christmases in town. So there are six past hiding places we've used before," she said tightly, tearing out the list she'd made.

They started in the study itself, in one of the lower cabinets, then proceeded to the unused nursery. There Miss Longstead looked under a cot and then inside a desk in the small schoolroom. Next, they stopped by Miss Longstead's floor. In her sitting room, she crouched down and opened the doors under an occasional table, to a space filled with notebooks and various boxes.

"I'm afraid I hang on to odds and ends, too," said Miss Longstead, her eyes once again darkened by grief. "Except I keep them in boxes, not heaps."

Charlotte got down on her knees and peered in. Her heart thudded. "That box in the back—do you recognize it? The one with ivory inlays."

Miss Longstead looked again. "Good gracious." She pulled out the box. "The pattern on the outside looks like another one of my boxes but the size is completely different."

The thickness—or the relative flatness of the box—was what had caught Charlotte's attention. A keyhole was visible but when Miss Longstead lifted the lid tentatively, it gave: The box was not locked.

Miss Longstead, with the lid open half an inch, glanced at Charlotte.

Charlotte nodded.

Miss Longstead bit her lower lip and opened the box the rest of the way. Inside lay a collection of small notebooks, about four inches wide and five inches long. She flipped through one. Its pages were pasted with newspaper clippings and telegrams.

She turned to Charlotte again, her eyes disquiet, her voice hushed. "But these are—these are all in code."

Charlotte let out a long, shaky breath. "As I said earlier, Miss Longstead, I will need your permission to take this box and its contents with me. For closer study—much closer study."

Twenty

It was nearly nine when Charlotte returned to Mrs. Watson's: 31 Cold Street had *not* been her last stop of the evening.

"Lord Ingram sent a message that you'd be late, so we decided to postpone dinner until you returned," said Miss Redmayne, pressing a cup of hot cocoa into her hands. "Mr. Bloom, Lord Ingram's expert, left not a quarter hour ago. He studied those accounts for a good five hours. And . . . he came and went by the back door—said Lord Ingram asked him to do so."

Charlotte shifted her gaze to Mrs. Watson on the settee, holding tightly on to a glass of whisky.

"We drove all over Reading this afternoon, searching for someone who could tell us something—anything—about the renovation and outfitting of the Cousins factory," she said, her voice disembodied. "The main contractor of record, a Mr. Fox, had listed an address in an industrial district. When we got there, we found only a place that sold crushed stones. We made inquiries with the owner of the place and in the surrounding area—and learned that Mr. Fox's office had been a temporary one, there only for the duration of the work.

"That in and of itself is not unusual. But this Mr. Fox, apparently, did not hire any local workers—and that did not go unnoticed. Most of his crew, it appeared, didn't speak any English—some of those we talked to today thought they were Germans; others thought they were Poles. They came. They did the work. And then they left."

Mrs. Watson took a healthy draught of her whisky. "The efficiency and precision of the operation bothers me more than a little. This was the first of the three factories acquired and renovated during the younger Mr. Cousins's tenure. They didn't entrust the work to anyone they'd used before. And this Mr. Fox, whom they did choose, was as quick as an assassin. Normally that would be good, except the end result Mr. Fox delivered, at least according to Mr. Bloom, was far less than what it should have been."

"And Mr. Fox was responsible for overseeing the modernization of all three factories?" asked Charlotte.

"Yes," said Mrs. Watson. "Because the crew worked so fast, there was an elevated rate of injuries on site. We spoke to a physician who saw to some of the men who were brought in. He studied medicine in Zurich and considers himself fluent in German. He said that one man, who died after an entire day in a delirium, kept saying in German, though in an accent he couldn't quite place, 'Two more, then Sheffield, then home.'"

She frowned—and did not smooth her forehead this time.

Miss Redmayne crossed the room to the sideboard and added a splash of rum to her own hot cocoa. She held out the bottle inquiringly toward Charlotte. Charlotte, who had been standing by the door of the afternoon parlor, joined Miss Redmayne at the sideboard. She didn't lace her cocoa, however, but poured a dram of rum into a small glass and tipped it back.

"In the places you went to, did you ask, Mrs. Watson, whether anyone had come before you to ask the same questions?"

"Are you wondering whether Inspector Treadles had been in Reading ahead of us? We wondered the same," said Mrs. Watson, her brow still furrowed. "But no, no one reported being asked similar questions, at least not anyone we spoke to."

An oppressive silence fell.

Mrs. Watson stared at the remainder of her whisky. Charlotte leaned against the sideboard. She should say a word or two of comfort to Mrs. Watson, but she was tired. And the night, in terms of the work they still had to do, was only beginning.

Miss Redmayne was the first one to speak. "Let me ring for supper. We can all do with a proper meal. And on a full stomach, things never appear quite as bleak."

Charlotte found herself smiling a little. There was a natural valor to the young woman, allied with energy and good sense.

Seeing Miss Redmayne take charge, Mrs. Watson sat up straighter—with a small groan—and set aside her glass. "In that case, let me put away all these letters for Sherlock Holmes."

Charlotte had seen Miss Redmayne convey a considerable heap of letters into the house in the afternoon—the public had responded to Sherlock Holmes's appeal for information on the murders of Mr. Longstead and Mr. Sullivan. The quantity of the missives had doubled, at the very least, in the hours since: The mound on the occasional table before the settee was an epistolary landslide waiting to happen.

"Anything useful?" she asked

"Not yet." Mrs. Watson blew out a breath. "A bit overwhelming, isn't it? It's been a while since we've done this."

Late in autumn, they had left London for a stay in the country, because Livia was to take part in a house party at a nearby estate. Before their departure, announcements had appeared in the papers, informing the public that Sherlock Holmes would be unavailable until further notice.

Since then, they'd investigated a case at Stern Hollow and taken a weeks-long trip to France. The small notices in this morning's papers were the first notification of Sherlock Holmes's return.

"A little odd, after all these weeks," continued Mrs. Watson, "to be back at what we used to do almost every day."

Charlotte's pulse quickened. "Mrs. Watson, do you still keep all the correspondence that has ever come for Sherlock Holmes?"

"Yes. Why—"

Charlotte was already out of the afternoon parlor.

———◆———

The study had once been the late Dr. Watson's domain. To this day, no one else used it regularly and his medical books still took up most of the space on the shelves. But for the enterprise of Sherlock Holmes, detective, and the volume of letters she received, Mrs. Watson had commissioned new storage drawers.

Even though Sherlock Holmes had officially been on a sabbatical, letters still trickled in. Charlotte opened the drawers and took out everything that had arrived after the end of the case at Stern Hollow.

Until then, Inspector Treadles had not asked any questions of his wife about her work, and had been thoroughly divorced from the goings-on at Cousins. Afterward, less so.

The letters had all been opened and read—most likely by Mrs. Watson, possibly by Livia, who had also spent some time in this house during that interval.

Standing before the storage drawers, Charlotte first scanned each letter, then checked the stated location inside against that on the postmark. To her disappointment, there were no mismatches.

Nevertheless, two letters caught her attention.

The penmanship on the two was not similar. One was done in block lettering, the other, a highly awkward script, that of someone who could barely hold a pen—or that of someone right-handed writing with the left hand.

The letters had not been forwarded to Charlotte's attention not because of their handwriting, per se, but because their contents were so transparently unoriginal. The one likely written by its sender's left hand purported to be from a young man who needed help deciphering clues from his beloved concerning what she wanted for a birthday present. The one in block lettering was even more obvious, the writer claiming to be the youngest of three elderly sisters who lived together and had their peace of mind regularly disturbed by seemingly rhythmic noises emanating from the attic.

Sherlock Holmes's first official client had been a young man trying to work out what his beloved wanted for her birthday. Sherlock Holmes's most famous non-murder-related case had been the discovery that a trio of septuagenarian sisters did not have spirits in their attic, communicating via Morse code, but deathwatch beetles making tapping sounds.

Both cases had been referred to in a newspaper article in the past summer, which wondered about what Sherlock Holmes had been doing since his thunderous arrival on the scene, and made the mischievous and perhaps malicious speculation that now his days would mostly be spent reassuring little old ladies about wood-boring insects.

Charlotte had not minded the article at all: It had provided excellent publicity and let people know that Sherlock Holmes was happy to deal with minor domestic cases, not just those the criminality of which shocked an entire city. The women around her, however, had been annoyed on her behalf. Both Mrs. Watson and Livia would have immediately interpreted the intention of the letter-writers as merely to mock Sherlock Holmes.

On the other hand . . .

If this was Inspector Treadles at work, and if he feared prying eyes, it could have been his way of making sure that these two letters were thought of as pranks.

What information had required him to take such care, so that it passed to her and only to her, undetected by any except her?

Should she steam open the gummed seams of the envelopes? Peel off the stamps? Perhaps even run a hot iron over the letters, in case he had written in milk or some other such substance that would darken at the application of heat?

Instead, she glanced again at the letters and headed for a shelf of atlases.

———❊———

Charlotte's emergence from the study coincided with Lord Ingram's arrival. To her inquiring gaze, he nodded solemnly: He had done what she'd asked him to do.

The company sat down to their very late dinner, where it took Charlotte a steaming bowl of mulligatawny soup, several beef-and-potato croquettes, and a modest slice of boiled mutton in caper sauce to give a condensed version of what she had learned this day.

"I can't judge, Miss Holmes, whether you learned a great deal or a great deal of nothing," said Miss Redmayne, sounding honestly baffled. "This case is like an underwater monster from *Twenty Thousand Leagues under the Sea*, full of tentacles that writhe and splash everywhere."

Mrs. Watson shuddered. "I dare say the dissection of the Sullivans' marriage made me feel as if *I've* been embraced by a giant cephalopod."

She pushed a croquette around on her plate. "We saw a few more of those flailing appendages today, between all of us. Does that, in fact, help?"

"To an expert in marine biology," said Lord Ingram, "the view of a single tentacle makes it clear what kind of monster lurks underneath."

As if remembering something, Mrs. Watson leaned forward. "Miss Holmes, Lord Ingram is of the opinion that you already know, with some certainty, what happened the night of the murders. Is—is he correct?"

Charlotte turned toward Lord Ingram—his confidence in her was very gratifying. But her attention was waylaid by the *bûche de Noël* that had been set near him, a splendid concoction, its chocolate buttercream striated to resemble tree bark, adorned with meringue mushrooms and real sprigs of holly. When her gaze finally reached Lord Ingram, he looked as if he were trying not to laugh out loud.

Alas, despite the covetousness she felt toward Madame Gascoigne's latest masterpiece, Charlotte knew that she needed more roughage.

"I have a hypothesis that does not conflict with any known facts," she said, spearing a brussels sprout with her folk, wishing that roughage tasted more like cake. "I believe that this hypothesis has merits, but I don't have enough evidence to present to the police and I don't know that I ever will."

"We are still gathering evidence every day," said Miss Redmayne. "Let's hear this hypothesis."

Charlotte ate her brussels sprout, the taste of which had been greatly enhanced by having been drenched in a lemon-and-parsley butter sauce. "I have been investigating the veracity of Mr. Longstead's appointment book. It's clear he was up to something in the final weeks of his life. I propose that his doings were related to the malfeasance at Cousins Manufacturing and I further propose that Inspector Treadles was assisting him in that endeavor."

"But Mrs. Treadles said that they'd only met twice," Miss Redmayne pointed out.

"That she *knew of*," Mrs. Watson answered for Charlotte. "Mrs. Treadles has been in the dark lately as to her husband's movements."

Charlotte inclined her head at Mrs. Watson. "Precisely. And because Mrs. Treadles doesn't know, and Inspector Treadles refuses to talk, we can't say with complete certainty what Inspector Treadles was doing at 33 Cold Street in the first place. Was he responding to the taunting notice in the papers that questioned his wife's fidelity, or was he there for something else?

"No matter his reasons, the fact is that he walked directly into that house, as did a number of other individuals that night. And this was normally a carefully locked house because two young women spent long stretches of time there by themselves.

"Four people were known to have keys to the back door of number 33. Miss Longstead did not approach number 33 that day. Mrs. Coltrane did at half past six in the evening, but only to check that all the doors were locked. A neighbor's butler also had a key but he assured me that the door was already open when he got there. That leaves Mr. Longstead."

Miss Redmayne whistled softly. Mrs. Watson might have reprimanded her under different circumstances, but Mrs. Watson was too busy setting down her knife and fork and pulling her chair closer to the table.

Charlotte calculated that she needed to ingest at least four more brussels sprouts before she considered herself virtuous enough for *bûche de Noël*. Thankfully, as an adult, she found vegetables increasingly tolerable, sometimes even enjoyable. Alas, not brussels sprouts in particular. Not yet.

"Mr. Longstead's evening jacket had jetted pockets and in one of them there was residue that smelled of peppermint," she continued. "He regularly visited an establishment of pharmaceutical chemists that does a brisk trade in confectionary. They sold peppermint lozenges. A similar powder clung to his set of keys, and his niece reported that, when he looked in on her as she was getting ready, something bulged in his jacket, to the dismay of their housekeeper.

"At this point it would be irresponsible not to conclude that Mr. Longstead had opened the back door of number 33. I further propose that he did it before the party started, so that it wouldn't interfere with his duties as the host. Who would he have opened it for? Everyone else we've spoken to was there illicitly. So he could only have opened the door for either Mr. Sullivan or Inspector Treadles.

"I inquired repeatedly into whether he could have been in league with Mr. Sullivan, and those closest to him repeatedly assured me he was not that kind of person. I was already leaning toward the notion that he opened the door for Inspector Treadles when Mrs. Treadles rushed in here this morning, all distraught, and said that her husband warned her, in no uncertain terms, from looking too deeply into the accounts at Cousins.

"Why would he warn her of such a thing unless he has been look-ing into them himself? And why would he, in the first place, when he didn't even ask any questions about her work for the longest time?

"The simplest explanation for Inspector Treadles's involvement? Mr. Longstead. But he was an engineer, not an accountant. He coun-seled Mrs. Treadles to have greater patience. His involvement with Cousins, even after his return, veered toward minimal. Why did he, out of the blue, develop an interest in Cousins's finances?"

Charlotte popped the next brussels sprout into her mouth, earn-ing her way toward the *bûche de Noël*. But no one else was eating any-more. All eyes regarded her intently, which made her feel obliged to chew more vigorously—and drink from her water goblet to wash everything down faster.

She coughed a little and slapped herself on the sternum. "I believe he found something by accident. I believe he found this."

She had brought her reticule into the dining room, and now she extracted the rosewood-and-ivory-inlay box that she had found at Miss Longstead's and passed it to Mrs. Watson.

Miss Redmayne and Lord Ingram left their seats to stand beside Mrs. Watson. Mrs. Watson had her hand on the lid but hesitated, as if she faced Pandora's box, and by opening it, she risked releasing great infelicity into the world.

"It's only notebooks inside," said Charlotte.

Which Pandora's box could very well have contained, too.

Mrs. Watson lifted the lid. Carefully and with no small reluc-tance, as if she were about to handle a sleeping serpent, she withdrew a small notebook. Miss Redmayne and Lord Ingram followed suit.

"Notice that the contents are in code," said Charlotte. "Each item pasted into those notebooks has a date written beside it. The oldest small notices date from six years ago."

Lord Ingram slowly set down the notebook in his hand. "When you told us about the Sullivans and their arrangement with Mrs.

Portwine, you mentioned that Mr. Sullivan became highly agitated when he realized that Mrs. Sullivan was trying to pick the lock of the study at Mrs. Portwine's. But later, when a similar incident happened, he no longer cared."

Charlotte cut a brussels sprout in two and soaked one resultant half more fully in butter sauce. "Indeed. When Mrs. Sullivan and I found a secret drawer in his study tonight, half of the drawer was empty, and the dimensions of that empty space were almost exactly those of this box. I believe that when Mr. Sullivan learned of the Longsteads' plan to no longer put their spare house up for let, at least not until they departed London, he had the idea to move the box to number 33.

"The Longsteads had not told him that Miss Longstead adored the studio and that it was the reason the house would no longer be advertised for tenancy. To his thinking, 33 Cold Street was perfect for his purposes. It would be vacant for some months, no one would be there, and he could always retrieve his box later, after the Longsteads left town, by booking another visit with the letting agent."

Mrs. Watson frowned. "It couldn't have been that easy to hide a box with the letting agent hovering nearby. This isn't a large box, but to take it out and put it somewhere, all without being seen?"

The butter-drenched half brussels sprout went down rather nicely. "That might explain why the box ended up in the attic. The studio there is the single largest space in the house, but it is two sections connected by a narrow passage. If he could situate himself in one part and the letting agent in the other part, that would have given him enough time to open the door of the storage closet and put this small box into one of the larger boxes of magazines that the previous tenants had left behind."

"The game!" cried Miss Redmayne. "The gift-hiding game the Longsteads played with each other."

Charlotte raised her water goblet in Miss Redmayne's direction.

"Mr. Sullivan's secrets might have remained safe, despite Miss Long-stead's occupancy of the studio, if it hadn't been for Mr. Longstead's search for a hiding place for his present. And what better place than the closet in the studio, right next to where Miss Longstead sat every day?

"This is entirely unsupported by evidence, but I think Mr. Longstead, when he first came across this box, believed it to contain Miss Longstead's gift to him. There is a chance that he took it to a locksmith to get it opened. And there is a further chance that after opening the box, he became even more convinced that it was not only a gift, but a grand gift.

"He'd tried to interest her in cryptography; she never loved it to the same extent he did. But hope springs eternal. It isn't difficult to imagine Mr. Longstead, when faced with this box of ciphers, happily assuming that, unbeknownst to him, his niece had been practicing cryptography on her own and prepared this tremendous surprise."

"Poor Mr. Longstead," murmured Miss Redmayne.

"The poor man," said Mrs. Watson at nearly the same time, shaking her head.

"I don't know when Mr. Longstead's delight turned to something else," said Charlotte. "But if you need further convincing that Inspector Treadles's current predicament is intimately linked to the goings-on at Cousins, remember he told me that what Sherlock Holmes typically did should have been good enough to help him?"

Everyone around the table nodded, in varying degrees of anticipation and apprehension. The gravest expression belonged to Lord Ingram, who knew more than the two ladies.

"Sherlock Holmes typically read his correspondence." Charlotte pulled out the two letters she had singled out and handed them around.

Mrs. Watson scanned the letters. "But these are—these are—what—" she stuttered, bewildered.

Charlotte smiled at her. "More than ever I am grateful for your policy, ma'am, never to toss away anything that comes addressed to Sherlock Holmes. I believe the letters are from Inspector Treadles, who chose the examples of these clients because they had been featured in a newspaper article. And if you look at where the letters were sent from . . ."

Mrs. Watson scrutinized the addresses on the letters and the postmarks on the envelopes. "I don't see any disparities."

"No disparities. But look at the locales themselves, please."

Lord Ingram lifted one envelope. "Headingley. Is that not near Leeds?"

Charlotte nodded. "Likely a part of Leeds itself now, but it probably still has a receiving post office with its own postmark."

Miss Redmayne took the other envelope. "This one is postmarked Sharrow. Where's Sharrow?"

"Sharrow—that's in Sheffield!" Mrs. Watson shot out of her chair. "Inspector Treadles was in *Sheffield*."

In Mrs. Watson's account of what she and Lord Ingram had learned in Reading, the name of this city had passed through the lips of a dying worker, mumbling deliriously in German.

Two more, then Sheffield, then home.

Miss Redmayne rubbed Mrs. Watson's arm gently. Lord Ingram poured a glass of wine for her. While they capably saw to Mrs. Watson, Charlotte finished all the remaining brussels sprouts on her plate.

The butter sauce had made them far more palatable. But alas, how virtuous could she feel, when she ate almost as much butter as she did brussels sprouts?

Mrs. Watson sat down again and drank from the glass Lord Ingram had set before her. The wine brought back some color into her cheeks, but the fine lines around the corners of her eyes deepened with her frown. "I'm more than willing to believe that Mr. Longstead and Inspector Treadles joined forces to scrutinize irregularities at Cousins—Mr. Longstead could have done far worse for a partner in such an endeavor. Not to mention that Inspector Treadles, having recently reconciled with his wife, probably yearned to render her a service, to make up for months of neglect. But why didn't they say anything to her?"

Lord Ingram poured a glass of wine for himself. "A trick of the masculine mind, I'm afraid. They probably thought it chivalrous not to involve her in something that could prove dangerous."

But that she had been so much in the dark had made life an order of a magnitude more difficult for her, when everything had gone wrong on the night of the party.

"I, too, am willing to accept the premise that Mr. Longstead and Inspector Treadles worked together and that Mr. Longstead opened the back door to number 33 that night," declared Miss Redmayne. "But if he was waiting for Inspector Treadles, how did he end up dead, together with Mr. Sullivan? And what was Mr. Sullivan doing there in the first place?"

Charlotte was eyeing the *bûche de Noël* again. Lord Ingram pushed it directly in front of her. She smiled at the cake, though she really wished to bat her eyelashes at him.

He said to Miss Redmayne, "While Miss Charlotte is busy with her one true love, I can venture a guess to your question."

Miss Redmayne laughed. Mrs. Watson chortled. Charlotte cut herself a slice of the cake. Ah, how scrumptious.

Lord Ingram studied her a moment, his gaze full of amusement and affection. But as he turned back to address the other ladies, all lightheartedness left his expression.

"When we began this investigation, we thought Mrs. Treadles in desperate straits. But the greater part of her current predicament arose from her husband's arrest. Knowing what we do now, if we go back to the beginning of that night, before anyone ended up dead, we can see that it was *Mr. Sullivan* in water so hot it was practically boiling, Mr. Sullivan who knowingly and recklessly abused the power of his office.

"His had not been subtle crimes. They had not come to light, because he oversaw all reports and the younger Mr. Cousins had been lazy and incurious. But then Mrs. Treadles took over the company and she wanted to know all about its inner workings. She was intelligent and tenacious, *and* she was entirely within her rights in making those inquiries.

"This must have terrified him. By exploiting the other men's hesitation about and hostility toward having a woman preside over their work, he could only stall her for so long. She was, after all, the owner of the company. Even a threat against her marriage was no long-term guarantee. He had to do something else.

"And I'm guessing . . ." He glanced at Charlotte. "Perhaps Mr. Sullivan didn't lie entirely to his wife. Perhaps he did intend for something to disrupt the party—ruin it, even—to distress Miss Longstead, infuriate her uncle, and cause a rift between Mr. Longstead and Mrs. Treadles."

Charlotte, her mouth full of airy cake and decadent crème Chantilly, nodded in agreement. "Mmm."

"But for Mr. Sullivan to cause that uproar at the party, wouldn't he need Inspector Treadles to be there?" asked Miss Redmayne. "But how could he be sure, even if he had put that provocative taunt in the papers, that Inspector Treadles would indeed arrive on the scene? And how could he anticipate what the inspector would do, even if he were there?"

She sucked in a breath. "Oh, so that's why he had Inspector Treadles's service revolver stolen!"

"Precisely," said Lord Ingram. "He didn't need Inspector Treadles to be there, only something that was unmistakably and identifiably his. As for what exactly he intended to do, I believe he planned to fire the revolver into number 31."

"What?" Mrs. Watson exclaimed.

"Not to injure anyone, at least not intentionally, but to cause a panic. He would make sure to leave the firearm behind and get out of number 33 quickly. And then, even better, once he was back in number 31, he could organize a sortie with a few other intrepid gentlemen to see what was going on. And when this cavalcade of heroes arrived next door, what should they find but Inspector Treadles's still warm revolver."

"Leading them to conclude that Inspector Treadles, who must have fled the scene, had been responsible for the shot. A diabolical plan," marveled Miss Redmayne. "But how did Mr. Sullivan plan to get into number 33 in the first place? He had no idea that the back door would be open."

Lord Ingram turned toward Charlotte and raised a brow. His timing was perfect: She'd just finished the small slice of cake she'd allotted herself and was looking mournfully at her empty plate.

"My guess is that he was prepared to shoot the door," she said, "taking advantage of the sporadic going-off of the fireworks, which he would have read about in the news. If everything went according to plan, Inspector Treadles would be blamed for damages to the door, too.

"And because he didn't expect Inspector Treadles at the party, he would have considered it a boon, when he spied Mrs. Treadles headed for number 33. If he could corner Mrs. Treadles for a moment and transgress upon her, then Mrs. Treadles, at least, would be much more likely to believe that her husband had actually fired the shot into number 31, dooming Miss Longstead's party.

"And Mrs. Treadles, after all, was the one Mr. Sullivan needed to evict from Cousins, as soon as possible. To his thinking a scandal of such a magnitude should have made Mrs. Treadles much too ashamed to leave her house again. And who knows, he might have succeeded. One reason Mrs. Treadles did manage to at last take over the reins at Cousins was because Mr. Sullivan was no longer there to oppose her. Imagine if he had still been there, with Inspector Treadles arrested as a jealous husband who would fire into a crowded gathering."

The room was silent.

"Is it terrible to be glad that a relatively young man is dead?" asked Miss Redmayne, her voice soft.

"Yes," said Charlotte, "but not as terrible as no one taking this man to account while he lived."

This time, it was Mrs. Watson who gently rubbed Miss Redmayne's arm. Miss Redmayne smiled radiantly at her aunt—her mother—and turned to Charlotte again. "But everything did not go according to Mr. Sullivan's plan. He never expected to be interrupted while he accosted Mrs. Treadles, for example. And we know now that he never caught the manservant who did the interrupting. What did he do after that?"

"I believe he went back to the party," said Charlotte. "Lord Ingram interviewed a number of guests. Miss Longstead's friend, Miss Elizabeth Yates, told him that during the party she had spoken to a cousin of Miss Longstead named Mr. Proctor. But when Lord Ingram tracked down Mr. Proctor, he couldn't recall any such conversation.

"After I left Miss Longstead's this evening, I stopped by Miss Yates's, and asked her to look at a photograph of Mr. Sullivan, whom she immediately identified as Mr. Proctor, Miss Longstead's cousin."

Miss Redmayne made a disgusted noise. "So he spoke to Miss Longstead's friend under false pretenses? Was there anything this man didn't stoop to?"

"Where his self-interest was concerned? Apparently not," said Lord Ingram. "Now if I recall correctly, Miss Yates and this 'Mr. Proctor' discussed Miss Longstead's studio, of all things. Was that how—"

Miss Redmayne almost knocked over a water goblet in her excitement. "My goodness. *My goodness!* Yes, that must be it. That must be how Mr. Sullivan learned that his secret was no longer safe."

She recalled herself and grinned sheepishly at Lord Ingram. "My lord, forgive me for interrupting and do please continue."

Lord Ingram waved away her apology with a smile. "You were absolutely correct in your conjecture. Miss Yates told me that she had been chatting with Mr. Longstead about the annual hiding of the Christmas present. No sooner had Mr. Longstead moved on to speak with another guest than the so-called Mr. Proctor appeared by her side. He claimed that he enjoyed this annual tradition between uncle and niece, and always liked to speculate as to where this year's presents would be hidden. He asked Miss Yates whether she had any ideas. And Miss Yates, not suspecting either deceit or treachery, said she thought there was a good chance that Mr. Longstead hid the present he had prepared in the studio at number 33, given that it was a new location not available in previous years.

"Mr. Sullivan left then. Not long after, Miss Longstead came and sat with her for a bit. I'm guessing this was the chat Miss Yates said happened at five minutes to one?"

Charlotte nodded. "Which tells me that Mr. Sullivan went into number 33, for the second time, somewhere between quarter to one and five minutes to one. Mr. Longstead, somewhat after one, because Miss Longstead spoke to him after she spoke to Miss Yates."

"Was Mr. Sullivan the one who shot open the door to Miss Longstead's studio and destroyed everything inside?" Miss Redmayne asked, holding on to Mrs. Watson's arm.

"When he couldn't find his precious box, he vented his rage on Miss Longstead's equipment and supplies. And I guess he'd just left the studio, headed downstairs, when Mr. Longstead arrived."

Mrs. Watson put her hand over Miss Redmayne's. "You don't mean to imply that Mr. Sullivan killed Mr. Longstead and then himself?"

"No, not at all. I meant to say that Mr. Sullivan fatally wounded Mr. Longstead and the latter, in his final moments, rallied and shot Mr. Sullivan in return."

Silence. The fire in the grate produced only an occasional soft hiss. Outside the window, the night was clear, and the stars were out, small, cold lights upon a dark vastness. Charlotte felt her body sinking into her chair, and her brain, following suit, drifting into a pleasant lethargy.

She straightened with a start. No, she couldn't let herself become sleepy yet.

"Given the way the two dead men had fallen, I can see that Mr. Sullivan shot Mr. Longstead first," said Lord Ingram, his hands tracing movements in the air. "And then Mr. Longstead threw his walking stick at Mr. Sullivan, probably not expecting that it would knock the revolver loose from his hand. But the revolver landed close to Mr. Longstead. He made a desperate lunge from where he lay, grabbed the revolver, and shot Mr. Sullivan, who also came for the gun. The shot struck the center of Mr. Sullivan's forehead and sent him staggering backward, cracking the back of his head as he fell against the windowsill."

Mrs. Watson, whose hands were around her own throat, slowly set them down. "But why? The box might contain evidence of Mr. Sullivan's crimes. But surely, even if he thought that Mr. Longstead had found him out, would he not have tried to see whether Mr. Longstead would be amenable to not turning him over to the police?"

"And did Mr. Longstead know it was him? Would he have invited him to Miss Longstead's party if he'd known?" asked Miss Redmayne.

"I think Mr. Longstead had suspicions, but nothing concrete. After all, Mr. Sullivan's name was not on or in the box," answered Miss Charlotte. "Or perhaps he did suspect, but didn't want to alarm Mr. Sullivan by suddenly cutting off contact. As for why Mr. Sullivan didn't think to negotiate with Mr. Longstead, perhaps he knew that what he had done was unforgivable. At least where Mr. Longstead was concerned."

Her gaze fell on the box that still sat in front of Mrs. Watson, an unremarkable thing, a most innocuous-looking object . . .

"What about Inspector Treadles?" asked Miss Redmayne, taking Mrs. Watson's hands into her own. "When did he finally arrive?"

"I'm not sure. We have inferred that he was assailed just outside the garden, where Lord Ingram and I found buttons from his coat.

The attack would have redoubled his determination to get into the garden—and into number 33."

She imagined Inspector Treadles racing across the garden toward what he believed to be a safe haven, a house the back door of which he had asked to be left open. Thankfully it was indeed open. He locked it behind himself and collapsed against it, panting.

As his pounding heart slowed, he gritted his teeth against the pain in his arm. The knife had slashed through three layers of sleeves. The smell of his own blood filled his nostrils.

And it was dark, so dark. Fog writhed outside. No light from number 31 fell into the empty house.

"He groped his way up the stairs. He knew of Miss Longstead's experiments in the attic studio. He knew that there he would be able to find some alcohol with which to clean his wound. And perhaps some cloth for bandaging. And then, an unhappy discovery—followed by a nasty surprise."

The jumble of smells in the staircase, growing stronger with each step, floral, spicy, spirituous, a bombardment of the senses. Did his eyes water? Did his throat grow irritated? Did a sense of foreboding crawl over his skin, only to be confirmed as his boots crunched over broken glass?

But what was that sound from below? Someone was coming into the house!

"He had locked the back door. But he couldn't have guessed that Mrs. Sullivan had departed from the front door and left it unlocked. His assailant walked in. The attic door was damaged and unlockable. He went down. And further down. Was the door to the chief bedroom open? Did a bit of streetlamp light come through despite the fog? Perhaps."

He slipped inside and locked the door. He could vaguely make out the hulking outlines of a bed. He moved forward, tripped, and landed in a spread of viscous liquid. The destruction in the attic had left his sense of smell temporarily overwhelmed, but he didn't need the pungency of blood to know that something horrific had taken place.

"I can only imagine how gruesome the discovery must have been," said Charlotte softly. "In that room he was not a dispassionate investigator arriving in broad daylight, but an already fearful man stumbling over dead bodies in the dark."

The pocket lantern on the windowsill, most likely brought by Mr. Sullivan, who'd had plans that night, would have already burned out. Did Inspector Treadles's hands shake as he struck a match? Did sounds of fright and distress burst from his throat when the feeble light illuminated crimson pools and crumpled bodies?

Was he able to make any sense of what he saw? Or was he too busy locking the door and taking up a defensive position behind the bed? He did also stumble upon his own service revolver, an ominous find, the significance of which he did not have the frame of mind to ponder, not with the assailant prowling just beyond the door.

"Then something happened that he didn't expect—the arrival of the police. Mrs. Sullivan had closed the front door, even if she couldn't lock it. But the assailant might have left it open. It's possible that he was still in the house when the police entered, but managed to slip out when the two bobbies were preoccupied with Inspector Treadles."

Charlotte took a long draught from her water goblet. "And the rest we know—or at least have eyewitness accounts."

"Poor Inspector Treadles," murmured Miss Redmayne.

Lord Ingram stared at a spot on the table.

Mrs. Watson patted her face with a handkerchief, as if she'd broken out in a cold sweat, in spite of the pleasant temperature inside the dining room. "Poor Inspector Treadles indeed. But who was that assailant and what did he want with Inspector Treadles?"

"To know that, I shall first need to do something about the box of ciphers." Charlotte rubbed her temples. "Have I ever told anyone that I'd already wearied of ciphers by the time I was sixteen?"

Twenty-one

Mr. Mears brought in coffee. But coffee was not enough for Charlotte to survive another late night; she must have cake, plenty of cake.

She took a fortifying bite—sponge roll, whipped cream filling, chocolate ganache. In a few hours, even this heavenly combination would pale before her need for sleep. But at the moment, the idea of staying awake long enough to merit an extra slice or two still excited her.

Mrs. Watson, Miss Redmayne, and Lord Ingram were already working, each dealing with a notebook from the box. Small notices from the papers often used fairly straightforward substitution ciphers. To be on the safe side, Lord Ingram had given the ladies a quick tutorial on transposition ciphers, which also appeared regularly.

Charlotte allowed herself another bite of cake and opened the notebook before her, the one with the earliest dates. In the carriage, as it drove through puddles of streetlamp light, she'd scanned the contents of the box and felt only dread at the thought of more ciphers, possibly convoluted and tortuous ones. But now, paging through this first notebook, pasted neatly with small notices in code and an occasional telegram, she was instead enveloped in a strange and strangely chilling sense of familiarity.

From the dates themselves.

The small notices were weekly—and punctual: In this notebook, which covered almost two years, only once did a notice appear one day later than usual.

She had come across something of the sort before.

Or had she come across this exact thing?

Lord Ingram looked up. "Holmes."

His voice was tight, an expression of incipient—or was it already outright—dismay on his face. "Look at these."

He had the most recent notebook, the small notices at the front of which were coded, but the last ten or twelve were not. They were in plain text—and they were biblical verses.

Posted every ten days.

"What is it?" asked Mrs. Watson, always sensitive to mood shifts in a room.

Lord Ingram waited for Charlotte. Charlotte's fingers tightened around her pencil, but she nodded. He handed his notebook to Mrs. Watson, who gasped as she saw the small notices inside.

"But these are—these were—"

She stopped, as if unable to continue.

These had been notices disseminated to Moriarty's minions, each notice pointing to a single word in a book, which acted as the key to any messages encoded during that period, until a new key was posted.

Miss Redmayne took the notebook from her aunt's hands and even her perpetually sunny expression darkened. "Moriarty. So Mr. Sullivan wasn't only lining his own pockets, he was lining Moriarty's pockets, too?"

All the while keeping this meticulous record.

On second thought, that he had done so didn't seem quite as odd. Mr. Sullivan's two leading characteristics had been malice and spite. He had likely viewed the rewards he had received from being Moriarty's minion as being less than commensurate with the work he had put in and the risks he had assumed.

This record then was something he had believed he could hold over Moriarty. Or, if not that, then at least must have felt that its exposure would have led to some headaches for his master, whom he'd probably never met.

Charlotte turned to Lord Ingram. "Can you tell me what Inspector Treadles knows about Moriarty?"

The inspector had been involved in several cases that had Moriarty looming in the background, but he would have only heard the name directly during the investigation at Stern Hollow.

The notebook with the biblical verses pasted inside had returned to Lord Ingram's hands. He leafed through its pages. "After I was released from police custody, before I took the children home to Stern Hollow, I met with the inspector for this specific purpose. He wanted to know more about Moriarty—mainly, whether Moriarty had anything to do with a case from this past summer that saw the death of a man named de Lacey, but he was convinced the body had been that of a random bloke, identified as de Lacey so that the case would close."

He shut the notebook and pushed it into the table, as if wishing it would never open again. "I agreed with Inspector Treadles that de Lacey was not dead—de Lacey was but a nom de guerre, taken on by whoever acted as Moriarty's chief lieutenant in England. I also told him to be extremely cautious if he was ever to find himself dealing with Moriarty or his underlings again."

"Did you tell him about the small notices in the papers? That they pointed to keys necessary to work out ciphers used by Moriarty's people?"

"No. He never asked me about them, and I don't believe his case in the summer concerned them either."

"If Inspector Treadles didn't know about them, then Mr. Longstead must have succeeded in deciphering at least some of the telegrams pasted in here on his own," said Miss Redmayne. "I wonder which ones."

"My guess would be the ones sent at the end of summer," said Charlotte. "The biblical verses are already in plain text, and the cipher key each verse points to is simply the title of the book it comes from. If Mr. Longstead realized that the telegrams from that time were wheatstone ciphers, then it wouldn't have been too hard for him to work them out. My lord, would you explain to the ladies how wheatstone ciphers work?"

While Lord Ingram did that, with the ladies taking notes, Charlotte copied the coded texts of the telegrams—there had been a number of them in the latter half of the summer. After she'd checked to make sure she had not made any mistakes, she distributed a telegram to each person at the table, with its key already written on the same sheet of paper.

The decoded cables, in chronological order, read:

If nothing else will put him off, you may proceed.

Expect cancer remedy delivered by tomorrow afternoon.

I trust you will have a plan for the sister.

Things are unstable here. Fend for yourself until further notice.

"Does 'the sister' refer to Mrs. Treadles?" asked Mrs. Watson, her voice low and raspy. "If so, would that make the 'he' in the first cable her brother, the younger Mr. Cousins? Did he know something?"

He had been such an uninspired man of business. Had he at last sensed something wrong at Cousins? Or was he *told*?

Charlotte's stomach tightened. She remembered her half brother, Mr. Myron Finch, who had once been Moriarty's cryptographer. Mr. Finch had been in London during that time. Had he tried to alert the owner of Cousins that his company had been hollowed out from underneath him?

She tapped her fingertips on the table. It had been too long since she last heard from Mr. Finch. Was he still safe? And if not . . .

Lord Ingram was watching her—she rarely fidgeted; her finger-tapping would have struck him as highly uncharacteristic. She took her hand off the table and gave him a nod to show that she was all right.

Mrs. Watson's voice remained strained. "It's easy for us to deduce the identity of those referred to here, because we already know it was Mr. Sullivan who received these cables and that he'd been up to no good at Cousins. How would Mr. Longstead have been able to tell what these telegrams were about?"

"He would have recognized the dates, or at least one of the dates," said Charlotte. "Miss Longstead said that her uncle was more affected by Mr. Barnaby Cousins's passing than he'd let on. The younger Mr. Cousins was the only son of his beloved friend, gone in the blink of an eye. And this third cable, the one about having a plan for the sister, was sent on the day he died."

"What was the cancer remedy for?" asked Miss Redmayne. "What did the younger Mr. Cousins die of?"

Her questions were usually launched with vigor and relish. This time her shoulders were hunched and she did not look at anyone, as if she already dreaded the answer.

"The papers said malaria." Charlotte was almost as reluctant to unearth anything else. She took a deep breath. "Mr. Longstead, by the way, inquired after cancer remedies at Sealy and Worcester, a pharmaceutical chemists' shop. He also spoke to Dr. Motley, the Cousins family's physician, around that time."

She now believed that when Mr. Longstead had written "physician" in his appointment book, he had not meant Dr. Ralston, his own physician, but Dr. Motley. What he'd recorded as meetings at Cousins had been his condolence call on Mrs. Cousins and his tête-à-têtes with Inspector Treadles, who was also inextricably related to both the Cousins clan and the Cousins enterprise. All those sessions at the "Reading Room of the British Library" would have been the time he'd spent deciphering the codes—or otherwise working on his own to find out the truth. And his visits to the chemist's had not involved pharmaceutical chemists, but *analytical* chemists.

Mrs. Watson pinched the bridge of her nose. "It just occurred to me. We know how almost everything fits together. But much of the evidence we have relates to Moriarty. I don't dare turn it over to the police, which would inform Moriarty of how much we know. I also don't trust that the police, with the exception of Inspector Treadles, wouldn't consider us fabulists. After all, who would corroborate the existence of Moriarty? The Marbletons and Lady Ingram were the only ones who would utter that name in public and even if they come forward, we cannot count on their testimony to carry any weight."

This time Miss Redmayne did look at Charlotte, her expression filled with foreboding, but also an anxious hope. Mrs. Watson's expression was more restrained, as if afraid to let herself hope. Lord Ingram, on the other hand, nodded, as much in promise as in encouragement.

Tell me what you plan to do, and I will help bring it to fruition.

"Is there still coffee left?" said Charlotte, resigning herself to a sleepless night. "And is anyone in the mood for a gamble?"

⁕

After a late-night call on Mrs. Treadles for her permission, Sherlock Holmes's representatives each visited a major London newspaper, with just enough time left before composition must be finalized, for their story to appear in the morning editions.

They told as much of that story as they dared: Mr. Sullivan's outrageous theft from Cousins Manufacturing; Mr. Longstead's audacious campaign to bring the truth to light; Inspector Treadles's tenacious investigation, after Mr. Longstead asked for his assistance.

Mr. Sullivan realized his peril before Mr. Longstead and Inspector Treadles could finish their work. He stole the inspector's service revolver, intending to fire it into a crowded party and then leave it behind as evidence in 33 Cold Street, to damage the standing of both Inspector Treadles at Scotland Yard and Mrs. Treadles at Cousins Manufacturing.

At this point in the telling, representatives of Sherlock Holmes took dramatic license. They painted a stirring picture of a confrontation no living person witnessed, of a revolver-waving, foaming-at-the-mouth Mr. Sullivan, and a calm, heroic Mr. Longstead. Mr.

Sullivan shot Mr. Longstead in the chest. Mr. Longstead, with a desperate rally in the final moments of his laudable life, put a bullet through Mr. Sullivan's forehead.

And Inspector Treadles, arriving late for his secret rendezvous with Mr. Longstead—because of Mr. Sullivan's goons, of course—stumbled upon the scene, an unfortunate bystander in this deadly quarrel between uncle and nephew, between the forces of good and evil.

With Charlotte still in her Sherrinford Holmes camouflage—she, Mrs. Watson, and Miss Redmayne had all performed their roles disguised as men—she and Lord Ingram made an unconscionably early call upon Lord Ingram's friend, an analytical chemist to whom Lord Ingram had entrusted the sample Charlotte had given him the evening before.

The bleary-eyed chemist handed Lord Ingram an envelope, along with a raspy "I'm sorry."

Lord Ingram's fingers tightened on the envelope. Charlotte briefly closed her eyes. Those two words told them everything they needed to know.

He saw her back to Mrs. Watson's, then left to catch an early train leaving from Euston station. Charlotte stripped off one disguise for another—the severe, monochromatic jacket-and-skirt sets were no less theatrical costumes than the large-bellied suits she donned to play Sherrinford Holmes—and called on Mrs. Treadles again.

She'd warned Mrs. Treadles that she might return in the morning. But the hour was so ungodly that Mrs. Treadles, though risen, had yet to dress.

"Please be ready to leave your house as soon as possible," said Charlotte, stifling a yawn behind her hand. The coffee must have at last worn off.

The next thing she knew, Mrs. Treadles, now ready, was shaking her awake. Charlotte, her eyes still mostly closed, shuffled out after her.

"You still haven't told me where we are headed," Mrs. Treadles pointed out as they approached the carriage.

"Mrs. Cousins's," mumbled Charlotte.

She dragged herself up inside the coach and fell onto a seat. Barely thirty seconds later—or so it seemed—Mrs. Treadles was again telling her to wake up. They had arrived at Mrs. Cousins's house.

As they were shown into the small drawing room, Charlotte saw herself in a mirror. She looked a fright, puffy and hollow-eyed. Good gracious, was her skin sagging a little? She was getting far too old for this staying-awake-all-night business. Sherlock Holmes, consulting detective, would only take minor cases of very little danger and imposition, until her countenance had fully recovered its usual radiance and elasticity.

Mrs. Cousins arrived shortly in a black wrapper worn over a voluminous nightgown, a maid with a tea tray following in her wake. "Alice, Miss Holmes, is everything all right?"

"I apologize for calling on you at this unreasonable hour," said Charlotte, feeling more awake now, not only from her two quick naps, but also from the unhappy nature of her task.

She had given plenty of bad news in the course of her work as Sherlock Holmes. She was better suited than most for the undertaking, her natural detachment shielding her from the worst impact of shattering her clients' illusions and breaking their hearts. All the same, she wished that she were elsewhere, still asleep.

"I do have news for the two of you and I'm afraid it's not joyful news."

All color drained from Mrs. Treadles's face. "You don't mean to say that the inspector—that my husband—"

"No, Mrs. Treadles. More than ever I am convinced of Inspector Treadles's innocence."

Charlotte gave an abbreviated account of what happened the night of the party, omitting all references to Mr. Woodhollow and Miss Hendricks. Mrs. Treadles listened and clutched at Mrs. Cousins's arm. At one point, Mrs. Cousins dropped the teaspoon in her hand and didn't even notice.

"When I presented this version of events to my colleagues last night, however, I still had an incomplete picture. Mrs. Cousins, I understand that your husband died of malaria?"

Mrs. Cousins took a moment to respond to this apparent non sequitur. "He did."

"Did he not take quinine?"

Mrs. Cousins sighed. "This was a recurrence for him—he first suffered a malarial attack after visiting Italy on his grand tour. Unfortunately, he developed a deep hatred of quinine from that experience, as it caused him to suffer from terrible tinnitus. Not to mention he was always convinced that he was developing cancer—my mother-in-law died of a tumor and that left a deep mark on him.

"Afterward, Dr. Motley concluded that he probably didn't have enough doses—hiding the tablets under his tongue and then spitting them out later, that sort of thing—because he detested quinine. And because he believed he wasn't suffering from malaria, but cancer."

Mrs. Treadles wrapped an arm around Mrs. Cousins's shoulders. Mrs. Cousins gave Mrs. Treadles's hand a squeeze.

Charlotte steeled herself. "I don't know whether Mr. Cousins took all his proper doses, Mrs. Cousins, but I do know that in his case it wouldn't have mattered."

"What—" Mrs. Cousins looked toward Mrs. Treadles, whose expression of incomprehension mirrored her own. An incomprehension that was rapidly becoming dread. "What do you mean, Miss Holmes?"

"Someone took advantage of your husband's fear of cancer and gave him some so-called cancer remedy. During this latest malarial attack, he took it. There is no such thing as an effective cancer remedy, and some contain small amounts of toxic substances. But this one was much worse, because most of it was arsenic."

Mrs. Cousins screamed, a short, sharp wail that hung in the air. Her mouth remained open, but mutely, as if her voice had been excised.

"No!" shouted Mrs. Treadles. She shot to her feet. "*No!*"

Charlotte proffered the results from the chemical analyst. "Mr. Longstead suspected this. That was the reason he called on you,

Mrs. Cousins, and obtained from you a piece of mourning jewelry. Because it contained your husband's hair. And Mr. Barnaby Cousins passed away recently enough that his hair could still be analyzed for the presence of arsenic."

Neither woman came forward to take the envelope from Charlotte. They only stared at her, as if they'd been turned into stone.

Charlotte exhaled. "I'm afraid it gets worse."

— ❈ —

"May I help you, miss?" asked the postal clerk, looking expectantly at Livia.

Livia's hands tightened around her package. Her throat was dry, her face was warm, yet her heart beat at a strangely sluggish pace, as if she—or it—were still asleep.

"This parcel," she said hoarsely. "And twenty penny stamps, please."

Lady Holmes had decided, in the end, that going to London with Livia was better than staying home. They were changing trains, and Livia had decided to send off her manuscript in the little post office just outside the railway station.

Once she stopped deceiving herself, everything became blindingly obvious.

Charlotte had told her that Mr. Marbleton was most likely Moriarty's son. Livia had never wanted to believe it. But it could not be a coincidence that right after they had burgled a Moriarty stronghold, Mr. Marbleton had abruptly bid her farewell.

Something had forced his hand.

Someone.

Moriarty.

That name alone chilled her lungs. She didn't know how she could possibly get news to Mr. Marbleton, but he had always said that no matter where he found himself, he would be on the lookout for her Sherlock Holmes stories.

If her story was published in a popular magazine, tens of thousands of copies would be printed and distributed to all corners of the world, making it that much more likely that one would find its way into his hands. And when he held it, this story that he had first met as a seedling, he would know that she had not forgotten him.

"Anything else, miss?" asked the clerk, handing over her stamps.

"Thank you, that will be all for now," she said.

For now.

"Happy Christmas, miss."

She gazed upon the clerk's ordinary but sincere face, and imagined that he was someone else's Mr. Marbleton. "A very happy Christmas to you, too."

Today and always.

Charlotte had needed to speak to Mrs. Treadles and Mrs. Cousins as early as possible in the day because she had wanted them to learn the worst from her, before they heard rumors from other sources. By the time she left Mrs. Cousins's house, paperboys were already abroad. An hour after early editions blanketed the city, a petty criminal confessed to stealing Inspector Treadles's service revolver on Mr. Sullivan's orders.

Two hours later, another petty criminal came forward to admit that he had entered 33 Cold Street—because the front door was open—on the night in question, hoping to steal something, only to see two dead bodies inside. When Inspector Treadles entered, claiming to be the police, the miscreant was so terrified of being arrested for murders he hadn't committed, he'd shoved the inspector from behind into the room and claimed he'd kill him, too! And then he fled after Inspector Treadles very logically locked the door against him.

Charlotte chuckled at the creativity of this account.

At noon she met Lord Ingram's train at Euston Station.

Since Inspector Treadles had given actual addresses in his two seemingly ersatz letters to Sherlock Holmes, Lord Ingram had decided to see those spots for himself. He reported that at the address in Sheffield, he'd had an excellent view of a large, modern factory, but had been far away enough that even had Moriarty's minions seized the letter, they might not have connected it to the factory, which had a large plaque that proudly declared, *De Lacey Industries*.

In nearby Leeds, the address Inspector Treadles had furnished had led Lord Ingram to an even larger, even more modern-looking factory, also under the umbrella of De Lacey Industries. Moriarty didn't simply siphon funds from Cousins—and likely other companies—he used the money to build himself new sources of wealth.

Charlotte remembered the photographic plates she had taken from Moriarty's stronghold outside Paris. There had been factories among those images. How many of them had been built this way, by draining the lifeblood of law-abiding enterprises?

She didn't want to dwell too long on the subject, so she turned to kissing Lord Ingram instead, a much more pleasant way to pass time.

Their carriage drew up before Scotland Yard. Lord Ingram planned to inform Inspector Treadles that Sherlock Holmes had done what Sherlock Holmes typically did. Then he was going to see about securing the inspector's release as soon as possible.

"What are you doing later in the afternoon?" asked Charlotte rather hopefully.

She didn't have a tea gown yet but he could still come by for tea—and for what the tea gown was infamous for.

"It's Christmas Eve, Holmes. I need to find my children some presents."

How could she argue with that? But she quickly brightened again. "Are you going to give me a Christmas present this year?"

They rarely gave each other presents.

He raised a brow. "Are you going to give me one?"

"Yes."

He stared at her for a moment. "Good heavens, I'm getting a hot water bottle cozy, am I not? The one you were knitting right in front of me in Paris!"

She laughed at his expression of mock horror. Her cheek in her hand, she said, "But I haven't the slightest idea what you are going to give me."

"The exact equivalent of a hot water bottle cozy," he warned darkly. "The exact equivalent, Holmes."

She was still smiling when the carriage drove away.

❖

Charlotte had barely reached home when a message from Lord Ingram caught up with her. The coup de grâce had come: a mountain of evidence of Mr. Sullivan's evildoing had been delivered to Scotland Yard, evidence not only of brazen embezzlement, not only of the poisoning of the younger Mr. Cousins, but of the murder of Mr. Mortimer Cousins two-and-half years ago, by ethylene glycol in the latter's tea, when it looked as if he might recover from his severe pneumonia.

It was as Charlotte had thought. Just as Mr. Sullivan had accumulated evidence to someday point an accusatory finger at Moriarty, Moriarty's lieutenants, who read his spiteful nature like an open book, had also secretly prepared to abandon him to the long arm of the law. After all, no investigation along that line could be allowed to proceed beyond Mr. Sullivan himself, certainly not when it might cause the confiscation of De Lacey Industries factories.

The news of the older Mr. Cousins's murder did not surprise Charlotte. In the morning, after she had informed Mrs. Treadles and Mrs. Cousins of the abundant presence of arsenic in Mr. Barnaby Cousins's hair, she had also warned them that she couldn't be sure Mr. Mortimer Cousins hadn't met a similar fate.

It didn't surprise her, but it still saddened her. She thought of the night of the party, of uncle and nephew in that room, Mr. Sullivan with Inspector Treadles's revolver pointed at Mr. Longstead's chest. Had he told Mr. Longstead everything then, so that he could revel in Mr. Longstead's pain and outrage before he killed him? And Mr. Longstead, an old man who had never been in robust health, how had he, with a bullet in his chest, found the strength to throw his walking stick at Mr. Longstead, scramble for the fallen revolver, and fire?

Because Mr. Sullivan had been responsible, at least in part, for the death of his beloved friend and partner, who had put Mr. Long-stead's health above profits, and had loved him more than a brother.

Thanks to all the revelations, Inspector Treadles was released just before sunset, in what the evening editions would hail as a Christmas miracle. Both Lord Ingram and Sherrinford Holmes were there to greet him, alongside his lovely and faithful wife.

"Thank you," said Inspector Treadles to Charlotte. "I knew that if anyone could save me, it would be you. Thank you."

She shook his hand. "I'm glad to see you restored to us, Inspector. Brilliant work, by the way."

"High praise indeed, to have that come from a representative of Sherlock Holmes."

"It is the opinion of Sherlock Holmes himself. There was never any need to doubt yourself."

Inspector Treadles blinked rapidly, shook his head, and said, his voice breaking, "Thank you again. Thank you always."

He and his wife left arm in arm, like a pair of newlyweds marching past a throng of well-wishers to their brand-new future. At their carriage, they turned around and waved. Mrs. Treadles reached up and touched her husband's cheek. He had tears in his eyes as he caught her hand and pressed a kiss into her gloved palm.

Charlotte remembered Lord Ingram's optimism about them.

Maybe it wasn't always a romantic outlook that caused one to be optimistic. Maybe sometimes it was simply the correct assessment.

She turned to the great romantic in her life. "How was your present hunting this afternoon, Ash?"

"Fruitful, I would say."

She narrowed her eyes. "I still don't know what you intend to give me."

He grinned. "I am beyond astonished."

"But I do know you bought yourself a hot water bottle—no, at least two—just now, so that you can put my present to use."

"And you are right." He laughed. "As you always are."

Epilogue

Dread invaded Robert Treadles. He was dreaming still— dreaming of waking up in his own bed, as he had done every night in his cell. But he was also awake enough to know that he was dreaming, and that the illusions of comfort, safety, and freedom would evaporate the moment he opened his eyes.

Even as his dream self hugged Alice tighter and buried his face in her hair, his thoughts returned to the evening of their second dinner with the Longsteads. After the ladies had departed for the drawing room, leaving only the men at the table, Mr. Longstead had brought out not only a bottle of port, but a notebook.

I found this notebook, and several others like it, in the studio at number 33, he'd stated gravely. *I hope you won't find it far-fetched what I'm about to say, but I—I believe the contents of the notebook has to do with Cousins.*

And so it had begun.

At first Treadles had listened only out of politeness. He'd been incredulous when the older man speculated that Barnaby Cousins, Treadles's late and very much unlamented brother-in-law, had been murdered. But then Mr. Longstead had produced evidence in the form of reports from not one but two analytical chemists, attesting to the presence of arsenic in Barnaby Cousins's hair, which Mr. Longstead had obtained from his widow.

After that Treadles had no choice but to be involved: Whoever had done this to his brother-in-law could do the same to Alice.

Mr. Longstead continued to speak, and it became obvious to Treadles that Alice had told him very little of the opposition she'd experienced at work. But at least her suspicions about the financial health of Cousins, as related by Mr. Longstead, formed the starting point of his investigation.

An information-gathering trip, visiting other factories that had been built by the main contractor who had renovated the Cousins properties, had led him to De Lacey Industries, at the sight of which his alarm grew to the full blare of fog horns.

He could not be sure this de Lacey was the same as Moriarty's chief lieutenant in Britain. But he made sure to notify Sherlock Holmes, however circuitously. And he met with Mr. Longstead to discuss the possible dangers they now faced.

They decided to inform the ladies in their lives after the first of January—let them enjoy Christmas and New Year free from Moriarty's shadow. Mr. Longstead hastened to arrange a debut for his niece, even as he redoubled his efforts to decipher the other small notices and telegrams in the notebooks, to uncover as much evidence as possible.

Treadles undertook another trip, to reconnoiter two other sites that had been worked on by the same main contractor. He'd found yet another De Lacey Industries holding in Manchester, but in Cornwall—he still wasn't sure what he had come across in Cornwall, other than that he'd barely escaped being captured.

He and Mr. Longstead had agreed that they ought to be more careful in meeting each another, but they had also agreed that a rendezvous at 33 Cold Street on the night of Treadles's return to London should be both safe and secretive, even if Mr. Longstead had to slip out of his niece's party. Treadles gave Alice a later date of return—he thought it might be a nice surprise for her to find him already home when she came back from the party.

But on the rail journey back he realized he was being followed. He changed trains rapidly and randomly. This delayed his return by several hours, but he thought he'd at last shaken his pursuer loose.

Only to be accosted a stone's throw from number 33.

The nightmare that had followed . . .

He opened his eyes—no point trying to sleep more—only to see, instead of bare walls and iron bars, a creamy bed canopy and flax-colored bed curtains, three quarters drawn. The air smelled not of the pervasiveness of vomit and other human wastes, but faintly and pleasantly of lavender water and floor wax, of a clean and well-maintained home.

Very carefully he turned his head. So the warmth next to him was also no illusion—Alice truly was in his arms. And he really was in his own bed, a free man once again.

Because of Charlotte Holmes. Bless that woman and every excessive flounce on her skirts.

It felt as if he was dreaming again, to recall his release from Scotland Yard. That lovely, lovely carriage ride home. The renewed grieving for Alice's father and brother, especially her father. The long, long talk they'd had, admitting to everything they'd been too afraid, too ashamed, and too unnerved to tell each other in all the weeks, months, and years before.

He'd felt clean and unburdened afterward, but also scoured raw, almost too shy to meet her eyes. He suspected that she felt the same, which was probably the reason she'd turned the topic to Sherlock Holmes.

"Do you suppose, Robert—I mean have you ever wondered whether there is any evidence, any real evidence, that there is an unwell man inside that bedroom at 18 Upper Baker Street?"

He'd chortled and poured them each a glass of whisky. "Let me tell you what I know, my dearest Alice."

Beside him Alice stirred. She opened her eyes and many of the same emotions he'd experienced just now charged across her face.

From an initial, automatic dismay, to the rush of relief at the realization that his arrest was now behind them and that they were together again.

She turned to him. "Robert, Merry Christmas."

"Merry Christmas to you too, Alice."

She cupped his face. "Today is the first day of the rest of our lives."

She had said this the morning after their wedding. He took her hand, kissed it, and gave the same answer as he had at that time, "Every day is the first day of the rest of our lives."

But this time, he would not forget it.

This time, he would do better.

—❖—

Christmas morning brought with it the lovely surprise of Livia at Charlotte's door.

According to Livia, their mother, having taken a few extra drops of laudanum, was still abed. So she had taken advantage of that and left their lodging house as soon as the place unlocked its doors.

Her arrival was greeted with riotous approval by Mrs. Watson and Miss Redmayne. The four women chatted with vigor and plowed through a large breakfast. Or rather, three of the women chatted with vigor and Charlotte plowed through a large breakfast.

The doorbell rang again. This time, it was Lord Ingram, his children in tow, Miss Lucinda happily informing Mr. Mears that they came to drop off presents on their way to the railway station.

Mrs. Watson's respectability might be questionable, but Miss Redmayne was officially a half sibling to Lord Ingram. Some would still frown upon his visit, but most would laud him as tenderhearted: A rich and striking man enjoyed a great deal of latitude in how he conducted himself.

But even he would come under fire if it became known that he'd exposed his children, especially his daughter, to a fallen woman such as Charlotte Holmes. The children knew her by sight and were too young to be trusted to keep secrets, so Charlotte slipped out of the afternoon parlor before the children came up the stairs.

As did Livia, who also didn't want it to be known that she was at Mrs. Watson's.

They sat for a while with Bernadine, their elder sister who could not take care of herself and whom Charlotte now supported. Then they decamped to the formal morning parlor.

There Charlotte waited for Livia to tell her what she now knew.

Which Livia did, with a long sigh. "Moriarty has Mr. Marbleton, doesn't he?"

It was always only a matter of time before Mr. Marbleton's kindly meant deception failed—and Livia perceived the truth for herself. "I'm afraid so."

Livia buried her hands in the fold of her skirts—it was cold in the morning parlor, where no fire had been laid. "What can we do to free him?"

"I'm not sure yet, but we'll come up with something."

Livia rocked back and forth in her chair. "Will it take years and years?"

Charlotte moved closer and took Livia's hands in her own. "Possibly."

Livia's hands shook. But she said, after a while, with her hands still shaking, "I'm ready for it."

Lord Ingram came and found them a few minutes later. They exchanged greetings. Livia presented him with monogramed handkerchiefs; he gave her a bottle of blue-black ink, the bottle engraved with her initials.

Livia, taking her present, diplomatically absented herself by saying that she would go try it at once.

Lord Ingram wasted no time in kissing Charlotte and Charlotte wasted no time in enjoying it very much.

She then proceeded to give him not one but two hot water bottle cozies. "See, I made one for you that looks almost exactly like my Christmas tree dress—I know how much you adore that. But since you bought an extra hot water bottle, I'm obliged to also give you the one I made for myself. Does it not look like the prettiest Christmas pudding you have ever seen?"

He laughed so hard he had tears in his eyes. "I see now I have no choice but to think of you when I hold my hot water bottles close."

She preened. "Precisely. Now what did you get for me?"

He went outside to the passage and returned with a sizable box, which she recognized immediately as a dress box.

A gentleman not related or married to her should not give her clothes.

Excellent.

Inside the box was a . . . a . . .

She shook the garment open and inspected it from all sides. No doubt about it. An open redingote in a shade of pink that did not exist before the invention of aniline dyes, and an airy white underdress? This was a tea gown, the laciest, ruffliest, most tucked and ruched tea gown she'd ever seen.

"How did you know I wanted one?"

"I didn't. But do you remember propositioning me at Stern Hollow?"

She had laid out the underdress along the back of a padded chair. He ran his hand down its front. Heat streaked down *her* front. "At Stern Hollow I did a lot more than propositioning you."

"Well, *before* we knew you'd be doing more than that, you invited me to come and visit you at your cottage while Mrs. Watson took her afternoon nap. I have been thinking about that invitation ever since. And even a stick-in-the-mud like me knows that ladies wear tea gowns for such occasions."

Was he turning up the hem of the underdress and putting his hand inside? Heat rushed up to her—

She cleared her throat. "So you intend there to be such occasions in our future?"

"Of course. When I come back to London for the Season, a free man, I hope to see you in a tea gown very, very frequently."

She had to put her hand over his to prevent him from doing anything else perfectly decent and respectable to the tea gown. Their eyes met; mischief gleamed in his.

But as seconds passed, his gaze turned serious. "Be careful, Holmes. We might not have ripped off the last veil of civility, but Moriarty must consider you an enemy now. Or at the very least, a highly inconvenient adversary."

She leaned in for another kiss. "Of course I'll be very, very careful. I have a tea gown I still need to wear in front of you, when you come back in spring."

USA Today bestselling author **Sherry Thomas** is one of the most acclaimed historical fiction authors writing today, winning the RITA Award two years running and appearing on innumerable "Best of the Year" lists, including those of *Publishers Weekly, Kirkus Reviews, Library Journal,* Dear Author, and All About Romance. Her novels include *A Study in Scarlet Women, A Conspiracy in Belgravia, The Hollow of Fear,* and *The Art of Theft,* the first four books in the Lady Sherlock series; *My Beautiful Enemy;* and *The Luckiest Lady in London.* She lives in Austin, Texas, with her husband and sons.

CONNECT ONLINE

SherryThomas.com